Copyright © 2025 by Torie Gaylord
Cover Design by Miblart
www.miblart.com
First edition October 2025
ISBN 9798992238952 (Paperback)
ISBN 9798992238945 (E-Book)

I0676537

Also by Torie Gaylord

Three Seconds
Three Seconds and Gone
Blink and You Miss It
Whispers of Moments

Watch for more at toriegwriting.com.

To those who face challenges that rock your world - may you keep finding the courage to take those steps forward and ignore the voices telling you that you can't.

WHISPERS
OF
MOMENTS

TORIE GAYLORD

Chapter 1

Lou – The Day Before Val's Kidnapping

I *– I shouldn't have done that. It's not like me.* I looked over my shoulder at the closed door debating if I should go back to explain myself. I don't know why I thought it would be like those times in my apartment where she pushed me away only to keep her feelings at bay. It's different now. My head's all over the place with her being back, and especially after talking about fating. I rubbed my face deciding against knocking on her door and headed to my room for the night. The last thing I need to do is force her to talk about something more than I already have. Besides, I've already made enough of an ass of myself.

After a fitful night of sleep, I drug myself out of bed. My hair was a mess and there was no hiding the fact I hardly slept. I sat on the edge of the bed for a couple of minutes. *Do I try to talk to her this morning? Do I give her space?* I decided against waiting, moving towards the door and making my way back to Val's room. I lightly tapped as I moved my ear closer to check for any signs of life. I didn't need to deal with a pissed off Val and Warrick. I waited a few more breaths before tapping again. Still nothing.

I cracked open the door telling myself if there were two outlines in that bed, I'd walk away. I poked my head scanning the room. There was no one in the bed, her bathroom lights were off, and it looks like one of her bags is gone. *Great, I fucked up this time.* I picked up on sounds coming from Jennie's and Chris' room, so I crossed the hall and knocked on their door. There was some mumbling I couldn't quite make out then Jennie opened the door. She had just gotten ready for the day while Chris was still rubbing the sleep from his eyes. Her usual perky smile was in place as she said, "Good morning, Lou. You look rough ... "

Her smile dropped after taking in the sight of me.

"Rough night. Have you seen Val?" I asked.

Her brows furrowed for a second, but I knew her concern was bigger than she let on judging by the way her entire demeanor changed. She rubbed her other arm throwing a look back at Chris who shrugged before turning back to me, "I think she headed out pretty early this morning. She's not back?"

I only shook my head in response.

"Maybe she's at the pub?" Jennie asked.

I backed away from the door, "I'll head there after breakfast."

I made my way downstairs making a mental checklist of everywhere I'd go to look for her after I was done, but my train of thought was interrupted by Chris, "Everything okay, man?"

We were at the island now getting a quick breakfast going. I shot a glance up the stairs to assess if Jennie was coming down any time soon, and when I was confident she wasn't, I leaned in lowering my voice, "I messed up last night, Chris. I should've stayed down here with you guys a little longer."

"What happened? I thought you went to sleep," his eyes were slowly widening.

I closed my eyes bracing myself for the reaction I knew I'd be getting, "I got caught up in things and decided to take a chance with Val, so my dumbass went in there and kissed her."

"Oh shit," Chris said with eyes so wide they looked like they were about to pop out of his head at this point. "You kissed her?"

"Who kissed who?" Jennie chimed in as she joined us.

I felt my jaw clench more out of annoyance that I dropped my guard than from her catching part of the conversation. Chris glanced at her then back to me keeping his mouth shut. *Damn it, I'm on my own for this one.* I rubbed my face as I confessed again, "I kissed Val last night."

Coffee spewed everywhere, including all over my face. "You did what?!" Jennie shrieked. "No wonder she looked upset this morning."

I snapped my focus to her forgetting about the hot coffee dripping from my face, "What do you mean?"

"Lou, why would you do that? Oh, no. No, no, no, no," Jennie mumbled under her breath gathering her things.

I moved from behind the island following her throughout the house, "Jennie, I need you to talk to me."

My frustration was quickly growing with each second I didn't get a response. We were back up to their room at this point when I snapped, my emotions getting the best of me yet again, "Jennie, I need you to tell me what's going on right now!"

Clearly that wasn't the way to handle this because she whipped around narrowing her eyes at me. She closed the distance between us jabbing her finger into my chest, "You don't get to demand *anything* from me right now, Lou. Do you know what you might've done?"

I removed her finger from where she was trying to dig a hole, "I probably pissed her off and she needed to get some air. She'll be back."

"What makes you so certain?" Jennie asked.

"She knows we're her safe house even if she doesn't want to be here. There's no other choice."

She threw her hands up, "Ugh! You are so thick headed sometimes."

I watched her finish storming around shoving things in a purse before she finally returned to jabbing her finger in my chest, "You couldn't have waited to see if she would come around. No, you had to go and kiss her without thinking about what that would do. Did you know Warrick, who is the only one keeping those damn vampires at bay, was going to be visiting her last night? Did it occur to you that that's the reason she probably went up to her room so early? No, you didn't. So now she's running around out there, her *life* at risk. We almost lost her once. I can't handle the thought of losing her again."

She pushed past me, jaw trembling from the emotions running through her head. "It was just a kiss, not the end of the world," I muttered behind her.

"Don't start with me, Lou," she threatened making her way to their car. I looked at Chris saying the same thing and all I got from him was a shake of his head and a shrug.

We had started our search for Val, Jennie taking the wheel. I don't know how many times I had to warn Jennie to slow down only to get a tense response in return. It didn't matter if my wolf didn't like it, she was going to drive however she wanted to get us to the pub as fast as possible. When we drove past the street, Jennie let out the loudest sigh after seeing Val's bike parked out front. She looked at me in the rear view still angry, but at least she was starting to calm down, "How do I get to Warrick's?"

"Why?"

"Just tell me how to get there, Lou." So, I did just that even though it went against all my instincts.

We pulled up to his ocean-front shack, his car parked out front to my dismay. Jennie jumped out of the car storming up to his front door. I watched as she was startled by Warrick ripping the door open before she had a chance to knock and gesturing to the car. He was pissed. Chris and I watched as the two of them got in a heated debate only able to pick up a couple of words here and there. Chris looked back at me every now and then asking the same question, "Anything?"

The answer was the same every time, "I'm only making out a couple of words, but he's livid."

When they were done, Jennie made her way back to the car letting out a breath as soon as she sat down. She glanced at me in the rear view, "I hope nothing happens to her for your sake, Lou."

"Why, what did he say?" I asked not entirely sure if she would tell me anything.

"Nothing worth repeating," she said starting the car. I took the hint and kept my mouth shut for the ride home. When we got there, we made our way back into the house, still keeping our mouths shut. It wasn't making sense why Jennie was all riled up. Val was fine, just needed her space. Warrick was mad at me, but what's new? She would see for herself when Val walked through the door tonight and we all talked it out.

Hours passed. We were gathered in the living room watching yet another movie when Jennie tossed her phone, "There's still nothing from Val and the sun's starting to go down. You think she's okay?"

"We can check again," I mumbled.

"Let's go," Jennie got up. "You're driving this time."

It wasn't long before we were back on the road. The possibility of something being wrong was becoming more apparent now, the guilt eating away at me. I could sense the other two in the car were feeling the same way. I can't believe I managed to do something so stupid thinking there wouldn't be any repercussions. The last time someone had consumed my mind like this was Melody, and clearly, she seems to be the root of what's going on here. My mind has been a mess since the day I saw her, and spending more time with her hasn't helped.

"Damn it!" I shouted slamming my hand on the steering wheel. Chris and Jennie jumped from the sudden outburst adding to my guilt, "Sorry."

"It's okay, man," Chris started. "She probably got caught up with things at the pub. We'll just go in and ask for her."

I drove the car to my usual spot in the parking garage across the street checking if her bike was still out front. It wasn't making the pit in my stomach feel any better when I didn't see it.

We were out of the car making our way to the pub. "Guess she decided to move her bike," Jennie said casually.

I looked in the direction she gestured, and sure enough, there was her bike. *Maybe I'm overreacting after all.* We walked into a busy scene, a wave of people at the bar, but there was Val still bopping around serving people. It was like a weight lifted off my shoulders and I let out a big exhale earning a pat from Jennie. Instead of staying, we made the decision to head back to the house now that we had confirmation we could wait it out.

It was definitely night now, dinner cooling on the counter, the three of us pacing with no sign of Val. Jennie kept calling only to be sent straight to voicemail while I kept texting getting nothing in return. I kept watching Jennie considering she was the one most riled up about this situation from the moment she stepped out of her room. Something had changed since we left Warrick's. She was still stressed and visibly worried, but her motions were calmer. I could tell Warrick had let her in on something, but I couldn't figure out what.

"We should go back to the pub," she mumbled.

"It's closed. Val would've left by now."

Jennie turned on her heel grabbing her purse and keys. She looked over her shoulder at me, "Then I'm going. You stay here in case she shows up."

Morning came and went with nothing still. Jennie somehow got Val's bike back without a word about what she saw, or didn't see, at the pub. I had another sleepless night in case Val turned up and needed help.

"Hey," Chris said thumping my shoulder. "You gotta stop messing with your hair like that. You're going to rip it out."

I dropped my hands. Staring out the window, I said, "This is my fault, Chris. If I had just listened for once, Val would be here. She'd be smiling and joking. Hell, we would probably be in a new world at this point reuniting her with more of her friends."

"You can't change what's happened. You can only hope for the chance to fix it going forward," he said then got up to grab something to eat.

Jennie was sitting on the couch staring out the windows while chewing on her nails. She hadn't said anything more since she got back last night. The fear was palpable between all three of us. There's a very good chance we'd never be seeing her again and that devastated me.

Chapter 2

Warrick – The Day Before Val's Kidnapping

A growl ripped from my throat as glass shattered around me. *What game did they think they were playing?* I was irate after seeing Val entangled with Lou, him kissing her the way I should've been. While I was angry with the both of them, I couldn't forget about being mad at myself for not being there sooner. This could have all been avoided. Yet, this could have been their plan. String me along this whole time. *Were those months with her even real?*

Another flash of anger and the coffee table was flipped. I pinched the bridge of my nose trying to calm my heart rate. It's like the Melody situation all over again except this one is more painful.

"Why the *fuck* does it hurt like this?" I yelled out to no one in particular clutching my heart. Her scent was all over this damn house making it nearly impossible to run from the memories. Everywhere I turn I picture her face, the way she laughs, the way she juts her chin out in defiance when she's cowering on the inside. Don't even get me started on the bedroom. I can't go in there. I'll sleep in my car before I'm confronted with everything that happened in that room, but I'll have to go in there to get my stuff before leaving here. *Just figure it out, genius.* I grabbed my head. This was all too much for me to process. Val and her damn tendencies leave my mind all over the place so I can't form a single, fucking coherent thought. It's maddening.

I was so in my head I didn't catch the sound of gravel or the familiar smell of blood associated with Cian and his group. The knock on the front door rang out, "Warrick, open the door. I can tell you're in there."

I yanked it open knowing full well Cian wouldn't wait to be let in. He stepped across the threshold with his usual ease laughing at the mess I made, "Remodeling?"

"Funny," I snorted. "What do you want?"

He slowly turned around to face me, a smile inching across his face, "I'm here one last time to see if you happen to know anything about the ashes left for me, or are you going to continue insisting it wasn't your precious Val?"

"You seem hell bent on damning her," I snarled. Even now I couldn't stop defending her. *It's the truth.*

"Is that a problem?"

"Just an observation," I responded not directly answering the question.

"When you first showed up, you were more than happy to try to take her out when I mentioned she could be a risk, but then you got entangled and now we're short on some incredibly powerful fighters. I'm not going to let my life get destroyed on behalf of your puppy love. Now, tell me what you know," he coolly demanded.

Cian wasn't going to leave until he got the answer he wanted regardless of whether it's the truth or not. I set my shoulders ignoring my internal voice, "Val and Lou worked together. She may have been with me, but it was part of their plan for Lou to finally go out so she could have an alibi to get out of this world scot-free."

My stomach turned with every word of that lie, but I delivered it flawlessly. Cian nodded his head seemingly satisfied with the answer, "That's what I thought. Your little lass you had there is a handful."

The minute the door closed, I slammed my fists against the counter. I sentenced Val to her death. And yet, a part of me had a hard time believing there wasn't some truth to the accusation I made. Especially after seeing her and Lou together.

Another growl pierced the silence with another piece of furniture upended. I grabbed my head sliding to the floor. I didn't know which path was the right one, Lou working with her or Val not being the one behind Cian's accusation. What I did know was that there would be a point where Cian would invite me over to gloat about his effective methods of torture which meant I would need to be mentally prepared to see her in pieces. Not only that, but I would have to convince him I'm done with her. She would no longer be a focal point in my life and my only purpose would be to carry out my mission.

As much as I tried to convince myself of what I was doing, a little voice called out in the back of my head not letting me be okay with completely walking away from Val. No matter how many times I repeated that I could get through this, that voice would counter every time.

I stormed into my bathroom to splash water on my face. Gripping the edges of the counter, I slowly lifted my gaze to meet my own eyes, "You're going to have to come up with something, Warrick. You always do. You're not going to let this one go as easy as you did before."

I dried my face then headed out to the living room. I laid on the couch, still not ready to be slapped with Val's scent consuming my room. I pushed the anger aside as I've done all too many times in my life to let sleep take over.

Throwing my arm over my eyes, a groan escaped my lips from the sunlight blasting my face. I forgot to close the damn curtains last night, so I was up the minute the sun decided to make an appearance. I rolled over to grab my phone. There were no messages from Val inquiring about where I was, but there was a message from Cian containing only a time to meet him at the cathedral tomorrow night. Nothing else. *Bingo*. I sent out a quick reply to him before typing out another message to the one person I know who could help me execute my plan. When I got a thumbs up in return, I tossed the phone aside.

I stood up, stretching and convincing myself I needed to pack everything up today which meant I needed to brace myself for entering that room. "No more outbursts today," I mumbled taking in the destruction I managed to do yesterday.

I had everything packed neatly away in my car to allow for a quick escape the minute I needed it then made my way to the pub. It wasn't open yet, but Conor would be there. Proving myself right, the pub's owner wore a disgruntled expression from being woken so early. Judging by the shadows framing his eyes, he didn't get a lot of sleep last night only further solidifying what I already knew. *Just play along. Don't give anything away.*

"Fancy seeing you here. Where the hell were you last night?" Conor demanded.

I nodded my head towards him, "Can I come in?"

"No," he answered filling up the doorway while crossing his arms over his chest.

"Alright," I sighed. "I had things to take care of last night."

"Did one of those *things* happen to be Val? Her bike's gone this morning and I haven't heard a word from her since she left last night. I've been worried sick."

My brows drew together in concern, "What do you mean?"

He ran his hands through his already-messy hair, "She left after dark when she lost track of time. My guys had to move her bike in the garage, so she had a further trek than what she planned. I'm worried one of Cian's guys snatched her, Warrick."

Anger involuntarily started to boil deep within my gut, but I kept my tone cool, "None of her friends were with her while she worked? Not even Lou?"

Conor shook his head as if that was the only thing he was able to bring himself to do. I was caught off-guard by Lou not even bothering to show his face after what I saw between those two. *Did that mean* – The thought of Lou forcing himself on Val out of spite made it even harder to keep my anger at bay, my jaw clenching in response.

I put my hand on Conor's shoulder, "You focus on what you need to do to run your business. I'll take care of everything else."

I started to turn as he opened his mouth, "You'll let me know she's okay, right?"

"Whether or not the message comes from me, you'll know."

I didn't give him a chance to respond as I settled back into my car. I had to keep myself from driving to Val's house. If I let my mind wonder for even a minute, my hands would take over directing the car down that all too familiar path. The number of times I had to backtrack just to head to my house was ridiculous. It doubled the time it normally took.

I burst through the front door, opening and closing my fists. I closed my eyes taking deep breaths to calm down. I would've at least expected Lou to be glued by her side. Now I'm questioning even more if Val and Lou were working together. When I was sneaking up to her room, I made sure I wasn't going to be detected, but now I'm wondering if I didn't do as good as I thought. Maybe Lou saw me which made him feel possessive. If he forced a kiss on Val as a power move ... no, I can't keep thinking about that.

It was too early to drink under normal circumstances, but I'm not facing normal circumstances. I swirled my whiskey while pinching the bridge of my noise. I kept going back and forth on what the truth actually was, my brain conflicting what my gut knows is true.

My train of thought was interrupted by a car approaching. I took a deep breath to pick up on any scents, my lip instinctively curling at the faint scent of Lou.

By the time the car was in park, I was moving towards the door. I yanked it open to be met with a shocked Jennie on the other side holding up her hand ready to knock.

"Why the hell did you bring him here?" I asked through clenched teeth pointing towards the car.

"Let's keep our voices down, Warrick," she pleaded quietly. "I don't want Lou to overhear. You're not the only one who's pissed at him. Now, tell me what you saw last night."

"You know damn well what I saw last night," I started raising my voice. I let out a breath before continuing, "Lou and Val were all over each other by the time I got up there."

"It wasn't real, Warrick," Jennie countered with her brows furrowed. "Don't tell me you think it is."

I thrust my finger towards the car again, "It wouldn't be the first time that asshole took someone from me. You think I'm okay with that happening again? With *Val*? No, you need to leave."

"Damn it, Warrick! It wasn't real," Jennie started. She glanced over her shoulder before bringing her attention back to me, "You want to know what really happened?"

Her pause for dramatic effect only added to my irritation, "Get on with it."

She sighed, "That kiss was all Lou. Val wanted nothing to do with it. You didn't see how upset she was this morning. I can't believe I'm telling you this, but she has genuine feelings for you, Warrick, and I mean, *big* feelings. I'm not going to say the words for her, but you know what I mean. She would do anything for you, and Lou crossing that line took away any chance he had at getting back with her."

My shoulders dropped a little as some of the fight left me. Jennie was telling me something Val wasn't ready to say and that I already knew to be true. I closed my eyes, "Go along with me and act like you're mad still."

"Okay."

"Don't get upset with me. Cian is going to be grabbing Val, if he hasn't already done it," I held up my hands signaling her to wait the second her mouth opened to argue. "I have a plan before you start chewing me out. There was no other way, believe me. I hate what I've done, but I'm going to try my hardest to make it up. I need you to be ready. Cian is going to put her through hell and it's going to fuck with her head. I'm going to have to go in there and sell it even if that means she'll hate me afterwards. I'll risk that to make sure she lives. You guys have to jump from here as soon as she's in the house and you better go back to my world so she can get some help. Don't say anything about this to Lou or Chris. Now, go."

Her mouth opened and closed a couple more times until she made the right choice by turning back towards her car. I threw the door closed for dramatic effect ready for things to fall into place.

The time for me to meet Cian at the cathedral came, dread filling me and making each step heavier. I had no idea what to expect when I finally got a chance to see her, but if the strong scent of blood and fear were any indication, it wasn't going to be pretty.

Cian was rambling on about next steps with our plan getting quick responses out of me. I couldn't focus on strategy right now. I had to make sure I didn't fuck up, checking things off my mental list as we kept walking further into the depths of this dark building.

"You're tense," Cian observed.

"It reeks in here. Why the hell have you not done anything about it yet?"

He only chuckled in response, "Give me a few minutes. I have something to show you."

I looked down the hall knowing exactly where it led, but kept my composure, "You get a few minutes head start, then I'm coming in."

I watched him walk away. As soon as he entered a doorway, I turned my head to focus my hearing. The distinct sound of punches bounced off the walls earning a wince each time. I couldn't stand it anymore, so I put one foot in front of the other making sure my steps were noisier than usual. Cian's cocky voice announcing me made my skin crawl. I rolled my head to each side earning a couple of pops. *Time for the show.*

Nothing could have prepared me for the sight before me: Val hanging with her hands chained above her head. Her body was coated in blood, and the parts of her skin not covered in blood, were black and blue. The last thing I looked at before opening my mouth were the buckets beneath her feet collecting what blood dripped from her. My heart shattered knowing I was the one who was responsible for her being trapped here.

But I put on the act I had practiced a million times, then left. I knew I didn't have long before Cian took her last breath. I dropped my head taking a few deep breaths before pulling out my phone to send a quick message. My phone started ringing instantly. I looked over my shoulder to make sure the coast was clear and brought it up to my ear, an all-too familiar voice on the other end of the line, "Took you long enough."

Chapter 3

Lou

We hadn't moved the entire day, not even to eat. I didn't know the exact time, but I knew it was late judging by the darkness that blanketed us. We hadn't heard anything, only adding to the worry.

A pounding on the door shook us out of whatever trance we were in. I nervously glanced between Jennie and Chris to see if any of them would make a move towards the door. When it became clear no one else was going to answer it, I wiped a hand over my face then squared my shoulders before heading over to see who was standing on the other side. I hated to think it was Warrick here to rub things in my face, or worse, it was Liam to break the news to us.

Another round of pounding rattling the door, "Come on! Someone has to be in there."

I knew that voice. Confused, I yanked open the door. I sucked in a breath trying to process who was standing before me. There was Melody propping up Val who looked like death. There was so much blood covering her from head to foot. Her head lolling to one side made me question if she was even alive.

"Are you going to let us in, or leave us out in the open?" Melody demanded.

"Y-yeah," I stammered moving to help Melody bring Val into the house.

"What's going on?" Jennie asked hurrying over to the door. Her eyes bulged out of her head at seeing her best friend. "Where are you taking her?"

"Up to the tub," Melody ordered. "I'm sure she wouldn't want blood coating every surface in here."

"Chris," Jennie called over her shoulder. "Shut everything down. We don't need people getting the chance to see what's going on in here."

The three of them kept barking out commands to get Val taken care of, but all I could focus on was the faint heartbeat next to me. I leaned my head down so only she could hear my voice, "I'm so sorry, Val. I promise you can yell at me all you want as long as you make it through this. I can't have you giving up on me now."

"Lou, are you paying attention?" Melody asked.

"Sorry, what did I miss?"

We made it up to the bathroom gently laying Val in the tub. A soft moan escaped her lips, but that was the only sign of life she showed. I brought my attention back to Melody who was standing there with her hands on her hips, "I was saying you guys need to jump. Now. Take her to Raf. I can't even begin to tell you the amount of blood she's lost and I'm sure she has broken bones. Make sure to let her rest."

"How did you get her out of there?" I asked noting Jennie darting out of view almost as if she was guilty of knowing something. *It has to be whatever changed after her interaction with Warrick. I'll ask her about that later.*

"Don't worry about that. Be thankful I was able to get her out at all," Melody said. She looked over her shoulder, "I have to get back. I'll be leaving my bloody clothes on the porch. Get rid of them. Don't leave them here. I took a huge risk carrying out this rescue operation."

She was gone as fast as she came in. I glanced back down at the tub not sure where to even start. Jennie hustled back into the bathroom, Chris behind her, "Holy crap."

Jennie shot him a glare. I put my hand on her shoulder, "What do we do now?"

"You heard her. We need to get back to your world ASAP. Go get the device and transport us."

I gave her a quick salute running to the office. The code for my world was second nature, thankfully making it easier for me to punch it in with no hesitation the minute I was out on the street, aiming it slightly above the house like I did when we left my world. I ran back inside as the familiar weightlessness took over, not allowing myself to get caught up in the shimmering portal that manifested itself before sucking us out of this world and placing us back into another. I almost didn't get back into the house in time before the portal whisked us away.

The second I felt more grounded, I ran out to the backyard to see if the view changed at all. I let out a breath of relief seeing the skyline I was so accustomed to. I hustled back to where Jennie and Chris were cramming themselves into the bathroom taking care of Val, "We're back."

"Then what are you still doing here?" Chris threw over his shoulder. "Get Raf. Her pulse is slowing."

"Fuck that," I said shouldering my way in between them. "Get the car ready."

I scooped her limp body in my arms wasting no time with getting her in the car. Not daring to let her go again, I ordered Jennie to drive like hell to the hospital while I told Chris to put Raf on speaker.

"This is a pleasant surprise," said the light-hearted voice belonging to my second.

"No time for pleasantries, Raf. I need you to meet us at the hospital now!"

"Got it, boss."

The call disconnected. I stroked the side of Val's face, "Stay with me."

She didn't move in response to my touch, she didn't even make sound. Panic started working its way into my throat. I couldn't lose her this soon after getting her back. Instinctively, I put my fingers to her neck holding my breath while I waited for the rhythmic thumping of her heart. It was there, but even more faint than when we had left the house. I held her closer to my body while barking out directions for Jennie.

It felt like I held my breath until we met up with Raf outside the hospital doors. Thank heavens for him, too, because he greeted us with a gurney. I ran out of the car, "You have no idea how much I appreciate you right now, Raf."

His eyes widened at the sight of the near-dead woman in my arms before he donned his mask of professionalism, "Don't speak so soon, Lou. Just put her here and I'll work my magic."

I did as I was told then grabbed his arm as he turned to wheel her away, "Don't worry about the secrecy on this one, either."

All I got in return was raised eyebrows, so I continued, "I'm sure Warrick's involved somehow and would like to get a report back. If it saves me from having to deal with a confrontation from him, then that's the way I want to go right now."

"Got it."

As soon as the words were out of his mouth, he was gone. Jennie and Chris caught up to me after getting the car parked, panting, "Where is she?"

"Raf's taking care of her. Now, we wait and pray like hell to whatever god you believe in that she makes it out."

We claimed a couple of seats in the waiting room making ourselves at home as much as we could. We'd rotate who was up to get either coffee or something to snack on from the vending machine. We eventually stopped paying attention to the clock after a couple of hours had gone by. I couldn't help but shake my head at how familiar this situation was, us waiting to hear any information on how Val is doing while doing our best to keep our nerves at bay.

Any time someone sounded like they were headed in our direction, the three of us would simultaneously lift our heads in the hopes a messenger would give us an update; only to be met with disappointment each time the steps faded away. Jennie and Chris nodded off a couple of times, but I couldn't let my guard down enough for sleep to sneak past.

The sun started making its ascent into the sky by the time Raf's scent filled my nose, letting me know he was moving towards us. He pushed open the doors, the three of us standing to greet him. He looked me up and down, sighing, "You need to get some rest."

"Not until I know," I gritted out between clenched teeth.

"I have some good news for you then," Raf said looking at each of us. "She's going to pull through. Not to say this is going to be an easy fight for her, but we were able to take care of the physical injuries. She has some broken ribs and lost a good amount of blood from the cuts we stitched back together. She took a brutal beating, and it looks like she had other injuries that hadn't quite healed before this either. Make sure she takes the time to rest to let her body heal. It'll take time, but she'll get there. Mentally, though, Val has an uphill battle. Whatever happened, Lou, they nearly broke her. She has no fight left in her. You know I've seen a lot, but this has to be one of the worst for how bad things are."

I didn't know it was possible for me to get so hopeful and so disheartened at the same time. I scrubbed my hands over my face, "Can we see her?"

"She's probably still asleep, but yeah. I'll tell you this – she looks a lot better than when you brought her in," Raf said over his shoulder leading us down the hallway lined with rooms.

Jennie glanced nervously around, Chris squeezing her hand for comfort. I knew how she felt because I was feeling the exact same way. We had no idea what we were about to see or what to expect out of this new version of Val.

Raf knocked on the doorway before entering, "You're awake. Are you up for some visitors?"

We waited until Raf signaled us to come in. Raf may have said she looked a lot better, but I wasn't completely sure if I agreed with his definition. The majority of her skin was covered in bruises. There were quite a few lines of stitches on various parts of her body, and that was what we could see. There's no telling what's underneath the blankets or hospital gown. The worst part, though, is how blank Val's face was. No reactions, no emotions, nothing. Just blank.

"I'll leave you all alone. I'm sure there's some catching up to do. If you need anything, Val, just hit that call button and I'll be in here before you know it," Raf instructed then made his exit to give us privacy.

Jennie was the first of us to speak keeping her tone soft and gentle, slowly making her way to the side of Val's bed, "Hey, how are you feeling?"

Val slightly turned her head towards Jennie, but didn't bother to look at her, "He left me there to die."

Jennie sucked in some air, quickly glancing in my direction before turning her attention back to Val, "You know he was the one who got you out, right?"

Val slowly brought her gaze to meet Jennie's before making her way to meet mine, "Leave."

And that was that. She dropped her head to the pillow behind her and closed her eyes. We remained where we were stunned at the abruptness in her tone, and when she realized we weren't making a move towards the exit, Val tapped the call button. Raf casually walked in a few moments later looking between us and Val as if trying to figure out what was going on. When he put two and two together, he swung his arm towards the door, "She can go home tomorrow. I'll call you when the time comes."

I gave a curt nod then led the way back through the hallway, out to the waiting room, and into the car. I slid into the driver's seat resting my head on the steering wheel. I felt Chris put his hand on my shoulder waiting for him to say something reassuring, but he never did. It was Jennie who spoke what we were all thinking, "What the hell was that?"

"Raf wasn't kidding when he said she has an uphill battle," I sighed. "If I had only listened for once, we wouldn't be in this mess."

Chris chimed in, "And if it weren't for your quick thinking, she wouldn't be alive."

"I only did what I was told," I countered.

Silence fell upon us again. I went into autopilot navigating us away from the hospital. I hadn't realized exactly where I was going until I was parked in the alley behind my place.

"Lou, you need some rest," Jennie said quietly.

"What did Warrick really say to you when we stopped by his house?" I mumbled.

"Rest and then I'll tell you."

I whipped around unable to keep my anger in check, "Just tell me, damn it."

She shrunk back in her seat, eyes wide with fear. Chris had tried to move like he was going to put himself in between us if I tried to attack her. I hung my head, "Sorry, you're right. I need to get some sleep."

I gripped the handle to pop the door open when Jennie started, "He was the one who confessed to Cian on Val's behalf which essentially gave Cian the green light to grab her, but Warrick had a plan to make sure she got out. He didn't give me specifics, only that she was going to be hurt mentally and physically and that he was going to have to sell a performance. Warrick screwed with her head to make sure Cian was convinced he was through with her. I'm sure she isn't wanting to see anyone right now."

"I'm going to kill him," I said casually.

"No, you're not," Jennie said. "You're going to let him live. He's the only reason we have Val right now, and that's enough for me."

I looked at her through the rearview mirror. There was finality in her tone that was matched by the set of her jaw. I didn't say anything else as I moved out of the car, grabbing the keys to my place and tossing the car keys in the driver seat so they could get back to Val's house.

I fell into my bed, reveling in being back home. I didn't bother with stripping down, fully aware of Val's blood still all over me. I knew Jennie was right, but I hated what she said at the same time. It went against every fiber in my body, and yet, I was going to convince myself that Warrick wasn't in the wrong here. I had to. For the sake of Val.

Chapter 4

Val – In The Cathedral

They finally left me alone to die. With each moment that passed, I could feel the cold embrace tightening around me.

More footsteps approached. When they reached the door, they paused before quietly opening it. I didn't bother to open my eyes. I didn't have the energy for it anymore. Whoever this mystery person was, they started messing with the chains above my head.

I cracked my eyes open just enough to see the person in front of me wasn't Cian or Liam. Melody was reaching above me trying to free me, cursing how well they did the chains.

"Why are you helping me?" I croaked out.

"Oh good, she lives," Melody whispered. "Keep your voice down."

"Aren't you in the camp of wanting me dead?"

"Not at all."

"Then why are you helping me?" I asked again.

She let out a sigh followed by the sound of the lock releasing. Her arms shot out to catch me, "Can you try to walk? We don't have a lot of time."

My legs had minimal movement, but it was apparently good enough for her because we started moving towards the doors.

Melody started, "I'm helping you because I care. When I saw Warrick storm out of here, I knew I didn't have long. If he gets the chance, he'll convince Cian to finish the job if Warrick doesn't do it himself. I know exactly how Warrick can be, and from what I understand, you do, too. Plus, I couldn't live knowing Lou went through that kind of heartbreak twice."

"What do you mean?"

"Val, that night Lou and I were talking in the pub, the night you accused him of cheating on you, he was telling me what you mean to him. His feelings are genuine," Melody answered.

We were getting to the sanctuary now, the front doors in sight. I couldn't believe I was about to escape from this hell, nor could I believe what Melody just said. Her tone was genuine. I tried to look towards her to see if her face would give anything away, but there was nothing except the steely determination to get me through those doors. I turned my attention back to her using everything I had to move forward as I said, "He wasn't hitting on you? Trying to rekindle the old flame you two had?"

Melody giggled, "Oh goodness no. I can't believe you thought that. Believe it or not, I'm happy where I am, and while Lou still holds a special place in my heart, him and I have both moved on. I'm not going to say it for him, I just want you to know that he doesn't have plans to go anywhere and would do just about anything for you. Although, you seem to have a hold over Warrick, too. *Shit.*"

With the way she ended that sentence, I thought we were about to be caught, but there were no signs of anyone else in the vicinity.

"Why'd you say 'shit'?" I asked.

"I'll tell you in the car. Give me a little more gas and we'll be there before you know it."

I did as I was told, counting down the steps until she nudged the door open not daring to look back. I immediately recognized the black car conveniently parked in front of the looming gray building, panic building in my chest. As I slowed my pace, Melody picked up hers, "We can't stop, Val."

"I'm not going in there."

"You have no other choice, you have to believe me. I'll explain when we get in," she said reaching for the door handle.

There was nothing in me to put up a fight. She got me situated in the car before running into the driver's seat. The ocean scent flooded me bringing memories to the surface I didn't want to see. Warrick made it clear back there that he was done. Not to mention, he caused me pain in more ways than one. *Why is Melody driving his car?*

We had put the cathedral behind us at this point. Melody was making random turns checking the rearview mirror to make sure we weren't being followed before she started explaining, "Warrick sent me in there to get you. Before you try to argue, he had to sell it to Cian so there would be no suspicions."

"Then why'd you say all that crap about Lou?" I asked fighting to remain conscious.

"Because it's true, Val," Melody said, all niceties from earlier gone. "Lou practically worships the ground you walk on, and you threw it in his face. The stuff about Warrick killing you? That I added to sell the story in case anyone was listening, but I slipped up right before we got out of there. I've never seen Warrick act this way about anyone in his life. He threw logic out the window by asking me to save you. The Warrick I knew would never have let someone survive after meddling with his plans, but he did this time. I hope you guys get it figured out, whatever's going on between the three of you."

I didn't get a chance to respond before I passed out. I faded in and out catching glimpses of what was going on around me: Melody dragging me to the front door, Lou apologizing, being laid in the tub, Jennie and Chris shouting, being back in a car, getting wheeled into a hospital. The next time I woke back up, Raf was knocking on my door asking if I wanted visitors. I agreed to that before I realized who he meant.

I couldn't bring myself to feel anything but numb. Jennie was trying to talk to me like we were the only ones in the room, but all I could think about was what Melody explained to me. I knew Warrick was the reason I survived, but he still left me there after digging his fingers into my side. He accused me of lying to him saying everything I had done was an elaborate ruse Lou and I had planned out. Even when Jennie confirmed what Melody said, that Warrick was the reason I was here, I couldn't bring myself to believe it. It was too soon after everything. I hadn't had time to process what I had gone through and what has been said to me. There was no way I was ready to hear everyone plead their case.

I didn't want to hear any more of it, didn't want to see any more of the concern in their eyes. "Leave," I coldly ordered them. When I knew they didn't move an inch, I called for Raf to make them leave for me.

When I could no longer hear the sound of them shuffling down the hallway, I lifted my head back up to find Raf pulling up a seat beside me. There was comfort in those brown eyes that had helped me once before. He put his hand on my arm, setting the clipboard I hadn't noticed on his lap, "I have to ask you some questions as part of procedure. What you say will stay between us. Val, I can only imagine the hell you went through wherever you guys were, so let me know when I've crossed a line."

I glanced at his hand unable to bring my eyes back up to his, "Please tell me I'm going to be okay." Tears started welling up. I didn't want to do this anymore. Since the start of this journey, I've had to deal with so much pain and I've shoved it aside every time, but now the gates faltered and everything I was holding back came crashing over me.

"Hey," he started with a gentle tone. "You're feeling something, so that's a start."

I couldn't bring myself to laugh or even crack a smile at that. I knew Raf was only trying to lighten up the situation.

"Let's get started with these questions, okay? And don't hold anything back. I need to know what I'll be working with here," he said bringing our focus back to the task at hand.

So, we started. We took turns going back and forth, Raf asking a question about everything that happened and me answering truthfully. By the time he made it through his list, he let out a sigh dragging a hand through his hair, "Most people wouldn't have made it through that, Val. Tell me, what's keeping you going even now? You could've given up back in the operating room. You and I both know that. There were even a couple of times you flatlined."

I may not have been awake to know exactly what he was talking about, but there were a couple of times where I stood between the operating room and grabbing hold of Gabriel's outstretched hand. Even I knew that meant I was on death's doorstep. I shook my head, "I have no idea what's keeping me going at this point. Believe me, I would've rather made that jump to the other side knowing I wouldn't have to deal with this pain anymore. Something tugged me back, though."

"Hmm," was the only thing Raf said in response to that. He knew something he wasn't willing to let on, but I didn't care to push. He added a few more things to his notes, talking as he did so, "I could've released you the moment you were awake, but I wanted to get a chance to talk to you alone first so I could get a full understanding of what's running through your mind. We wouldn't have had that opportunity at your place. Here's what we're going to do. I'll give Lou a call to pick you up tomorrow. You'll go home, you'll eat, and I'll be back before you know it to do a therapy session."

"Fine," I said. "Can I sleep now?"

"Yup, I'll get out of your hair," Raf said moving to leave.

He shut out the lights leaving me encased in darkness. I sighed letting my head drop back on the pillow. I have no energy to deal with anyone right now and the thought of going back to the house once again plagued me. All I wanted was to be left alone, but going back in there would mean that Jennie would fret and fuss to fix things, Chris would be her shadow, and who knows what the hell Lou would do. Even the thought of jumping to another world made me anxious. I don't want to risk going through anything like I just did. I wouldn't have had to if I just kept my head down and focused on reuniting with my friends.

Mark, Lilly, Joe, and Bev are still out there. They wouldn't get the same Val they're used to, though. No, she's gone and left in her place is an empty shell of a person.

The thoughts kept rambling through my head not shutting up. I huffed in frustration pressing the call button hoping Raf was still around. My wish was granted when his head popped in the doorway, "You rang?"

"Do you have something that plays music or something? I don't want to watch TV or deal with a screen being on, but I can't get the thoughts to stop and I want to sleep," I complained.

He moved into the room towards one of the cabinets pulling out a radio, "Here." Raf tuned it to a classical station turning the volume down so that it was more background noise than the center of attention.

"Thank you," I mumbled.

He was back out into the hallway, "Sure thing. Rest up, Val."

The soothing twinkle of a piano danced out of the radio slowing the never-ending train of thought until I was finally able to drift off. Images of the last 48 hours flickered behind my eyelids in place of any dreams. I woke up screaming, covered in sweat, Raf and a nurse holding me down.

"Val! You're here, you're safe. Breathe. It's okay, you're going to be okay," Raf shouted while straining to hold my arms down.

"Get off of me!" I yelled. Tears started streaming down my face and the scream became replaced with sobs. Raf dismissed the nurse before pulling up a chair next to my bed.

He wiped my tears for me then handed me a tissue, "Talk to me, Val."

"I-I can't," I stuttered in between sobs. "I can't do this, Raf. If I have to relive that pain over and over again, I'll break."

"I'm trying to help you, but I can't if you don't tell me what you saw."

I shook my head wiping away the fresh set of tears streaming down my cheeks. Raf brought his chair closer, now talking in a soothing tone, "It's going to take a while for you to move past this, I'm not going to lie. This is why I'm trying to figure out what's going through your head, so I can help give you some coping mechanisms to work through this."

I nodded my head taking a steadying breath. If I don't show any progress, there's a good chance he might not let me out of his sight, and as much as I like Raf, I don't want to have to stay in this cold hospital.

"Alright," he said sitting back in his chair. "Can you tell me what plagued your dreams?"

"Images of hanging there kept going through my mind. All the cuts, punches, stabs repeated over and over again."

"I want you to know you're in a safe place. That's not going to happen here, the threat is gone," he said trying to reassure me.

I brought my gaze up to his, "What happens when I leave here?"

"You're not planning on going back there, are you?" Raf asked.

"No," I said shaking my head. "Only moving forward."

"Okay, I think the chances of you having to go through that again are very low."

I looked at him skeptically, "You have a little too much certainty."

Raf put down his pen, "Hear me out. When you detailed out the events that led up to the grand finale, there was one thing that kept sticking out to me. You were killing Cian's vampires and it sounds like that was making him desperate. When someone gets desperate, they'll take drastic measures to protect themselves. I think that's what happened there. Staying low in the next world you go to will greatly minimize the chances of something like that happening."

"And if Warrick's there?" I asked almost dreading the answer.

"I don't think it's you that needs to worry about Warrick. He was the one who got you out. Lou's the one who should watch his back, if we're being honest here."

I nodded my head trying to process what he was saying. The part of me being ruled by fear wanted to be convinced that Raf's assessment is wrong. I'll get kidnapped and tortured no matter what I do or don't do. The other part of me trying to rise to the surface understood Raf's logic. I almost laughed at how obvious that was. I knew if I hadn't killed any of those vampires, Cian would've left me alone and I could still be with Warrick. The minute the thought crossed my mind, the golden sound of his laughter flitted through the air.

"Where'd you go there, Val?" Raf asked, pen poised to start writing. "Don't tell me I was able to break through so quickly."

"There's a part of me that knows you're right, but there's a greater part of me who doesn't want to hear it."

"It'll take time. Tell me what you thought about when that dreamy look crossed your face."

"I don't know if I'm ready to go down that path yet," I said quietly.

He nodded in understanding, "That's okay. Was there anything else besides the torture that ran through your mind last night?"

My throat started closing. I looked down at my hands watching my hands tug at the edge of the blanket, "Warrick."

"What about him?"

I let out a breath closing my eyes, "Him snarling at me, the hurt on his face at thinking Lou and I were working together, but also the hesitation I saw when I would say something to make him doubt what he convinced himself of."

"Okay, that's a good start. Do you think your history with him is also playing into this image you have in your mind?"

"I guess? I mean he has tried to kill me several times," I trailed off.

"But?" Raf asked trying to prod me to continue.

"But he's also given me love I've never felt before. Raf, I got to see him actually laugh and smile rather than the usual cold and calculating version of him. He became more gentle with me, never hesitating to make sure I was taken care of."

Raf chuckled, "You mean he has a human side?"

Even that got a little laugh out of me, "You wouldn't recognize him if you saw that version."

"You know? You just lit up talking about him like that. What happened to make things go cold?"

I frowned, "Lou happened."

"And what did Lou do?" he asked, encouraging me to go on despite the voice in my head telling me to stop.

I squeezed my eyes shut, shaking my head, and swallowing. I felt Raf place his hand over mine, "You don't have to keep going if you don't want to. We've already made good progress and your friends will be here soon to get you."

"I can do it," I gritted out. "Give me a second."

I took a few more deep breaths to calm whatever emotions were stirring in me. The reignited hope within me started to think I could potentially make it past this, that I wouldn't be woken up covered in sweat and screaming every day.

I looked at Raf's clipboard, "I had to move back into my house after one of the vampires almost got his hands on me. It was the second night back and I was ready to head up to bed because Warrick was going to be coming over again, but after my shower, it was Lou in my room. He ended up kissing me and Warrick saw."

"Was the kiss consensual?" Raf asked like he already knew the answer.

I shook my head, "No. He forced himself on me, and honestly? I was scared he wasn't going to stop."

"Dumbass," Raf muttered under his breath. "No wonder you shoot daggers at him every time you look his way. And I'm sure Warrick was irate given their history."

I found myself staring at the other end of the room, "What do I do if that happens again?"

"That's a hard question to answer," Raf said thoughtfully. "I'll have a talk with him and your friends, separately of course. I think he probably learned his lesson and will keep his distance unless you initiate, but I would also just make sure you lock your door when you go into your room by yourself to avoid any unwanted visitors. As for overcoming the negative emotions associated with that event, I'll have to think on that a little more. I'm hoping tomorrow I'll be able to have something to help you, but for today, I want you to focus on telling yourself that you're out of danger's way. Try different methods. You'll know when you've found the one that works. I'm partial to meditating, but I know others really like journaling."

He cocked his head towards the door then moved to stand up, "You ready for company?"

"I guess," I said noticing the monotone voice was back. Raf noticed it, too, a little frown tugging at the corners of his mouth.

A knock sounded followed by Jennie poking her head in, "How are you doing today, Val?"

"Better, I guess."

"Can we come in?" she asked.

I looked at my lap, "Do I have a choice?"

Raf gestured for them to come in, Lou taking up the rear. He looked better than yesterday, but you could tell he hadn't slept well. Raf put his hand on Lou's chest backing him out. Their hushed voices drifted in the room even though I couldn't pick up on the words. I didn't have to, though, because I knew Raf was talking to him about leaving me alone.

I glanced at Jennie to see her focus was on the two in the hallway. *Good, keeps me from having to talk.* Jennie was still looking out the door when she said, "He didn't stay with us last night."

I glanced between her and the doorway. Her voice was distant as if she was worried about Lou leaving our new group. It never really occurred to me how close they all got until now. They spent a lot of time together with Jennie spending the majority of that helping Lou work through his feelings. They had deep conversations and got to know each other the way Jennie and I know each other. Not only that, but Lou and Chris developed such a strong bromance I'm sure Jennie is a little worried at how Chris will take the news if Lou decides to move on.

"Sorry, Val," Jennie said shaking herself out of whatever tried to take hold. "You feeling ready to come home?"

I only shrugged my shoulders.

She sat in the chair Raf left near the bed grabbing my hand, "I'm not going to force you to talk or whatever, I just want you to know that I'm really happy you're alive. I know it came at a cost, so I'll do whatever you need to help you get back."

"Jennie, I don't know if I'll be able to get back to the same old Val you knew."

She squeezed my hand a little bit, "You said the same thing when Gabriel died and we're still thick as thieves. I think it's safe to say I'm not going anywhere as long as you want to keep me in your life."

"Where's Chris?" I asked purposely changing the topic.

"He stayed at home. Didn't want to overwhelm you with too many people. Plus, I think after seeing you last night, he was a little freaked out."

"Can't say I blame him," I replied faintly.

Raf and Lou were coming back in the room stealing the focus of our attention. While Raf had his usual doctor smile plastered on his face, Lou looked grumpy telling me everything I need to know.

Jennie turned to me, "I'm going to give you guys a minute."

I gave a quick nod watching Jennie make her exit. She glanced nervously over her shoulder at Lou which didn't do anything to calm my nerves.

"I'll follow her lead," Raf said pointing towards the direction Jennie went.

Lou and I watched as Raf also made an exit. Awkward silence filled the space between us for a little bit, Lou not knowing where to look. I found myself not wanting to be the first one to talk again.

"So," Lou started. "You're getting out of here today. Bet you're happy about that."

All I did was scoff in return. Little did he know the mess of thoughts wreaking havoc on my mind.

He grabbed his hair then dropped his hands, "Look, Val, I really am sorry. I don't know how many times I can say that before you believe me, if you ever will."

"Lou, stop," I said. He snapped his head towards me finally meeting my gaze. "Things got messy. I'm not going to blame you any more than I blame Warrick. Hell, more than I blame myself."

"No, I almost couldn't stop myself when I was kissing you. I don't know what took over, but you were all I could think about. It drove me crazy that you were with Warrick, and I just wanted you for my own."

I held up a few fingers hoping he would pick up on my signal to stop. Him bringing up that night stirred something in me I didn't like, something dark I was trying my best to push aside. "Lou," I started. "Let's not talk about that, please. A lot of things have happened in a short amount of time. I'm struggling with processing all of that."

"Stop. Stop trying to be okay with everything," he said with pain clearly etched in his voice. "I can't take this back and forth anymore."

"You can't take this back and forth anymore? Imagine how it is for me. I don't want to be with someone who just fucks with my emotions all the time, but I'm always drawn to him. When it comes to you," I shook my head. "You always stir something within me."

"What do I stir in you, Val?" he asked, his voice getting husky.

"I'm not going there," I said reaching for the call button knowing Raf was right outside the door.

"Wait," Lou said holding out his hand. "I shouldn't have said that. I'll be whatever you need, but know that I'm not going to stop helping you until everything gets sorted out."

I only nodded my head. Raf chose this moment to come back in. "So," he started by clapping his hands. "Discharge. You're going to take Val home and let her rest. That's going to be the best medicine for her in her current mental and physical state. I'll stop by every day before my shift here to run through some exercises. Sound good?"

I gave a nod seeing Lou do the same out of the corner of my eye.

Raf clapped his hands together, "Good! Lou, go take care of the paperwork. Val, do you think you could walk?"

I moved to stand on my feet, wincing the moment I put weight on my bad leg. Raf met me the instant my face showed any signs of pain, "Sit back down, I'll get you a wheelchair. No need to make you feel more pain than you already do."

As if on cue, a nurse came in with a wheelchair. Raf guided me into the chair, then pushed me out to the front desk where Jennie and Lou were both waiting. Lou still couldn't look at me whereas Jennie couldn't stop looking at me. The contrast was enough to almost make me laugh. Almost.

It didn't take long for us to get back in the house. Jennie was helping provide me extra support since it seemed like my body wasn't quite ready to hold itself up while Lou started to move around the kitchen to prepare some lunch.

I sighed, "Don't bother. I just want to sleep right now. Raf put me through a lot this morning and it wore me out."

Lou looked stunned, but quickly regained his composure, "Okay. I have to run to the pizza place anyways and tonight's a full moon. I'll try to stop by tomorrow, but as you know, that's dependent on how I feel."

"Do what you need to, Lou. We got it here," Jennie said over her shoulder.

I was thankful for Jennie to be the one to respond. She helped maneuver me up the stairs, being patient as I put one step in front of the other. By the time I laid in bed, my eyes were already half closed. She brought the blankets up to my chin and that was all it took for me to drift off.

I woke up with Lou's concerned face filling my vision. The more I woke up, the more I was able to take in my surroundings. The sun was starting to go down and Lou was dressed like he was ready to leave. I knew I was in my room and that we were in the werewolf world, but I couldn't shake the images of Cian sneering into my face with Liam right behind him. My throat was raw presumably from screaming which would also explain why Lou was in front of me.

"Are you okay, Val?" he asked with a hand hovering over my shoulder.

I threw the blanket over my head while nodding at the same time. I didn't need him feeling sorry for me. He should focus on himself given that he was going to be changing tonight.

"Got it," he said. I heard him leave, closing my door behind him. I wasn't going to try to listen in case him and Jennie were talking about what just happened, so I just laid there. I turned so I was looking out the window to take in the view of the city below the house. I didn't dare let myself think about everything that was pushing at the boundaries I set in my mind. This was my time to feel numb.

I watched the sun set, the moon taking its place with howls ringing throughout the night. It would be the first time Jennie and Chris truly got to experience what it was like to be in a world that was filled with werewolves as opposed to vampires.

I allowed myself to pay attention to the sounds emanating from the first floor: pots and pans clattering indicating it was time for them to eat, the subtle bass from the TV now that we were back in a world that worked with the same connection as what was in the human world. Every now and then, I would catch some laughter floating up the stairs to remind me they were having a good time whether I was there or not. *Was this what it was like when it was Lou and them?*

As soon as that thought floated into my mind, I shooed it away. It wasn't like me to want the situation to always be centered around my thoughts and me in general, so no need to start now.

I couldn't bring myself to move despite the tempting scents of food drifting into my room under the closed door. Even when Jennie knocked on my door, I pretended to be asleep until she left. This was how I spent the rest of the night and the next day until Raf came over.

His face filled my vision interrupting my stare into the void, "Did you really not get out of bed this entire time you've been back?"

"No," I whispered feeling as though I was in trouble.

"C'mon, Val. Let's go down to the pool. We'll work on your leg today and use it as an opportunity to do a little therapy at the same time."

Instead of responding, I slowly moved out of the comfort my blanket provided despite the protest from my body. Raf left the room so I could get changed, moving to shed the cozy shield of my pajamas. Every motion was heavy and laborious.

It felt as though years had passed by the time I made it down to the pool. On the walk there, Jennie and Chris watched me in a way that made me think they saw a ghost. Raf tapped his wrist with his goofy smile in place, "I thought I was going to have to wait another couple of hours before being graced by your presence."

"Can we get started?" I asked in a monotone voice.

"By all means," Raf said stepping into the water.

I followed his lead, closing the distance between us before whispering, "Can we go to the far edge, please? I don't want curious ears to overhear."

He frowned a little at that, but still nodded his head.

When we got as far as we could from the house, Raf started leading me through exercises to start strengthening my leg again. I had lost a lot of muscle there, struggling with a lot of what he was guiding me through despite everything being so simple. When I finally got the hang of one exercise, Raf started me on another putting me back at square one. More soreness than pain was working its way into every muscle fiber, my leg starting to feel fatigued. Frustration was building until I finally had enough. Slapping my hands on the water, I dropped my head, "I can't do this."

"Considering you've been doing this for a while now, I would say you can," Raf countered offering a hand to lead me to the far wall overlooking the city. "You finally want to talk about something that isn't reps, or form, or breathing through the ache?"

"I don't know."

He gazed towards the city, "Our last conversation got me thinking. There was a time I was so in love with a woman, I would've done anything for her. And I did. I met her after I turned. I was so convinced that no one would love me at this point because of what I had become, so I hid behind my humor and poured myself into my work. One night, I went out with some of the other doctors, relieved I didn't have to be by Lou's side for once. That was when I saw her. She was so beautiful and made everything look effortless. I couldn't take my eyes off her. I was always drawn in her direction, even after I secured her number. Man, I felt on top of the world after that. The feeling didn't go away even when we were well into our relationship."

I was sucked in to his story by now. I placed a hand on his arm, "What happened?"

"Oh, it was a storybook romance. We were so in love with each other you couldn't separate us. We eventually got married in a charming ceremony. She was glowing and all I could see that entire day," he said, a faraway look taking over. "We both had no idea it would turn ugly so fast. She ended up getting brain cancer that was detected too late. By the time we got the diagnosis, she only had about a month to live, but that was the best month of our lives."

Raf was fidgeting with the wedding band I had just noticed. I glanced back up at him wondering why he would just tell me this story rather than ask me questions. Despite the confusion, something hit me. "Were you fated?" I asked.

That was enough to bring him back to reality, his focus fully on me now. "What do you know about fating?" he asked more curious than anything.

"I know it's basically the same concept as a soulmate. You're drawn to someone that you're meant to spend the rest of your life with, and no matter what you do, you can't avoid it," I answered.

He nodded in approval, "We were fated. Let me tell you, Val, I haven't ever felt anything like that since."

"Was she a human?" I asked selfishly. If he was fated to a human, that meant it was possible for me, too. On the other hand, it meant Raf knew a level of pain so deep after losing someone who was his world. He had no way to avoid what was going to happen, and yet, he's still standing here able to joke, be lighthearted, and keep moving forward. It was suddenly starting to make sense why he told me that story.

"You already know the answer to that one," he said quietly. "So, do you want to tell me about the feelings you have for Warrick and why they're causing you trouble?"

Chapter 5

We finished our session that day, me talking through everything I felt towards Warrick and him helping me dissect what was going on in my head. When we got out of the pool, I was so tired I could barely keep my eyes open anymore.

Raf glanced up at the sky then back to me, "It's nice enough out here, you should enjoy it."

I knew he meant I should get some rest because I clearly wasn't going to be able to make the trek back upstairs. I nodded laying on the outdoor couch. I had barely gotten comfortable when Raf laid a towel over me muttering his goodbyes. He felt like a brother to me now, and the only one who I was willing to talk to at the moment.

And that's how the routine went for the rest of the week: Raf would drag me from my Fortress of Solitude to help me strengthen my bad leg while also working through the trauma so that I wasn't spending my days lying in bed. He started picking up that I wasn't eating, so he would bring a protein-packed lunch over for us to eat after the pool session. Jennie and Chris would try their best to pull me out of my room, but I would only leave for Raf because I felt he wasn't trying to convince me I was wrong about something. Jennie and Chris had good intentions, don't get me wrong, but there was something accusatory in their tones. I don't blame them with how I treated them back in the vampire world, yet it still hurts. Raf wasn't judging me for my choices or past actions, only trying to help me move forward. Most of all, he wasn't looking at me with pity in his eyes. As much as I love Jennie, I was tired of her looking at me with that sad expression on her face as if she knew about anything I had gone through. Then there's Lou who hasn't made an appearance at all this week seemingly taking Raf's advice to heart.

We finished up another session, Raf bringing over the light blanket we were keeping outside for this reason. I only seemed to be able to sleep without nightmares or flashbacks outside.

"I'll give you a break tomorrow, but I'll be back the day after that. I need you to eat and not stay cooped up in that room. It's going to kill you and we're not going to be doing all this work for nothing," he scolded.

I nodded my head, my eyes closing and I willed my mind to not let me have a nightmare. The last thing I needed to do was to break the streak of not screaming bloody murder while I napped outside.

My mind seemed to have listened once again with Lou nudging me awake, "Hey, it's starting to get cold out here. Let's go inside."

I slowly sat up, wiping the sleep from my eyes picking up on the darkness around me. I had slept the rest of the day away.

I only showed my agreement by moving towards the door. The stiffness from being in the pool for so long, and then sleeping set, in making it even more difficult to move, but when Lou reached for me, I pushed his hand away.

"Where's Jennie and Chris?" I asked walking into a quiet, empty house.

"They're out exploring the city."

"Oh," I said stopping in the middle of the living room.

"Val, I'm only here to keep an eye on you. Jennie's really worried and this was the only way Chris could get her to agree to go on a date. Raf is buried at the hospital otherwise he'd be here," he said moving towards the kitchen.

I wrapped the towel tighter around my body. I watched his movements, restricted and tense. I made my way upstairs to get cleaned up not taking my eyes off Lou for a moment until I was safely behind my locked door. I came back downstairs freshly showered and back in my pajamas noticing he hadn't moved from where he was at.

"Have you eaten anything today?"

I nodded my head still watching him closely. I held up one finger to indicate I had only eaten one meal.

"I brought a pizza," Lou said pushing the box more towards the middle of the island.

When I still hadn't shown any signs of moving towards him, he sighed running his hands through his hair, "I don't care how you feel about me right now. You need to eat."

"Fine," I huffed out.

I tentatively stepped in his direction making sure to keep the island between us. He watched every movement with sadness etched in his features. The same damn sadness Jennie looked at me with, but I knew if I let go of what had happened between us, we'd be able to move forward. Yet, there was a part of me not willing to let that happen so soon. The constant back and forth was exhausting.

I laid my eyes on the pizza before me, all slices still intact. Lou turned towards the fridge fishing something out so I took my chance to grab my slice and sink my teeth into the greasy pizza with extra cheese. Closing my eyes, I savored every flavor coating my tongue. Lou somehow manages to get the perfect ratio of sauce to cheese to seasonings. Every part of the crust is coated with a layer of garlic butter that adds a nice crispiness to every bite.

When I opened my eyes again, Lou was watching me doing his best to hold back a grin. He gestured towards the glass of amber liquid in front me, "Good to know you still like my pizza at least. Join me in a drink?"

I raised an eyebrow. I hadn't watched him prepare my drink and my trust wasn't there to let me bring the glass to my lips.

He saw my hesitation. He grabbed his glass then went to the couch, "You don't have to drink it if you don't want to. I'm going to enjoy my drink after a long day. Do whatever you need to do, I'm just happy to see you eating."

Lou did just that. He flopped onto the couch not losing a single drop of whiskey then turned on the TV. It didn't take long for him to zone out practically forgetting I was sitting there, so I went back to eating and eyeing the glass in front of me. Eventually I got thirsty enough that I made myself a fresh glass.

I had forgotten the warm burn of whiskey as it slid down my throat. It was as refreshing as it was dangerous. I didn't know what game Lou was trying to play by bringing harder liquor over, but I knew it would temporarily numb the emotional pain. *You're entering into dangerous territory, Val. Just walk away and go up to your room.*

I pushed my thoughts aside throwing the rest of the glass back and refilling it. "This isn't one you want to drink fast," he chuckled.

I hadn't even heard Lou move, so when he spoke next to me, I jumped, "Don't do that."

"She speaks," he said leaning against the cabinets.

"I'm going upstairs," I said draining the next round of whiskey.

"Before you go," he started. I stopped mid-step before turning to face him. His face had grown serious, "Everything I did back in that vampire world was wrong. I royally screwed up and I know nothing I do will make it up to you, but I will try my best. In the meantime, can we focus on the path ahead?"

Raf's voice was in the back of my mind telling me that agreeing to Lou's request would help in this healing journey I'm in, but it was going to be a hard battle to get to the part that allowed me to agree. At the same time, the whiskey was starting to hit. My thoughts were going a little fuzzy, the world started spinning, and I started feeling warm. Most importantly, I was feeling light and free from inhibitions.

In the time it was taking me to respond, Lou had already taken a few steps closer to me. I didn't move, but I didn't like it either, "Did you do something to the alcohol?"

Lou paused, not acting like he was caught, but more to give me some time, "No. You've hardly eaten anything all day. You expect a half-eaten slice to counteract two glasses of whiskey you decided to take as shots?"

I glanced back at the pizza instantly wanting more to help offset the alcohol. When I brought my attention back to Lou, he was right in front of me. He slowly raised his hands to my shoulders, "This is as close as I'll get unless you want more. Val, do you think we can move on from what happened back there?"

I looked at both of his hands before meeting his grey eyes again. The whiskey was doing a damn good job at blocking the voice screaming for me to stay away. Not sure I could trust my voice, I nodded my head.

"Thank you," he said dropping his hands and moving back to the couch. "Eat more."

I did as I was told, making another fresh glass. *At least the bottle's empty at this point.*

I watched Lou for a few moments. He was sitting there, head resting against the back of the couch completely entranced by what he was watching. The longer I looked at him, the more I could see how tired he still looked.

"Have you been sleeping?" I asked noticing my tongue starting to feel thick.

Lou lazily looked at me. Clearly the whiskey was hitting him, too. He moved to stand up so he was standing across the island from me, his glass empty. Lou put both hands on the island, bracing himself, as he said, "Jennie's been keeping me updated on everything that's going on in addition to Raf. My worry for you has been keeping me up, so to answer your question, not really. When Chris texted me about coming over tonight, I jumped at the opportunity so I could see what's going on for myself. They were right."

"What do you mean?"

"Val, the circles under your eyes are worse than mine. You've clearly lost weight by not eating and only moving when Raf comes over which is why he's been here every day. You hardly speak to anyone. Just come back to us," he pleaded. It was the same tone he'd used when they rushed me to the hospital. There were a couple of moments that I came to, and in those times, Lou was begging me to stay with him.

I got up moving to Lou. I slid my arms around his waist feeling him tense at my touch. It must've had something to do with the sessions with Raf or something to do with the whiskey muting my internal arguments that led me to hug him. Maybe it was a combination of both.

Lou cautiously wrapped his arms around me as if he was afraid I was going to lose it, but when he was confident I wasn't going to, he tightened his grip pulling me as close to him as he could. I felt him lower his head so his cheek was resting against the top of my head. That's how we stood for a couple of minutes. No words were exchanged, only the mutual understanding that I was ready to move on and let go of what happened. The tense man who had been standing before me only moments ago was now replaced with someone who was finally able to relax.

"Thank you," he whispered.

I pulled my head away to look up at him, "I'm so – "

"Don't," he said cutting my apology off. "There's no reason for you to be."

We stood there watching each other. I was feeling myself being pulled to him again. Knowing the whiskey was the one behind that, I dropped my arms then moved back to my seat to eat some more. I may be ready to put the past behind us, but that didn't mean I wanted to kiss him. If he felt disappointed, he didn't show it. Instead, he went back to his spot on the couch after opening another bottle of whiskey to refresh his glass.

I ate a couple more slices following Lou's drinking advice and taking sips in between bites. We both moved to refill our glasses at the same time. At this point, I was most definitely drunk.

"Wanna dance?" Lou asked with a slight slur indicating he was at the same point as me.

"Sure," I said letting him lead me to the living room. He put some music on the TV, the first song being the one we had danced to the first time in his apartment.

Lou gently moved me towards him still being careful not to scare me away. I wasn't going to say anything, but any feeling of hesitation or lack of trust were long gone.

"Jennie and Chris have been gone a while," I said most definitely slurring my words.

"They're going to be staying at my place tonight."

"Why?" I asked not daring to say anything more.

That lopsided grin of his tugged at his lips making it hard for me to not want to kiss him, "I offered it up to them in case they drank too much tonight. Didn't want them to risk their safety and my place is a lot closer than yours for them to walk."

"They probably wanna break from me," I mumbled, struggling to keep the world in focus. I wanted to curse the alcohol, but it was doing too good of a job numbing the pain.

"Hey," Lou started lifting my chin up forcing me to look at him. "That's not it at all. They haven't been on a lot of dates and Chris wanted to treat her tonight. No more of those self-deprecating thoughts. Let's have some fun."

I nodded my head, "Okay."

We danced for a few more songs letting the conversation die until we moved downstairs to play some pool. I was getting ready to break when Lou asked, "Do you play pool like you play poker?"

"Only one way to find," the words trailed off as I smacked the cue ball into the triangle further down the table scattering the rest of the balls. We didn't move, waiting for the balls to stop moving. A couple of solids found their way into the pockets making me smile, "Still got it."

"Shit," was all Lou could say.

I moved around the table on a mission to sink as many solids as I could while Lou watched me his mouth open in disbelief. I got down to the eight ball when Lou was suddenly behind me. I felt his breath against my neck sending shivers down my spine, "I may not have been able to distract you during poker, but I think I have a better shot here."

He was careful not to touch me as he placed his hands on either side essentially trapping me where I was. I smirked knowing what game he was starting to play, but little did he know, I was all too familiar with this tactic. I slowly bent to get ready to take my shot, my ass barely making contact with him. I heard a sharp intake of breath that made me miss my mark. *Damn it.*

I turned so I was facing him, "Don't think that will work again, Lou."

I ducked under his arms to position myself on the opposite side of the table, stumbling a little bit. I hated to admit I liked being close to him again. I liked feeling the warmth of his body. I knew this was the whiskey talking again and I had to be careful.

He started making his run eliminating obstacles for me. He was about to sink his last ball before joining me on the quest to take out the eight ball when he hit the ball a little too hard, sending it on a dance around the table. I knew this was my chance to end it. I lined up seeing exactly what angle I needed to strike the cue ball at to put the eight ball in the pocket I called when Lou took off his shirt. Not moving from my position, I lifted my eyebrows, "Really?"

"Just getting ready for a swim, that's all," he casually said.

I rolled my eyes, but had a hard time not thinking about the hard lines of his muscles. It may have been obvious that I haven't been eating as much as I should be, but it was clear Lou had been spending more time at a gym. *Damn it, why did I let myself drink like that?*

I smacked the cue ball putting the eight right where I wanted to, ending the game. Putting my cue stick away, I moved back upstairs to finish my last glass of whiskey. Lou took his outside, wading into the pool. I followed him, ironically not wanting to feel alone when I was drunk. Anything keeping me from making a move on Lou was out the window now. Besides, Warrick made it clear we were done even if he was the mastermind behind getting me out of Cian's clutches. I needed to hear it directly from him that he wanted to be with me, and in the meantime, I guess I could let myself have a little fun. *Jeez, you sure get over things quickly, Val.*

My feet got the best of me, making me stumble the last couple of steps. Lou held out his hands ready to catch me if I fell in, but after steadying myself, I took a seat at the edge dropping my legs into the water. Lou took a swig from his drink not taking his eyes off me. I shifted under the weight of his stare, "You're not trying to shoot your shot, are you?"

"I'm not here to take advantage of you, if that's what you're implying," he answered.

"Good."

He took a step closer to me, taking another drink. I gave him a little splash and we both had to hold back some laughter. Another step closer and another splash. This game continued until he was in front of me, once again placing his hands on either side while being mindful to not touch me, "I would say you're having a good time."

"I would agree," I nodded my head, my tongue still thick, making it hard for me to form any words.

Lou lifted one of his hands debating about touching me. I looked at his hand then at him, "You can touch me, you know. I'm not going to hiss and shrink away."

The moment I gave him permission, he started rubbing my arm then moved to tracing some of my new scars, "I hate that this happened to you."

"Nothing we can do about it now. Raf says I need to leave it in the past," I said doing my best not to melt into his touch.

He frowned, "Why do you have feelings for someone who has repeatedly tried to kill you?"

All filters were off, I guess. I must've made a face because Lou followed up his question, "Shit, don't answer that. In fact, let's not talk about that stuff tonight. I don't want to ruin the fun we've been having."

I put a hand on top of his, "I can talk about it. It's hard ... to describe how I feel about Warrick. I don't know what it is ... that brings me back to him, but that's probably over now."

"What do you mean?"

I let out a laugh, "I'm probably never going to see... him again and that's fine by me. It's time I moved ... on."

I looked down to Lou. He moved his hand back to the ground and lifted himself out of the pool. Water dripped all over as he straddled me. His face was inches from mine. I felt my heart rate pick up threatening to beat out of my chest. Lou brought a hand up to my cheek tracing the scar there. I moved my head back, the memories of what happened trying to take over. "What are you doing?" I choked out.

"I hoped you would never get scars like this," he said not noticing the panic creeping into me.

I brought a hand up to his chest fighting through the alcohol-induced fog to keep my bearings, "Lou."

That seemed to have snapped him out of whatever trance he had been in. He dropped his hand, but still kept his face close to mine, "Sorry."

"It's ... okay," I slurred.

I pushed him back into the pool finally able to breathe now that there was distance between us. After taking a swig from my drink, I felt a tug on my leg and found myself in the pool with him. I pushed my hair back spitting out the water, "What ... the hell was that for?"

"You didn't think you'd be able to get away with pushing me into the water without facing some consequences, did you?"

I immediately recognized the playful look on his face. Throwing that brief sober moment out the window from earlier, I closed the distance between us pushing him under the water for a second. When he popped back up, Lou was laughing. Unable to keep myself from getting drawn in to the sweet sound of his laughter, I looped my arms around the back of his neck while wrapping my legs around him.

"Val," Lou started protesting. "Please, I want to respect you."

He put light pressure on my stomach trying to push me away only to get a shake of my head in return, "I ... can appreciate that, but I want ... to be close."

"You're drunk."

"You are too, but I'm aware enough to make my own decisions," I said lifting my chin up in defiance.

Lou sighed closing his eyes, "It's really hard to listen to Raf right now."

Sucking in some air to keep myself from slurring, I responded, "Then don't."

He snapped his eyes open, pupils fully dilated. In a voice filled with desire, Lou asked, "Are you sure? I'll only do what you give me permission to."

"Kiss me, Lou," I whispered.

And he did. He was gentle at first, letting me dictate how this was going to go until he finally took over. His hands tightened their grip on my waist keeping me where I was and acting as a restraint for him. The amount of effort he was putting in to avoid crossing another line was not going unnoticed. I pulled back to come up for air for a second, "What did Raf say to you?"

"What?"

"At the hospital," I was trying my best to catch my breath. "What did Raf say to you to make you have this much restraint?"

"He just said to give you distance and listen to when you say no. The rest of this? It's all me. I hated how you looked at me and despised my actions that night. I never want to stoop to that level again."

"You don't need to hold yourself back ... like you're scared you're going to break me. I'll tell you to stop if you're crossing a line," I said brushing my thumb over his bottom lip.

I leaned in brushing my lips against his, "Kiss me, Lou. Really kiss me."

And he did. He moved us to the edge of the pool to have something to brace me against so he could angle my face to give me a deeper kiss while entangling his other hand in my hair. *Back to usual activities ... get drunk then fall into bed with someone to try to fill this hole in my heart.*

That thought stopped me, Lou picking up on my hesitation. "Everything okay?" he asked searching my eyes.

"As long as you're okay with this not meaning anything," I said startled by the truth coming out.

I expected Lou to be as startled as I was, but all he did was cock his head to the side, "Don't worry, I'm not going to be falling in love tonight. I may be drunk, too, Val, but I can recognize when we're hooking up because we're sharing something versus when it's just physical to fill a need."

"Good," I said relaxing a little knowing there weren't any strings attached. Lou downed the rest of the whiskey in his glass almost as if he was proving a point then grabbed my face to bring it back to his.

We were entangled in each other for a little while longer before moving to the couch where I spend my afternoons napping.

His hands started roaming my body, his kisses becoming more intense. Lou was showing me a side he hadn't before. A side more focused on fulfilling a need rather than getting lost in the moment. This is the proof he was giving to assure me he wasn't going to be letting his feelings resurface.

Lou peeled off our wet clothes then went back to giving me a type of attention my body craved. As he worked me, I had a hard time keeping my mind from wandering to Warrick and how I missed the feeling of him kissing me, his hands finding all the right places to caress and tease.

We went at each other for several hours before the alcohol finally left our system and we fell asleep in a mess of tangled limbs. I woke up a few hours later. Lou was still sound asleep next to me as I moved to get up. I grabbed my wet clothes, made sure the blanket was still covering him, and snuck my way into the house. I looked back over my shoulder to make sure he hadn't moved then climbed the stairs to my room.

When I tucked myself in my bed, it felt like I could breathe a little again. I didn't like the fact I just slept with Lou again, a part of me filled with guilt at the thought of being with someone who isn't Warrick. *What would this do to Lou and I?* Before I could keep going down that path, sleep took over.

I walked down the street, leaves drifting to the ground as a cool breeze brushed past me. At first, I didn't know where I was until the black Ducati came into view.

Home. Our home.

My pace picked up into a jog. I threw open the front door, "Gabriel!"

I paused for a moment to see if I could pick up any noise. When there was nothing, I moved further into the house. Pictures of us lined the walls, all smiles and kisses and laughter.

I forgot the warmth this place brought with its light blue walls, sandy colored flooring, and simple decorations. No one was in the front of the house, so I wandered back to the bedrooms noticing a trail of rose petals. Smiling, I turned the corner into our bedroom. My heart swelled at the sight in front of me: Gabriel in his loose, black button-down shirt and black skinny jeans holding a bouquet of roses as candles flickered around the perimeter of the room.

He beamed at me, "There you are."

"What are you doing here?"

"I've heard you, Val, baby. I can't stand to see you crying anymore, so I wanted to give you something special."

My hand shook as I brought it to my lips, "Ar – are you real?"

"As real as I can be."

"You're not something I conjured up in a fit of sadness?" I asked still not trusting what I was seeing. This wasn't real. One of the monsters following me would burst through the door at any moment.

His smile faltered for a moment. Gabriel put the roses on the bed moving towards me. He brushed my hair behind my ear, his thumb stroking my cheek, "I'm real. I'm here."

I leaned into his touch, tears welling. I felt whole again, something I hadn't felt in ages. I breathed him in, the scent of the ocean mixed with pine overwhelming my senses. I wound my arms around Gabriel to hold him so tight you would have to pry me from him, "I've missed you more than any words could describe. Please tell me you're coming back and this isn't just a dream."

He chuckled, "I've missed you, too." He pulled away holding my face, "Let's go for a ride."

I didn't hesitate to let him pull me back outside. He put my helmet on then helped me onto the bike before getting on himself. After a couple of quick revs, we were off. Riding with him was unlike any feeling I had before. I was flying, relishing in the freedom. On a straightaway, I let go of his strong chest to spread my arms out. My head dropped back and I closed my eyes. Everything was right with the world again. He glanced back shaking his head. I'm sure he was smiling as much as I was in this moment.

I let out a groan of disappointment when he pulled off the road, killing the engine. I gave him a pouting face when he pulled my helmet off. His honey-sweet laugh filled my ears, "I'll take the long way home. I promise."

"You better," I jabbed him in his ribs.

"I do need to talk to you before you wake up," he said patting the seat. Something shifted in me not ready to push our happy reunion aside. He stood close to me rubbing a hand on my thighs to bring me comfort, "You know I love you way more than I could show you, right?"

I nodded not liking where this was going.

"I don't ever want you to forget that love you have for me. I do want you to find someone you can share the love only you can give, though. I can't be the only one to know what it feels like to have that, and you know you have to do it, too. I see it written all over your face. Hell, you already know who that person is."

"What are you saying?"

"Baby, I'm always going to be watching over you and loving you. I hope you feel when I wrap my arms around you at night, because every time I do that, I'm at peace. There's nowhere I'd rather be than around you. It hurts me to be practically shoving you into someone else's arms, but it hurts me even more seeing you throwing yourself at others just to put a band-aid on a gaping wound."

I reached up to caress his cheek. He leaned into my hand taking his turn to close his eyes for a moment. I couldn't say anything without running the risk of my emotions taking over. Tears started spilling from my eyes, Gabriel wiping them as they came, "Don't cry for me, mi amor. I will always, always be with you. Nothing will change that. In the land of the living, though, please love. Love this man with all your heart. Tell me about your adventures, your sorrows, and your deepest wants. I'll be here listening and waiting until the time is right for you to come join me."

He kissed my forehead to end his speech. I held on to him even tighter just to know he wasn't fading away, and when I was confident I wasn't losing him, I pulled back, "Why now?"

"Because you're trying to fade away and it's not your time yet. Believe me, there's no one who would want this reunion more, but there's still a few things you need to take care of."

"But I'm messing up," I countered, my lips trembling.

He pulled me in so my head was against his chest. My eyes widened at the sound of his heart that I almost didn't hear him, "You're doing exactly what you need to be. It may not seem like it, but you have to trust me. Did you know I saw Daryl?"

"You did?"

"Yeah. He told me everything I had already witnessed, and he also told me how he should've listened to you. Even if you feel like you're messing up, I don't want you to forget how damn impressive you are. I knew it when we first met. You're incredibly strong which is how I know you'll make it through this, too."

"I can't, babe. I can't do this anymore," I sobbed.

"Shhh," he said stroking my hair. I forgot how much I missed this comfort. It made my heart shatter into a million pieces knowing I was going to have to return to the land of the living without him. "You are capable of so way more than you know. I love you, Val. Now, you're going to need to wake your badass up and conquer your day, okay?"

"No, I'm not leaving you," I pleaded.

He gripped my face so I was looking at him, "You are, but that doesn't mean we're separated. Remember? I'll be right here."

Gabriel tapped my heart. His head whipped up suddenly, his focus elsewhere. He looked the other way before looking back at me, "Listen to me, Val. I need you to wake up, now. I need you to get out of here and trust me when I say I'll be waiting for you, okay? You have to go, baby."

He kissed me with urgency then pulled back, "I love you, mi amor."

His hands dropped and he turned towards whatever he heard. I started to turn around to the void behind me assuming that's where I needed to go when I heard bones snapping. I spun around screaming when I saw the Gabriel crumpled on the ground and Liam standing over him. Liam looked at me, "Fancy meeting you here."

I kept screaming as the dream faded hearing the faint whisper of Gabriel's voice, "I'll always be here waiting for you."

"V al!" someone shouted at me. My eyes were still closed, but I could tell I was still screaming. I was shaken and yelled at again, but I couldn't fully tear myself away from sleep yet.

"Val, I need you to wake up right now!"

There was another shake and my eyes shot open. I flailed around wildly ready to fight. *He can't be here. There's no way.* My breaths were heavy. I reached towards my throat not getting enough air. I looked all over my room until my eyes finally landed on Lou. I grabbed his arm, "He's here. We're not safe. We have to go!"

"What are you talking about?" he asked.

Jennie was standing in the doorway looking panicked, Chris with the same facial expression behind her. Jennie glanced at me then back at Lou, "What do you need me to do?"

"Call Raf. Now!" he ordered.

"He's going to kill us! We have to go," I shrieked. My throat was raw from the screaming, so as I repeated the last sentence, I whispered the words rocking back and forth.

"Val," Lou said reaching for my cheek. I jerked my head back, my wild gaze landing on him. "Val, I need you to tell me who you're talking about. The only way I'll be able to help you is if you talk to me. Please."

"Liam. He's going to kill me. He killed Gabriel."

"Liam isn't here. I checked every inch of this house and property. The coast is clear," Lou said doing his best to keep a calm tone.

Chris popped up in the doorway, "Raf's on his way. He'll be here in five minutes."

"Good. Can you guys check around for anything suspicious?"

"You got it," Chris said turning to head back downstairs.

I was still rocking in my spot. Lou turned his attention back to me. "Can you tell me what happened?" Lou asked sitting on the edge of my bed.

"He killed him. Lou, he killed him," I couldn't bring myself to say anything else, only repeating this new phrase.

Lou reached out for me again only to get me drawing back again. He let out a breath he had been holding on to. "This isn't going to be easy," he muttered to himself. "Gabriel is dead, Val. He has been for years. Liam is back on the world we just left with no way of getting here. You're safe."

"But I'm not, Lou. I'm not safe," I said looking at him again.

"I'm not going to let anything happen to you."

"Lou, I'm here," Raf said rushing into the room. He took one look at me then demanded Lou leave. Raf closed the door behind him then crossed the space. He sat down where Lou had been moments ago, "What happened, Val?"

"He killed Gabriel right in front of me," I started crying. "It hurts, Raf. Make the pain go away."

"The only way I can do that is if you tell me everything."

I buried my head in my arms debating if I actually wanted to go through with recounting my dream. *He's going to think I'm crazy. He'll just tell me I'm making something up to rationalize my thoughts.*

"You don't need to say anything to the group standing outside the door. It's only you and I in here. They won't be able to hear us, I'll make sure of it. I won't judge you or doubt anything you say, so I'll repeat myself, the only way I can help you is if you talk to me," he said.

I thought about it a little longer before finally recounting the dream I just had. By the time I was done, Raf nodded his head, "I believe you, Val. If there's one thing I've learned, it's that you don't ignore the messages of the dead. You know what you have to do, so when the time comes, you do it, okay? In the meantime, I'll give you this sedative. Take it and rest today."

Chapter 6

The sedative Raf gave me knocked me out into a dreamless sleep for the rest of the day. I had no idea what was going on around me, but Jennie, Chris, and Lou were busy doing something downstairs. I could hear them running around as if they were preparing for something.

It was night by the time I was finally able to wake up. I was empty, not wanting to move again. When I caught a whiff of Lou's pizza, I went on autopilot wrapping the blanket around my shoulders and slowly making my way downstairs. Raf's voice was the first one to drift up to me, "You guys have to jump. If what I'm hearing at the hospital is right, things are getting worse in other places. There's a war going on, as I'm sure you know, and it's spreading to these other worlds. Find her friends, and more importantly, find Warrick."

"Why the hell would we want to do that?" Lou spat.

Raf didn't back down, "If you want Val to make any sort of improvement, you'll find him."

Jennie stepped between the two wolves. *Bold move.* Her back was to Lou as she asked Raf, "Where do we even start?"

"The only thing I know is that he's somewhere tropical. I couldn't get any more details than that. Something about me being in the rival pack and all."

"Thank you, Raf," she said. Jennie turned to Chris still ignoring Lou, "Go check the list of codes so we can start figuring out potential places to go with what we know."

"C'mon, man," Chris grabbed Lou. They were heading towards me. There was no turning back now. Lou stopped when he saw me at the top of the stairs. He jogged up to me lowering his voice, "Hey, I'm happy you're up. Pizza is on the island. I made it just like last night. Please, eat."

I watched after him as the two men passed me. Raf had heard Lou say something so now his attention was fully on me, "How are you feeling?"

I headed toward the island, "Numb."

Jennie slid me a slice of pizza and some water, just watching me. Raf pushed a chair underneath me, "Did you and Lou really drink through two bottles of top-shelf whiskey last night?"

"Yeah," I said taking a tentative bite of pizza. "Don't you dare suggest that's why I had that dream."

Raf shook his head, "Hey, I said no judgement here and I mean it. Just impressed, that's all."

"I don't want to see Warrick," I blurted.

Jennie buzzed nervously around the kitchen keeping her head down. Raf put on his doctor mask, "I know you don't, Val, but you need to. Remember what we talked about earlier about not ignoring messages?"

He was purposely being vague meaning Jennie had no clue about what Raf and I discussed earlier. *Add another point to Raf for keeping his word.*

I glanced at Jennie who was frozen at the sink clearly listening in before bringing my attention back to Raf, "Doesn't mean I want to see him."

"You say that now," he trailed off as Lou and Chris rejoined us at the island.

Chris looked excited as he said, "There's only one code with notes around it that go to a tropical place. We'll start with that and start bouncing around if we need to."

"You look excited," Jennie remarked.

"I've always wanted to go someplace warm and tropical."

I gave a panicked look to Raf. He picked up on what I was worried about, "These three have been brought up to speed on what they need to do to help you make more progress. You're in good hands, Val. These people really care about you."

Jennie reached for my hand making me jump, "We won't let anything else happen to you, okay?"

I swallowed the lump in my throat looking down at my barely touched pizza slice, "Fine."

"Can we have a moment alone?" Raf asked.

Everyone cleared out and Raf waited a few more beats until he turned to me. He motioned for me to come closer then dropped his voice, "I know you don't want to see Warrick, but believe me, when you do, you'll never want him out of your sights again. If everything you told me was true, you'll feel a thousand times better. Don't let Lou try to get in your head, okay?"

"Okay," I whispered.

He settled back in his seat pointing to my plate, "At least eat half of that before you retreat back to your room."

I did as I was told and finished the slice before retreating. The other three hadn't come back yet, so I said my goodbye to Raf. When I got upstairs, I found another slice waiting for me with a note from Lou. I didn't read what he wrote me nor did

I touch the pizza. Instead, I turned on my TV to let the noise distract me from my thoughts as I fell asleep once more.

The next morning, I woke up to my balcony doors open with the sound of the ocean drifting up to me. I slept through the jump. I gingerly stepped out onto my balcony squinting at the bright sun.

"Morning," Lou muttered making me jump. He was wrapped in the blanket I had used after the therapy sessions with Raf.

"Did you sleep out here?" I asked quietly.

"Yeah. Raf said you might be a little jumpy coming off the sedative, so I wanted to make sure I was close by in case anything happened."

I wrapped my arms around myself feeling a little uncomfortable. He picked up on that, "Don't worry. I stayed out here the entire time."

"Are Chris and Jennie downstairs?" I asked looking out over the water. This ocean was the bluest I had ever seen. The house had landed on the beach. I swept my gaze away from the water taking in the colorful buildings that looked to be the hub of activity noting it was within walking distance.

"No, they went to check things out. They should be back soon, though," Lou answered moving to get up.

I watched him moving towards the door. Lou paused in the doorway, "How are you feeling today?"

"A little less numb, if that makes sense."

"Yeah," he said offering a soft smile. "It does. Let me know if you're up for exploring."

He turned making his way to the door. "Lou?" I called out.

His hand hovered over the door handle, "Yeah?"

"I'm sorry."

His brow furrowed, "Sorry for what?"

"For you having to see that yesterday," I said gesturing towards the bed. "That probably wasn't how you wanted to wake up the next day after having drunken sex. And, for everything else. It wasn't fair how I treated you back in Cian's world."

Lou dropped his shoulders making his way back to me, "There's nothing you need to say sorry for. You've been through more than you should have. If you weren't waking up screaming, I'd be more worried. Plus, I already told you, we're leaving that stuff in the past."

"Thanks," I mumbled.

He crossed his arms over his chest, "I'm making an executive decision. Get dressed. We're checking out the town. People sound way too happy for me to want to sit in here all day."

"I – ," I opened my mouth to protest, but Lou shook his head. "We're going, Val, whether you want to or not. Doctor's orders from Raf," he said over his shoulder on the way out of my room.

A frustrated groan escaped my lips as I threw my head back. After my mini protest, I threw on a pair of running shorts, a light hoodie that belonged to Gabriel relishing over it still smelling like him, and some flip-flops. I met Lou in the entryway and looped my arm through his. This action surprised him, his eyes widening, "You sure?"

I nodded my head, "Yeah, I need someone to help ground me and you're the only one here. You have no idea how terrified I am that we're going to walk out there."

Lou patted my arm, "I got you, Val."

He opened the door and I took a deep, steadying breath before letting him drag me outside. Just as it was when we were on my balcony, the air was fresh with the hint of salt from the ocean lingering. Birds were singing all around us seemingly following the rhythm coming from the steel drums playing in the distance. We started our trek by walking along the pristine, white-sanded beach occasionally feeling the warm embrace of the water around our ankles.

I stopped, tilting my head back to let the warmth of the sun wash over me. "Have you ever seen water so blue, yet so clear?" Lou asked.

I brought my gaze back to the scene in front of us. This water would put the Bahamas to shame. I had never seen water so vibrant. Taking in the sight of the clear water, we pointed out a few of the fish, commenting on how colorful they all were. There were even a few new fish, if we could call them that. They may be swimming in the water mingling with the other schools of fish, but that was the end of their similarities. Seeing this served as a reminder there were a lot of things we needed to learn about this world.

We continued our walk towards the town, our conversation becoming easier with each step. Stopping when we reached the main road, we observed what was playing out in front of us. The buildings we could see from the house were a mix of homes and shops, all different colors from pink to blue to yellow and anything in between. It looked like there was a market going today with stalls set up filled with a variety of goods, but that wasn't what caught our attention. The people were all shapes, sizes and colors. Some had wings and others didn't. They all, however, had pointed ears. Lou leaned down to me, "Where are we?"

"Do you remember the notes next to the code you put in?"

"Something about the Caribbean and maybe fairies?"

I smiled at Lou, "We're on an island filled with fairies. That also means there's going to be a lot of magic, so we'll need to be careful."

"Let's go," Lou said tugging me with him.

As soon as we passed the first couple buildings, the air was filled with the smell of cinnamon and other food aromas. My mouth started watering with each food stand we passed. Mixed with the colorful building and vendor stalls were huge tropical flowers, palm trees, and plants that looked like they were around when dinosaurs roamed the Earth.

Everyone around us was smiling and laughing carrying on light-hearted conversations. It was like there wasn't a care in the world here, everyone's on island time and living their best life. *Maybe this is where I needed to be all along.*

We kept making our way down the street, no one paying us any extra attention than what they would to any potential shopper. The closer we got to the town center, the happier and lighter I felt. Anything weighing me down before was gone. I glanced up at Lou sure he was feeling the same way based on the lazy grin and his relaxed posture.

The music that's been accompanying us got louder, and when the street finally opened up to what I assumed to be the town center. We were greeted by the sweet sound of steel drums directing the rhythm of the people dancing around a giant fountain. We positioned ourselves in the audience clapping along with everyone else, full blown smiles taking over our faces.

Next thing I knew, I was being pulled into the group dancing. I closed my eyes lifting my face towards the sun again as I let the music drive my movements. The fairies around me let out several whoops signaling their excitement at getting someone else to join them and I mimicked their sounds caught up in the moment.

I went from outstretched arm to outstretched arm completing a full circle laughing the entire time. The moment I was back in front of Lou, I pulled him to me still keeping some space between us. I could do this every day if it meant I could leave my troubles behind. Being completely carefree took me back to the days when Gabriel and I were just living life. There wasn't a war, there wasn't the looming date of him going to the frontlines, and there wasn't as much death and abuse. Even the thought of him didn't make my heart heavy like usual.

A break in the music signaled for those of us dancing to disperse. Lou and I were laughing, my arm linked back through his. We took a few steps away from the fountain when Jennie's laugh rang out. I looked up at Lou, "Shall we go find them?"

Lou pointed nodding his head in the direction of where we heard her, "I don't think we'll have to look far."

The person blocking my view finally moved revealing Jennie and Chris looking about the happiest I've seen them. My heart swelled knowing they were free of whatever burden I had placed on them.

Their backs were to us and they were clearly engaged in a conversation. We approached them slowly trying not to interrupt, but I couldn't keep myself from reaching out to tap her on the shoulder as soon as she was within arm's reach. She whipped around, eyes wide surprised to see us. Her infamous squeal filled the air as she threw her arms around me.

"Hi, Jennie," I said laughing.

"I never thought I'd hear your laugh again," she said into my hair. "And you're here with Lou!"

She ended our hug to give a quick one to Lou before stepping back. Chris and Lou did the typical guy thing exchanging a complicated handshake before going in for a hug.

There was no hint of concern or worry in her eyes for the first time since I had been rescued. She did a little jump and let out another squeal before saying, "You'll never believe who we ran into?"

"Who?" I asked unable to think of anyone she'd get this excited about.

She took a step aside revealing who they had been talking to when we were walking up. My eyes widened in shock, "Joe? Bev?"

"It's so good to see you here! We thought we'd never see any of you guys again," Joe said while Bev moved in for a hug.

After Bev released me, I reached towards Joe pulling him in, "We have *a lot* to catch up on."

Bev glanced at Lou then back at me, "We can tell."

Joe thrust a hand out to Lou, "I'm Joe, nice to meet you. This is my wife, Bev."

"Lou. Nice to meet you guys, too," Lou said shaking both Joe and Bev's hands.

"How do you two know each other?" Bev asked.

"Well, that's part of what we need to catch up on," I answered. "Come over tonight."

"We'll be there, but where are you exactly?" Bev asked.

I pointed in the direction where Lou and I had come from, "Follow the road out of here and head towards the beach. I think you'll recognize the house when you see it."

Joe's eyes widened, "The house came with you?"

"Thankfully, yeah," I nodded.

Jennie jumped back in, "I just can't get over the fact you guys were transported to this beautiful island. There isn't a care in the world here."

"It has been a nice break, for sure," Joe smiled.

Jennie, Joe, Bev, and Chris went back and forth for a little while longer. Lou and I were nodding our heads and laughing when the time came in the conversations, but I finally got to a point where I needed to take a break. Despite leaving all my cares behind me, I still needed some breathing room. I mentioned to Lou I was going to check a store out then made my quiet escape.

I headed into the nearest storefront admiring all the little trinkets. I ducked under some wings and dodged around small faeries running around my feet as I moved from shelf to shelf. The store itself was nowhere near as colorful on the inside as it is on the outside. The shelves were pieces of wood hung up by a couple of brackets, but the glass trinkets sitting on top sparkled and shined in a way I've never seen before. I was completely mesmerized.

I eventually moved to the back corner opposite of where the register was with a staircase behind it. I caught myself staring at those stairs thinking about how simple it would be to have an apartment above the little shop I own. I'd spend my days making sales, chatting with familiar faces and new, and be able to take things at a slower pace. Not that I've done much hard work since my life flipped upside down. Being a server isn't exactly the hardest job, at least when I compare it to the office job I had back home.

I shook myself out of my little daydream and brought myself back to the present. I took another step over, completely focused on what looked like a crystal whale-type creature. It was reminiscent of a whale shark, but it looked like there were flowy ribbons coming off its back and two extra sets of fins lining its sides. There were a couple of antennas slightly behind its eyes. This particular crystal seemed to move when you changed what angle you were looking at while also sending rainbows around the space as light refracted through the middle of it.

I was still holding the whale shark creature when everyone around me started bowing. I turned my head from left to right wondering what the hell was happening. I bent at my waist to follow suit lifting my head slightly to see what was causing people to react this way.

The sound of steps echoed as the owners of the feet slowly descended into view with the smell of cinnamon growing increasingly stronger despite there being no food in this store. There was a group of five led by the tallest woman I've ever seen. She easily towered over everyone around her, her skin so dark she could blend in with a forest at night. Contrasting with her skin was her hair. It was long and straight, the platinum color practically shining. There were several crystals threaded throughout for what reason I wasn't sure. Next to her were two men, one whose skin was a lilac color and the other a deep tan. Their ears were pointed also, one of them with earrings jingling with every step he took. Both men were scanning the room giving me the sense they were the protection for the women in the group. Following the three in the front were another pair, a man and a woman. The woman looked very similar to the one in the front, just shorter and instead of platinum hair, hers was a light blue without any crystals. She was smiling up at the man next to her and she was dazzling. I was immediately drawn into her presence, wanting to be close to her and have her attention on me. Her smile was blindingly white, every feature of her face perfectly placed, topped with cotton candy pink eyes.

The man was the only one without the signature pointed ears which immediately snapped my attention to him. He was about the same height as the gorgeous woman hanging on his arm and had black hair. You could see the outline of muscles through his tight t-shirt. He was saying something, but I couldn't get a glimpse of his face. I felt myself slowly rise as I found it harder and harder to shake the feeling of familiarity as I took him in. He turned to her returning the smile, but then continued turning his head to look behind him. At me. With eyes that could rival the bluest glacier. I was standing at full height now, my lips parted with shock, his eyes slightly widening at the sight of me. *Warrick.*

Chapter 7

Discovering Joe and Bev was one thing, but seeing Warrick here with a woman draped over his arm was another. It was hard to fight the light and happy feeling that's been filling me since the minute Lou and I stepped into the town, but I knew something was stirring underneath everything else. I was caught completely offguard, thankful I didn't drop the crystal whale still in my hand. I waited for the group to clear the shop and head in the opposite direction from where I would be heading before returning the crystal back to its place on the shelf. Everyone was back to normal, too, as if nothing had happened. *Must be a regular occurrence for royalty to walk through the town.*

Judging by the reactions everyone had, I would assume the woman leading them was the leader of this world. That would be the only reason Warrick would be with her. My mind tried to go back to focusing on the dazzling woman with him, but I couldn't let myself do that. *Get to Lou. I need to warn him.*

I quickly made my exit from the store careful not to bump anyone to keep from drawing attention to myself. I picked up the pace of my walk the minute I was outside of the store. I glanced over my shoulder to see the group still slowly putting more distance between us, the onlookers bowing in waves as they passed. Every now and then, Warrick would glance back looking for something, or someone. I didn't care to see if he laid his eyes on me again. I was all jitters wanting to return to the safety of home.

I nearly smacked into the back of Lou, letting go of my breath I didn't realize I was holding.

Lou jumped, turning around. He must've sensed I was unsettled because his hands found their way to my shoulders again to steady me, "Val, you okay?"

I forced a smile, "Yeah, just thought I saw something. Can we head back?"

"Yeah," he agreed, his brow furrowing slightly. He turned to the rest of the group, "We're going to head back. Jennie, Chris, don't feel like you need to cut your reunion short. Joe, Bev, it was great to meet you and I look forward to seeing you tonight."

"Enjoy your walk home," Jennie said giving us a couple of quick hugs. When she had me in her grasp, she whispered, "It's great seeing you and Lou back on speaking terms."

I nodded my head as she let go, giving Joe and Bev quick hugs of their own. Lou held out his arm and I hooked mine in it reminded of how Warrick was with the mystery fairy. Lou matched my hastened pace following the path we took to get here except skipping the dancing this time. When we finally got out of the town, it was as if everything good back there got sucked out of me. I doubled over making Lou stop with me. He put his hand on my back, "Are you okay?"

"What was that?" I said in between breaths. Panic was creeping up mixed with the sadness I've grown so accustomed to since getting away from Cian's.

"I don't know, but I felt it, too. There has to be some sort of magic around there. Val, what happened?"

"Warrick," was all I could gasp out. I squeezed my eyes shut feeling some tears escape with the sudden movement. My hands started shaking as panic threatened to take a firmer hold.

Lou squatted in front of me, grey eyes filled with concern. He reached for my face, "Hey, look at me. Take a deep breath."

I did as I was told, inhaling the air that now smelt of ocean more than the aromatic smells that surrounded us a few feet back.

"Good, now let it out. Do it again a couple more times," he instructed.

The breathing exercises managed to keep the panic attack at bay, but didn't completely eliminate the feeling.

Lou grabbed my arm putting it back in his, "Let's get you home. Besides, we have guests to prep for. That'll be a nice distraction."

He led me back, keeping the hurried pace from before. We were on the beach with the house in sight, making note of the few people lying out to enjoy the sun and sand. We kept our distance so we didn't disturb anyone. I was watching the sea again counting the number of seconds for the waves to push onto the beach using a method Raf taught me to try and calm myself.

Lou tightened his grip on me causing me to look up at him. "Shit," he mumbled.

I followed his gaze to one person who was laying out in the sun. He was the only one between us and the house, far away from everyone else. This clearly wasn't the first time he'd been out here judging by the tan on his skin, but the panic I worked so hard to tuck away crept back in. All of a sudden, I felt incredibly hot and my stomach flipped threatening to empty whatever small amount of contents were in there.

Warrick propped himself up on his elbows watching us approach and greeting us with a little finger wave, "Fancy meeting you here."

"How the hell did he get here so fast?" I asked in a hushed tone.

Lou looked at me, "I'll take care of this."

We inched closer to him and I became more worried I was going to empty my stomach on this beach.

"You two make a lovely couple," he quipped.

That was all it took. I snatched my arm back so I could double over, vomiting behind Lou. There wasn't a lot that surfaced, but I was still embarrassed.

"I'd have that reaction if I were involved with Lou, too, love."

I wiped my mouth with the back of my hand standing up to face him. Lou started saying something, but I cut him off, "No. You don't get to sit here making those kinds of comments."

"Really? Tell me what I get to say, then. By the way, it's lovely seeing you, too," he smirked. I thought I was imagining things since my mind was all over the place, but it looked like there was some relief behind that mask of his.

"I'm not dealing with this," I said starting to storm off making sure to keep distance from Warrick in case he tried to grab me.

"Wow, that's a first."

"Warrick, shut your ass up," Lou snapped.

I whipped around, "I'm sick and tired of your shit, Warrick. Every time you come around, I almost die. I'm not doing that anymore. Go fuck yourself."

"Feisty," Warrick said. "Don't fuck things up for me this time, either. You found your friends, now move on. Remember, it's not just about you two," he called behind me.

I rolled my eyes bristling at those comments, but continued my trek back to the house. I wasn't going to let him see my emotions get the best of me again. The second I stepped foot on my property I collapsed into one of the chairs. I sat there dry heaving, willing the happiness from earlier to come back. When my body calmed down, I stripped down to my underwear craving the calm from the pool. I glanced in the direction of Lou and Warrick who were clearly still arguing on the beach before diving into the cool water.

My eyes were closed under the water filled with images from when Cian was holding me hostage. The scar on my side where Warrick dug his fingers in burned with the memories consuming me. I came up to take a breath then immediately went back under to scream so no one would hear me. By the time I resurfaced, my throat was raw and Lou was sitting at the edge of the pool. He was holding his head in his hands, "I'm so sorry, Val. We'll get out of here tonight. We'll tell Joe and Bev everything, get them to grab their things, and join us."

I could've lashed out. I could've blamed Lou for what had happened in the past, but Raf's voice was in the back of my head reminding me to let that go. I swam over to rest my chin on my arms next to Lou, "We can't control his actions. I do appreciate you trying to look out for me, though. Please, don't say sorry. We've said that enough and it's time to move on."

His grey eyes slid over to me, "Really? Not the reaction I was expecting since you left your stomach contents on the beach and came back here to scream under the water."

I don't know what I was expecting, but that wasn't the reaction I thought I'd get from him. I jerked my head back like I had been slapped by the anger lacing his voice then pushed away from the wall to get distance between us.

"Shit, Val," he started, his voice filled with regret.

"Don't. Just don't," I said lifting myself out of the water feeling very self-conscious about him being able to see through my impromptu swimwear. "Don't bother checking on me. I'll come down when I'm ready."

I stomped into the house slamming the door shut behind me. I instantly wanted to go back to town to replace these negative emotions with positive ones, whether they were mine or not, but instead went upstairs to shower and crawl back in my bed.

Exhaustion took over, my eyes unable to produce any more tears after emptying in the shower. Eventually my eyes shut, taking me back into the dream where I had met Gabriel. This time, I was cuddled in his arms in our bed letting him draw soothing circles on my back. No words were exchanged, just comfort. I didn't want to leave. Being here let me breathe. There were no feelings of panic, anger, sadness, or anything else threatening to take me under.

I faintly heard the knock on my door ripping me away from what finally brought me true peace. I didn't stir even when I felt someone sit at the foot of my bed.

"Val," Jennie said softly. "Lou told us what happened. Are you still up to hang out with Joe and Bev?"

I moved the blanket away from my face to look at her. "I can do it," my voice full of sleep.

"Here's a cup of peppermint tea," she said scooting up closer to me. "They're already downstairs, but don't feel rushed. Chris is keeping them entertained."

"And Lou?" I asked.

"He's keeping quiet, but mentioned he heard it's supposed to be a full moon tonight, so he'll be making his exit sooner rather than later."

"Good," I mumbled.

"You don't have to tell me if you don't want to, but what happened in that time between us saying goodbye and now?" Jennie asked still using a calm tone.

"I thought you said Lou told you," I responded while moving myself into a seated position to take the cup of tea from her.

She shrugged, "He talked about the confrontation with Warrick, but that was it. I can tell something's up since you're back up here and he's grumpy."

"He snapped a little at me for the reaction I had from the confrontation."

"Why the hell would he do that?" she asked scrunching her nose the way she does when something annoys her.

It was my turn to shrug my shoulders, "I don't know, but I didn't want to deal with that with what has been running through my mind." I dropped my head trying to take a steadying breath. "I'm trying, Jennie. I really am, and if I'm making it seem like I'm not, please tell me," I said with those last few words coming out laced with emotion. Tears started welling in my eyes making Jennie move even closer.

She placed a hand on my leg, "We know you are, Val. You've been through so much in such a short time. This is your safe space, don't try to play tough in here, okay? Screw Lou if he's going to be an asshole about things."

I wiped a tear away. When Jennie knew I wasn't going to say anything, she continued, "Talk to me whenever you need to. Hell, talk to Chris if I'm not here. You've already made *amazing* progress, don't let this bump in the road take away from that."

There was another soft knock at the door. Jennie and I both jerked our heads in the direction of the sound seeing Bev standing there, "Hey, Val. Can I come in?"

I gave her a soft smile, "Of course, Bev."

"Gosh, I miss this," Jennie said as she rearranged herself on the bed so her back wasn't facing Bev.

"Me too," Bev said giving Jennie's hand a squeeze. She returned her attention on me, "You've gone through hell, Val."

I looked at Jennie who shook her head telling me she didn't say anything. Bev picked up on the unspoken questions and gave my leg a squeeze, "I'm not blind. I can see the new scars on your face, and arms now that they're not under your sweater."

I blew out a breath, "I guess you could say that."

"Do you feel comfortable telling me what happened?" Bev cautiously asked.

I took a sip of my tea letting the warm liquid settle in my stomach before starting, "I'll give you the CliffsNotes version so I don't make you guys wait too long for food."

Bev shook her head indicating that she didn't care how long we were here, so I continued, "As I'm sure you know by now, we're not in a world filled with humans and it's not the only world out there."

"Yup, Joe and I kind of figured that out, but we'll get into that later. Please, go on."

So, I did. As I was telling her about the other two worlds, I noticed Lou had made his way up to my room and was leaning in the doorway. He was staring down in his cup, not quite willing to make eye contact. I brought my focus back to Bev as I explained what happened to Daryl, who Lou and Warrick are, and kept what happened to me at a high level intentionally skipping the gory details. The expression on Bev's face took me back to the night Jennie and Chris came over for dinner the first time, too.

"You take all the time you need before coming down. I'm going to go back down to Joe to talk to him about grabbing our things," Bev explained.

Jennie raised her eyebrows at the willingness of Bev moving in here while I opened my mouth to protest. Bev held up her hands stopping me, "Don't. You probably picked up on it being nice here and are wondering why we'd be so willing to leave, but eternal happiness wears on you after a while when it doesn't belong to you. There's a heaviness in the air we all work to avoid, the leader clearly not letting us in on what she knows. Plus, this isn't our home, Val. We'll do anything to help if that means we can get back."

Lou was watching her very carefully still not leaving his spot from the door. I glanced at him only getting a nod of approval before I reached over to squeeze her hand, "It's good to have you guys back."

Bev patted my leg, "Joe and I will be right back, okay? Don't start eating without us."

Jennie and I watched her leave. Jennie looked back at me jerking her head in Lou's direction, "I'll give you two some alone time, but scream if you need me."

She got up, pausing in front of Lou, "I'm not happy with you."

"Yeah, put me in the doghouse. It's not the first time," he joked.

Jennie shook her head making her way out of my room. Lou took her place at the foot of my bed. He stared up at the roof trying to figure out what to say before his eyes met mine, "I was an ass earlier, Val. I was all riled up because of Warrick and the change getting ready to come on. I took it out on you. It was immature. I also couldn't stand seeing you like that, though. I'm not trying to take away from what you've been through, so please don't take it that way. I've been through the ringer, too, and I've struggled with getting my mind back in the right headspace. I can only imagine what you've been having to deal with."

I glanced out the balcony doors seeing the sun setting, "You know tonight's my birthday?"

"Why didn't you say anything?" his voice etched with something I couldn't quite place my finger on.

"There's been enough attention on me. All I'm saying is, I'm going to sit on the beach for a little bit tonight. Before you warn me about Warrick being a loose cannon and knowing where to find us, I need to do this for me. Don't stand vigil, don't stay in the shadows watching me. Just let me do what I need to," I warned.

Lou glanced away, "Got it. I'm going to head out, so I'll see you in the morning. We'll do something to celebrate, okay?"

"Sure," I said still unable to bring myself to look at him.

Lou lingered a little longer before finally getting up to leave. I took another sip of my tea then made my way to my closet to change out of my pajamas. I put on something comfortable grabbing my tea as I made my exit from my room. Jennie and Chris were the only two left downstairs while waiting for Joe and Bev to come back. Chris looked over at me watching me approach the table, "Jennie says it's your birthday?"

"Yeah, but don't worry about it. I'm not really in the mood to celebrate tonight," I said waving him off.

"You sure?" Jennie asked.

I nodded my head. I glanced over at the food lining the island grateful for an opportunity to change topics, "What's for dinner?"

Jennie knew what I was up to, but didn't press the issue any further, "We have some fish tacos. We wanted to change it up from the usual."

My stomach growled only a little bit showing some signs of life. As if on cue, Bev and Joe let themselves back in with their arms loaded with their belongings. Jennie and Chris didn't hesitate to take their things upstairs for them while Joe and Bev took another trip to get the remainder. I was shocked with the amount of stuff they had accumulated, but when Bev came back in with a plate full of cupcakes, I understood why.

"You didn't have to do that," I said moving to take the plate from her. "But, thank you."

"There was no way Bev was not going to do anything," Joe reminded me.

When Jennie and Chris made their way back downstairs, Bev threw up her arms, "Happy birthday!"

The rest of the group chimed in, all smiling at me. The energy was infectious that I found myself smiling, too. They all came in to give me a group hug, Bev still being the one to talk for the group, "We don't have to celebrate tonight, but we wanted to at least acknowledge the special occasion."

"Well, thanks guys," my voice muffled. I pulled away pointing to the island, "Now, go get food."

If I thought it felt like old times when I was reunited with Jennie and Chris, then I was mistaken. The feeling was intensified with two more of our group back with us making me a little excited for when we caught up with Mark and Lilly.

They were all laughing and joking around me, getting the occasional smile, but they never pressured me into forcing the lightheartedness. This was why these were my friends. There was no pressure into being someone I wasn't, yet they didn't hesitate to make sure I was part of the fun. I reached out grabbing the hands that were available and interrupting the conversation, "I love you guys. I really wanted to remind you of that."

"We love you, too!" Jennie shouted. Her response made us all break out in laughter.

Bev moved to bring us cupcakes each with a candle lit on top. Everyone started singing around me, and when the song was complete, I carried out the tradition of closing my eyes to make a wish before extinguishing the flame. They all waited for me to take the first bite, Bev anxiously waiting to see my reaction. Bev had made my favorite flavor: Funfetti. Not only that, but she made the best homemade buttercream frosting. I licked my lips, "Bev, don't tell me you spent all day making these."

"Definitely not all day, but I wanted you to have your favorite flavor."

"Thank you. I couldn't have asked for anything better," I smiled at her.

She beamed in return, "If it gets that kind of reaction out of you, then it was more than worth it."

After the cupcakes, Joe and Chris headed downstairs to start a game of pool. Jennie and Bev moved to start cleaning, not letting me join in. I leaned back against the island behind them, "I think I'm going to go for a walk on the beach alone if you guys have it in here."

"Go enjoy. You won't regret it," Bev said over her shoulder.

Jennie didn't miss a beat as she added, "Yeah, and we'll watch a movie when you get back if you're up for it."

"Sounds good. And seriously, thank you. I needed this night," I said.

"Now go," Bev said jokingly whipping a towel in my direction.

I ran upstairs to grab my necklace holding the engagement ring from Gabriel and throwing my favorite sweater on that was a gift from him on the last birthday we celebrated together. I glanced out my balcony doors to check if the coast was clear. There were no signs of wolves meaning Lou had listened and Warrick was hopefully preoccupied with something else.

I headed out the back door walking the short distance to the beach to find a comfortable place to sit down. I could still hear the faint notes of music from the town, but barely. The waves crashing against the beach demanded my attention more. I glanced around me one more time confident that I was the only one out here. I looked up at the stars, "I wish you could be here to see this, Gabriel. You would be at home in this place."

A slight breeze ruffled the palm trees almost in response.

"Birthdays aren't the same without you, you know?" I let out a small laugh, "At least I'm not getting shitfaced and partying until the sun comes up."

The wind picked up enough to ruffle my hair. I could've sworn I heard a male voice telling me happy birthday and that he loved me.

I rubbed my arms and ended my one-sided conversation just taking in the ambiance. It was an eerily quiet night with not even signs of life in the ocean. I hadn't been out here that long, but I was ready to get back to the house. Something in my gut was telling me it was time to move.

I was on my feet, dusting myself off when I heard something crunching behind me. I whipped around readying myself to run if I needed to. At first, I couldn't see anything, but when my eyes were able to focus, I could see two blue eyes staring back at me.

"Oh no, Warrick," I shook my finger at him. "You're going to leave me alone tonight."

He took another step closer causing the hairs on my neck to raise. I didn't dare move a muscle not knowing how he would react. He wasn't acting aggressively, but that didn't mean anything with him.

I took one step back and suddenly slammed to the ground. I had no idea what happened and was looking around wildly trying to locate the massive black wolf who was my biggest threat. I didn't dare scream out of fear of dragging my defenseless friends out here. That was when I felt something gripping my leg growing increasingly tighter.

I looked down still unable to figure out what was holding on to me. I tried pulling at it, biting down my scream when I discovered it was a decaying hand that had shot out from under the sand, skin flapping from the bones and nails biting into my skin. Panic gripped my throat when I was being pulled closer to where the hand had shot out from. There was no way I was going to let myself see the owner of it. I clawed at the sand in front of me trying to find something, anything I could use to counter this force dragging me under.

I felt the sand inching higher on my legs which meant I didn't have long before I was consumed. That's when I felt the teeth close around my arm. My head whipped towards Warrick. At first, I thought he was taking advantage of this situation to attack me, but he wasn't putting enough pressure to hurt. Even in his wolf form, I could see the concern in his eyes.

He tugged with enough force that he stopped me from inching further into the pit, but another hand shot out to aid the first one. I watched the hands now working in double time to bring me closer. I turned back to Warrick reaching for him with my free hand, "Please don't leave me here to die this time. *Please*."

Warrick hesitated for long enough to make me start crying, still begging him to just do anything. I was in the same situation I had been in when Cian got his hands on me. It was far too soon since that had happened.

He let out a growl then I felt the tugs. We weren't moving very far which frustrated him even more. Warrick dropped my arm running to where the hands kept their firm grip on my legs doing his best to pry their fingers loose. While he was working on my attacker, I did everything I could to try and pull myself away. It came to no surprise that there wasn't anything for me hold on to, but I eventually dug enough sand away so I could start inching myself further from the pit.

It didn't take too long after our joint effort for the hands to finally free me. There was a high-pitched scream sound and the last thing I saw were those decaying hands flailing in the air before plunging back under the layer of sand that kept them hidden.

I scrambled away to increase the distance between myself and my attacker. My breaths came out in shudders fully displaying my panic. I ran my hands all over my body to make sure I was still intact since adrenaline still flooded my senses. Warrick cautiously approached me and I threw my arms out, "Don't. Come. Any. Closer."

He dropped his head, his ears following suit expressing sadness. A quiet whine escaped from him. Warrick clearly wasn't trying to hurt me at this point, but I couldn't see past the harm he had done before.

I held my head in my hands as my body was wracked with sobs. A wet nose nudged me eventually, breaking through the barrier I created with my arms. Warrick's warm tongue lapped up my tears. I pushed him away taking a steadying breath, "Okay, okay. Thank you."

He put his head under one of my arms on the side with my bad leg to help me up. As I was brushing myself off, I let out a chuckle, "This is not how I pictured my birthday."

Warrick nosed my hand again letting it rest at the base of his neck. I ran my fingers through his soft, thick fur missing his presence. He pointed his nose in the direction of my house bringing me back to the present and I nodded, "Don't worry, I'll gladly lock myself away tonight."

He let out a snort of approval and matched my pace. I couldn't bring myself to say anything else on this walk back, afraid emotions would get the best of me again. The last thing I needed was for Jennie and Bev to think something was wrong when they've already been going out of their way to give me a fun night.

We made it to the edge of the property line stopping to go our separate ways. I took my hand back even though I didn't want to. "Thank you," I croaked out.

Warrick nuzzled my hand in acknowledgement. I gave him one last pet before turning to head back to the house. I gave my eyes one more swipe to get rid of any lingering wetness, brushed as much of the sand off that I could, then set my shoulders to head back into the house.

I reached for the door handle stopping at the sound of something rustling in the nearby bushes. Warrick was where I left him now growling in the direction the sound came from.

I was frozen in place praying there wasn't another threat about to head my way. My limit is one incident a night and even that's pushing it. Out of the corner of my eye, I saw Warrick lower himself stalking towards the bushes. I shifted to get a better view while making sure my hand was firmly on the handle to allow for a quick escape.

I sucked in a breath as I saw another wolf emerge from the bushes. "Oh fuck," I let out. I've seen this play out before and I knew it wasn't going to be anything good.

There was a flash of brown fur and Lou was on Warrick faster than I've seen anything move. Teeth were snapping, fur flying, and that familiar flash of silver were all I could see. Warrick threw out a paw connecting with Lou's face sending blood flying. A growl ripped through the night so loud I saw Jennie and Bev making their way over to the door to come see what was happening. I shook my head willing them to stay where they were. They looked at me confused so I mouthed them instructions to stay inside. Joe and Chris were coming up the stairs behind them looking equally confused, so I went through the routine again, shaking my head and telling them to stay inside.

The few moments I had taken my eyes off the fight almost cost me. Warrick's body was thrown against the side of the house, his head smacking against the glass smearing blood as he went. *This is going to be so stupid, Val.*

I took a step in between the two wolves giving Warrick the chance to get to his feet. Lou barked at me and I could almost hear him telling me to move. Warrick lunged at Lou over my shoulder knocking me to my knees. It didn't take long for them to get back at it, and for the second time tonight, I feared for my life, rolling to one side hoping I was getting out from under the two. *Not exactly how I pictured myself between two guys.* I hated myself for thinking that, but I was clear. I ran for the door, Jennie throwing it open for me and slamming it shut behind me to make sure the fight didn't come inside.

"What the *hell* were you thinking, Val?" Jennie demanded.

I whipped around, "I wasn't! I don't need to you to reprimand me." I held my stomach trying to hide my shaking hands. I glanced out the doors seeing the fight carry on, "I hate seeing them like this."

"I don't blame you," Jennie said sliding an arm around my shoulder. "We just have to let them get this out of their system."

"Damn. If you would've told me this is what Lou can be like, I would've never believed you," Chris said.

"How do you think he became an alpha?" I asked, wincing as Warrick threw Lou against the glass and raked his claws down Lou's side sending another spray of blood on the cement. "Did he ever tell you about when he was Warrick's second? He had to fight him all the time."

"He had to fight that guy?" Chris' eyes were wide.

I held his gaze, "Why do you think he can hold his own in this fight? This is going to go on the rest of the night. I just hope we don't end up with a body in the morning."

I turned away from the door making my way over to the fridge to get myself my one birthday glass of wine. Jennie and Bev followed me, Bev asking, "So, you've dated those two?"

Her question stopped me, my eyebrows rising, "That's what you're going to ask me with two alphas trying to come through that door?"

"I'm honestly impressed," Bev said earning a look from Joe. He decided to chime in, "Your dating history has always been interesting, but I think this takes the cake."

"We're really going to be analyzing my love life? Guys, come on," I rolled my eyes.

The snarling continued outside making us fall silent. I took a swig from my glass letting the alcohol settle in my stomach before answering Bev's question, "It's complicated."

"Are you setting your Facebook status?" Bev asked causing Jennie to choke on her drink and rush over to the sink in case wine started coming out of her nose.

"Jeez, Bev. What's gotten into you tonight?"

"What? I want the details," she shrugged nonchalantly.

"Yes, I've dated both."

She winked her eye, "Don't blame you. Lou's incredibly handsome, and if the other guy is anything like that, I'd be all over him, too."

"Yeah," I said letting my gaze drift back outside where the noise had quieted. I moved back towards the door to stand next to Chris and Joe who were scanning the yard to see if there were any signs of the wolves.

I reached for the door again, Jennie scolding me. Ignoring her, I took a step outside careful to avoid the blood that had been spilt.

The night was quiet letting me finally relax. I headed back into the house to change out of my bloodied clothes and into my favorite pajama set and joined Bev and Jennie on the couch grabbing the bowl of popcorn. With the action done, Chris and Joe resumed their game downstairs and we hit play on the movie.

Another bottle of wine later and the credits rolling, Jennie and Bev headed upstairs to go to sleep. Joe and Chris followed them leaving me alone in the living room. I got up to grab the first aid kit knowing I would have to stitch Lou up when he finally returned in the morning. I snuggled under my favorite blanket starting another movie I've seen a hundred times and fell into a dreamless sleep.

Chapter 8

The sunrise blasted through the backdoor waking me up in time to see Lou limping back. His naked body was dripping with blood from fresh wounds that hadn't healed thanks to Warrick's silver coated claws and teeth. I opened the door holding out a towel I brought down just in case to keep as what blood I could off the floor.

"I'll clean all this up today," Lou grumbled.

Closing the door behind him, I asked, "Happy now?"

"Not particularly."

"Why, Lou?" I led him up to my bathroom so we didn't freak out the others in the house when they woke up to use the bathroom in the hall.

He settled in the tub not able to look at me, "I can't always control what the wolf wants to do, and he wanted revenge for you. I'm sure Warrick would've started something anyways."

I shook my head in disapproval as I got to work helping him clean up. I reached behind me for the first aid kit when Lou put a hand on my knee, "No stitches. They're already closing up."

Turning back, I took a closer look. He was right, his wounds were closing even if it was incredibly slow. I lifted his chin with a fresh towel in my hand to clean the cut slicing through his eye. He winced the minute I made contact making me pause, "Does it hurt? I can stop."

"Don't," he said bringing my hand back to his face. "It hurts, but I need this to be clean. Too close to my eye."

"Did he get your eye at all?" I asked bringing my face closer to his.

"Thankfully, I closed it in time," he said holding my gaze with those grey eyes of his.

We stared at each other for a little bit, Lou slowly moving closer. My heart rate picked up, my voice only coming out in a whisper to protest, "Lou."

He squeezed his eyes shut laying back in the tub, "Sorry."

I went back to cleaning his face wound shaking my head to tell him it's okay. When I finished, I went to Lou's room to grab him some clean clothes then curled up in my bed while he finished up in the bathroom.

"Val?" Lou called.

I sat up, "Yeah?"

"This is embarrassing," he laughed. "But, can you help me out of here?"

"Sure."

I went back into the bathroom to see Lou still in the tub. He had hardly moved from where I left him and he was looking up at me. I maneuvered myself under his arm to start lifting. Lou put the majority of his weight on me catching me off-guard and almost making me fall over before we made our way to my bed.

"Are you sure?" Lou asked.

"I don't know about you, but I don't exactly have the strength to carry you down the hall to your room," I huffed.

I helped him get on the covers then went to his room to grab the blanket he'd been using along with the extra blanket he packed. I tossed the two to him, "Don't get blood on my bed."

"Got it."

I curled back up under my covers forcing my eyes closed. Lou shifted around for a few minutes before finally settling in and throwing an arm over me. I was too tired to fight it and just told myself to calm back down. It was in that stillness I was able to finally go back to sleep. My dreams quickly turned into nightmares of being tortured, but instead of it being Cian and Liam, it was Warrick reminding me over and over again about how I would never cut it. His torture, however, was 100 times more intense than what Cian and Liam put me through.

I was being shaken, Lou trying to wake me, "Val! You gotta wake up. It's nightmares, nothing real."

I could feel myself being pulled out of the hell I was going through in my mind, but I wasn't completely awake. I knew I was screaming, but I couldn't stop as if some invisible force was holding me hostage.

"Val! I need you to wake up. You have to meet me halfway," Lou shouted again.

My eyes finally snapped open to find Lou on top of me. I threw out a punch connecting with his face. His head went to the side and my hands flew up to my mouth, "Oh my – shit, Lou, I'm so sorry. I didn't mean to do that."

He rubbed his jaw, "I deserved that. I should've known better than getting in your face when an unknown force had a hold over you, but I panicked. Hell of a right hook, though."

I lifted my head up, "Are you okay? I really shouldn't have hit you after the night you had."

Lou grabbed my hands, "I'm fine, Val. Really."

I dropped my head back on my pillow rubbing my face sighing, "These nightmares have to end sometime, right?"

"They will."

Our conversation paused for a moment before Lou said, "Everyone else is awake."

"We should probably head downstairs which means you need to get off me and get dressed."

"Right," Lou said looking down.

I took in the sight before me. His wounds were closed a little more than they had been earlier, but he was definitely going to be adding a few new scars, especially with the scratch on his eye. When he didn't show any signs of movement, I gave his knee a nudge to add some encouragement.

I approached the island alone, everyone looking at me with concern. Jennie was the first one to break the silence, "Another nightmare?"

I rubbed my face again more to hide myself from their pity than anything else, "Yeah, but I don't want to talk about it. Sorry if I woke you all up or startled you with my screaming. I'm trying to get it under control."

"We know," Bev said. She slid a plate of pancakes and fresh fruit in front of me as Lou walked up.

"You're looking rough," Chris observed.

Lou gave me a quick smile before responding, "Looked worse this morning, but Val helped clean me up."

"I'm sure," Chris said giving Lou a fist bump.

"Not like that," Lou countered. "Anyways, I have a mess to start cleaning up."

Bev slid a plate in front of him, "Not without food."

"If you insist."

Lou kept the conversation from being focused on me or the fight that happened last night. I gave his leg a squeeze under the island to share my appreciation for his ability to change topics.

My attention shifted once again when the doorbell rang. I was halfway to the door before I realized what I was doing, "I got it."

Everyone was watching me carefully, Lou already halfway out of his chair in case I needed backup. I had no idea who would be hitting our door when we don't really know anyone and no one knows Bev and Joe are here besides us, unless they had been watched. That wouldn't make a lot of sense considering they have no enemies here.

No one was standing on the other side of the door when I cautiously opened it. Instead, there was a card, a cupcake, and a medium-sized wrapped box complete with a bow sitting on the ground. I quickly scanned the landscape outside of the house to see if there were any signs of someone lurking, so when I deemed the coast was clear, I scooped everything up and brought it back inside.

Jennie moved closer to my side as I sat back in front of my plate, "What is that?"

"I think it's a birthday gift?" I answered.

"Open it," Chris said.

I glanced around at everyone who was watching me closely. I started with the card hoping I would have some indication who this was from. As I pulled it out of the envelope and opened it, I shielded it from Jennie and Lou trying to peek over my shoulder.

Warrick's familiar writing scrawled across the card: *Val, love. I know I'm a day late, but happy birthday. I'm sorry it ended the way it did, and if it were up to me, I wouldn't have let that happen.*

Anyways, enjoy this cupcake (it's the chocolate cake recipe I've made you before) and I hope you love the gift. I have something I want to show you, and only you, so meet me on the beach tomorrow night. I figured you'd want to celebrate with your friends at the bonfire tonight. I hope to see you at that, too. It may not have seemed like it, but I felt so much relief seeing you stand before me.

His writing felt sincere with no signs of a threat. I didn't know if I was going to meet up with him, though, but maybe it'll help keep the nightmares at bay. According to Raf, at least. I tucked the card away then casually started peeling the wrapper away from the cupcake. I took my first bite letting it melt into my mouth. My eyes fluttered closed as the rich chocolate flooded my senses. *How does he know how to make the world's best cupcake?*

When I opened my eyes, everyone was watching me expectantly. "What?" I asked with a mouth full of cupcake.

"Well?" Jennie asked, looking at me impatiently.

"Well what?"

"You're being dense, Val. Are you going to clue us in?" she asked smiling. I could tell she already knew who it was from, but she wanted me to say it out loud for everyone else to hear.

I swallowed and casually said, "It's from Warrick."

"You sure you can trust that?" Lou asked pointing to the cupcake in my hand.

I looked at it before looking back to Lou, "It seems alright to me."

"If you say so," he shrugged.

I went back to eating the rest of the cupcake then moved on to opening the present. The ribbon fell away as I tugged on one side of the bow. I pulled the top of the box off and was greeted with the whale shark creature crystal I had been holding in the shop that day Warrick walked through the shop.

"What is it?" Bev asked craning her neck.

Lifting the crystal creature out of its box, Jennie and Bev both started gushing about how beautiful it is while the guys were trying to understand what they were looking at. While everyone was carrying on around me, I couldn't take my eyes off what was in my hands. My heart swelled when a little bit of sunlight trapped itself in there only to send rainbows throughout the room. I got up, still held in a trance, and made my way up to my room to put this on my nightstand. I admired it a little longer when Lou's voice made me jump, "Hell of a gift he got you there."

I whirled around, hand clutching my chest, "When did you get up here?"

He was leaning against the doorframe with his hands in his pockets, "Not too long ago."

"Shouldn't you be eating?"

"Shouldn't you?" I countered.

"Look, Val. All I'm going to say is that you need to watch your back with him."

"Trust me, I'm fully aware. I can also admire a gift that turned out to be something I was planning on buying myself."

Lou held his hands up, "I'm not here to attack you, only to remind you."

He left after that. I cast another look towards the crystal knowing Lou wasn't wrong, but I also came to the conclusion that I was going to meet Warrick alone in a couple of days and I'd keep that to myself. The last thing I want to do is cause another fight.

I took my seat next to Lou again and finished the food in front of me when Jennie set a bottle of champagne in front of us, "Bev tells me there's a big bonfire tomorrow on the beach. We're going. No ifs, ands, or buts about it because I want to party and I can finally feel like I can let my hair down a little bit. Val, you need to actually let loose and celebrate your birthday. So, I'm declaring we have a pool party here and do whatever we want with no judgement before we go over there."

I started to open my mouth only to be stopped by Jennie wagging her finger, "No. Go get changed and get your cute ass out there. Lou, clean up your mess."

Lou gave her a little salute. I rolled my eyes, but did as I was told.

When I got downstairs, everyone was outside and there wasn't a sign of blood from last night. I took a moment to watch everyone laughing and having a great time. Champagne was flowing, the guys (minus Lou) were flirting with their other halves, and it was like we were all ten years younger again. My feet finally found the motivation to head outside, but my arms instinctively wrapped around my exposed body to hide the more aggressive scars.

The minute I stepped outside everyone cheered. Waving them off I jumped into the deep end. Jennie thrust a cup in my hand as soon as I surfaced and I gladly chugged it down followed by another one. Lou was next to me with his eyebrows raised, slowly sipping on his drink.

"What?"

He shook his head, "Nothing, just surprised you downed that."

"Just wanting to feel good, that's all."

Lou gave me a little splash, "Could've saved you the trouble and made you feel good myself."

I returned the splash, a little giggle slipping out as I did so. I had no time to react to him wrapping his arms around my waist and tugging me in closer. "But I can tell you'd rather let alcohol do the job," he continued, dropping his voice. "Scared to get close to me again, Val?"

Heat rose to my cheeks and pooled throughout my body. "Lou," I warned sounding a little breathless. He had clearly been drinking, too.

He wrapped my legs around him pressing me gently against the wall, "No judgements and we do whatever we want, remember?"

"I have to want it, too," I protested.

Lou brought his hands out of the water in defense, "There's no pressure. You tell me what you want and I'll listen. If you asked me, though, I would say you do want it."

"If 'it' means a refill of champagne, then yes," I said untangling myself from him. I swam over to Jennie before he could say anything else to lure me in closer. Her and Chris were clinging so tightly to each other that I felt awkward tapping on her shoulder. She looked over at me, "What's up?"

"Sorry to interrupt. Where's the champagne?"

"Over there," she pointed to the edge nearest the chairs where Bev and Joe were lounging. "Everything okay?"

"Yeah, just need some alcohol to help loosen me up. Did I tell you I almost got attacked by fairies last night?"

"No, but no wonder you were screaming this morning. You're okay, right?"

"Yeah," I nodded.

"Good. Go help yourself. We have plenty more where that came from."

I left those two to get back to whatever they were doing, glad to get out of their airspace. When I reached for the bottle, Bev was there to fill up my cup. I smiled at her, "Thanks, but you didn't have to."

"You know I'm more than happy to. So, you and Lou? Or is it you and Warrick? And when can I see this other guy? Because if he's anywhere near as good looking at Lou, then I can understand the trouble you're in."

I glanced over my shoulder at Lou who was watching me before turning back to Bev, "Honestly, I don't know the answers to any of those questions."

"Well," Bev said reaching for my shoulder. "Be careful and protect your heart. You'll know who you want, I'm sure of it. If you need to talk about any of your feelings, let me know, too. I don't know these guys as well as Jennie may know them, so I can at least offer a more unbiased viewpoint."

"Thanks, Bev," I said swimming away.

The music Jennie had blaring over the speakers became quieter as I rejoined Lou sipping on my drink this time. We looked out over the ocean watching people playing on the beach. I could see a lone figure laying out again and I swore they were looking in our direction, but Lou brought my attention back to him, "Bev and Joe are good people."

"Yeah, they're my favorite out of this friend group. Don't tell Jennie and Chris."

Lou laughed a little at that, "Don't worry. I don't want to get on Jennie's bad side more than I already have."

"She takes a while to forgive."

"Do you?" he asked locking eyes with me.

"Depends on the situation," I said bringing my cup up to my lips.

"You don't have to hide your scars, by the way," Lou said abruptly changing the topic.

"What?"

"When you came out here, you were covering up your scars," he said grazing the edges of where I had been cut. "Don't cover them."

I traced the angry line of what was about to become a new scar for him. He tried to pull away until I took a step closer, "If you get to touch mine, then I get to touch yours."

"Okay," he whispered.

"Does it hurt?"

"No. Do yours?"

"Only the memories," I answered.

He nodded while I took another sip. Lou grabbed his cup, "I need a refill."

He took off, and as I watched him swim away, I couldn't help but notice my feelings were getting all tangled up again. I couldn't deny what I was feeling towards Lou at the moment, but I wasn't sure if that was the alcohol or something else. Then there's Warrick, who makes me want to vomit and fall in love all at the same time.

"Damn it, Val. You only have yourself to blame for this one," I mumbled to myself.

I watched as Joe refilled Lou's cup while Chris was sneaking up behind Lou. Jennie and Bev were fighting giggles until Chris caught up to Lou dunking him under the water. Everyone was full on laughing at this point, including me. I swam closer to the group finishing what I had in my cup and joined in on the fun.

Lou came up with a smile on his face looking wildly around for whoever it was who attacked him. He started heading towards Chris who was now back at Jennie's side when Chris pointed in my direction.

"Oh no," I said with Lou prowling in my direction. "You know damn well it was Chris."

"Don't think that's going to stop me," Lou smirked. He pulled me under with him, my cup choosing to stay on the surface. While we were under the water, I opened my eyes to see Lou doing the same as we became entangled with each other. He pointed to his lips then mine and I nodded. His lips brushed against mine teasing me a little bit to see if I would fall over the edge and fully kiss him. When I didn't, Lou pulled back almost asking again. I gestured that I needed air before going back up.

Lou was maybe a second behind me, but in that second, Chris had positioned himself to be ready for the moment Lou came up. Lou had just enough time to get another round of air when Chris dunked him under again. He retreated back to Jennie as Lou broke the surface again.

I shrugged my shoulders, "I tried to tell you it wasn't me, but you didn't want to listen."

"True," he said then turned around to Chris. "You're up."

"Not if you're going to try to kiss me under there," Chris joked while backing away.

"Pucker up, handsome," Lou responded making us all burst out in laughter. The two of them played around with Joe eventually joining in on the fun while the three of us women retreated to the calmness of the hot tub with what was left in the bottle. When we settled in, Jennie asked, "So, what did Warrick write you?"

"You two are obsessed with my love life, you know that?" I laughed.

"It's finally getting good again," Bev chimed in.

I rolled my eyes, but answered Jennie's question, "He just told me happy birthday and let me know he made my favorite kind of chocolate cake in cupcake form."

She narrowed her eyes slightly as if she knew more than what she was letting on, but thankfully decided not to press the issue. I happily changed the topic when I had the chance, "Bev, have you gone to one of these bonfires before?"

"Yeah, they're a lot of fun. Reminds me of partying in college, honestly. Everyone's having a good time drinking and dancing. Not a care in the world."

"Is that partly because of the magic around here?" I asked.

"Yeah, it's tied to the woman who runs the town. Wherever she goes, there's a bubble of that eternal happiness I told you about. She wants her people to have a good time," Bev said looking distant.

"Everything okay?" Jennie asked.

"Yeah," Bev smiled. "Just looking forward to when I don't have to have a feeling forced upon me anymore."

I raised the bottle, "I hear that."

The guys didn't give Jennie any time to respond jumping into the hot tub with us. Chris and Joe slung an arm over their partner making Lou and I feel even more awkward. Small talk filled the space until Jennie fixated on the bonfire tonight wondering what it'll be like, what to wear, and worrying over any other detail Bev was willing to give up. While they were focused on that, Lou looked at me mouthing, "Wanna get out of here?"

I nodded letting him take my hand. Little did I know the mistake I was making. Lou let go of my hand and pushed me in the pool instead, completely catching me off guard. He jumped in behind me, and when we both came up for air, I sent a wave of water in his direction, "What was that for?"

Lou pulled me in, "You were looking too serious. I needed to see that smile again."

He leaned in for the kiss starting off gentle then picking up the passion when I reciprocated. When he pulled away, he was positioned so I couldn't see the reactions of everyone in the hot tub and they presumably couldn't see me. Lou lowered his voice, "We're going to grab some food, go upstairs, eat and then fall asleep. I know I'm not the only one who could use that before tonight, but I wanted them to think we're going to do something else."

Matching his volume, I asked, "Why?"

"Because Jennie wouldn't let us just go upstairs to go back to sleep."

"You have a point there."

I leaned into the act, pretending to be all into Lou as we headed out of the pool. I gave a little finger wave before disappearing in the house. Lou immediately headed to the kitchen grabbing whatever would help him recover energy the fastest while I grabbed a big cup of water to help offset the champagne.

"Let's go," Lou ordered keeping up his fast pace despite the limp he now had.

We got into my room hunkering down so Lou could eat a little and I could relax into bed.

"You ready for tonight?" Lou asked between bites.

I shifted my focus from the movie playing to him, "What do you mean?"

"Ready to potentially see Warrick tonight?"

"Oh, I'm sure he'll be there."

Lou cocked his head, "What makes you so sure?"

I sighed, "When I saw him, I was in that store. He was in a group that came down a set of stairs and had a woman hanging off him. My hunch is that he's found the leader of this place and he's letting her daughter hang all over him so he can get what he wants."

"And he's leaving you love notes?" Lou asked, anger creeping into his voice.

I shook my head laughing a little bit, "Down boy. I'm not reading too much into any of this right now. We're going to take a nap and go have fun tonight, trying not to worry about what Warrick's doing."

I got out of bed leaving Lou to his snacks to take a shower. I locked the bathroom door behind me in case Lou wanted to get any ideas again and let the water wash over me. I wasn't ready to see Warrick tonight, and I definitely wasn't ready to try to keep Lou from picking a fight. I rested my forehead against the wall doing my best to settle the ball of nerves in my stomach to keep myself from getting sick again.

I eventually wrapped up finding Lou putting away his food. He started another movie and had his back to me. I tapped him on the shoulder, "Shower's yours if you want it."

"Thanks."

I curled back into bed, my towel still covering my body, and drifted into another dreamless sleep. I hadn't realized Lou crawled into bed next to me until an alarm went off a couple hours later. Startled awake, I immediately sat up in bed. Lou slowly rolled over letting out a groan, "It's just the alarm, Val. It's okay."

"Sorry," I mumbled.

"Don't say sorry," he said sounding more awake this time. "Let's just get ready to go."

So, we did. I threw on a cute crop top T-shirt with some shorts while Lou threw on a plain white V-neck shirt and ripped jeans. He gathered all his things to take back to his room and we headed back downstairs to meet everyone out back. Jennie and Bev went all out with their makeup and outfits clearly ready to have night out. Chris and Joe both took the same casual approach Lou did. Chris and Jennie looped their arms around each other, Joe and Bev lacing their fingers together, and I rested my hand in the crook of Lou's elbow.

It was obvious where we were headed judging by the giant fire a little way down the beach surrounded by a hoard of people dancing to the music provided by the steel drums and other instruments.

As soon as we entered the bubble created by the leader's magic, all our worries were washed away. It wasn't hard to laugh or lean into Lou more. It was like being drunk without the dizziness or aftereffects. I started dancing in time with the music the closer we got, pulling Lou with me like I did the first day we went into the town.

I was dancing on him like no one was watching. Jennie, Bev, and I changed dance partners every now and then just to have fun. Some of the fairies around us pulled us in with them and even I had to recognize that this was the best I had felt since getting here. Lou didn't let me stay away for long, though, pulling me back so we were close to each other again. His hands found their way to my waist sending shivers throughout my body. He moved closer to my ear, "You look beautiful tonight."

"Thank you, Lou," I said with a soft smile on my face.

"I'm not just saying that so I can get lucky tonight, either. I really mean it. You're finally smiling and just being you."

I took a step back, "I appreciate the compliment. I'm going to get a drink real quick and I'll be back."

I made my way over to where everyone else seemed to be grabbing something to drink just to be greeted by the leader. In a rich, soothing voice, she said, "I knew I'd be running into you tonight."

"I'm sorry?" I asked confused. I have never met her before and was pretty sure she hadn't seen me in the store. Yet, she was looking at me with certainty in her white eyes.

"Val, right?"

"Yeah, have we met?"

She chuckled, "I'm sorry, we haven't. At least not in person. I'm Sarind. Welcome to my island."

"It's nice to meet you," I said skeptically. "What do you mean we haven't met in person?"

"I have the ability to get glimpses of the future, but keep that between us. I don't typically tell people that. You've been through a lot, child. You're going to go through more, but hold on to that resolve that's gotten you to this point. I'm glad you and your friends are here. Enjoy your night."

Before I could say anything or ask her any questions, she disappeared back into the crowd. Her quick, cryptic message rang in my ears, leaving me frozen for a few moments. There was just a sea of happy people who were dancing and drinking. When I could finally move again, I scanned the faces for her coming up with nothing. I was ready to head back to my group, but my gaze landed on those ice blue eyes I had been hoping to avoid all night.

No amount of magic could have kept me from being impacted by what I saw. The woman who I assumed to be Sarind's daughter, and who I saw with Warrick in the shop, was grinding on him. My stomach churned every time her back arched more so she could be closer to him. She slung an arm behind his head closing her eyes clearly lost in the moment while Warrick was locked on to me. He kept his hands firmly in his pockets so as to not touch her any more than he wanted to. My heart shattered, surprising me since I wasn't sure about my feelings for him, so I put my cup back down and left.

Chapter 9

I put enough distance between myself and the bonfire so I could double over and emptied my stomach on the beach again. Warrick had been keeping his distance from me here, but he was still able to get in my head as easily as he did when he was attacking me. All he had to do was have a drop-dead gorgeous woman throwing herself at him. There was no way I had any chance anymore, the hope of rekindling anything with him gone. She was flawless and I was yesterday's trash all scarred and beat up. He had his fun with me, but that was all it would ever be.

"Why do you care, Val? Why is it getting to you this badly?" I asked myself.

I glanced over my shoulder in the direction I had seen Warrick thankful I couldn't find him in the sea of people. I continued the trek to the house gradually feeling sadder with every step.

When I made it back to my room, I stood at my nightstand staring at the crystal whale Warrick gifted me. Convinced of the thoughtful gesture just this morning, I wasn't so sure what I thought of it now. *Was this just his new way of playing with my head?* I moved it to the set of drawers under the TV to put some distance between myself and any thoughts of Warrick then stripped down and crawled into bed.

Instead of falling asleep, I just laid there still staring at the whale. He had told me he hadn't been with anyone since the beginning because I was the one for him. Could I trust that now? Could I trust him to not try anything when I meet him on the beach tomorrow? This could be a ploy to get me alone so he could finally end things, but I wasn't entirely convinced of that either. Also, I don't know why I was letting this bother me considering I didn't think we were technically together at this point.

A wave of homesickness washed over me. If my dad were here, I would be able to go to him for solid advice on what to do and get some comfort at the same time, but no. He's not here and I have no way of reaching him.

"Ugh!" I screamed out sitting up. A gentle knock on my door snapped my focus back to reality. Gathering the blanket around me, I said, "Come in."

Lou poked his head through the door, "You okay in here?"

"Just frustrated, that's all. My head's a jumbled mess," I put my head in my hands.

He slid an arm around my back pulling me into him, "Does it have something to do with why you ran off tonight?"

I leaned into him feeling some level of comfort by the warmth coming off his body, "Yeah."

"Is that something named Warrick?"

Groaning, I nodded.

Lou sighed, "We all saw him tonight with his, uh, date. Needless to say, Jennie's pissed and Chris and Joe are having to do damage control. Bev tried talking to him, but didn't get anywhere. It's going to be an interesting one."

"That's a nice way to put it," I chuckled.

"As much as I'm enjoying sitting here like this with you, you might want to put clothes on because I have a feeling Jennie's going to be storming in here any minute."

I nodded moving to stand up. I hugged the blanket tighter noticing Lou looking away. I threw on a big T-shirt just in time to hear yelling outside.

Lou ran out to the balcony right behind me. He wasn't wrong about Jennie, she was irate. Instead of yelling at Joe and Chris like I expected, she was jabbing a finger in Warrick's chest.

"Oh, shit," Lou mumbled, running out of the room.

I watched him leave then returned my attention to the scene unfolding in front of me.

"You asshole! I've been defending you ever since you clued me in on your plan and then you turn around and do this? You're always toying with her. Was anything between you guys real?" Jennie screamed at Warrick jamming her finger at him. Chris did his best to get a grip on her while Joe tried to contain her arms without any luck.

I sucked in a breath worried about what might happen if she kept going like this. Warrick looked up in my direction, eyes widening a little bit at the sight of me before looking back at Jennie. His mouth set in a hard line, but he didn't move anything else as he coolly responded, "I suggest you stop poking me and sober up to have an adult conversation about this. There's more to this story."

"I will not stop until you turn around and *leave*," she spat, jabbing her finger into him with every word.

Lou made his way outside stepping between Warrick and Jennie. Warrick looked over Lou's shoulder gesturing up to me, "Can I at least talk to her?"

She lunged toward him again, Lou putting his hands on her shoulders to stop her, "If you want to talk to her, you go through me first."

Warrick's smile crawling across his face made me want to be sick. I knew that smile and knew nothing good was going to happen. He was focused on Jennie as he said, "I've killed someone close to her before, it won't be hard to do it again, blondie."

"Motherfu – " Jennie jumped at him, her shout cut off by Lou hefting her over his shoulder to remove her from the situation entirely. Lou turned around so he was facing the other wolf, "Do us all a favor and get out of here, Warrick. Please."

"Nice scars, Lou," Warrick said, then turned around to leave. I heard the door downstairs close, and as soon as it did, Warrick glanced back at me. His sinister facial expression replaced with one of regret, he dropped his head and walked away disappearing into the night. I knew he was hoping to explain what I saw with probably a million excuses, but that didn't change the fact that he told me I was the one for him and now he was with someone else.

There was a whole bunch of commotion going on downstairs snapping me back to reality. Jennie was still screaming while the guys were shouting at her to calm down. I was in the hallway when Bev reached the top of the stairs looking exhausted, "I'm sorry this is how your celebration turned out."

"It's okay."

We didn't say anything else as I continued to make my way downstairs while Bev started to retreat to her room. I stopped to give her a hug. "Thank you for just being here, Bev," I whispered.

"Anytime, Val."

We released and Bev looked grateful to have a place to escape to. I, on the other hand, steadied my shoulders doing my best to mentally prepare for the chaos I was going to be stepping in to. On my first step down the stairs, something shattered. I picked up the pace finding Joe sweeping up the broken glass, Chris trying to calm Jennie down, and Lou holding her against the wall so she couldn't do anymore damage.

"I'm not letting him get away with this," she exclaimed through clenched teeth.

"You're also not going back out there after he threatened you, J. I'm not losing you," Chris responded in a calm tone. "Look at me. I need you to take a breath. I can guarantee you that Warrick isn't even interested in the woman he was with. Besides, Val can handle her own fights. This one isn't yours."

Lou agreed with Chris, "He wasn't even trying to touch her. She was the one all over him."

Joe nodded his head affirming what the other two had said.

"He's right, you know," I said still not moving from my spot at the base of the stairs. I was ignoring what the guys were saying wanting to focus on what I knew would get her to calm down, "This is my fight to have with him. You've already done so much for me, Jennie. It's time to take a break. Relax and enjoy being on a tropical island."

Her wild eyes settled on me as she still fought against Lou's hold, "I'm tired of seeing him hurt you."

"We all are, but she can handle this one," Lou grunted clearly putting in more effort to restrain her than I thought he would be.

I took a step closer being mindful of what Joe was cleaning up, "We're not even together right now. He's allowed to be with whoever he wants. Seriously, Jennie, it's okay. I'm not even upset right now."

Lou shot me a look over his shoulder that I did my best to ignore. I had already pushed all those emotions from moments ago into a box before I descended the stairs. That was the only way I'd convince Jennie to drop it.

"Don't spoil a night of fun and partying because of me," I shook my head. "Give Chris the ride of his life or do whatever it is you two do behind closed doors."

Chris' cheeks turned a bright red and Jennie finally laughed. She relaxed enough that Lou felt confident in letting her go. I closed the distance between us and gave her a hug. She gripped me tighter, "I thought something bad happened to you when we couldn't figure out where you went. Then I saw him with that woman all over him and went crazy."

I pulled back pushing some of her hair out of her face, "I know. I should've told you guys I was heading back, but I didn't want you to feel like you had to leave early. I'm good, I promise."

Lou gave me another look that I chose to ignore yet again. I gently pushed Jennie towards the direction of Chris, "Now, seriously, go. Don't waste the rest of your night. And Joe? Go take care of your tired wife. I'll clean up the rest."

They all nodded then migrated upstairs. When the coast was clear, I pinched the bridge of my nose, "I shouldn't have let them get so involved."

"Please, tell me how you were going to keep them from diving in too deep," Lou chuckled.

I picked up the broom and dustpan from where Joe was cleaning up and resumed his task, "Fair enough. Thank you for keeping that from escalating any further. She had no idea what she was getting into or what line she was about to cross out there, but I felt that change in him almost like feeling a shift in the wind."

"I know," Lou started. "I felt it, too. She may have been able to act that way towards him previously, but that was an entirely different situation."

"What do you mean?" I asked as I moved to get the vacuum to finish cleaning.

Lou sighed as he sat on the couch, "Back on the vampire world when we had no idea where you were, we all drove over to his place. It was Jennie who got out and confronted him jabbing her finger the same way she did tonight. He didn't threaten her, though, which makes me wonder if it was all an act. Jennie mentioned something about Warrick having a plan to get you out, and he told her that when we were at his place. I'm starting to think the whole fighting thing they did there was all a part of his act."

"What act?"

"She said he mentioned something about having to sell his performance to Cian in order for his rescue operation to go smoothly."

I rolled my eyes, "Sure, whatever. I'm leaving that behind me. I'm just happy you were there to stop anything from going any further. If you hadn't stepped between them, I might've lost everyone tonight."

Lou got up and pulled me in for a hug, "Hey, don't think about that, okay? It didn't happen so we're in the clear."

We let go and I put everything away before sinking into the couch, Lou doing the same next to me. Staring up at the ceiling, I asked, "Feel like doing guard duty tonight?"

"Unfortunately, yeah. Won't complain about the company, though," he answered.

I gave him a playful shove, "You never stop trying, do you?"

"No, not when it comes to you. I have a big hole to dig myself out of."

Shaking my head, I said, "I don't even know anymore, Lou. Before you go getting your hopes up, all I'm saying is my heart and head are a mess. I don't think it's the best idea for us to explore that path any further right now. I just need a break from it all. What I do need is the support you and everyone else in this house has been giving me. You have no idea how that's helped."

"I get it," he said sounding a little distant. "It's just been nice seeing you come back to life. You would've thought we were enemies when we saw you in the hospital back in my world."

"Well, that's because that's what I saw you all as. I felt so betrayed. Not to mention all the actual pain I was in. I mean, I had been hanging by chains for quite a while getting sliced up and tortured."

"What really happened there?" he asked.

"This is a conversation that requires some wine," I said moving to get up.

"Probably won't help us stay up to keep watch over everything," he laughed.

I gestured for him to go around the house, "Then make sure everything is locked up and draw the blinds."

He didn't respond, but I heard him get up to check on things. By the time he returned to the couch, I was sitting there with the open bottle on the coffee table and two full glasses in hand. I offered him his then took a long sip of mine. I grabbed a blanket more for comfort than anything else.

"Where to start," I mumbled doing my best to procrastinate.

Lou cocked an eyebrow at me while a smile tugged at the corner of his lips, "The beginning would be a good place."

I gave him a playful shove, but quickly frowned after that, "Alright. I was heading out of the pub after Conor practically chased me out of there since I stayed well past my curfew. I had parked my bike right outside the entrance because I wasn't walking the best and wanted to have a quick getaway if I needed it, but it wasn't there so I checked with Conor if he had seen anything that happened. I thought it was weird when he said he got it moved because people were checking it out and driving too close and he didn't want anything to happen."

"That explains why it was in the garage," Lou interjected.

"Yup," I continued taking a deep breath. "So, I headed that way making sure to check my surroundings keeping my head on a swivel in case anyone wanted to jump out at me. I wasn't checking the ground, though, or I probably would've noticed the rope that trapped me. I was hanging upside down trying to find a way out while also pushing aside the pain since the rope was wrapped tightly around my bad leg."

"No one saw this going on?"

"No, but that's because Liam used whatever magic he had to basically put us in a bubble. No one could see us, hear us, or even have any signs we were there."

Lou shook his head, "That's insane."

I gulped down another sip of wine nodding my head in agreement. I tightened my grip on the glass as I went back in on the story, "He put on this whole show about basically capturing me and there was nothing I could do about it because he's that good. Then, he knocked me out. I woke up still upside down, but in a dark room. I figured out they were holding me up by chains and saw there were buckets under me to drain me of my blood, something Cian had promised he would do if I continued killing his vampires. Lou, all the cuts they had on my body stung. I can't begin to describe the amount of pain I was in, but that's what got him and Liam off. There were several rounds of them slicing me, punching me, and playing head games. After each round, Liam would be sent in to heal me up just enough so I wouldn't die yet."

"I take it he didn't just do that from a distance," Lou said, his face grim.

I stared down into my wine trying to persuade myself to keep going. Lou saw me struggling and placed a hand on my knee, "You don't have to keep going if you don't want to."

"It's okay," I said patting his hand. "I have to. It'll help me move on."

"Okay," he said not moving.

"To confirm what you just said, Liam didn't heal me from a distance. In fact, he took advantage of me being helpless and kissed me. Thankfully, that's all he did, but if I were there any longer, who knows what he would've tried to do."

"Shit, Val. You had me try to take advantage of you and then Liam does the same thing not to long after. I'm so sorry."

I waved him off, "You? I've worked hard to forgive. Liam? Not so much. Anyways, at some point, Warrick comes in. He was convinced you and I were still working together. Convinced that all the time I spent with him was just for show. The biggest scar on my side?" I lifted my shirt to point it out even though Lou knew which one I was talking about, "It's only that way because Warrick dug his fingers into it making it bigger. And yet, I still begged for him to turn around and help me. Little did I know he actually was helping in that moment, in his own twisted way, but the minute he walked out of that room, a little piece of me died. I was finally broken, and Cian knew it, which is exactly why he sent Warrick in there. Melody came in to save me and she was the one that cleared the air, but I couldn't hang on to consciousness too long as you know."

Lou's face was set like stone, showing no signs of expression except for those grey eyes that looked like storm clouds brewing. I downed the rest of my wine then set down the glass. Avoiding eye contact, I settled back into my seat, "Now you know."

"I know if I was in that room going through what you just described, everything would be a million times worse. The fact that you survived that ... hell, the fact that Raf was able to bring you back as good as he did ...," Lou trailed off.

"Raf knows what he's doing, but I will say I was very close to death. Mainly because I gave up. I didn't want to live anymore after that."

"Do you still feel that way?"

I brought my eyes up to meet his, "Not anymore, I don't think."

"I'm glad that feeling isn't still consuming you, Val. These worlds are better with you in them and I don't want to lose you."

"I know," I said starting to move closer to him. "I heard you on the way to the hospital. When you told me to stay with you, my heart pumped a little harder to avoid death a little bit longer."

Lou opened his mouth to say something and was interrupted by the sound of a moan and a couple of smacking noises. Our heads both turned in the direction the sound was coming from then giggled when we realized what was going on. In between laughs, Lou said, "I guess Jennie must be feeling better."

"Hell of a way to make us change topics," I smiled. I gave his hand a squeeze, "Thank you for listening and letting me get through that story."

"Thank you for sharing it," he responded.

We did our best to ignore the sounds coming from upstairs while Lou sipped on what was left of the bottle. I shook my head, "I can't let their sex noises be the only thing we're listening to right now. Dance with me?"

"Sure," Lou smiled.

We made our way downstairs to add more distance between the floors. Lou started the music and I instantly recognized the song as one of the ones we danced to in his apartment. He held his hand out to me pulling me in tightly as soon as I placed my hand in his. We swayed back and forth for a few moments before I looked up at him, "This takes me back."

"It was a much simpler time back then, believe it or not," he said caressing my cheek.

I leaned into his touch, "And it wasn't that long ago, either."

"No, it wasn't," Lou said, his voice dropping to a hushed tone.

"Why?"

"You put this music on and managed to bring me some comfort when I was in pain, so I thought it might do the same for you."

I rested my head back on his chest, "Thank you."

He gently kissed the top of my head then rested his cheek there. We stayed like that for the rest of the song and even a little bit into the next song. I let out a yawn and Lou scooped me up, "I think it's time you got some sleep."

I nodded unable to keep my eyes open any longer. He carried me back up to the living room and laid me on the couch. After covering me with a blanket, he turned to sit in another chair when I reached out to stop him, "Don't leave me."

"Okay," he whispered crawling in behind me on the couch so we could spoon. Lou wrapped his arm around me pulling me in close. I let the steady beating of his heart lull me into a restful sleep.

Chapter 10

Morning came a little too quickly, but Lou was still there with his arm over me. His deep breathing confirmed he was still asleep, so I only lifted my head to see if anyone else was awake. Joe and Bev gave me a little wave from the island as they sipped on their coffee, but Jennie and Chris must have still been up in their room. I gave them a quick smile then laid my head back down.

My thoughts drifted to the invitation from Warrick since there was nothing else preoccupying my mind. To go or not to go. That was something only I could figure out. I had no plans to mention anything about this to anyone else in this house, especially not Jennie after the way she acted last night. I still had no idea if I wanted to face him after seeing someone all over him. Warrick could be using this as an opportunity to finish what Cian hadn't, I reminded myself, but he could also be using this as a way to explain his side of the story. *I'm going regardless of what's going to happen.*

As soon as I reminded myself of my decision, Lou started stirring behind me. He let out a soft groan as he did a little stretch and I could tell he was enjoying the sleeping arrangement judging by what was pressing into my back. He gave me a kiss on my cheek whispering, "Good morning."

"Good morning, Sleeping Beauty," I said rolling over to face him.

He somehow brought me closer to him reminding me of those first mornings in the vampire world. His hands started to trace my body when I said, "We've got company."

Lou's hands froze as he lifted his head. I did the same and we earned another wave from Joe and Bev. They moved to get up to join us in the living room handing us each a cup of coffee. We sat up taking a sip waiting for the first jolts of caffeine to hit our system.

"Thanks for, uh, not giving us a show this morning," Joe said.

"I take it Jennie and Chris kept you both up, too?" I asked.

Bev nodded, "You can say that. I'm sure if there was anyone out on the beach, they would've heard them, too. You two look cozy."

Lou glanced at me, "We might be, but there's nothing going on here. Just fell asleep making sure no one was trying to break into the house to carry out their threat."

I gave his knee a quick squeeze, "Yeah, and I was starting to have a rough night, so Lou was making sure I didn't add to the sounds coming from our house."

"Sure," Bev said skeptically. "Speaking of that threat, do you think he actually would've gone through with it with all of us right there?"

"Bev, honey, I don't know the guy and even I know he would've killed her," Joe answered.

"He's crazy," she shook her head.

"That's why you don't mess with Warrick," Lou sipped on his coffee. "I think the only person I've seen successfully get away with pushing his buttons is Val, and even then, she hasn't come out unscathed."

"It's something I've learned the hard way, but Warrick's not one to be messed with," I said.

We carried on small talk for a little while longer until Jennie and Chris eventually found their way downstairs. I gave them a grin and asked Jennie, "Feel better?"

She blushed a little, "Sorry about my outburst last night."

I waved her off, "Warrick has a way of bringing that side out of people. Just, please, don't try to do that again."

Jennie winced a little, "Wasn't my brightest move."

We took our turns poking fun at her, thankful she was in the mood to play along. We collectively decided to head into town to get some food since none of us were up to cooking after the craziness of last night. As we approached, I braced myself for the happiness that was about to wash over me. We were laughing and joking more easily the moment we entered the bubble.

Our day went on just like that. We carried on like we had nothing to care about and were just living life. Even when we got back to the house, the artificial happiness translated into something real as we hung out in the pool catching some sun.

By the time evening rolled around, everyone was doing their own thing: the guys were downstairs playing pool while Jennie and Bev were having a mini spa session. I looked out towards the beach knowing I would need to eventually make my way out there, but I wasn't quite ready to go yet. I made my way over to the kitchen to grab some water and to glance outside for any signs of Warrick. I wasn't seeing anything, so I figured I would go take a walk out to the beach to see if he was there.

Reaching for the handle, I told Jennie and Bev, "I'm heading out for a walk. I'll be back."

"Want us to go with you?" Jennie asked with a nail polish brush poised above her toes.

"No, don't let me interrupt your mani-pedi," I smiled. "Besides, I won't be far."

"Alright, but scream if you need anything and leave just the screen door closed so we have a better chance of hearing you."

I gave her a thumbs up then headed out. The cool breeze caught me off-guard as I wrapped my arms around my exposed stomach. The crop top and shorts almost weren't enough for this evening.

My toes hit the sand and my steps grew cautious as I was reminded of almost being taken under a few nights ago. I scanned the ground for any signs of the fairies lurking beneath, but when I felt the coast was clear, I went back to looking for Warrick not having to look too hard.

He was standing there, in a black V-neck shirt and ripped up jeans watching the ocean. He looked relaxed, one hand in his pocket with the other one was holding a cupcake. My gut was telling me to run while my heart was telling me to stay. The fight between the two made me want to just turn around so I didn't have to deal with whatever onslaught of emotions I'd have to sort through after this.

Apparently, though, my body was on the side of my heart because I took a few more steps closer. I took a glance around the beach noting we were the only ones out here and feeling thankful Jennie asked me to keep the door open.

He turned his head at the sound of my approach, his icy blue eyes softening as he met my gaze, "Hi, love."

I recoiled at the sound of the familiar name thinking of what I saw since being here, "You don't get to call me that."

He turned around so he was fully facing me, remorse filling his eyes, "You weren't supposed to see me like that last night, Val. If anything, I was hoping I could catch you alone even for a few moments back there, but then you ran off."

I wanted to keep my composure already mentally kicking myself for having that type of reaction right out of the gate. I did my best to keep my poker face on as I responded, "We're not together. Do whatever, or whoever, you want."

He winced a little at that, "What I say next probably won't do anything to convince you, but I have no interest in her whatsoever."

When I didn't say anything in return, he took a step closer to me. I held my ground replaying the words from Lou, Chris, and Joe about him, matching what Warrick just said – he had no interest in her. I guess if I kept repeating that to myself, it eventually had to be true, right? Warrick reached toward me, my body tensing and eyes closing. He was completely aware of the change in my body language as his hand hovered slightly above my face. When I didn't make any other movements, he gently caressed my cheek tracing his thumb over one of my many new scars. I heard him swallow, his voice full of regret, "I didn't mean for this to happen to you, love."

It was the first time he called me that with actual sincerity since seeing him in this world. I slowly opened my eyes to meet Warrick's gaze, "You were the one who sent me there."

Warrick winced, "I knew I shouldn't have. Damn it, I really shouldn't have."

"I have never felt so alone, Warrick," I started. The gates were open at this point so I figured it was time to get things off my chest. My voice cracked as tears started welling in my eyes, "When you walked out leaving me in the worst situation I've ever faced, I wanted to die. I wanted Cian and Liam to just end it. Hell, I almost begged them to. You want to know what I felt when you walked away? Something damn near close to the heartbreak I felt when I was presented with Gabriel's flag and dog tags. All the smiles I've been pasting on my face? They've been fake so everyone in that damn house can continue living their lives and hold on to the hope that things will get back to normal. But, it wasn't just when you walked out on me. It was when you dug your fingers into a fresh cut, when you sliced me yourself. It was all the times you *attacked* me, and yet, I still want you. I want to love you. I'm so drawn to *you* and I just don't know *why*."

I didn't bother to steady myself as sobs wracked my body, "I don't know whether to run or love. I don't know if you're going to kill me or make me the happiest woman in whatever this crazy, twisted universe is. I need someone to tell me what to do because I sure as hell can't do it anymore."

Warrick held on to my hands not breaking eye contact as he said, "Then *love* me, Val."

"Why? Why should I love you? I don't even know if I can trust you not to snap again. I don't know if I can trust that you won't leave me like everyone else has."

"Because we're fated," he said a little too quickly.

Those three words stopped my world. My mouth opened and closed a couple of times before I finally asked, "We're what?"

"We're fated, love. There's no denying it no matter how much we want to," he gave me a soft smile.

"W-we can't be," I stammered. "I-I mean you've tried killing me. Multiple times. How do you know?"

It was one thing to have the idea of being fated to him sitting in the back of my mind, but a completely different thing to hear him say those words. The part that was throwing me off the most was not knowing how I felt about Warrick and now, all of a sudden, I'm being told I'm fated with him. Even though I had a hunch this might be the case, I couldn't bring myself to fully admit it because of how all over the place I was.

"I've known for a while," he dropped our hands taking another step closer. "I had my suspicions after we first met when all I could think about was you. All I wanted to do was see you and be around you. And yes, I felt that way immediately after we met in the pizza place. As time went on, I met with Raf to know for sure since he had fated. Before you question that, Raf is Lou's second, but he's the only one I know of who's gone through this and I needed to confirm what I've been feeling. My craziness when I saw you in Cian's world? I was trying to process what Raf told me ... after you stabbed me, I was having a hard time convincing myself I was supposed to spend the rest of my life with you. Hell, I think I spent even more time trying to tell myself you'd want to spend the rest of your life with me. I acted out in the worst way possible. I shouldn't have done that, and I don't blame you for not trusting me."

My breath hitched with our proximity. Warrick's hand moved to cup my neck slightly tilting my head up so I was forced to look at him. "Losing you would break me, and it almost did back there. Talk to me, love," he said softly.

"This is a lot to take in," I whispered. My mind was racing. I went back to the conversation Raf and I had in the pool where he told me about his love. We dived into the feelings I had for

Warrick, but he never confirmed if what I was feeling constituted as being fated.

"I know. You don't have to tell me anything right now. I wanted to get that off my chest, especially after you saw me with Marin. That's only part of me trying to get Sarind on my side, and even then, I set the record straight after leaving your house last night."

"You haven't slept with her?" I asked.

"Have you slept with Lou?" he asked searching my eyes.

"You answer first."

"Yes, once when I first got here to convince her mother I was serious about our deal. Sarind may seem kind and want everyone around her to have happiness, but she's not above making people do some dirty work."

"What do you mean?" I asked not picking up on what he was trying to say.

Warrick stroked my cheekbone again, "Answer my question first. His scent is all over you, and if that's the direction you want to go, then I'm not going to stop you. I just want you to know that you're not getting rid of me that easily."

"Yes, once. I was drunk off my ass after having a nightmare."

"We're even then," he said still holding me. "Sarind cares about everyone's happiness, as evidenced by the magic she keeps around the town for everyone to feel light. More than anything, she cares about her daughter's happiness and will do just about anything to get Marin what she wants. When I stepped foot on this island to finally meet with Sarind, Marin made her intentions clear. Sarind said she would join my cause if I dated her daughter for a little bit because I was all Marin would talk about and it was driving Sarind mad," Warrick shook his head.

"Her parenting skills aren't the most effective ... if anything, Marin annoys the crap out of Sarind which is why she'll do anything to shut her up. Anyways, after I got back to the bonfire last night, Sarind pulled me to the side letting me know she finally met you and that I could end things with Marin if I wanted to so she wouldn't be coming between you and I. That's what I did. You have to believe me that I had no interest in her whatsoever."

"What's your cause?"

He hesitated debating what he was actually going to tell me, "I'll tell you more about that soon, but my whole purpose for inviting you out here tonight is to celebrate your birthday, love." Warrick offered me the cupcake he'd been holding on to this entire time, "Did you get my gift?"

I accepted the cupcake and took a step back to start eating it, "Yes, thank you. It was beautiful."

"There's a couple of reasons I got that for you. One, I saw you clutching it so tightly at the shop I knew you had fallen in love with it. Two, on this specific night, that creature makes an appearance and should be showing up any time now. And three, it's a peace offering. No more crazy fighting between us."

I nodded taking in what he had just told me while making my way through the cupcake. Warrick studied me while waiting for a response, his eyes drifting to my exposed skin and landing on the scar. He came closer to me his fingers touching the spot, "I hate that I did this."

Taking a step back I looked toward the water, "How am I supposed to see this whale creature in the dark?"

He turned his head moving to stand next to me, "Just wait."

While we stood there, I said, "You know? This place has been about the most peaceful world I've been to since this whole thing started. It's so calm."

"Don't be fooled by everyone's chipper attitude," Warrick countered. "Remember the other night when those fairies were trying to drag you under?"

"Yeah," I shivered. He instinctively put an arm around me, but when he felt me flinch, he dropped it.

"They're one of the few who would love to snack on human flesh, and you were very lucky to get away from them. You have to remember there will always be threats no matter where you're at or what kind of magic there is."

We fell silent for a few beats, then Warrick continued, "Despite those threats, this is a beautiful world. I had to share it with you."

As if on cue, the water lit up. I took a step closer so the tide would wash over my feet. I glanced at Warrick who smiled at me then nodded his head in the direction of the water. I looked back in time to get a full, clear view of the whale-shark-like creature making its entrance. I now knew why the crystal was cut in the way it was to capture some of the light that hit it. This creature emanated light like a glow-stick gracefully floating through the water, the edges of its fins and the spots along its body contributing their own light.

Not only did the water glow with the creature, but it also glowed with bioluminescence as the water rippled. The sea had come to life by simply being in the presence of this whale.

It moved closer and everything around it illuminated. It swam over what looked like an underwater city teeming with life. There were blues, greens, pinks, yellows, and almost every color in between filling my vision. Coral jutted out acting as skyscrapers in this marine city. Normal fish swam alongside other creatures in various shapes and sizes like those fairies on the land. Not only that, but I could see all the way to the bottom no problem.

"This is stunning," I said completely captivated by the scene unfolding in front of me.

"They say you'll be blessed with good fortune after seeing this whale swim by," Warrick said watching me.

"She's even more beautiful than I could've imagined," I went back to admiring the whale who seemed to be doing small circles in front of us. I took a small step forward suddenly pulled back by Warrick. I threw a look over my shoulder at him, "Why can't I go?"

"You don't know what's out there and I'm not risking you getting hurt, love," he said not taking his arm back.

I turned back to the water. "I can't believe I'm seeing this," I said with a voice full of awe.

"Happy birthday, love," Warrick said tugging me even closer to him.

I stiffened at the proximity with him again. Noticing my body tensing up again, he whispered, "Is this okay?"

I wanted to say yes. I wanted to give in and make love on this beach. It would be so easy with him opening up to me for once and for going out of his way to celebrate my birthday, but something was still holding me back. The threat to Jennie was still bouncing around in the back of my mind. His accusations while I begged him to free me stung like they were being said to me for the first time again.

"Warrick, I – "

He dropped his arms letting the cool air rush between us as he took a step back, "I'm not going to push you any more than I already have. I will leave if you want me to, love."

Despite all my hesitations, my heart breaking at the thought of him leaving me again was enough for me to change my mind and turn around. I stepped up to him, grabbed his arms, and wrapped them around me, "Don't leave me again, Warrick. I believe you about being fated. Why else would I be out here after all that's happened between us? There's a part of me that doesn't want to trust you, but it's small compared to the part who's ready to let those walls come back down. I don't know what's suddenly come over me, but I can't let you walk out of my life again. Screw the people who want to judge me for this decision. My heart is saying this is what it wants, so I'm giving it what it wants."

Warrick grabbed the back of my head and kissed me. The cliché fireworks went off all around us as I leaned into the kiss more letting the sparks radiate through my body. He entangled his fingers in my hair deepening the kiss. I wrapped my legs around him not giving the night air a chance to get in between us again. You would think we were reunited after years of being apart rather than weeks. The longer we kissed, the more I started feeling whole again as the pieces of my heart put themselves back together.

"You are the best thing that's ever happened to me, love," Warrick said quietly after pulling away. "It's like I can breathe again."

"Stay with me," the words rushed out of my mouth before I could get a grasp on what I was saying.

He smiled, "I would love to, but do you think that's a good idea with Lou in the house?"

"Can you two set aside your differences for a little while?"

Warrick gave me a quick kiss, "I would do anything for you. I just don't know if he'll be able to do that." He set me down before continuing, "He was the one who initiated that attack the other night. I was going to walk away. And as much as I would like to put him in his place, it makes it harder for you which is the last thing I want to do right now."

"Let's try it," I said grabbing his hand starting to walk back towards the house. I didn't want to give him the chance to leave me again. "Promise me one thing?"

"Anything, love."

"Don't kill any of my friends," I commanded thinking about the interaction between Jennie and him last night.

Warrick nodded as he let me tug him towards the house. This wasn't going to be the popular choice given how things had escalated, but we all have to move on. If everyone kept telling me to forget what happened in the past, then they would have to follow their own advice, too.

We approached the door greeted by the sounds of Jennie and Bev giggling about something. I slowly opened the door, Warrick and I both a little cautious. Jennie beamed at me, "Val, how was your walk?"

Her smile faltered when she saw who was behind me. Jennie's eyes narrowed and her usually cheery tone was gone when she asked, "What the hell is he doing here?"

Lou must have heard what she asked because he suddenly appeared at the top of the stairs storming over to where we were standing. Warrick dropped my hand right before Lou shoved him against the wall pinning his neck with his forearm, "You have a lot of nerve to walk in here with Val. I don't give a fuck if you were the reason she got out of Cian's torture chamber, you were the reason she was put in there in the first place."

Warrick gave Lou one of his signature cocky smiles, "Fact check yourself, Louis. Cian wouldn't have been hunting her if you hadn't killed a couple of his vampires."

I tried pulling on his shoulders to get him to release Warrick, "Lou, don't."

"No, Val," he said through gritted teeth. He pushed harder on Warrick's throat now cutting off his air, "You don't get a say in this. He's manipulating you to get what he wants. Once he has that, he'll kill you. I'm not letting that happen. I'll break if I lose you."

I stopped trying to pull him off Warrick for a split second shocked by him using the same words I heard back on the beach moments ago. Shaking my head, I yanked on his shoulders again, "You don't get to decide for me, Lou. I get to make my choice here. Please, just let him go."

Panic was creeping up into my throat as I watched Warrick frantically clawing at Lou's arm. His face was starting to turn blue from the lack of air which motivated Lou to press even harder. "Lou!" I screamed. "You have to stop!"

He wasn't listening to me anymore. I looked to Jennie and Bev for any signs of help only to see they were just as shocked as I was. Warrick tried kicking out missing Lou by inches. My head whipped around looking for anything to end this situation. At this point, Joe and Chris were back upstairs frozen in their spots. They had their pool cues in their hands, but I knew those would snap in half if I hit Lou with them. I frantically glanced back at Warrick who was now starting to go slack, eyes trying to roll back in his head. I was losing precious seconds.

I ran into the kitchen grabbing the heaviest pan I could find before running back over to the two wolves. I smacked Lou as hard as I could in the back of the head hoping that would do the trick. He immediately collapsed, freeing Warrick from the hold he had on him. Warrick crumpled to the ground and I ran over to him dropping the pan. I gave him a couple of light pats on the cheek, "Warrick, I need you to wake up."

I put my head to his chest growing increasingly worried when I couldn't locate a heartbeat. I laid him flat on the ground interlacing my fingers and got to work performing CPR, "Warrick, don't do this to me. It's going to take more than that to take you down. C'mon. Come back to me."

I kept up the steady rhythm pausing momentarily to check for breathing or his heartbeat. Nothing yet. I kept going, my friends starting to surround me. I wouldn't let myself cry, not when I wasn't ready to give up on him. "Jennie, I need you to check on Lou. I don't think I did anything to cause damage," I commanded.

"He's fine," Joe said. I looked over my shoulder at him to see that he was examining Lou's head. "He's going to have a pretty good knot and maybe a massive headache, but he's fine."

I nodded shifting my focus back to Warrick, "Don't you dare give up on me now. You can't go down this way, Warrick."

I put my head down to his chest straining to hear anything. I moved a fraction of an inch to give myself a better vantage point when the loud *thump* rang out in his chest cavity. I sprang up in time to catch Warrick inhale a giant mouthful of air, eyes snapping open. He grabbed for his throat looking wildly around. I laid my head down on him, his arms instinctively wrapping around me as I said, "Thank goodness."

"What the fuck was that?" he asked in between breaths.

"Lou," I said. "It was Lou."

He moved to sit up, so I sat back on my heels. The surprise was gone from his face, replaced with the collected expression Warrick typically wears as he smoothed his hair back. Joe and Chris drug Lou's unconscious body away to avoid any other attacks when he woke up.

"Hell of a welcome," he said with a shaky voice.

I looked back towards Lou, "I don't know why he acted that way."

Warrick let out a bark of laughter, "I have an idea."

"Don't tell me," I said closing my eyes pinching the bridge of my nose.

Jennie flung her arms out, "Well? Care to share with the class?"

Warrick laughed a little more, "It's going to get a lot more interesting in here. Lou's fated to Val."

Chapter 11

Hearing Warrick confirm what had popped into my head only minutes ago made my world spin. Jennie and Bev's jaws dropped open.

Joe was the only one who seemed to have the ability to talk, "Is that even possible?"

Warrick shrugged, "I haven't heard of that happening before, but that doesn't mean it's impossible. It could be that he thinks he's fated and he's not really, but usually when a wolf acts that intense, there's a reason. Besides, it's just a hunch at this point. He probably isn't, but I'm not ruling it out."

I put my head between my knees struggling to handle this news. That would explain Lou moping around in the vampire world when I left. That would explain why he was being so patient with me, and when I heard him utter practically the same words as Warrick, something clicked in my head.

I was starting to put together a mental list of question for Raf: Is this even possible? Does fating in fact make a wolf a little more unstable? How am I supposed to know who I'm fated with? How will I even know what it feels like?

Everyone was debating around me whether or not Lou was actually fated with me, but with Warrick, things have been different. Lou's been around me all the time without really having to deal with separation, so it's not like we were constantly being drawn together. Even when I went into the pizza place the first time, it wasn't like I felt a magnetic pull. Not the same way I've felt pulled to Warrick.

I waved my hands, signaling everyone to stop talking, "Good theory, Warrick, but I don't think that's the case. He may think he's fated to me. He may be acting crazy because he feels the need to protect me since we've spent a good amount of time together. Lou's someone who takes people under his wing, that's his nature. We happened to feel a connection, so I think that amplified his protective personality."

"You're probably right, love. That makes more sense anyway and makes me breathe a little easier. I'll still want to check with Raf when I can, though."

Lou started stirring making us shift our focus from the conversation to him. He sat up rubbing his head and groaning, "What the hell did I get hit with?"

I lifted up the pan, "This."

"Why?"

"Because I can't have you killing Warrick."

Lou jumped up lunging for Warrick again. I stepped in between them putting my hand on Lou's chest to try to calm him down, "Alright, all of you need to listen to me. Warrick hasn't done anything to make us want to welcome him with open arms, but that's what we're going to do. He'll be staying with us for a little bit. Warrick, you need to keep those asshole remarks to yourself. No fighting, no squabbling, no mind games, and no passive aggressiveness. We're turning over a new leaf. I'm done with the drama."

Not giving anyone a chance to respond, I made my way upstairs making my way out to the balcony sinking into one of the chairs. This was going to be hard having two rival alphas under the same roof. I don't know what I was thinking asking Warrick to stay with me, it just felt so right at the time. I sighed dropping my head in my hands.

"Love?"

I shot out of my chair in a defensive stance. Warrick had moved so quietly I hadn't heard him come in. He held up his hands stopping in the middle of the room, "Didn't mean to scare you. I didn't know where I could go, so I came up here."

"Sorry," I shook my head. "Yeah, make yourself at home. Do you think this was a mistake?"

"It's your house, you get to make the rules. I can put aside my differences for now if that's going to help you sleep better."

"Thanks, Warrick," I walked up to him reaching for his neck. "How are you feeling? You can't even tell you were just choked."

"We heal fast when the conditions are right," he said pulling my hand away. "I'll grab all my stuff tomorrow, but I think I'm going to take a shower. It's been a long day."

"Yeah, go ahead."

I turned on some music, turned the lights off, and flopped onto my bed while Warrick shut himself in my bathroom. *Why did I let the one person who causes me to have physical reactions in my house?*

I don't know how long I laid there staring at the ceiling when there was a soft knock on the door. I propped myself up to see who was going to be letting themselves in mentally prepared for a fight. Lou poked his head into the room, "Can I come in?"

"Depends."

"On?"

"On whether or not you're going to keep your temper under control."

"Val," Lou sighed. "I was caught off-guard, but can you blame me? The guy has almost gotten you killed more times than I can count at this point. He's played more mind games with you. Do you even know which way is up at this point? Why bring him here? Why the sudden change? I can't bring myself to trust him. There's no part of me that could, but you're letting him waltz right into this house where he could have access to whatever the hell he wants. So, why, Val?"

"Yes, why, Val?" Warrick interjected from the doorway to the bathroom. He was drying his hair, a towel wrapped around his waist and eyes trained on Lou watching every move.

Lou let out a small growl, but didn't move from his spot. I noticed Warrick wasn't leaving his spot, either. *At least there's hope that it's not going to be a constant fight between these two.*

"Because Warrick has information that could help us. There's something he's not telling me and I want to know what that is. I can't ignore the fact I feel some level of comfort in his presence despite everything, so maybe I'll be able to get some sleep without waking everyone up every other day screaming," I finished.

"No," Lou shook his head. "There's more to it than that, but neither of you are going to say anything."

"Is that a problem?" Warrick asked.

"Yes, it is. It'll come out someday," Lou turned to leave. He turned his head, his back facing the room now, "I just hope you know what you're doing, Val."

He closed the door behind him no doubt going back to the rest of the group. Warrick put the towel over his head, but still didn't leave the sanctuary of the bathroom. I watched him a little longer before saying, "You can sleep in here."

"You didn't say anything to him about us being fated, love," he said raising his head to look at me.

I shrugged, "Neither did you. Anyways, I didn't feel like giving him another reason to go after you."

"I can handle Louis, love."

"Warrick, I really don't want to do this right now. Be my guest if you want to break that news to everyone downstairs," I shot back at him laying back down on the bed.

Warrick sighed, "I'm starting to feel like this was a mistake."

I propped myself up on my elbows again, "Don't say that. We don't have to shout from the mountains what we know especially when things are a little rocky. I want us to have this time to ourselves, Warrick. We need to be united before breaking the news to everyone or they're going to immediately accuse you of mind games again. My trust isn't like a light switch, I can't just immediately trust you because of what you said on the beach back there."

Warrick crossed the room dropping to his knees in between my legs and putting his hands on my knees, "Then how do I get that trust back, love?"

"Let's go with the obvious – start by telling me what you're doing jumping between worlds tomorrow. Tell me what your plan is. Loop me in so I can try to help," I said running my hand through his damp hair.

"I'll try."

"Thank you," I said. "I'm going to check on things downstairs, feel free to join me or stay here."

"Do you have pants I could borrow? As much as I'd like to be naked in the same room with you, I think I'd feel more comfortable going downstairs without the risk of flashing everyone" he gestured to the towel still clinging to him.

"Um," I said getting up. "Come with me."

I led him across the hall to my parents' room and started digging through my dad's clothes. I had some of Gabriel's clothes in boxes, but I wasn't ready to share those with anyone.

I held up a pair of flannel pajama pants getting a nod of approval from Warrick. I tossed them to him then made my way back downstairs greeted by the smell of freshly baked cookies.

I immediately headed over the island where Joe and Bev were talking in low voices plucking a cookie off the plate. Glancing around the room, I noted Chris and Jennie were probably downstairs and Lou was out in the pool. I turned back to the two in front of me, "Everything okay?"

"Jennie's pissed and Chris is trying to calm her down. Judging by the bickering, it's not going so well. Lou's out there drinking his sorrows away just walking around the pool," Joe said. "We're good, though."

Savoring the melted chocolate from the fresh chocolate chip cookies, I used this time to think about how I was going to tackle this conversation. I sat in the chair I was standing next to not able to bring myself to look at them, "I didn't think this one through. Warrick's up there trying to act like nothing happened between us; Lou's pissed because his enemy is now living with him and now I have to be ready to step in between the fights; Jennie's pissed more out of fear since Warrick threatened her; and I drug you guys in the middle of this mess."

"You didn't drag us in the middle of this. We kind of had no choice due to circumstances. Jennie is Jennie and she's going to make a big deal of things because that's her personality. I don't know too much about Lou and Warrick, but I'm sure Warrick is trying to set things right where Lou is too caught up in his feelings to think rationally. Val, you need to stop beating yourself up because you're still recovering from something you should've never gone through."

"You should listen to them, love," said the familiar British voice from behind me.

I sucked in a breath. *He really needed to stop doing that.* Warrick settled in the chair next to me grabbing a cookie. He took a bite and a smile formed on his face, "I haven't had a cookie this good in years. Thank you,"

Bev straightened up a little bit smiling in return, "Of course."

Jennie stormed up the stairs yelling something at Chris. She paused seeing us all in the kitchen then threw her hands up with frustration, "Ugh!" She continued storming out to the pool jumping in to join Lou quickly grabbing the bottle of whatever he had out there and throwing some back.

"Here she goes," I mumbled.

Chris slowly made his way up looking exhausted. He started at the sight of the four of us, but quickly regained his composure, "I think I'm sleeping on the couch tonight."

"We're sorry, Chris. Come grab a cookie," I said. Warrick pulled out the seat next to him ignoring Chris' hesitation. Chris eventually moved to the seat taking a cookie off the plate Joe was offering. Silence hung over us as we sat there munching on Bev's snack. My gaze drifted out towards the pool to where Lou and Jennie were talking. The door was closed making it hard to make anything out outside of the occasional raised voice to match the gestures toward the house.

Chris shook his head, "Part of me wants to hear what they're saying, but another part of me is fine with not knowing."

"You really want to hear what's going on out there?" Warrick asked.

Chris' eyes widened, "You can pick up what they're saying?"

"I'm surprised this is catching you off-guard, but yes."

I got up to grab some water offering a glass to everyone else, "Be careful what you wish for, Chris. Jennie can be a loose cannon when she's drunk."

Warrick chuckled as I passed him a glass. Chris looked back out at the pool debating if he wanted to know when he nodded his head, "Hit me."

"She doesn't understand why I'm here," Warrick started. "She's going on and on about how rash Val is being while being mad at you for not taking her side. Jennie's saying she doesn't want to be with someone who won't support her. Well, this is interesting," he trailed off.

"What?" Chris and I asked in unison.

Warrick glanced at Chris, "You're not going to like this, but she's also trying to flirt with Lou. Meanwhile, he's just going on and on about how Val betrayed him by bringing me here."

Chris looked hurt, so I reached across Warrick to give his arm a comforting squeeze, "What happened down there?"

"She started tearing into you, but I countered everything she said which opened up the doors for her to throw our kiss in my face as an excuse that I had some sort of lingering feelings. It's not true, but she wasn't having it. Ultimately, she told me she wanted a break, so I'm giving her some space."

Warrick raised an eyebrow towards me and I waved him off.

Bev jumped in, "Jennie's been acting all over the place lately, so she's clearly struggling with what's going on. I'm sorry, Chris. She'll come back around."

"I know," Chris said looking hurt. "Doesn't change the fact that she's now trying to throw herself at someone new as a way to get back to me."

We all looked out to watch those two for a little bit. Jennie would clearly do something to flirt with Lou then look back towards the house. She couldn't have made it more obvious if she tried. Lou, on the other hand, had no idea what was going on. He finished the bottle and started to make his way out of the pool.

"He's coming to get more," Warrick murmured.

Joe grabbed another bottle that matched what was in Lou's hand, "I'll take this out to him. I'll sit out there for a little bit to hopefully keep things from escalating."

"This damn fridge has a never-ending supply of alcohol," I remarked.

That got a couple of chuckles out of everyone around me. At least I could help lighten the mood a little bit in here.

We watched as Joe handed Lou the bottle who immediately chugged half of it. Joe settled into one of the chairs trying to talk to Jennie who kept waving him off. I could tell Lou was starting to get tipsy with an obviously drunk Jennie inching closer and closer to him. She can get vindictive when she's not getting her way, and things have not been going the way she'd like.

"My bet is on Jennie kissing Lou in the next 30 minutes," Chris said surprising us all.

Warrick was the first one to jump in on the bet by clinking his glass with Chris', "She'll kiss him in the next 20 and he'll storm out of the pool scared he's going to lose all the progress he's made with Val."

"You're on."

Bev and I looked at each other confused by what happened. I guess the first alliance with Warrick and the crew here had been made. I grabbed another cookie and continued watching it play out. At this point, Warrick and Chris were giving a play by play, ad-libbing what was playing out in front of us despite Warrick being able to hear what was being said. There were a couple of times all of us laughed a little, and a couple of times where we commented on how uncomfortable Joe looked.

Joe made his way back in at the 15-minute mark shaking his head, "Sorry, Chris. It's like I'm not even out there."

Chris clapped a hand on Joe's back, "It's all good, man. I'm not surprised by what I'm seeing. I've seen her act this way before. I just never thought I'd be on the receiving end."

Bev brought Joe up to speed on the bet, Joe joining in to Bev's surprise. I noted how much time had passed as we got closer to the 20-minute mark. Warrick was about to lose the bet when Jennie grabbed Lou's face and planted one on him. They kissed for a little bit until Lou recognized what was happening and pushed her away. He lifted himself out of the pool grabbing his towel as he hurried back towards the house.

Lou ripped the door open realizing we had all been watching them. He focused in on me as I raised my glass to my lips taking a slow sip. "Val," there was panic in his voice. "That was all Jennie. One minute she was talking to me, the next kissing me. I swear, that was the last thing I wanted to do."

I shrugged, "I know."

He kept stammering trying to explain himself, but when I was done hearing it, I turned towards him, "Lou, stop. You're freaking out over nothing. Jennie kissed you because she wanted to get a rise out of us in here. You're innocent, we get it. I'm tired and have had my fill on dealing with drama. We can talk more about it tomorrow if you want. Goodnight."

Lou's mouth opened and closed a couple of times before he eventually hung his head making his way up to his room. We waited until we heard his door lock before going back to the quickly diminishing plate of cookies.

Warrick and Chris clinked glasses together, Chris saying, "You were spot on. I think I'm going to bed. Val, is it cool if I sleep down in the basement?"

"Knock yourself out. Let me know if you need anything."

He left the room before Jennie walked in ignoring us as she went upstairs leaving Warrick, Bev, Joe and myself as the only ones still up. A yawn hit me hard signaling it was time to sleep, so I started cleaning up. No other words were exchanged outside of telling each other good night.

Warrick followed me to my room, "What a night."

"Yeah," I laughed. "See what you do to people?"

A genuine smile tugged at the corner of his lips warming my numb heart a little bit. *I've missed that smile.*

I started to get settled in bed, Warrick still standing near the door, "Are you okay with me sleeping in here, love?"

I patted the space next to me nodding my head, "Just grab a blanket out of the closet. I want you comfortable, but I need to be comfortable, too."

"Got it."

I rolled over feeling the bed dip as Warrick laid next to me, careful to keep some space between us. His breathing slowed, and once I knew he was asleep for sure, I let myself close my eyes.

M y eyes opened to my room slowly lightening as the sun inched further into the sky. I felt groggy from not getting the most sleep, so I didn't immediately notice Warrick no longer next to me. Rubbing my eyes, I sat up resting against the headboard. Everything was how I had left it last night except for the balcony door being open. I made my way over to the open door wondering if I'd find Warrick standing there. I hid myself behind the billowing curtains confirming that's where he went. I watched him for a little while taking note of something not sitting right with me.

"I know you're there, love," he said without moving.

"Good morning to you, too," I said as I inched my way out. "How are you feeling this morning?"

Warrick looked at me out of the side of his eyes, "Neck's a little sore, but I'm fine."

"I hope Lou keeps it together today. I'm trying to make it all work for everyone."

"About that, has Lou been keeping your bed warm?"

I flinched at the sudden change in his tone, "Yes, but only when he was recovering from the change because I couldn't help carry him to his room and I think there was another night when I couldn't sleep alone. Nothing more than that."

He stood up to full height turning to face me, "Still doesn't sit right with me, love."

My chance to respond was cut short as Warrick grabbed me then held me over the railing of the balcony. I was dangling there, upside down, panic taking hold. I looked up to his sneering face, begging, "Please, Warrick. Don't do this. Don't let me go."

"All this talk about trust and you're here snuggling up to Lou the minute I'm out of the picture. I don't think so."

His hand around my ankle was gone and I screamed as the cement below me got closer until I landed on my head, my neck snapping. In no time at all, the world went black.

Chapter 12

My eyes snapped open to Bev's concerned face. I jolted upright and pushed myself back, the panic from the latest nightmare not quite out of my system yet. My eyes shot around the room frantically taking in the scene: Bev and Joe are the closest to me looking like they just woke up, their faces full of concern; Jennie behind them hungover, but worried; Chris trying to pull Lou off Warrick; Lou trying to pin Warrick who for once wasn't looking fully composed. Lou was shouting something at him, but Warrick's focus was fully on me. He looked horrified and I immediately knew what happened.

"Val, hey, are you alright? Did he do anything to you?" Bev asked quietly.

"N-no," I stammered shaking my head. "I'm fine. Really. I just had another nightmare, that's all. I'm really sorry I caused all of this."

My head dropped into my hands, tears taking their familiar trek down my cheeks silencing the room. The constant conflicts and general stress was stacking up. My friends didn't deserve to have this burden placed on them. Warrick and Lou could get them back, they wouldn't need me any longer.

Warrick who was no longer being held back by Lou, rushed back over to me. He tried to lift my face, but I wasn't moving. "Please go," I whimpered.

"No, love. I'm staying right here."

"Why? Clearly, I scare you. I make everyone feel like they have to walk on eggshells and put everyone on edge when it's time to sleep. I've caused more problems than I can count. Just look at last night as an example," I countered through tears.

Warrick pulled me into his arms while everyone was trying to talk me off the ledge I was clearly walking towards. Warrick was being so gentle, his arms putting enough pressure around me that allowed for me to get out with a simple movement if I wanted to. He had me angled so I was turned away from the rest of the people in the room with my head resting on his chest.

He turned his attention to our audience, "Can you all give us some time alone?"

Joe quickly agreed, ushering everyone out including Lou who was protesting with every step he took. He kept mentioning that Warrick had no idea what to do to help, that Raf hadn't explained the techniques he was using to help me, but that didn't stop Joe from pushing him out of my room. The door closed signaling Warrick to put his whole focus back on me, "I didn't know what to expect, but those nightmares are something else. Tell me, did I do something to hurt you, love?"

"How do you know it was you?" I asked quietly.

His hand came up to stroke my hair, "Because you screamed my name."

"You threw me off the balcony."

He tried lifting my head again, successfully this time. His eyes searched mine, brows furrowing the longer he took in my distress, "I would never do that to you. We started off on the wrong foot, but you know I'm never going to hurt you again. I'm not going to let you give up on us, either. You may think you're placing a burden on everyone, but you're not. We wouldn't be here without everything you've done. You've reunited with five of your friends, you put together a device to jump worlds, you've started decoding the combinations to get us to other worlds, you've helped me get further along with reaching my goals which I need to bring you and Lou up to speed on today. Don't you dare tell me you're a burden. I know things have felt chaotic and there are most certainly things you shouldn't have gone through. Just. Don't. Give. Up. On. Me."

"How can I trust that you're not going to leave me again?" I asked holding his gaze.

"What can I do to earn that trust?"

"Keep your word. Prove that you want to love me. Take me back to the Warrick I had to myself in that house back in the vampire world."

He grinned at me, eyes softening, "I can do that, love. Are you ready to go downstairs?"

I squeezed my eyes shut to push past the wave of emotions, "Not really, but do we have a choice?"

"There's always a choice," he whispered stroking my cheek. "I'll bring you anything you want to eat."

"No, I should go," I sighed.

"Are you ready to face a gauntlet?"

I looked up at him again, "What?"

He nodded towards the door, "Your friends may have left the room, but they're all out in the hall listening. I'm sure that's mostly to make sure I wouldn't actually cause you any harm."

"Let's get this over with," I said moving to get out of bed with a sigh.

Warrick was already at the door opening it when I made it over to him. He wasn't wrong. Everyone was standing on the other side of the door trying to act like they weren't just creeping on what I thought was a private conversation. Surprisingly, Jennie was the first one to speak up, clearing her throat, "He's right, you know. The last thing you are is a burden on us."

Everyone nodded in agreement making heat rise to my cheeks, "Well, thanks, I guess. Sorry you had to deal with yet another one of my episodes."

"You're recovering, Val," Lou chimed in. "It's not going to happen overnight. Also, sorry for going after you Warrick."

"All good," he responded, not without an edge to his voice. Warrick gave me a nudge to start moving toward the stairs. Obeying, I lifted my cement-laden feet to head to the kitchen.

Warrick got to work making a breakfast. I didn't know if his initiative was more out of habit or as a peace offering. Bev scooted next to me lowering her voice, "My unbiased opinion in the short amount of time he's been here is that Warrick really cares about you and would genuinely do anything for you. May not be what you want to talk about right now, but I wanted to uphold my promise."

I smiled a little at her comment, "Thanks, Bev. I appreciate you letting me know."

"It also helps that he has a hell of a body. Don't tell Joe I said that," she giggled. A laugh tried to escape my lips earning a raised eyebrow and a secretive grin from Warrick in return.

Shaking his head at what Bev said, Warrick asked, "Love, are you up to leaving the house today? I have a couple things I need to do which involve your participation, and one of those things is heading into town."

"Sure, I guess," I said.

He paused, "You don't have to join me if you don't want to."

I shook my head, "No, I'll go with you. The fresh air will do me some good."

Warrick nodded, "Lou, are you good with taking some time to talk with me and Val? I have to bring you two up to speed on some things."

Warrick was wasting no time getting down to business only proving to me that he's making an effort to stay true to his word. It would be nice to finally get a glimpse into why he's been keeping so many things under wraps.

I looked over to Lou who nodded his head. He may have agreed, but his jaw was set, clearly not happy about the forced proximity to Warrick. I had to give them props for one thing – they were at least starting to make an effort to play nice.

Warrick outdid himself on the breakfast spread. There was a full line of food with everything from pancakes and waffles to bacon to fruit. I had never seen people go after food the way everyone was now. The only person who was hesitant was Lou. Not surprising considering his history with Warrick, but he would have to eat eventually. I also couldn't help but think back to breakfast the day the bombs had hit where things felt eerily similar to how they do now.

We finished with breakfast, Lou offering to clean up so Warrick and I could head into town. He changed into yesterday's clothes while I threw together a quick outfit. I had no idea where he was taking me or why he needed me, but I didn't have the energy to think about it today.

Warrick led us back to the crystal shop and up those mysterious stairs I thought led to an apartment. I was surprised to find the space above the store wasn't an apartment at all. Instead, it looked almost like an office building where fairies were working away at whatever they had been assigned that morning. The space was open with tables thoughtfully placed around the room. There was a kitchen in the corner next to the only walled off room in the space. He walked us over to that room knocking on the door.

Sarind cracked open the door, her white eyes assessing the two of us before motioning for us to join her in the office, "I'm glad you stopped by today, Warrick. I was starting to wonder if you forgot about my meeting request."

I was caught a little off-guard by the formality of this interaction. There was a whole other side of this world I was learning about today with the office workers buzzing around on the other side of the door and now Sarind is holding herself like someone who's running a company, not someone who is viewed as a world leader.

"How's Marin holding up?" he asked.

Sarind shrugged, "She's not happy, but she needed to go through this experience." She looked at me, "How are you holding up, Val? I'm sorry you had to see Warrick like that. It was purely for business."

I was caught off-guard by the sudden change in topic, nervously glancing between her and Warrick. He put his hand on my knee, nodding his head in encouragement for me to talk with her, "I've been better."

"I'm sure. Alright, pleasantries aside. Warrick, you want to know if I've seen anything that would indicate your war going one way or another. I'm sure you also want to know if we're fully committed to your cause. Did I miss anything?"

"No. Your answers to the above will take care of my last question," he said matter-of-factly.

"Which is?" she inquired.

"If I can move on to my next stop or if I'm needed here any longer."

Sarind folded her hands in front of her, "Understood. Well, I haven't seen anything that gives a clear indication. There are too many variables at play, as I'm sure you're aware of. With that, we are committed to your cause. Here's your signed document back for your records. I can't put these people's livelihoods at risk without at least trying to stop the evil you say is coming our way. Val, I understand there's a war raging in your world, is that right?"

I had too many other questions running through my mind to be able to answer her right away so I ended up staring at her for a little while until only a single word came to me, "Yeah."

"And how has that affected you?"

"Well," I swallowed. "It completely turned my life upside down to the point where I don't know if I'd be able to go back and pick up where I left off."

She nodded satisfied with my answer, "Exactly what I'm trying to avoid. Warrick, I know you feel the same way. We have to put an end to this before it gets any worse."

"I'm sorry," I interjected. "What's going on here?"

Warrick turned to me, "I'll explain later with Lou, I promise. I brought you with me to get you out of the house and to add more evidence showing I'm telling the truth."

"O-okay," I stammered. I squirmed a little in my chair wanting to move on with the day so I could pester Warrick with all of my questions. I couldn't help but think about Raf telling us we needed to find Warrick and talking about the war.

Apparently, that's all connected, but I'm still missing a lot of context. Shaking my head, I focused back on their conversation.

Sarind looked back at Warrick, "Does that help you with your last question?"

"I think it does," he said reaching across the desk to shake her hand.

She gave him a smile before turning to me, "Val, I understand you saw one of our most rare creatures while you were here?"

"I did," I answered right away. "It was the most amazing animal I've ever seen in my life."

"There's a saying around here that they'll make an appearance for those who need good fortune. Everything I know about you, you could use some of that. May you be blessed in your adventures."

That signaled us all to conclude the meeting. We all shook hands then made our way back out of the shop. Instead of heading back to the house, we headed further up the street to a small, tan townhouse. Warrick fumbled with some keys eventually unlocking the front door. As he led the way in, I asked, "This is where you've been staying?"

"Yeah, it's time I cleared out of here and bring my stuff over to your place, if that's okay?"

"Sure."

I stepped across the threshold scanning the space I was now standing in. The first thing that greeted me was the stairs up to the second floor. The walls were a light blue fitting in with being this close to the ocean. This place was the most decorated I've seen of any of the spaces Warrick owns with trinkets and art scattered around the space. The furniture was all a light color, too. I stayed rooted to my spot waiting for him, so I didn't get to see if the rest of the space matched what I could see from my vantage point.

He jogged down the stairs carrying a couple of duffle bags, "Ready?"

I nodded my head following him to the back of the house where his car was parked. I settled into the passenger seat running my hand over the soft leather, the smell of new car flooding my nose, "How many cars do you have, Warrick?"

"Enough to get me around," he grinned as he drove the car back to my house.

We got back to a surprisingly quiet house. I poked my head around various corners until spotting motion out in the pool. I headed out there leaving Warrick to settle in and plopped myself in the chair next to Jennie, "How are you?"

"Fine," she curtly responded.

"What's your deal, Jennie?" I asked cutting to the chase.

She slowly turned her head in my direction, "Just pissed at Chris, that's all."

I tugged at her arm, "Let's take this conversation inside."

She didn't say anything, but she got up to follow me. I wanted to set the record straight with her so she didn't keep doing something stupid. Last thing I need for Jennie is to channel her inner reckless Val.

She huffed sitting down in one of the few chairs in the basement. I had no idea where Warrick was, but I was hoping the rest of the group stayed outside so they didn't spy on our conversation.

"Okay, tell me why you're pissed at him," I said watching her carefully.

Jennie rolled her eyes, but eventually sighed, "I know what you're going to say, but he was completely ignoring the fact that my *life* was threatened by the crazy you just waltzed into the house with. He wasn't on my side at all, and if I'm not going to be able to have the support I need, then I don't need to be in a relationship with him."

I had a hard time keeping the annoyance out of my voice, "First of all, you're an adult, Jennie, so act like one. Chris is his own person, even when he's in a relationship with you. He's allowed to have his own opinions and feelings. That just means you need to have a healthy conversation with him about that to communicate how you're feeling, not screaming at him then ending the relationship. Second, it sounds like you're angry with me too, so let's figure that out. Third, don't try to repeat that stunt of getting drunk and kissing whoever you like. That's my job."

Jennie narrowed her eyes at me making me brace myself for whatever fury I just unleashed by calling her out. Instead, she took a deep breath, closing her eyes, "You're right, Val. I need to have a level-headed conversation with him to work through how I'm feeling. As for you, yeah, I'm mad. It's like you've thrown out everything that has happened recently and welcomed the one person in here with open arms who's been trying to kill you. Why?"

"Did I tell you about the dream I had? The one that made Lou call Raf over to give me a sedative?"

"No, but I've been wondering what happened."

I sighed, a ghost of a smile flirting with my lips, "Gabriel showed up." I heard her open her mouth getting ready to say something, but I continued with my story not giving her the chance, "He was really there. I could touch him, feel his beating heart more than I ever have whenever he popped up in my dreams. We went on a ride to our favorite spot where he told me to love Warrick with all my heart. Then, Liam came in and snapped his neck killing him right in front of me. I know you're going to think I'm crazy and tell me it was only a dream, but it felt so real."

"I'm so sorry, Val. I don't think you're crazy, and I'm not just saying that to put your mind at ease," she said reaching for my hand. Before she could hold it, Jennie took her hand back to rest on her lap. "I still don't understand why you didn't think twice about bringing Warrick here."

I chuckled, "Believe me, I did. I had so many doubts. I still can't fully trust him, but Raf also said we needed to find Warrick, if you remember that. We need him to explain what's going on. And to add another layer to all of this, he confirmed we're fated which is something Raf hinted at, too. Warrick's not trying to play head games with that."

Her mouth hung open for a few beats before closing allowing her to regain her composure, "You fall very easily, so it's surprising to hear you mention any sort of doubt." She sighed looked off at something on the other side of the room, "I still don't get it, but I'll play nice."

"That's all I ask," I said moving to get up. "Are you and Chris going to make up?"

"Not sure yet, but probably, eventually."

I gave a quick nod of my head turning to leave. I was counting my steps up the stairs to help calm some of my jitters that I didn't notice Warrick standing there leaning against the entryway blocking my exit. Almost smacking into him, I jumped, "Oh! Were you listening to that?"

In a quiet voice, he said, "Yeah, your friends are lucky to have you to care for them, love. And you're lucky to have them, too."

"Don't exclude yourself from that," I said squeezing his arm.

It felt like time froze in that moment with us staring at each other in such close proximity. My breath caught in my throat as he caressed my cheek. His voice dropped to an even more hushed tone, "Can I kiss you?"

Unable to say anything, I nodded. His lips grazed mine tentatively to make sure I still wanted this then his lips covered mine in a soft, passionate embrace. It hadn't been that long since we kissed last, yet it still caught me off-guard when my body wanted more. It was almost as if I was trying to make up for lost time, and when he pulled away, I almost whimpered. Almost.

I kept myself together only letting my blushing cheeks indicate how he made me feel. Warrick tucked a strand of hair behind my ear, "I've missed you."

"The feeling's mutual," I croaked.

"Do you think you're up to talking about what's going on with Lou?"

I cocked my head, "I mean he's being a little more dramatic than usual, but I don't think it's anything we need to talk about."

He chuckled, "No, love. I'm more talking about what I've been keeping secret from you. Are you ready to dive into that and grab Lou so we can all talk about it together?"

"Are you two done with your make out session?" Jennie asked behind us.

I instantly moved out of the way to create more space for her to get by with Warrick mirroring my movements. She muttered her thanks as she passed still giving us a little bit of the cold shoulder.

"Um," I stared, watching her leave. "Sure. I'll go grab him."

"No, I'll grab him. Do you have a space in this house we can talk?"

"We can go in my dad's office," I suggested.

He nodded, "That works. We'll meet you up there."

I headed in that direction shaking my head to get the little voice to stop scolding me for offering up the space that holds a gold mine of information for Warrick. On one hand, he could take advantage to try and get a hold of as many details as he wants. On the other hand, though, he would end up stumbling across this room at some point, so might as well rip off the Band-Aid.

I settled into my dad's desk chair as the two of them walked into the room. Lou was clearly unhappy with being summoned by Warrick, the last person he wants to deal with here. Warrick wasn't looking the most relaxed, either. They pulled up chairs on the opposite side of me and we sat there in an awkward silence for a couple of minutes.

Clearing my throat, I asked, "So, where should we start?"

"Why doesn't Warrick start from the beginning?" Lou asked anger lacing his voice. Lou was staring Warrick down challenging him with Warrick returning the stare. I could've sworn I saw them bristle.

I abruptly stood up hoping to get them to change their focus with no such luck. I moved in between them, "Warrick, go sit in my chair. I'll sit here. This isn't a discussion that's going to turn into a fight. Now, Warrick, please just tell us what's going on."

Still not letting his eyes leave Lou's, Warrick jumped into what he's been hiding, "As you know, there's a war going on. Don't roll your eyes." Lou stopped mid-eyeroll signaling Warrick to go on, "It's not only focused on your world, love. There's a huge threat of this war expanding beyond your boundaries. It puts everything at risk. If the enemy wins, life as we know it is done, if we even survive, that is. Sounds dramatic, but it's not. I'm trying to go around to these different worlds to gain support to fight back. No one has been able to stand up to this enemy, but my hope is to put together an army to put an end to this. I'm being very selective about who I recruit which is why it was a *huge* breakthrough that you were able to figure out some of those codes, Val. You saved me so much time."

"Gald I could help. I take it Cian is one of those who you've recruited. Who else?" I asked.

Warrick nodded his head, "Yeah, which is why he wasn't the happiest about you taking up the vampire-hunting profression. Every fighter is important and we didn't want to lose anyone, so now he's having to up his numbers again."

I winced now understanding why Cian was acting the way he was after what I had done, "Sorry."

Warrick reached towards me earning a low growl from Lou. Ignoring the warning, Warrick held my hand, "It's okay, love. You had no idea what was going on in the background and I should've told you before we went to that ball."

He sat back in his chair continuing, "You know I've recruited Sarind, but there's a couple of others. I won't dive into too many of the details right now, but we're slowly building our numbers. It has been a slow process up until this point, thanks to you fixing my device, love."

"Who's next?" Lou asked. "And why tell me?"

"Well, you see, as much as I don't like it, Louis, there's a reason why I haven't killed you yet," Warrick said nonchalantly. Lou started to get out of his chair, but was stopped when I threw out an arm. Warrick, chuckling at the reaction he got out of Lou, went on, "You're a hell of a fighter. The more strength I can add to our side, the better. I hate admitting this, but you're on the same level as me which is going to come handy when the time comes to face off with our enemy."

"What do we know about the enemy?" I interjected. Warrick frowned at my question not willing to be as forthcoming with this piece of the puzzle as the other parts.

"Before you answer that, I just want to make sure I'm getting this. You're asking me to join up with you? The guy who's been attacking me, the people in our world, and killing for fun?" Lou asked.

"That's correct," Warrick answered with no hesitation.

Lou shook his head, "There's a screw loose in your head or something. I'm only agreeing because I don't want anything to happen to the people in our world, but don't think this means I trust you."

"Always the saint," Warrick grinned.

Another growl sounded next to me. I instinctively put a hand on Lou's to calm him down earning a growl from Warrick. I groaned, my head dropping back before looking at the both of them, "What do you two want from me? I'm only trying to keep the peace so we can make it through at least one conversation."

Warrick was the first one to surprisingly back down. He ran a hand through his hair to push it back into place, "Sorry, love.

I'll do my best to push aside our differences so we can find a path forward. Lou?"

Lou's jaw muscles twitched as he thought through how he was going to respond. He eventually hung his head in surrender, "Same. We have bigger fish to fry than who's hand your holding."

"Alright, thank you. So, what do we know about this enemy?" I asked again.

The frown returned to Warrick's face, "He's not one to be messed with. I've squared off with him before and nearly lost my life. I'm not playing around with this one."

"Him? As in one person? And you need a whole army?" I asked, surprised considering Warrick is no slouch when it comes to fighting. Lou gave me a shocked look, too.

"Yes, one person. I need an army because he's a master at manipulating people to be on his side. Just look at what's happened to your world."

That last remark quieted me. When I was ripped from my world, everything was a mess. I had never seen the amount of fighting that was going on and it was on a global scale. If one person was behind that, I couldn't blame Warrick for his urgency and for trying to pull together his own army.

"You should have no problem with understanding how he works, then, given your own manipulation abilities," Lou quipped, bringing me back to the present.

I didn't give Warrick the chance to respond when I interrupted, "Is the enemy the person you had pictures of? The grainy ones that looked like they were from security footage?"

"There's pictures? Maybe I can help add any intel I have on him," Lou offered.

Warrick stood up signaling we were done with the conversation, "That's not relevant right now. I've brought you up to speed on what I've been doing. I appreciate you both for being willing to help me. Now, excuse me while I get a drink."

He left without waiting for us to follow. Lou and I sat there for a few moments shocked by the sudden departure, but also letting what Warrick just explained soak in. I brought my attention to Lou who still looked zoned out, "Thank you for trying to be civil and for agreeing to help."

Lou slowly brought his gaze up to meet mine, "I've never heard of him losing a fight, let alone losing one so badly he almost died. He's always come out on top, and usually without a scratch. I also smelt fear on him when you asked about who the enemy is. This is worse than we thought, Val."

"You've never seen him scared or hurt?" I asked probing to get more background.

He shook his head, "Never. Warrick is one who's always made it clear that he's top dog. Even just now when I dropped my head, I submitted. I may be an alpha to my own pack, but Warrick still has a hold over me and always will."

"I'm going to check on him," I said standing up.

Lou grabbed my arm pausing my exit, "Be careful. Usually, when he's in a mood, he'll lash out. Never seeing him like this before, I have no idea how he'll react."

"Thank you for looking out," I patted his hand. He let me go so I could head downstairs to find Warrick. Everyone else was still out in the pool oblivious of what was really going on. Hell, I was oblivious until a few minutes ago, but I was going to keep it that way for them. Warrick wasn't out there, so I moved through each room of the house until I found him sitting on my balcony slouched over the large bottle he was nursing. Heeding Lou's advice, I spoke while still in my room, "Hey."

He didn't lift his head, just took a sip then waved me out to join him. When I was standing on the opposite end, Warrick looked up at me, "Is that what you were looking for?"

"Thank you for being open about what's really going on."

"Please don't ask me any more questions about our enemy right now. I'm not ready to dive into that more until I get more info," he said dropping his head.

"Got it. Are you okay?"

"Yeah, love. I have my demons, too."

"You did mention that you'll probably be heading out of here soon. Where are we going next?"

Warrick motioned for me to sit next to him and I obliged as he took another long sip. He angled his chair so he was fully facing me now, "I need to check in on my pack, so I'm planning on going back home and would suggest you join me to recoup for a little bit. After that, we'll be going to the witch world. I've got a hunch you'll want to stick with me for that one."

I left Warrick to be alone, not wanting to risk poking the bear any more than I might already have. I was downstairs on the couch watching them all enjoy hanging out in the pool oblivious to what's going on around them. Jennie must have taken my advice because she was back to being all over Chris while Bev and Joe were wrapped up with each other. There was no denying the love written all over their faces and here I was about to pop their bubble of bliss.

"Makes it hard to want to go out there, doesn't it?" Lou said from behind me.

Shoulders slumping, I said, " I hate being the bad guy especially after everything I've put you all through."

"Val, you really need to stop thinking you're ruining all of our lives. This was bound to happen at some point. If anything, you're saving us from having to go through even more pain. What did Warrick say when you went to check on him?'

I glanced up at Lou, "He just said we're going to be leaving soon and not to ask any more questions about our enemy."

Lou returned his attention to the pool, "There wasn't anything else he talked about?"

"Nothing you need to know about."

He gave a quick nod, "Got it."

"Might as well get this over with," I reached for the door handle.

He patted my back, "I'll help you get through this one."

We joined the rest of the group, Lou and I sitting at the edge of the pool dipping our feet in. I checked to see if Warrick was still outside to see him finishing his bottle and watching me a little too closely for my liking. Lou must've sensed the stare down because he put some more space between us while not missing a beat talking to Chris.

"So, Jennie, who kisses better? Lou or me?" Chris asked, puffing his chest out a little bit. Clearly, he wasn't one to dwell on their breakup and her hasty kiss with Lou for too long.

Jennie took the question in stride, throwing her head back and laughing, "You would like to know, wouldn't you?"

"I mean, I'd like to know," Lou said with his lopsided grin. The somber wolf standing next to me was no more. "It's not too often that you can get this kind of feedback," Lou winked. I watched him for a little bit longer. It didn't seem like he had any intention of bringing up any of the topics we had just discussed with Warrick. *So much for having my back.*

Joe swam up to me rested his head on his arms along the edge of the pool, "What's up with the sourpuss up there?"

I looked over my shoulder at Warrick again who still hadn't taken his eyes off me before returning my attention to Joe, "He's just having to process some things. Actually, I came out here to let you all know we're going to be heading back to the werewolf world for a little bit to reset before going to the next world."

Jennie overheard what I said, pouting at my announcement, "We're leaving so soon?"

"Unfortunately, so enjoy the rest of today. We'll be leaving tomorrow."

Joe gave me a thumb's up, "Works for us. We're excited to see Lou's pizza place anyways."

Making my exit from the pool, I headed into the sanctuary of the kitchen unsure if I would be safe going back upstairs with Warrick watching me. Whatever was making him drink like that had to have been pretty bad, and knowing how touchy he can be, I didn't want to risk anything.

I rested my head in my hands feeling incredibly tired all of a sudden. This was one of the rare moments I had peace and quiet, but it was cut too short by the stairs creaking.

"There goes any chance of secrecy," Warrick chuckled.

I stood up straight, "You're drunk."

"Not quite, love," he grinned. "I can change that if you'd like."

"No," I responded rooted to my spot. "Is this how you handle your demons? Because in my world, that's when you know you have a problem. Trust me, I would know."

Warrick was standing in front of me at this point tracing his thumb along my jawline and sending shivers down my back despite my inner voice screaming to run, "The only way I can tame these demons is if I burn them. What better way to do that than with alcohol?"

He licked his lips wetting them, a move I had seen so many times before. Electricity charged between us and I was having a hard time not giving in. Warrick could see my hesitation. Cocking his head to the side while bringing his thumb to my bottom lip, he asked, "What's stopping you, love?"

Shivers rippled through my body making me almost give in right there. With the small amount of resolve I had left in me, I took a step back putting a hand on his chest, "The fact that you can be very dangerous and I don't know if that gets worse when you've been drinking away bad memories."

A predatory smile crept along his face, "Is someone afraid of the big bad wolf?"

I looked out the back door hoping Lou was able to hear what was going on in here in case things escalated a little more. He was still talking with Jennie and Chris as if nothing had happened, but his back muscles tensed picking up on the potential threat.

I brought my gaze back to Warrick's noting he had taken a step to negate the one I had just taken. I put my hand back on his chest, "Why are you acting like this?"

"Just listening to what my wolf wants"

That was all that needed to be said for Lou to make his way back inside. He closed the door softly behind him, "Warrick, back off. She wants space and you need to respect that."

Warrick whipped around, "Always the knight in shining armor, aren't you, Lou?"

"You're not thinking clearly. You need to take a deep breath and take your mind back over," Lou started clenching his fists bracing for a fight.

Warrick let out a slow chuckle, "My wolf and I apparently have a better relationship than the one you have. My human side also wants Val, so in all honesty, my wolf is just heightening that desire."

"Val," Lou said keeping his eyes on Warrick. "You need to get out of here now."

Warrick moved so fast neither of us had time to react. He pulled me in tightly against him, the alcohol on his breath and the heat radiating off his body was overwhelming. I felt the possessive grumble start low in his chest as he said, "She's not going anywhere, especially not with you."

"Lou, I'll be fine. I can handle this," I tried to sound as convincing as possible.

"See? She's in safe hands. Go back to your pool party, I have things handled in here," Warrick said while moving his hand down to grope my ass. I jumped when he squeezed harder than what I expected making Lou lunge in our direction.

A sinister laugh filled the space as Warrick moved me further from Lou, "I don't think so. She's *mine*."

The way he emphasized that last word sounded inhuman. Lou picked up on that, too, because he was now moving towards Warrick, not caring about being careful anymore. I felt Warrick's arm release as he grabbed Lou by the back of his neck slamming him down on the kitchen counter. Lou let out a growl trying to push himself up, but Warrick had too much leverage over him for Lou to be able to do anything. I took a couple of steps back to get myself out of the range of Warrick.

He eased up enough for Lou to put some space between his face and the countertop only for Warrick to slam him back down again. I had to do something or Warrick would keep torturing Lou the way only he knew how to.

The second Warrick felt my touch, he whipped his head in my direction, eyes wild and bright indicating his wolf was just under the surface, "Hey, let's go upstairs."

He thought about brushing me off to continue going after Lou, but ultimately decided against it. Lou picking up on what I was doing protested, "You don't need to sacrifice yourself to come to my aid."

"I'm not, Lou. I want to try to make him forget about the woman we saw him with at the bonfire."

I never broke eye contact with Warrick making sure he wasn't going to go back to tormenting Lou. The edge was gone in his eyes replaced with anticipation. I laced my fingers through his then started tugging him up the stairs. I had no plans of having sex with him at this moment, but I would figure something out to keep him occupied.

We got into my room, Warrick crashing into me the second I got the door closed. The breeze drifting in the room reminded me the balcony door was still open. I had to put an end to this sooner rather than later. The last thing I needed was for my friends to hear me being intimate. I pulled my head back doing my best to act out of breath from being caught up in the moment, "Go over to the bed."

"I like where this is going, love."

Warrick did as I told him to, sprawling on the bed, his motions loose and heavy clearly being influenced by what he drank earlier. "I'll be right back," I said winking as I made my way out of the room.

I rushed into my dad's office and started searching the drawers for the pair of handcuffs I knew had to be around. I had seen them a couple times before, once when I was sitting in here talking with my dad and another when Lou and I were looking for anything to help us. They probably wouldn't keep Warrick tied down for long, but I had to try something to keep anything from boiling over and this would at least continue to give Warrick the idea he was about to get laid.

By the time I walked through the doorway of my room, Warrick was fast asleep. A sigh of relief escaped my lips. Glancing down at the handcuffs in my hand, I debated if I would go through with trying to restrain him or not. The voice in my head convinced me to let him sleep, so I put the handcuffs back where I found them. I hopped in Warrick's car heading to the place he called home in this world.

Chapter 13

I shut the car off taking in the simple house in front of me. It was a tan color with white steps leading to the small porch topped with a white railing. I had no idea what I was doing, but I figured I would enjoy being here to have some well-deserved alone time. I carried myself up the stairs surprised to find the front door slightly open.

"Hello?" I asked poking my head in. "Anyone in here?"

I was shocked to see the place ransacked. Gone was the orderly appearance I've come to associate with Warrick. It was almost as if someone was looking for something they couldn't find. I stood there for a few more moments checking to see if I could hear any sounds to indicate if I wasn't alone.

"Come in, Val," a familiar, smooth voice called out.

I did as I was told, careful to avoid any of the broken glass scattered around the floor. Sarind stepped around the corner to meet me in the entry way. I continued scanning the room, "Did you – ?"

She let out a small laugh, "Did I do all this? No, but I'm afraid Marin did. I just came to assess the damage and make sure Warrick wasn't caught in the crosshairs."

I folded my arms across my stomach, almost as if there was a chill in the air despite it being a typical warm, humid tropical day. I brought my gaze back up to hers, "Marin did all this?"

"Unfortunately, she hasn't been handling this heartbreak too well. I'm happy this is all she did," Sarind said gesturing to the damage.

"What do you mean?"

Sarind took a seat on the only cleared off couch cushion motioning for me to sit in the chair sporting a giant gash. I did my best to get comfortable, and when I finally stilled, Sarind started talking, "You're aware there's magic here. Each one of us carries the ability to do something extraordinary with that magic. Part of the reason Warrick has asked me if my people would be willing to join the cause is that some of us have stronger abilities than others. For example, not only can I see the future and manipulate emotions, but I can also bring in storms. Marin has been fortunate enough to inherit some of my elemental abilities and can control lightning, amongst other things. She hasn't learned enough restraint yet, so when she does decide to pull on the electrical currents around her, the damage can be quite devastating."

I nodded my head now understanding her earlier comment about Marin making a mess of the place. Seeing my understanding, Sarind continued, "Needless to say, Warrick was smart to get out of here when he did. I don't need to know if he's staying with you or returned back to his home world," she said. "The less I know, the better for when I face Marin later today, but a word of advice?"

"Sure," I muttered.

She leaned forward holding my hands within hers, "You may want to head out of here sooner rather than later. That war isn't going to be waiting before it spreads, and from what I can tell, there's a lot more that still needs to be done."

I took in her words realizing this might be my one chance to get the information Warrick was holding close, "Do you know anything about the one behind the war?"

"That is not my information to tell. Warrick will tell you when the time is right, but in the meantime, I suggest you, Warrick, and Lou take the time to put aside your differences and start working together."

She stood up moving towards the front door. I followed behind her deciding not to ask any more questions since there was a good chance I wouldn't be getting any helpful answers anyways. When we were on the patio, she turned back to me, "It was good to see you, Val. I hope we can see each other again in the near future."

"It was good to see you, too, Sarind," I said in return. I started getting back into Warrick's car, taking one last look at the house and noticed Sarind was already gone. In that conversation, she confirmed one thing: it was time to go.

I pulled back up to my house with Lou waiting outside the front door. He looked exhausted and I could tell his patience had run out. *Great, Warrick must be up.* Lou lifted his head up when I cut the engine. He ran his hands through his hair before walking over to me. Avoiding eye contact, I started to move around him, "What's up, Lou?"

He grabbed my arm, stopping me, "Let's go for a walk."

"Didn't realize I did anything wrong," I joked, following him as we made our way down the beach.

"I can appreciate the joke, Val, but I'm not really in the mood," Lou started, dropping my arm. "Where did you go?"

I squinted my eyes as I looked over the ocean, "I just needed to get some air. He's a lot to handle when he's had that much to drink."

"So you decided to leave him to us," he said with no hints of a question.

"Did something happen, Lou?" I asked.

He let out a sigh, his cool grey eyes resting on me. I finally saw the beginnings of a black eye, "You tell me."

"Shit," I muttered dropping my gaze.

Lou lifted my chin so I was forced to look at him, "He woke up, still drunk despite his protests, and was hell bent on finding you. When you weren't there, well, he decided to take it out on us. I wasn't going to let anything happen, so I stepped in. I think it's time for us to go, so we can get some space between myself and Warrick."

"That isn't the first time I heard that today," I said removing my chin from his grasp. "We'll go."

"Thank you," he said turning back towards the house.

"On one condition, Lou," I said reaching for his arm. He turned back around to face me, "What's that?"

I dropped his arm, "I need you and Warrick to start putting aside your differences."

Lou let out a bark of laughter, "You say that like it's going to be easy."

"Oh, I know it won't be easy, but I've been thinking about this war. It's weighing on me, Lou, and I want it to be over. We're not going to get there if you and Warrick keep bickering. He's clearly trying to do anything to stop it."

"Can you trust him?" Lou asked, his tone serious.

I brought my eyes up to meet his and nodded, "I have to right now."

"Trust isn't something you can fake. You either trust him or you don't," Lou said, calling me out.

I sighed, "How often have you seen him drink like that?"

Lou's eyebrows knit together in confusion at my sudden change of topic, "Maybe once or twice before. What does that have to do with this?"

"He didn't start drinking until after he got done telling us about what he's doing and the war that's going on. Whoever 'the enemy' is has some sort of hold on him," I explained.

Lou nodded, "Maybe you have a point, but I'm not going back in there acting like everything's all sunshine and rainbows. It's going to take some time."

"I'm not expecting you to drop everything the minute you walk back in there. I know it's a slow process. I just appreciate you being willing to take baby steps," I said starting to head back toward the house. "We'll stick to the plan, but head back to your world tonight instead of tomorrow."

Lou was quiet for a few steps then asked, "Why didn't Warrick just leave on his own? He has his own device."

"I thought about that, too. I don't know why. Maybe he wanted some more time in this paradise," I said trying to keep the conversation light. I really had no idea why Warrick didn't just jump back to his world after he got Sarind's buy-in.

"Are you sure you can trust him?" Lou asked again.

"Lou, I don't know what's running through his mind or why he didn't leave right away. Maybe he really did want to spend some more time here listening to the ocean crash on the beach. Maybe he wanted to try to clear the air with me before having to go right back to work. It's something I can ask him about when we get back in the house," I finished.

"What are you going to ask me, love?" Warrick casually asked. Lou and I jumped not realizing we were already back at the house. I took in the sight of Warrick who looked better than when I left him, but not completely sober yet.

I debated how I wanted to respond, whether I cut to the chase or beat around the bush for a little bit. Lou tapped my arm interrupting my thoughts, "I'm going to head back inside."

Warrick shifted to let Lou walk past him, surprisingly not messing with Lou at all. When we were alone, Warrick looked at me again, "You were going to ask me something."

I let out a sigh finally deciding which tactic I wanted to use, "You have your own device, Warrick. Why didn't you just jump back to your world after the meeting with Sarind?"

The corners of his mouth slightly turned up, "Ah, I was wondering when you were going to ask me that. I guess I wasn't ready to go back quite yet. I wanted to talk to you some more, spend some time with you. I also wanted to see how things would go with Lou and the rest of your friends as a little bit of a test."

"And?" I asked starting to grow impatient.

"Don't worry, Val. Things went as I expected them to. Lou's not happy, your friends don't seem to trust me, and you're on the fence."

"I'm only on the fence because you're not telling me everything. You come in here, tell me we're fated, then continue to play your games. I need you to show me I can trust you," I started to reach for his arm and decided against it. He looked down at my hand then guided it down to his arm.

He stroked the back of my hand with his thumb, thinking about what he was going to say next, "I'm not telling you everything. Not yet, at least, but you will know when the time is right. I'm sorry for giving you reasons to not completely trust me, and I'm especially sorry for playing games, love. I have old habits I need to break and I'm not doing very well at making progress. To be honest, I stayed here a little longer because I wanted to spend that time with you. I know when we all get back to my world, I'm going to be diving right back into work and I didn't want to miss an opportunity to have some quality time with you."

"Why do you do that?" I cut him off. "Why do you go from asshole to someone who actually has feelings in seconds?"

Warrick sighed, "It's a defense mechanism. You're the first person in a very long time to get me to drop my walls."

I held his icy blue gaze as I asked, "Why are you so afraid to show others this side of you?"

He glanced away, "That's something I'm not ready to talk about quite yet."

I stood up straight pulling my hand away in the process, "Let me know when you are. By the way, we're leaving tonight."

I turned toward the door when Warrick gently grabbed my arm, "Val, you visited Sarind today, didn't you?"

"Yes," I answered, noting the change in topics. "She said the three of us need to start working together which means we have to move on from whatever feuds we have."

"Anything else?"

"Yeah," I looked at him as I removed my arm from his grasp. "She said you were lucky to not be in the house when Marin decided to pay you a visit. Your place got trashed, but it was still standing. You knew she would be showing up, didn't you?"

It was Warrick's turn to look away, "Yes."

"Is that the real reason you decided to hole up here?" I asked.

"It played into the decision, but like I said earlier, I wanted to spend some time with you."

I watched him a little longer to see if his body language would betray him. When nothing changed, I gave his arm a squeeze, "Thank you for being honest with me, Warrick."

I didn't hang around to see if he would say anything else. Once I was back inside, I headed to the island where Lou had gathered everyone. Jennie watched me through slightly narrowed eyes, Chris looking happy to be next to her. *They clearly made up.* Bev and Joe offered some of the snacks they set out with a glass of wine. Lou watched me carefully while leaning against the island. I acknowledged him first, "Did you tell them?"

He gave a quick shake of his head, "Nope, I was leaving that to you."

The front door opened and closed behind me indicating Warrick decided to join the party. Everyone tensed a little as he pulled up a seat next to where I was standing, still with enough distance from the others to not pose an immediate threat. I glanced around at everyone as I said, "We're leaving tonight."

Jennie was the first to say something, "Why'd you bump up the timeline?"

"I think it would be good for us to all have a little more space. Warrick and Lou would be able to go back to their apartments, and hopefully, that will allow us to hang out with a little less tension influencing our actions."

She only nodded in return. Joe clapped his hands together, "Well, I think it's a good idea. As nice as this place is, I'll be ready to go somewhere that's a little more normal."

Jennie let out a bark of laughter, "Normal? You think we'll be going somewhere normal? There are werewolves there, and even if we went back to *our* world, it's not like it would be normal either." Her eyes were wild. Everything she's seen and gone through up until this point was getting to her and I felt responsible. Maybe I shouldn't have suggested that friend's weekend in the first place. She must have realized her reaction was starting to cross a line because she quickly started back-pedaling, "Sorry, I shouldn't have reacted that way. It doesn't help that the last time we were there, we were trying to nurse Val back to health. I'm sure you want a change of scenery when you've been living on an island that forces you to be happy."

"It's okay, Jennie," Bev draped an arm around Jennie's shoulders to pull her into a side hug. "It's hard to define normal now that all of our lives have been shaken up. Maybe what Val was getting at was that we'll be able to do some more 'normal' activities, like eating out, going to clubs, and laughing around the dinner table again."

"Thank you, Bev," I jumped back into the conversation. "Look, Jennie. It'll be a lot different than what it was last time. I'm still standing, I'm not bleeding from anywhere, and I'd like to enjoy a little break form the chaos, too. We'll be able to explore a little more and hang out this time. Plus, I know a few good places for food."

"Please tell me the pizza place is one of them," Lou said.

"It could be," I joked.

"I guess that would be a nice change of pace," she dropped any signs of hostility. "Clearly, we could use the break."

"Alright, that settles it," I looked around at everyone one last time. "We're heading back."

Lou retrieved our device from its hiding place and stood outside to start the process of returning back to his home world, bumping up our timeline even more. Why hang around for a few hours when we're all ready to go? No one else moved from their place at the island. I knew from experience that it wouldn't take long for us to be whisked away.

I hadn't gotten the chance to experience the feeling of moving through the portal to a new world very often, but it always felt the same. All the air was taken from the room, the scene going from bright sunshine to pitch black in an instant only to be replaced with the familiar modern city stretching below the hill the house was sitting on. Lou was breathing a little harder from his sprint back into the house after he punched the code in our device, and Warrick took a casual sip of his water as I said to them, "Welcome home."

Warrick lifted his glass in acknowledgment while Lou pulled out his phone. Joe and Bev made their way to the windows overlooking the backyard to take in the new city before them while Jennie and Chris looked from their seats in the kitchen.

"Hey, Raf," Lou said. "We're back for a little bit and we'll be stopping by the pizza place in a few minutes. Meet us there?"

The conversation was kept short, and as Lou put his phone back in his pocket, he said, "Let's go."

"I'll go with Warrick," I said.

At the mention of his name, he lifted his head up, "I need to make a stop by the office first, love."

"That's fine. We're not all going to fit in Lou's car, so I figured I would go with you, if that's okay?"

"Sure," he said as he stood up. He wasn't in a very talkative mood and I was beginning to wonder if that was because of our conversation we had not too long ago. Warrick was avoiding eye contact with me, but still reached a hand out. I placed my hand in his as he led me out to his car.

The crisp chill air was polar opposite of the warmth we were just in. I rubbed my arms to generate some sort of heat while I settled into Warrick's car. He saw what I was doing and reached into his backseat, "Cold?"

"I don't know why, but I wasn't expecting it to be so cold here."

He placed a jacket on my lap, "Unlike where we were at, we have more defined seasons here. You're at the tail end of fall and the beginning of winter."

I thought about it for a moment. I knew my birthday was later in the year, but I also knew that meant Christmas was right around the corner. I'd have to set up the tree and decorations to try to add some extra joy in our downtime.

The car ride to the office was silent, giving me time to take in the vibrant golds, oranges, and reds of what leaves were still clinging to their branches. A light drizzle started to fall, coating the car in a thin layer of water. While I appreciated the tropics, there was something so comforting about this kind of weather. It was perfect for snuggling up under a blanket, a warm drink in hand while a fire crackled in the fireplace.

My daydream was interrupted when Warrick cut the engine, "Would you like to head up with me, love?"

"Sure," I said letting myself out of the car. "What do you need to do anyways?"

"I really wanted to let them get a head start. I also have a new assistant, so I wanted to check to see if she's doing alright before she heads out for the night."

"When did you get a new assistant?" I asked while following him into the elevator.

"After the vampire world. I had to come back here due to some drama with my old assistant which meant I would have to hire someone new," he said not sounding entirely happy with this topic. "I haven't had a lot of time to help her get up to speed, so I'm hoping this little break from world-hopping will do the trick."

"Makes sense," I nodded. The elevator dinged, welcoming us to the top floor. There weren't a lot of lights on making the space darker and more ominous given the sun had just set, but as we approached Warrick's office, I could hear the familiar sounds of someone typing away. We approached her desk, and I was able to take in his new assistant. She was young, probably early twenties, and breathtakingly beautiful with glowing skin, long eyelashes, high cheekbones, toned body, and long blonde hair currently half up and half down.

I shifted myself so I was hidden behind Warrick in time to see her whole face light up with a smile the minute she laid eyes on him. She stood up, holding out her hand for Warrick to shake, "It's good to see you again, Warrick. Anything I can get for you?"

"No, thank you, Holly," he answered with a warm grin that didn't quite reach his eyes. "Just stopping in to see how you're holding up. Sorry I haven't been here to help with the onboarding."

She giggled and waved him off, "Don't worry about it. You've been busy with your own work. Did you have good travels?"

"I did, but you'll unfortunately be stuck with me for a little while. I'm taking a break from traveling," he said with the same tone of voice that told me he was still grinning. "You can head out if you want. Looks like a storm is blowing in."

"I'll just wrap a few things up then head out," she said, not missing a beat. She sat back down in her chair turning her focus back to whatever she was working on before we got up here and I silently followed Warrick into his office.

He shut the door behind me and I waited for the both of us to get settled before saying anything. I pretended to examine things on his desk, but Warrick picked up on my thoughts before I could vocalize them, "Yes, I know she's flirting with me. No, I'm not interested. Yes, I think she may try to give you some problems when she realizes who you are. No, she doesn't pose any sort of threat. She's fresh out of college and one of those people who have had everything given to her in life, but despite that, she's a hell of a worker who follows instructions well. Did I miss anything?"

He didn't look up from his computer as he said all that, sounding mildly annoyed. I scoffed as I pushed myself away from the desk to look out the windows as he often did in the early days of me being here. The lights on the pizza place filtered out on the street, but Warrick wasn't wrong about a storm making its way into the city. Clouds were starting to obscure my view reminding me how high this building is. My stomach growled at the thought of food and I turned to face Warrick again, "No, you didn't, but thank you for filling me in. How long do you plan on spending here?"

With his attention still on his screen, Warrick said, "Not too much longer. I'm just checking to see if there's anything urgent that can't wait until tomorrow."

His tone was cold again. I turned to look back out the window, "Your walls are back up."

Warrick slapped his desk catching me off-guard. I let out a small yelp as he started to raise his voice, "Dammit, Val! What do you want from me?"

Holly, his assistant chose this moment to poke her head in his office, "Sorry! I didn't realize you had someone else with you." She turned her attention to me, "Is there anything I can get you?"

"No, thank you," I answered in a quiet voice.

"Alrighty, I'm headed out, then. See you tomorrow," she said cheerfully. I couldn't help but wonder if she heard the commotion since her timing was a little too coincidental. I shook my head to clear the thoughts happy that the chances of someone lurking outside his office door was little to none now.

As soon as the door was closed and the sound of her heals faded, Warrick started talking again, this time at a normal volume, "I shouldn't have raised my voice. You're not doing anything wrong."

"I'll just head across the street," I muttered as I made my way to the door. I gripped the handle and turned around to face him, "It seems like you need to be alone. I'll just tell the others you got caught up with work."

"Val, wait," Warrick said as he started moving towards me.

I took his jacket off, immediately missing the warmth it provided, before making my way out of his office space, "Goodnight, Warrick."

I closed the door behind me hastily heading towards the elevator. I was halfway down the hall when I heard the door open and Warrick call out, "Val!"

Ignoring him, I repeatedly pressed the elevator button even though it never makes it arrive any faster. I cursed under my breath when it still hadn't arrived and Warrick was now right behind me, "Love, please. I shouldn't be taking any of this out on you."

"I just don't understand what's making you act this way," I said with my back still to him. Out of the corner of my eyes, I saw him place both of his hands on either side of the elevator as he sighed, "There's no reason. I'm letting small things get to me."

"Like what?" I asked squirming as his body heat settled around me.

"Like the fact that I'm having to open up in a way I've never done before. It's not the most comfortable or easy thing to do. The fact that you and Lou looked really close while you were strolling along the beach. The fact that I can tell you feel insecure around my new assistant even though there's no reason to be. The fact that I acted like an idiot after drinking and that seemed to push you away, rightfully so. Need I go on, love?"

I shook my head. "No," I whispered.

"Please look at me," he pleaded.

I turned to face him, "I still stand by what I said earlier. It sounds like you could use some time alone to sort through what you just said and to sober up."

The elevator finally opened behind me. I glanced back at it before giving Warrick a light kiss on his cheek, "Goodnight."

He didn't plead with me this time. Instead, Warrick stood there watching until the elevator doors closed. When I was finally alone, I let out a sigh pinching the bridge of my nose. *Why did I think going with him would be a good idea?*

Chapter 14

C heers erupted when I walked through the doors of the pizza place. Everyone looked happy, pizza in one hand and a beer in the other. I let a smile spread, unable to fight the happiness oozing from everyone in the space.

I did my best to wipe off the excess water from the rain now pouring outside. Lou greeted me with a towel and a steaming mug, "Forgot to tell you to grab a jacket on your way out. Dry yourself off before you bring all that water in here and enjoy some hot chocolate. Where's Warrick?"

I shrugged my shoulders, "He got caught up with things in the office. Thank you for this." I lifted up the mug he handed me before taking a sip, appreciative of the warmth pooling in my body. I settled in the only open seat between Raf and Lou grabbing a slice and watching the quiet world outside. I started to wonder if Warrick would ever make his way over here despite me telling him not to, but after an hour, I watched his car drive off in the direction of his apartment. I didn't realize it, but I let out a breath of relief getting Raf's attention, "Everything alright, Val?"

"Oh yeah. It just feels good to be here not on the verge of death or running from it," I answered with a smile I hoped was convincing enough. Thankfully, it was because we were back to joking around and laughing in no time. I hadn't realized how fast the time had passed until I got up to help Lou clean and could finally see a clock.

"It's late," I observed.

Lou looked over his shoulder from the dishwashing area, "Yeah, but I wasn't going to be throwing you all out when we were finally enjoying ourselves."

Raf came in carrying the rest of the beer glasses, "It's good to see you standing on two feet, Val. Everything getting back to normal?"

"For the most part," I smiled at him. "I still have the occasional nightmare, but I'm finally not scared of my own shadow and the pain is gone."

"I'm calling that a win," he turned to head back out to the dining area. "Need a ride? Lou's car is full and I don't think you're going to be walking tonight."

"Yeah, that would be great, thanks," I answered sensing he wanted to talk about topics that would be better discussed without Lou's presence.

Raf tapped the doorframe and went back out to the rest of the group. I made my way over to Lou leaning against the countertop next to him, "So, still need someone to help out around here or does your pack have that covered?"

Lou did his best to hide his grin from me, but I still caught a glimpse of it, "Be here to help me open up."

"You got it, boss," I said then headed back out to join the rest of the group.

My friends were laughing at the story Raf was in the middle of telling. As I settled into my seat, Raf continued, "Lou had just taken ownership of this place after being freed from Warrick's pack. He took one step out of the kitchen, arms loaded up with several pizzas and slipped. Pizzas went flying straight up in the air, Lou's feet not far behind them. As soon as he thudded against the ground, the pizzas landed on him one at a time. The icing on the cake was that he sat up when the last one landed right on his head, sauce and cheese dripping off him. Hell of a way to meet his new pack."

In between giggles, Jennie asked, "Wait, that's how you guys met your new alpha?"

Raf nodded his head, smile taking over his face, "Oh yeah. We had no idea how this clown was going to be our alpha. Kind of hard to let someone give orders when he's coated in pizza."

"Raf, stop embarrassing me," Lou said wiping his hands as he leaned against the entryway into the kitchen. Despite his tone, he was sporting a smile, too.

"Oh, you know you thought it was funny," Raf waived him off. "It was a nice icebreaker, that's for sure."

"Everyone ready to head back home?" Lou asked changing the topic.

We all nodded our heads and made our way out to the cars. The rain was starting to turn into snow and I made a mental note to take some time tonight to move my car so I could get out. There's no way I'm riding my bike in this kind of weather.

Raf guided me to his car, opening the passenger door for me before he headed to the driver's side. Out of habit, I looked towards Warrick's office building focusing on the garage instead of his office window since the clouds were blocking my view. There were no signs of life so I slid into Raf's car.

"So," Raf started when the doors were closed and we were on our way. "Did you and Warrick have a chance to talk?"

I twisted my hands together watching the snow pelt the windshield, "Yeah, and you were on to something. He admitted to us being fated."

"How are you feeling about that?"

"Honestly? I don't know how to feel. A part of me wants to dive right into a romantic relationship with him where another part of me can't believe it and wonders what sort of cruel game the universe is playing."

"I can see that, especially with him," Raf said. "I know you're already aware of this, so feel free to tune me out. No matter how much you ignore him, you two will always be drawn to one another. You could very well move across the country or go back to your world and Warrick would pop up not too long after that."

"I know," I sighed looking down into my hands. "I'm just tired of the back-and-forth with him, Raf. It's exhausting. Factor in my friends' dislike for him and the tension with Lou, and there are days where I don't want to deal with it. I mean right before I came in to eat, he freaked out on me for a second and I told him to stay there. I didn't want to be the reason everyone stopped having a good time."

He pulled the car to a stop in front of the house and put it in park. Raf turned to look at me, "It's going to be hard. Very hard. Trust me, though, when I say it'll get a lot easier. You'll need to be patient."

I nodded taking in what he said, "Thank you for the ride, Raf. Oh, I do have one more question for you?"

"What's on your mind?" he smiled back.

I sat there thinking back to what Warrick said about me and Lou the first night he was in the house trying to figure out how I was going to ask Raf. I brought my eyes to meet his, the smile slowly fading from his face. I took a deep breath, "Could it be possible to be fated to more than one wolf?"

"Why do you ask?"

"Warrick claimed Lou's fated to me," I blurted.

"Ah," Raf chuckled. "Well, rest easy in knowing he's not. Lou's just formed a connection with you and doesn't want to see anything happen."

"How can you be so sure?"

"What Lou has described to me is nowhere near being fated. He's only described feelings, and ones of infatuation at the most. Lou doesn't like losing to Warrick, so the thought of you throwing everything you guys had out the window and going to his biggest rival drives him mad. It's hard to explain, but you have to trust me on this one, Lou's not fated to you."

I felt like I could breathe a little easier with Raf confirming my suspicions. I nodded my head and gave him a grin, "Thanks again, Raf."

"Anytime," he smiled at me.

I made my way back into the house, the rest of my friends not too far behind me. We settled on the couch for a few minutes, Jennie turning to me, "You're right, Val. I think this time around we're going to enjoy this world even more. It helps that Joe and Bev are here, too."

I grinned at her, "Good! They'll be able to keep you company when I'm working."

"Working? What do you do here?" Joe asked.

"I help Lou out in the restaurant. Nothing too glamorous, but it fills the time."

"I wouldn't have pegged you for a waitress, but I'm glad you're keeping yourself busy," he nodded.

I shifted in my seat, "I was thinking we could start putting up Christmas decorations."

Jennie's eyes got wide, "Is it really almost that time of year?"

"Yeah," I laughed. "I had the same thought when we got here and the storm came in."

"Do we need to do anything with the pool?" Joe asked.

I jumped up and ran over to the backdoor, "Shit! We need to winterize it."

"We won't be able to take care of that tonight, but we'll get it taken care of for you tomorrow," Joe said.

I turned back towards them, "I can't let you guys do that."

"Why not?" Chris asked. "You'll be working and we'll be sitting around here. We can at least take care of the pool before we go off exploring."

The rest of them nodded in agreement. I settled back into my chair feeling appreciative for the people in my life, "Well, thank you. After that, though, you guys better relax and start to have some fun."

"Yes, boss," Bev joked. Everyone laughed at that before we all broke out into yawns. I stretched my arms out, "Time to turn in for the night. See you all tomorrow."

"Goodnight, Val!" they called out in unison.

I got ready for bed happy when I could cuddle under my blankets. I turned on my side to watch the snow fall feeling as if I were living in a snow globe as the large, fluffy flakes made their slow descent to the ground. My eyes eventually closed and I drifted off into a peaceful sleep.

The next morning, I woke up disappointed the snow hadn't really accumulated which means it must've been the first snow of the season. *It should make taking care of the pool easier.* I stared out my balcony window a little longer taking in the low fog snaking around the hills with the clouds keeping up their moody disposition contrasting the bright and colorful leaves still trying to give something enjoyable to look at.

I checked the time noting I still had a few hours before my shift got started, so I made my way downstairs noting everyone else was still asleep. I had the quiet house to myself and I was going to enjoy every minute of it. I moved outside after I wrapped breakfast up so I could get a head start on taking care of the pool. I appreciated everyone else offering to do it, but I didn't want to add one more thing they have to do for me. They've already gone above and beyond, and I couldn't ask for anything more.

I grabbed the cleaning equipment to start the deep clean of the process, thankful I had grabbed my coat and gloves. I knew this would be the longest part, but it gave me some time to figure out what I wanted to accomplish while we were back here. I knew I needed check for any updates on my dad. Not knowing if there were new developments was killing me. I also needed to talk to Warrick about what was going on last night and how we're going to approach this whole fated thing. Raf was right, we'd only continue to be drawn together and that's going to make any opportunities I get to date other people more of a challenge than what I want to deal with. I knew with Lou things would start going back to normal with time, so I guess I can cross that one off my list. I did need to talk to him about working with Warrick, though. *Everything has to go back to him, doesn't it?*

I shook my head to clear any lingering thoughts as I took the last pass of cleaning the pool when a voice called out making me jump, "Val, I thought we were going to take care of that for you?"

My hand on my chest, I turned to face Chris and Joe, "You guys almost gave me a heart attack!"

"Sorry," Joe shrugged with a grin. "Although, it's kind of fun to sneak up on you."

"Yeah, sure, fun," I rolled my eyes. "I figured I'd get a head start on this since I had some time before work."

"What can we do to help?" Chris asked.

I headed towards the shed, "Let me grab a few things."

I came back out to meet the two guys handing them water test strips and the various chemicals while walking them through the remaining steps. I finished cleaning the last few sections and took a moment to check the time. I was now down to about half an hour before I needed to be at the restaurant. I checked in with Joe and Chris one more time before heading back inside to finish grabbing what I needed for the day.

Armed with a mug of tea to help keep me warm, I settled into my car taking a few steadying deep breaths. This routine felt more comforting to me than even before I came to this world the first time. I laughed a little at that realization then got my car in motion. It took me no time to get to Lou's, so I was at least ten minutes early. *Boss man will be happy about that.*

I let myself in calling out to Lou as I set my coat and tea on the bar, "Hey!"

Lou poked his head out of the kitchen, "You're early."

"Figured it wouldn't hurt. Where do you need me?" I asked taking a quick scan of the place. The chairs were already down, silverware rolled, tables set, and the smell of pizza wafting out from the kitchen.

"Can you get the beer glasses ready then meet me in here?"

"You got it."

I wasted no time with getting the glasses readied behind the bar then slowly made my way into the kitchen. Lou was cranking out more pizzas than I thought was necessary, "Why all this food?"

"Something you'll learn about this place – when the weather starts turning, people want their comfort food and that's the business I've worked so hard to make myself the best in, so orders are going to be increasing. Plus, the order history while we were away painted a good picture that we're going to need more pizza ready to go," he explained without slowing his pace.

I started slicing the pizzas that were ready to go, throwing what was done under the heat lamps noting opening time was right around the corner, "It's no news to me that people gravitate towards pizza when the weather starts getting worse. People don't like to cook all the time and their time is taken up by other things during this season. Speaking of, if there's a lull today, can I take a little break to take care of some errands?"

Lou cast a glance over his shoulder, "Do those errands involve Warrick?"

I pretended to look at my nails, "Believe it or not, they don't. I want to get some gifts for everyone."

Lou wrapped up his prep work, turning to face me while drying his hands. He was back in his signature flannel, hair messier than usual. I noticed he was sporting dark circles under his eyes indicating he hadn't slept very well last night. Lou furrowed his eyebrows, "Gifts? For what?"

"Christmas," I answered.

"What's Christmas?" he asked.

I cocked my head, "You don't celebrate that here?"

"No, we mostly celebrate the solstices with the winter one coming up soon. We mostly just spend time with family cooking and playing games keeping it low-key. The only solstice we really go all out for is summer because of Warrick's ball. What do you do for Christmas?"

I leaned against the wall, "It's a pretty big holiday back home. We go all out with decorations, putting up a tree and covering it in lights and ornaments. The house gets covered with lights on the outside. Garland and tinsel go up. We hang stockings over the fireplace to be filled with gifts. There's a lot of significance that goes into it, but I don't have time to get into all of that. Essentially, we hang out with friends and family like what you do for the winter solstice, but there's also gift exchanges. I figured since my friends are away from their families, I could still give them a decent Christmas, so I want to get them gifts."

"Sounds like a lot of work for one day," Lou observed.

"It is, but Lou, it is so worth it. It's my favorite holiday and just putting up the lights and the tree makes me so happy. All the decorations bring joy and warmth during a season that's so cold and dark," I said relishing in the fuzzy feeling I get when Christmas rolls around.

Lou opened his mouth to say something, but the door opened ending the conversation. We headed out to the dining area to see a large group of workers from across the street hoping to get some lunch. We fell back into the easy rhythm we got so used to before we jumped from here: I grabbed their orders while Lou took care of their drinks and making sure we had enough food prepped. More people filtered in throughout the lunch hour, but I noticed one person still hadn't made his way over. Disappointment was starting to settle when the door opened and Warrick waltzed in with his assistant in tow.

As soon as he crossed the threshold, he locked eyes with me, the corners of his mouth subtly turning up almost as if he was saving that just for me. He pointed his assistant in the direction of a table to sit at still not taking those icy blue eyes off of me.

Lou started heading over to him clearly letting tension creep into his shoulders. I put a hand on his shoulder, "I'll take care of this one."

I checked a couple of my tables before finally approaching Warrick, "How does it feel to be back home?"

He leaned against the bar resting on his elbow, "Good. I've missed the routine."

"You've missed pizza every day and the constant bickering with Lou?" I asked.

He let out a small laugh, "Believe me when I say I'm as surprised as you, but I have."

I cocked my head in the direction of his assistant, "How is she doing?"

"She's picking up on things, but there's a lot she still needs to learn. Figured I would take this lunch hour to go over some more things with her while I have a break in the day."

"Well, I know what you probably want for lunch. What'll she be having?" I asked cutting to the chase. I didn't want to take up any more of his time if he was needing to take care of training.

"Just give us a large pepperoni pizza and a couple of waters."

"Got it," I said. I started to open my mouth to ask another question, but decided against it.

Warrick picked up on my hesitation. Reaching out to gently touch my arm, he asked, "Something else you wanted to talk about, love?"

I glanced around catching a glimpse of Lou out of the corner of my eye intently watching us. Just seeing that took me back to the early days of being here when we were trying to get information out of the man before me. It's crazy to think about everything that has changed since then. I turned my attention back to Warrick, "Everything okay after last night?"

Warrick's eyebrows started to come together before relaxing again, "Yeah, everything's good. There was a lot running through my mind and I appreciated the alone time."

I offered a kind smile in return, "Good. Let me get your food going so I don't keep taking time away from your working session."

He gave my arm a squeeze before making his way over to the table. I headed into the kitchen to see if there was a pepperoni pizza ready to go. Lou intercepted me, "Who's he with?"

"That's his new assistant. Apparently, he's doing some training with her right now," I said brushing past him.

"She's pretty," Lou observed.

I bristled at his comment, catching myself by surprise since there wasn't anything like that between us anymore. Maybe it was more the fact that Lou commented on her looks when she's sitting across from Warrick. I armed myself with a full pizza, a couple of glasses and a pitcher of water. Before I could stop myself, I glanced at Lou, "If you think she's so pretty, then you should be the one waiting on their table."

He held his hands up in defense, "Didn't realize that was a sensitive topic."

I was out the door before I could say anything in response. Taking a deep breath to clear out the emotions Lou stirred up in me, I set the pizza down and filled their glasses, "Anything else I can get for you two?"

They shook their head signaling the time for my exit and I went to check on the rest of my tables again. I got to my last one, the one with a bunch of guys from Warrick's office, and was picking up the cash they paid with when one of the guys decided to be bold and grab my ass. I instinctively grabbed his arm, "I don't think so, pal."

He gave me a toothy smile, "Just had to show my appreciation."

I dropped his hand curling my lip in disgust, "You can do so by giving a bigger tip."

"I'll show you a bigger tip," he said starting to move closer to me. I didn't have a chance to say anything in return because Lou was now in between us grabbing the guy by his shirt, "It's time to go. Next time I see you in here harassing my waitress will be the last time you breathe."

The guy let out a laugh, "At least the last thing I see will be something enjoyable."

Lou wasted no time picking this man up and throwing him out of the restaurant. The rest of his friends kept their eyes down while they hurried outside and didn't look back as they made their way back across the street. Everyone was silent at this point, Warrick watching us very carefully. I could feel the tears threatening to spill, so I headed back into the kitchen doing my best to hold my head up high. Lou was right behind me not giving me the chance to wipe away my emotions, "You okay?"

"Just caught me off-guard, that's all. Bold move considering Warrick wasn't too far away," I said trying to keep it light.

"Asshole didn't do anything to come to your defense," Lou grumbled.

I put a hand on Lou's arm, "It's fine, Lou. I just need a breather before I go back out there."

"Got it," he said leaving the kitchen to give me space.

My breath came out shakily, my hands following suit. I let a few tears fall when there was a quick knock on the doorway, "Are you okay, love?"

"Yeah, I'm fine. You should get back to your training," I said not turning around to face Warrick.

I felt his hands rest on my shoulders, his voice dropping to a low volume, "Are you sure?"

I only nodded as I reached up to wipe away the tears. He started to rub my shoulders in a soothing motion, "Don't think he'll go unpunished. I didn't step up because this is Lou's domain and I'm trying to be respectful of that. Please don't think it was because I don't care."

I finally turned to face him, "Thank you for clearing that up."

His thumb chased another tear away then he pulled me tight into his chest, "We need to figure out what's going on between us, but now's not that time. Stop by my office in a couple of days and we can talk a little more. Does that work for you?"

"Sure," I said thankful he was taking the initiative to dive into what's next for us.

Warrick placed a gentle kiss on the top of my head then made his exit. I took one more steadying breath then headed back out there.

Lou was behind the bar refilling some drinks and gestured toward another table filled with new customers. Thankfully, they were people I knew and loved. Jennie was throwing her head back in laughter at some joke Chris said while Joe and Bev chuckled. I walked up to their table, "I hope you're not laughing at my expense. Do I have toilet paper on my shoe or something?"

Jennie laughed harder while Bev shook her head and filled me in on the joke. I needed a good laugh after what just happened, and when we finally composed ourselves, I grabbed their order getting back to work. It was well past the normal lunch hour and only two tables were occupied: the one with my friends and the one with Warrick and his assistant. I went back in the kitchen to find Lou prepping more orders for this evening. He gave me a quick glance, "Go take care of your errands. I think I can handle this crew."

"Thanks," I said wasting no time to with getting out of there before he changed his mind. I gave everyone a little wave then snuck out, driving in the direction of some stores I was hoping would have something for everyone. Lou let me know to be back within an hour since delivery orders were already pouring in and he needed help in the kitchen, so the clock was ticking.

This had to have been the quickest shopping trip I've ever done, especially when it came to finding gifts for others, but I did it. I was heading back to the pizza place feeling accomplished knowing I got everyone a good gift and the tree wouldn't be empty, but that feeling quickly evaporated the minute I walked through the door to pure chaos.

"What took you so long to get back?" Lou asked me as he rushed by, arms loaded with food.

I grabbed a water pitcher to start refilling glasses following his path, "I was only gone for an hour."

"Didn't think to check your phone?"

"No, I left it in the car. This is a little early for a dinner rush," I observed trying to change the topic from him scolding me.

"I don't know what's going on, but I'm not going to say no to business."

We eventually got everything caught back up, but the number of customers didn't decrease until about an hour before closing. Lou was wiping the sweat from his brow, leaning against the bar as I was starting to work on cleaning things up, "Sorry about earlier. I had to keep my head down to get through everything and I probably didn't come off the best."

I waved him off, "Don't worry about it. Just took me back to the first day I met you, that's all."

Lou chuckled leaning closer to me, "You could say we've both changed a lot since then. Speaking of change, the Val I knew wouldn't have let that ass-grabbing incident get to her. You doing okay today?"

"Yeah, it just happened to pile on to other things running through my mind, that's all," I said avoiding eye contact. To be honest, I didn't like being taken advantage of when I was already in such a vulnerable state with my insecurities clouding my judgment. I don't know why, but I can't quite trust Warrick's new assistant. It felt like she knew exactly who I was and was going to do her best to make my love-life hell when there are already so many question marks.

"What's going through your mind?" Lou asked pulling up a chair after cleaning a few tables. The restaurant was empty at this point, leaving the two of us alone to apparently have a deep conversation.

"That's a loaded question," I nervously laughed. "Um, well, I think the biggest thing is what the hell am I going to do about being fated to Warrick? I tried to get some sort of advice out of Raf, but he was more happy about the fact that Warrick and I had a conversation than what I should do next."

"What do you want to do next?"

"I don't know if I should try to be in a relationship or not. I struggle with being able to trust someone like that, Lou. On the other hand, there's a part of me that feels warm, and ironically, safe around him," I let out a sigh. "Add a hot, new, young assistant to that and I'm an insecure mess."

"I don't know why you feel insecure," Lou mumbled.

That got some laughter out of me, "It's different when you're in my shoes. So, when that guy grabbed my ass and Warrick didn't do anything, I had a million things run through my mind. Even though he came back to check on me, it didn't do anything to cut down those negative thoughts."

"Can I offer my opinion without you ripping my head off?" Lou asked, tapping the table. "He could be going through a lot, too. I'm sure this whole fating thing is weighing heavily on him. Add to that the fact he's feeling like he not only has to shoulder this world from a war, but others? That's a lot for anyone to do. Don't forget he runs a wildly successful company and that success is dependent on him actively working. I'm sure he's having to dig out of a pile of issues, questions, wins, you name it."

"You know?" I started to narrow my eyes. "I don't like you being on Warrick's side. It makes me feel like there's something really wrong with this place."

Lou chuckled, "It feels good to joke with you again, Val."

He moved to lock the front door and draw the blinds signaling he was officially closed and I had survived my first shift back.

Chapter 15

After a refreshing conversation with Lou, I carried myself out to my car, taking a moment to catch my breath since the busy day was finally catching up to me. I opened my car door, looking up towards Warrick's office building more out of habit than curiosity. There was his shadow standing guard over the street below, a sight all too familiar to me when I was trying to convince him I wanted to explore a relationship.

In the short time I stood there staring up at him, another shadow creeped over to meet Warrick where he was standing. Judging by the shape of this other shadow, his new assistant was bringing him something. There wasn't anything necessarily romantic in her gestures, but she was standing a little too close to him for my liking. *Why am I getting jealous?*

I shook my head ducking into my car and driving back to my house ready to tuck myself in the sanctuary of my room. The more distance I put between myself and the city, the better I felt. Plus, I had Christmas presents tucked away in my trunk and I couldn't wait to share those with everyone. I'm bound and determined to make sure this is a damn good holiday despite everything that's happened.

As soon as I walked through the garage door into the house, my breath was taken away. Lights illuminated the house with their soft glow. The tree was set up in its usual home in the corner of the living room decked out in lights and ornaments. Garland was wrapped around the banisters and stockings were hung. My friends had found all of my parents' decorations and not only got them out, but made the place look like something out of a magazine.

"Surprise!" Jennie yelled out.

I don't know if it was the exhaustion or the emotions running through me from the day, but my hand inched towards my mouth while tears prickled my eyes, "You guys really didn't have to do this. A winterized pool would've been amazing and all I could've asked for."

"With your jumpstart on the pool, it took us no time at all. Jennie was the one who realized how close to Christmas we are and mentioned we should decorate. It wasn't hard for all of us to get onboard with that decision considering everything that's been going on," Chris shrugged.

I held out my arms signaling them to come in for a hug, "Thank you. You guys have no idea what this means to me after the long day I had."

They all crushed me in a loving hug where we swayed with one another, laughing. When we finally let go, everyone's laughs turning into yawns. We migrated to our respective rooms settling in for the night. Walking through the door into my room, my face once again sported a smile at the sight of a smaller Christmas tree fully decorated sitting by the balcony door. *Jennie remembered.*

Morning came and I had to appreciate another dreamless night. I rolled over in bed flipping through the notifications on my phone not surprised when there wasn't anything noteworthy. I laid there for a little bit longer checking for any other signs of life throughout the house. The only noises I heard were the sighs of the house settling as it adjusted to yet another new world. Knowing no one was awake, I snuck out of bed this time for something more positive than trying to avoid a barrage of questions. Acquiring my friends' gifts from my car, I ran back up to my room tucking them away in my closet for another time when I could hunt down wrapping paper.

I settled back into my bed reveling in the warmth of my blanket and turned on a movie to fill some time since I wasn't quite ready to start my day. A quiet knock at my balcony door almost sent me to the floor.

"You almost killed me, you know," I hissed. "What the hell are you doing here anyways?"

A cocky smile crept along Warrick's face, "Good morning to you, too, love. Can I come in? I brought breakfast."

I moved to let him in mostly because I wasn't dressed appropriately for the cool air rushing in, "Sure. I'm surprised you're not at the office already. Don't you have a lot you're trying to catch up on?"

"Perks of being the CEO," he said brushing past me, shedding his coat and shoes while he settled on the end of my bed. "I can start my day from home when I can't sleep anymore. It's nice when I don't have to field hundreds of questions all day. It works wonders for my productivity."

"Does that mean training is going well?" I asked doing my best to keep the snark from creeping into my tone. His assistant hadn't been doing anything to motivate me to like her and I'm sure Warrick was well aware of that.

"She's been a test of patience, that's for sure," he said handing me a bagel sandwich. He unwrapped his own and dug right into it. When he realized I still hadn't moved, Warrick patted the bed next to him, frowning when he realized I wasn't making my way over to him.

"Why are you really here, Warrick?" I asked keeping my tone as neutral as possible. I didn't cross my arms or give off any other signs of being defensive which was a lot harder to do than I thought it would be.

He dropped those blue eyes, sighing, "I felt bad for not doing anything more after yesterday especially since it impacted you so much. Then I saw you last night and couldn't imagine what was running through your head when you saw Holly well after working hours in my office."

All hopes of keeping the defensive posture at bay were dashed. My arms crossed and the tone changed, "So, you decided it would be a good idea to show up here unannounced to remind me of things that sting knowing I'm going to be hung up on that stuff. Do you know how much I'm struggling with this idea of us being fated? Do you know how much it drives me crazy that I get jealous when I don't even know what's going on between us?"

Warrick was standing up now debating about crossing over to me as he answered, "You know you're not the only one who is having to come to terms with being fated. I know that sounds like something an asshole would say, but I guess the better thing to say is I'm struggling with the idea, too. This is not easy to be sorting through when I'm coming back to way too many fires at work and this war putting even more pressure on us. I know those are not excuses, love, and I'm really trying to keep things separate. It's hard."

I softened a little opening the door for him to stand in front of me now. I really looked at him now that he was close and he clearly hadn't been sleeping well. My crossed arms dropped, meeting Warrick's hands, our fingers intertwining, "I'm sorry, Warrick. I feel like I'm being selfish by not thinking about what you're going through."

"Stop, love," he said giving my hands a soft squeeze. "You're allowed to process your feelings and emotions, too. We're both having to work through something that's pretty heavy while also balancing a lot of stress. We could both do better. Now, please eat."

He turned to sit back on the bed where his bagel sandwich was abandoned. I watched as he took another bite then patted the bed next to him. I slowly moved over to sit next to him while starting to eat the sandwich he brought me. I had to admit, it was pretty good. Nodding, I said, "Thank you for bringing me breakfast. I wasn't quite ready to get up, but I was getting hungry."

"I wasn't coming over empty-handed. What's with the tree and the lights on the outside of the house?"

I had to think a moment since he changed the topic so fast. I glanced over to the tree, smiling, "I can't believe they got the lights put up on the outside of the house, too."

"Is there some sort of significance?" Warrick asked snapping me back to the present conversation.

"Yeah," I said meeting his eyes. "It's something we do called Christmas."

"Ah," Warrick nodded. "I need to brush up on the holidays in your world, but from what I remember, Christmas is a pretty big one and I believe it's your favorite."

My bagel stopped halfway to my mouth. I slowly turned to face him again, "H-how do you know that?"

"Look, love. I'm doing something new where I try to be more honest with you. You know I did a lot of research when it came to you, and one of those things was learning about your likes and dislikes."

"Well," I was making sure to choose my words carefully. "Thank you for being honest. And yes, Christmas is my favorite. One of the reasons it's my favorite is because of the decorations and the warm, fuzzy feeling I get when looking at the soft glow of the lights, the ornaments that carry a lot of family memories. It still bugs me that you know a lot about me already and I don't know hardly anything about you."

He didn't flinch at that. Instead, he moved closer to me so we were barely touching, "What do you want to know?"

I was caught off-guard by how willing he is to jump right into sharing about himself. This isn't the Warrick who likes to play games and dodge any of the personal questions. This isn't the Warrick I know.

I tore off a little bit of my bagel and chewed it slowly while I figured out what I wanted to ask him. There were so many things from his family to his childhood, his dating history (even if I know a little bit about that one), where he grew up, school, the list goes on. I finally looked at him, "Tell me about your parents."

If I wasn't so close, I would've missed the flash of pain across his face. He took a deep breath and closed his eyes, "That's a tough one, love."

"I didn't mean to open old wounds. You don't have – "

Warrick patted my thigh, cutting me off, "It's okay. I have to work to build up trust and part of that is being honest with you, right?"

I only nodded my head not wanting to do anything to deter him from opening up to me. He didn't meet my gaze, but started saying, "My parents were everything I could've asked for. They were kind and understanding. They had my back and would do just about anything for me. They made sure my childhood was filled with so many good memories from the trips we went on to just staying in the house and building castles while watching movies. My mom was the best baker I knew. Anytime I came home from school or a friend's house, the place would be filled with the warm smell of some sweet treat baking in the oven. She'd pop her head around the corner beaming as she welcomed me back in. She would want to hear about every part of my day and would listen to the smallest of things. She always knew what advice to give, too. Then, there was my dad. He always helped me with my homework. He'd help me practice for whatever activity I was doing at the moment, whether that was a sport or something at school. His jokes were top-notch. He never let anything sit too long when it came to house projects.

"And the love those two shared was on another level. Their eyes lit up whenever the other walked in the room. They were always helping each other and making sure to talk through everything so nothing was left on the table. I don't think I ever heard them fight. They were amazing enough to show me what true love looks like," Warrick trailed off.

I placed a hand on his knee, "Were they wolves, too? Do you think they were fated?"

He shook his head, "They weren't wolves, but the way they loved each other, you would've thought they were fated. It was like they were inseparable."

"Do you mind if I ask what happened?" I asked cautiously knowing this was an already difficult subject, but I couldn't help myself since he was talking about them in the past tense.

"They were murdered," he choked out, squeezing his eyes shut. "Right in front of me when I was twelve."

Warrick didn't say anything else and I didn't dare press him to. My heart lurched at the thought of seeing my parents' lives taken while I was in the same room, especially if they were the same picturesque couple Warrick described his as. What got me even more was the fact that he was alone at such a young age. No wonder he had to be cutthroat. He had to make sure he survived and I'm sure he did that by whatever means necessary.

I set my bagel down so I could wrap my arms around him. As I turned, a single tear fell. He tried to turn his face away, but I guided his head to my shoulder. He stayed there for a few moments while steadying his breathing before pulling away and watching me. The only part of him showing any traces of sadness were his eyes. I cradled his cheek, "Thank you for sharing with me."

"Of course, love. Now, no more questions today. You came out swinging, not that you would have known what happened, and I need a moment to recover."

His phone rang out in the room making us both jump. Warrick brought it up to his ear, standing up so he could pace as the person on the other end talked his ear off. When he hung up, he came back over to me pressing a kiss on my forehead, "I have to run, but promise me you'll stop by today?"

"Sure," I said going back to eating my breakfast.

He grinned at me as he moved toward the balcony to make his exit, "I'll text you when to come by if you can manage to sneak away."

I nodded, "See you later, Warrick."

He was gone. I stared out the door marveling at how quickly and quietly he can climb up and down my balcony before moving over to lock the door. I finished the bagel sandwich he brought over to me checking the time. There was still a couple of hours before I needed to be at the pizza place, but I decided to get ready to head out. When I made it downstairs, Bev was sitting at the table sipping on a cup of coffee watching the world go by out the window.

"Morning, Bev," I said quietly knowing the others were still asleep.

She jumped a little, but recovered and shot a smile at me, "Morning. Come sit with me, Val. We haven't seen a whole lot of you since getting back here."

I did as I was told, settling into a chair across from her. Her hair was pulled back and she was wearing a robe over her pajamas, but you couldn't really tell she just rolled out of bed. *Must be nice to wake up ready to go.*

"Have you guys gotten to explore?" I asked.

"We went out to a few places last night since Jennie wanted to party after we got everything set up," Bev chuckled. "They all got a little hammered, but I'm enjoying the quiet this morning. Lou's got a good place. I don't know if I've ever had pizza hit the spot like that. I think we're going to try to go shopping today. It's almost like Jennie is scoping the place out to be her new home or something."

I shrugged, "I wouldn't blame her. This world is pretty tame and there's only a few nights where you lock up the doors and stay out of the wolves' way."

"Plus, it's nice to have an in with the two most powerful here," she said watching me over her mug. "By the way, how is Warrick? Did I hear you two talking in your room earlier?"

I glanced out the window, "Yeah. He's doing alright, I guess. Things have been a little rocky since before we got back here, though. I'm struggling with what to do."

"I get it, Val. He can be a lot and I'm sure you're worried about that temper of his, and if I were you, I'd have a hard time moving past all the crap he did. On the other hand, though, you can see he truly cares about you. The few times I've been able to watch him I've noticed he's really battling with himself by trying to keep his crazy reeled in," Bev explained.

I put my head in my hands, "It's so hard to figure out what to do. I feel like I'm putting blinders on by trying to explore what's between us. Every time I see him, I have to bury the pain he caused me way down and I can't trust that he's not just going to flip a switch and lose it again."

"It doesn't help that you still have Lou pining after you," she casually noted.

"Ugh," I slumped back in my chair. "Don't remind me. Lou is so kind and true to himself. He takes care of others and wants to help. He's not bad in bed either, but there's just something missing in general for me. Something that's not missing when I'm with Warrick."

Bev smiled a little, "Sounds like you already know your answer."

I couldn't bring myself to say anything in response, so I looked at her and nodded. She was a lot more confident than I was.

Bev reached across the table, "Look, Val. Warrick may be a little unhinged, but he's wrapped around your finger. Even after he acted like an idiot back in the fae world, he was filled with guilt and remorse. He just wanted to make it up to you, but was worried he'd push you away some more."

"How do you know this?"

"I do what I do best," she smiled. "I talked to him, and from those conversations, I know he cares about you more than you think and values your opinions. Try things out with Warrick. We have your back here, so if anything goes wrong, we'll jump in to help. I may not have been able to see how you were with Gabriel since he was already deployed by the time we met, but judging by the way you look at Warrick or how your features soften when his name is mentioned, your feelings for Warrick are on par with what you felt for Gabriel or even a little more intense."

"Bev," I started. "You blow my mind with how much you pick up on people in such a short amount of time. You've never steered me wrong yet, so I guess I can try this out."

"Good," she said taking another sip of her coffee. "Now, you looked like you were about to head out, so don't let me stop you."

I stood up, "Thanks, Bev. Tell the others I said good morning."

I made my exit and headed towards the pizza place. I parked my car, sitting there for a few minutes then getting out to find a coffee shop. I figured I'd get Lou and I some coffee since I'm here earlier than usual and I'd have the chance to scope things out in case I wanted to bring Warrick something later. I walked to one of the last buildings on the block when I found a cute coffee shop. Pushing the doors open, I walked into a cozy space with light blue walls and cute signs with witty sayings about how coffee is the fix for everything. A barista greeted me with a smile and I placed an order for a couple of black coffees.

I headed back to the pizza place surprised to find the front door unlocked again, "Lou?"

"You're here early. It's almost like you're trying to impress the guy who runs the place," he said leaning against the doorframe leading to the kitchen while drying his hands.

"Okay, that was corny and you know it," I said setting our coffees down on a table. "Why is the door unlocked this early?"

Lou locked the door behind me then joined me at the table, taking a sip of coffee before saying, "I saw your car parked out there when I came down this morning and figured you'd be wandering in at some point. Thanks for the coffee, by the way. I haven't been to that coffee shop in ages."

"Even though this is a simple coffee, I like it. Anyways, would it be possible if I skipped out for a little bit again today?"

Lou looked at me skeptically, "What for and when?"

"Warrick mentioned he'd like to see me today if bossman would be willing to let me take a little bit of a break and I have no idea. He said he'd text me."

"I don't know. I let you run around for a bit yesterday and all hell broke loose. Are you going to pay more attention to your phone this time if I tell you I need you to come back?" he asked.

"Yeah, I'll be better about that this time, I promise. Plus, who knows what's going to happen. Maybe I'll want to come back sooner rather than later anyways," I casually said.

"Sure, just let me know when you're leaving."

I gave him a small smile, "Thanks."

"So, you're really going to try to make this work with Warrick then?" Lou asked.

I nearly choked on the coffee I just drank. Getting the last couple of coughs out of my way, I asked, "Haven't we talked about this before?"

I was hoping we'd be able to avoid this topic and let it be some unspoken understanding between Lou and I that we weren't going to work romantically when I compared how I feel to Warrick.

Lou leaned back in his chair stretching his legs out in front of him, "Yeah, but I need to know if you're all in on trying something out with Warrick or if you're still being wishy-washy. It'd help me out if I could move on. I'm still holding on to the hope that you're still interested in me that way."

I dropped my shoulders, "Lou, I'm sorry for stringing you along. I think I'm going to try this with Warrick which means I'm only interested in being friends with you."

"You think or you know?"

"I know I want to try this with Warrick. It just scares me, that's all."

He nodded, "I appreciate you being honest with me even if it wasn't the news I was hoping for. Know that I'm still here for you, Val. If anything goes wrong, I got your back. My promise still stands. I'll protect you."

I flashed a warm smile at him, "Thank you, Lou. That's really big of you to take this so well."

"We're all adults here, and it's kind of hard to compete with someone you're fated to," he winked at me.

I let out a laugh taking another sip. We fell into easy conversation for a while after that with no signs of getting friend-zoned bothering Lou. Either he was good at hiding his true emotions or he really does move on that fast. My bet was on hiding his emotions.

"Lou?" I asked when we were starting to get up to put the final touches on getting everything ready for opening. "Can you point out the best places to go shopping here to our friends?"

"Yeah, I take it they ended up going out last night?"

"How did you know?" I asked, surprised.

He let out a couple barks of laughter, "Because I gave them suggestions. Believe it or not, they like me, too."

"I know," I rolled my eyes. "Just surprised me, that's all."

Our conversation ended the minute we unlocked the doors and the hoard of hungry people waiting outside stormed the place. I was flying between tables again, alternating between drinks and food. There was a little bit of a lull, if you could call it that, where I was able to take a break behind the bar to check my phone. Warrick texted me to come over around two since that'll be the first free moment he'll have all day which meant he wasn't going to be making it over here to grab lunch. Almost as if on cue, Holly sauntered in tapping furiously at her phone screen.

Barely glancing up at me, she said, "I need a couple of pepperoni pizzas."

"Medium, large, or ?" I asked even though I knew the answer. I just wanted her to treat me with an ounce of respect rather than a nuisance she was forced to deal with.

She gave me a look that could kill, annoyed I was even asking her that question. She waved her perfectly manicured hands at me, "Whatever Warrick always orders, I don't know. All I know is I needed them five minutes ago and you're still standing here."

"Listen, *Holly*," I felt anger rising. I wasn't about to let this little blonde Barbie think she could treat me like shit just because she's working on the top floor of the nicest building in town. As soon as I opened my mouth to tell her off, Lou put a hand on my arm and flashed a toothy smile at her, "We have the pizzas ready, Val will bring them right out. In the meantime, can I get you anything else?"

She immediately dropped all hostilities, leaning across the bar to get closer to Lou and show off her cleavage. I gave another eye roll, but headed into the kitchen to grab the two to-go boxes mocking me for not having them out there to be picked up. When I made my way back to the bar, I couldn't help but notice Lou was flirting back. They were so engrossed in their conversation, they didn't hear me approach or clear my throat. I finally got their attention when I slammed the food down, my words dripping with poison, "Here's the order. Don't want to leave Warrick and his team waiting now. I'd hate to see that negatively impact your performance."

Holly jumped before scrambling to grab the food and scurry back across the street. No goodbyes to Lou, no extra sass to me, just hustle. *I guess she has some common sense after all.* I turned to face Lou, my hands on my hips, "What are you doing?"

He shrugged, "I don't know what you're talking about."

"Who you choose to flirt with doesn't bug me, but what does bug me is that you let her walk all over your employee then basically told her it was okay to do that by giving her all sorts of positive attention," I lectured. "I'm not going to be putting up with that bullshit if she keeps doing that. There's plenty of other places I can get a job around here."

"She won't be treating you like that again," Lou said, crossing his arms.

"You're pretty confident about that."

"Because I'll handle her every time she comes in from now on."

"Oh, I'm sure you'll handle her," I said giving him a hard time about his word choice. He caught on and blushed a little. I waved him off, "You have fun, Lou. Just means you can't give me a hard time when it comes to Warrick *and* I can outright flirt with him when he stops by."

"Wouldn't be any different than what I saw when you first got here," he playfully bumped into me. "Now, finish taking care of these customers."

"Aye aye, captain," I returned jokingly.

Two o'clock rolled around a lot quicker than I thought it would. I glanced at Lou tapping my wrist getting a nod in return. I wiped my hands off then quickly jogged down to the coffee shop to grab a couple of drinks for us before making my way across the street. The familiar ding of the elevator signaled I reached my destination. Surprisingly, Holly's desk was empty at the end of the hall and Warrick's office door was closed.

I knocked lightly then waited to be let in. When I didn't hear anything, I carefully opened the door, poking my head in just in case he was still in a meeting. To my surprise, the office was empty. I let myself in then settled in the chair opposite of his. I pulled out my phone to send a quick text to see where he was at. Maybe I could meet him rather than waiting in his office. It didn't take long for him to respond, letting me know his meeting is running late. I snapped a quick picture of his coffee to inform he that he doesn't have long before his drink gets cold. That earned me a thumbs up and a floor to venture to.

I hopped back on the elevator scanning the many buttons for the one that matched what he sent me: B2. I don't know why it took me so long to find it when it was clearly going to be one of the bottom options. The doors opened to a dark, windowless hallway leading to an open space at the end. The lights were dim, but just enough to guide you.

I slowly approached the room, keeping my steps as quiet as possible given the crowd gathered around the perimeter. There were at least fifty people leaning against the wall, mostly men, but a few women were sprinkled throughout. They were all watching something in the middle of the room. Following their gazes, my eyes landed on a smaller circle. I craned my neck to try to see what was going on when Warrick's voice filled the room, "Alright, where was I. Ah, yes. Being a wolf is a huge responsibility. You want to become one in this pack, you have to understand the deal you're making. We are in charge of the crime in this town. Something happens, we take care of it. Lou's pack comes in and cleans it up. We also don't engage in any conflict with his wolves, got it? It's as simple as that. I do expect that you hold your position here and you do it well. You break any of those rules I just said, and you're done. I won't be forgiving. Once you're changed, you'll be at the bottom of the pack until you work your way up. You ready?"

I heard a muffled yes in return. Understanding flooded me. I was about to witness a change. It was at this time the smaller circle disbanded, and as they joined their pack mates in the outer circle, curious glances came my way. I tightened my grip on our coffees forcing myself to stare straight ahead. I had literally walked into the lion's den and was completely defenseless. I had to trust that Warrick would protect me if anything bad happened.

Word must've started spreading that I was here because more and more of Warrick's wolves started looking at me. The men watched me hungrily while the women didn't hide the fact they weren't happy with my presence. There were only a few familiar faces in the crowd. The men who had lunch at Lou's yesterday were huddled in a corner whispering to each other with the one who grabbed my ass smirking at me. Warrick picked up on some of the things being said and snapped his head up in my direction. He didn't look happy, but I don't think that was because I followed his invitation. I had no idea what as being said about me, but I didn't think it was good judging his reaction.

Warrick returned his focus to the task at hand. The guy kneeling before him watched every movement with admiration. He was young, but looked so eager to please that he would do just about anything, including getting changed into a wolf. Warrick yanked him up and bit into his shoulder so fast that the guy didn't have any time to react.

Chapter 16

Realization sunk in and a scream rang out causing Warrick to drop him. Warrick wiped a hand across his mouth and watched as the soon-to-be new wolf writhed around the floor. His body contorted in ways indicating how painful this process must be as everything about him changed. He started panting before finally passing out. Warrick knelt down to check his pulse. I'm assuming this was normal since Warrick signaled some of his other wolves to take the body out so this poor guy could recover somewhere.

Warrick scanned the room as he casually unbuttoned his shirt. I had no idea what was coming next, but my grip tightened a little more on the coffee cups. Warrick cleared his throat, "It has come to my attention that we're a little distracted by the presence of a human here. I'm sure a few of you already know Val, but for those who don't, she works across the street at Lou's and helps supply us with our lunches. For those who do know her, step forward."

The women curled their lips at me no doubt wondering why their alpha was paying attention to little old me. Some of the guys who were gawking earlier cast glances towards their friends before looking down at their feet while others, including the ones from yesterday, only focused on me more. The ones from yesterday didn't break their focus as they obeyed their alpha's orders and stepped forward. At this point, Warrick had his shirt off and was walking a circle so he could look at every one of his wolves, "Some of you are wondering why she's even down here when this space is reserved for pack only. Well, simply put, she's here because I invited her down here since pack business was taking a little longer than usual. Now I have to make her wait even more, and let my coffee go cold, because some of you want to play games. I don't take very kindly to my wolves making comments about someone who's very important to me. I especially don't appreciate someone trying to make moves on her either."

I was surprised he hadn't said we were fated, but also relieved. I didn't know how they would all react but I wasn't holding my breath for being welcomed with open arms, and as far as I knew, there was only one way out of here.

Warrick walked over to the group of guys from the restaurant, their faces now pale including the one who grabbed me. He stopped only inches in front of his face, "Any of you feel like challenging me? That's the only way you're going to get to Val."

The other guys backed up a step, violently shaking their heads and keeping their attention on their feet. The one who was smirking only moments ago hesitated before he shook his head which set Warrick off. He picked this wolf up by his collar and said through gritted teeth, "Your hesitation just dug your grave."

He tossed this guy into the middle of the circle, a laugh building on his lips, "I mean, I don't blame you for wanting to take a shot. Look at her." Warrick wrenched this guy's head in my direction forcing him to look at me. A sneer formed on Warrick's lips as he continued, "She's gorgeous and I can tell you from experience that she's no slouch in bed, either."

Everyone's head whipped in my direction. I felt slimy and crossed my arms to cover my body. No one needed to know that. I hated when Warrick was like this and that he made me come down here just to watch him be an asshole. Anger mixed with panic started creeping up my throat making it hard to breathe, a feeling I was all too familiar with. I took a step back, but didn't dare turn to leave in case that added fuel to the fire.

Warrick shoved his "challenger" down, standing to his full height, "What are you waiting for? Take a shot. Let's see what happens."

I don't know what clicked, but this guy finally moved to sweep Warrick's legs out from under him. Warrick easily dodged by jumping up. Insane laughter ripped from him, "I'll go easy. Take another shot."

He lunged at Warrick, landing a hit square into his diaphragm. Taking advantage of Warrick trying to recover, he kneed Warrick in the face knocking him back. Instead of continuing the attack, this guy stood there in disbelief. I'm sure he wasn't expecting to have landed some good blows on someone at Warrick's level. Yet, that hesitation was all Warrick needed to launch his own series of attacks.

It became very clear to me that Warrick was being dramatic because he was on his feet charging the challenger in no time. Warrick knocked him to the ground and began throwing punches. Left, right, left, right. The sound of bones snapping filled the air mixed with the smell of blood. No one dared to make a sound or move as the scene was unfolding out of fear they would be viewed as the next challenger. He didn't let up even as blood started splattering, the guy was unconscious and defenseless. I was quickly reminded of how ruthless Warrick can be. I knew he wasn't going to stop until this guy was dead in order to send the message to his pack not to mess with me, and that only made the panic worse.

Warrick gave one final punch before standing up, covered in blood. He smiled as he spun around again, arms outstretched, "Anyone else up for the challenge today?"

Warrick took the silence as everyone's answer, "Good. Now, get back up there. I've held you all a lot longer than I needed to."

I scooted to one side to let his pack filter out. I heard several people mutter "whore" under their breath as they walked past me, but I kept my eyes trained on Warrick. One of his wolves brought him a towel so he could clean himself off while a few others moved to discard the lifeless body. I hadn't realized I was holding my breath until my head started pounding and the sides of my vision started going fuzzy. I sucked in some air hoping that would ease the panic a little more.

I was alone with Warrick now, but didn't dare move a muscle. Surprisingly, I still held on to the coffee cups that no longer provided warmth to my hands. He finished buttoning up his shirt before making his way over to me. He reached for my face, but changed courses to grab the coffee cup instead, "Sorry about that, love. I didn't mean to make you wait so long."

"Why did you have me come down here?" I asked.

Warrick placed a hand on my lower back to guide me back to the elevator, "I honestly thought I'd have everything wrapped up by the time you got down here. I didn't want to leave you hanging in my office just in case anyone tried anything."

"I don't know if I buy that. I feel like there was a part of you who wanted to show off your ruthless side again," I claimed, not letting my panic show in my voice.

His hand pressed harder on my back as we walked into the elevator. Warrick lifted his coffee cup out of my hand, "Damn it, it's cold. I'll warm it up after we get upstairs. I'd be lying if I said I didn't want you to see what happens when we change someone. I wanted you to know that we're not just crazed, bloodthirsty wolves running around killing people for fun on a full moon. I hold my pack to certain standards and I know Lou didn't share any of that with you in the early days. So, yes, I was a little selfish in that regard."

"And the guy you just killed for fun?" I asked not knowing if I truly wanted an answer.

"Love, I don't kill for fun despite what you may think. He was making lewd comments about what he'd do to you if he had the chance. Mix that with the other murmurs I was hearing and I wanted to send a message. I wasn't planning on any of that happening today, especially when it impacts the time we can spend with one another."

The elevator opened back up on Warrick's floor. Holly was happily typing away at her desk and smiled as we walked by asking Warrick how his meeting went. He gave a quick answer, then ushered me into his office so we could continue our conversation. I was amazed at how he acted like nothing happened.

He settled into his chair, smoothing his hair back then pouring his coffee into a mug so he could reheat it. Warrick settled into his chair, "Thank you for this, love. I'm sure you don't believe me about what I said earlier, but it's true. I hate killing."

"Then why do it? And why do you look like you're having fun?" I asked, standing instead of making myself at home.

"It's how I keep such tight control over a large pack. That wasn't even a quarter of my pack down there today, but those who witnessed what just happened will be sure to spread the message. While I hate it, there is a part of me that enjoys it when I'm hurting people. It gives me a rush, and I know that's morbid and will probably push you away, but I can't always help it. Part of being alpha is being able to maintain my position which means I have to be stronger than everyone else, so when I say it gives me a rush, I mean it's referring to the alpha side of me that needs to know my position isn't threatened."

My phone took this moment to buzz and relief flooded through me when Lou's name popped up on the screen. Typing out a response, I said to Warrick, "I have to go. Restaurant's getting busy again and Lou can't hold it down."

Warrick jumped up, "You're not just saying that to run, are you?"

I held out my phone for Warrick to read the message, "No, I'm telling you the truth."

He nodded and started walking me to his office door, "Okay. Come over tomorrow night."

"I don't know, Warrick. I haven't had a lot of time to hang out with my friends and explore the city with them," I said hoping I could convince him with my excuse. Honestly, I just wanted some space again.

"Please, love. I want some solid, uninterrupted time with you," he pleaded looking worried.

A small part of me felt bad for having him worry like this. I'm sure I was giving him flashbacks to when Melody ran out, but I wasn't ready to dismiss him quite yet. Why? I'm not sure considering he's given me every reason to run. I reached out to give his arm a squeeze, taking a closer step so our bodies were touching, "I'll let you know, okay?"

"Okay," he whispered.

We stayed there a few moments longer. Warrick looked like he wanted to kiss me, but I could tell he wasn't going to make the first move out of respect for any boundaries I may still have. Appreciative of him not trying to force anything, I gave him a quick kiss then made my exit.

When I was back in Lou's place, I completely forgot I was still carrying my cold cup of coffee. My stomach growled and I had to stifle a yawn when Lou walked back over to me, "You listened."

I scanned the nearly empty restaurant, "Why'd you tell me to get back over here? Were you testing me?"

"A little bit," he admitted. Lou sniffed the air then moved closer to me taking one more inhale, "You smell like blood. And fear."

I winced, "Can I have a salad or something? I'm starving. And I need my coffee warmed up."

"Got it," Lou said moving to take care of the things I just listed. I collapsed in our favorite booth debating what I wanted to tell him as I rubbed a hand over my face. He returned with a Caesar salad, probably one that was already made, and my coffee now steaming. I gratefully accepted the warm cup, wrapping my hands around it to soak up the warm comfort.

Lou cocked his head to the side, "Now, you want to tell me what happened in the thirty minutes you were gone."

"It was only half an hour? I could've sworn I spent a lot longer over there," I said in disbelief. How could he do all of that so quickly?

"Earth to Val," Lou waved a couple of fingers to get my attention.

"Sorry. I just lost all track of time, that's all. Anyways, I got to witness what happens when someone's changed," I blurted.

Lou raised his eyebrows, "Warrick let you see that? It's a pretty sacred thing, so not a lot of people get to see what happens."

"Well, he thought everything would be over by the time I met up with him, so it wasn't like it was his main goal for me to see that. Although, it kind of freaked me out seeing someone's body react like that," I said.

"There's a lot going on when the change happens. Did he die?" Lou asked.

"No, why?"

He pushed my food towards me reminding me to eat, "Well, I thought I smelled a little bit of death on you, too. I wasn't sure, so I didn't want to say anything, but it's not uncommon for people to not make it through the change. Especially when Warrick does it."

"What does that have to do with anything?" I asked confused.

"He's aggressive, Val. He'll change people then leave them to fend for themselves because if they can't fight through the change, then how are they supposed to make it as a wolf? How are they going to be able to handle the full moon when it comes around," Lou said getting lost in his memories. Continuing, he brought his steely grey eyes to meet mine, "When someone goes through that, they need monitoring by a medical professional who is up to speed on what happens to the body when someone has been bit, especially when someone as powerful as Warrick initiates the change. The more powerful the wolf, the more intense the change is."

"How do you not know if Raf is being pulled in? Or if any of his pack that works at the hospital isn't doing that?" I asked in between bites.

"Raf was already a wolf and a very well-respected doctor when Warrick decided to change me. I didn't have anyone checking on me or making sure I would live to see another day. No, I was abandoned, and when I finally showed back up to work, Warrick only nodded his head and carried on with his day," Lou said curtly.

I held up my hands, "Alright, sorry I touched on a sore subject."

"It's okay. It's important for you to be aware of these things. What else happened? You didn't seem to scared when talking about what you saw there."

I grabbed my mug again, thankful for the warm coffee to give me some energy to make it through the rest of the day. I lowered it back down to the table, "Warrick killed one of his wolves basically right after he changed someone."

"One for one," Lou observed.

Ignoring him, I went on, "It was the guy from yesterday who grabbed me. Warrick forced this guy to fight him and turned into usual asshole-Warrick. He didn't stop, Lou. He didn't stop hitting him until he was beyond dead then made a big show to the rest of his pack down there that I was off-limits."

"No surprise there. I'm shocked you didn't come running back here after all that."

"I'm not Melody," I snapped.

Lou flinched at that, "Right, I know."

I started to reach across the table, but stopped when the little voice in the back of my mind reminded me that Lou didn't need to be comforted after that, "Sorry. Look, I didn't run because every instinct in my body warned me that if I ran, I'd probably be dead before I could make it to the elevator. I decided to stay for that reason and to hear Warrick out. I really didn't want to set him off again."

Lou watched me for a few moments after I finished my explanation, "You're a lot smarter than most, Val."

"Thanks," I rolled my eyes.

"No, seriously," Lou said then lowered his voice despite there being no one else around us. "You'd be surprised how many people run after seeing something like that only to provoke the wolves that lie just beneath the surface. I'm guessing he had about fifty people down there, and judging by your facial expression, the answer would be yes. I probably don't need to say this to you, but I will anyways. Never turn your back on a wolf in a tense situation. Never. That'll only provoke them."

"Told you that you don't have to worry about me," I reminded him.

That remark earned a smile from Lou, "I'm just glad nothing crazy seems to have come out of that whole interaction. Maybe Warrick is changing a bit."

"You're welcome," I said, standing up to greet the customers that just walked in. I got them all settled with their drinks and a couple of quick slices before returning to the table with Lou. "In all seriousness, I hate when he gets like that."

"I know. A lot of people do. On the bright side," Lou mentioned as a way to change the subject. "I think your friends got excited about where I told them to go shopping."

"Good, thank you for doing that," I said. "Are you doing anything in a few days?"

"No, why?"

"Come over to the house. It'll be Christmas and I'm sure everyone will be more than happy to include you in the celebrations."

He pretended to think about it, "I mean, I'll have to check my calendar, but I think I can make it. I'll have to get someone to run this place, though."

I waved him off, "That'll be easy. Your pack will jump at any opportunity to help you out."

"That's what you think," he said.

I rolled my eyes and got back to work. The coffee and salad were working wonders on me and managed to carry me through the rest of my shift. I headed to my car happy I didn't take a moment to look up towards Warrick's office, then made my way home.

Everyone was hanging out talking and laughing. When I grabbed a plate of food and joined them, they all cheered a little. Jennie beamed at me, "I never thought we'd see you again. Been avoiding us?"

"Ha, no. You'll never believe the day I just had," I said.

"Go on," Jennie encouraged.

"Saw someone get changed into a werewolf and another person get killed," I said more causally than I meant to.

Everyone stared at me with their jaws gaping open. Chris was the first to break the silence, "Not what we were expecting. You okay?"

I nodded, "At this point, yeah. If you had seen me right after it happened, probably not. Anyways, I invited Lou over for Christmas."

"If you need to talk more about what you saw, that's okay," Jennie invited. "That's some heavy stuff."

"Seriously, I'm good. Lou and I talked through a lot of it and I'm just giving myself some space from Warrick. Although, he wants me to go over to his place tomorrow night."

"That's Christmas Eve," Bev mentioned.

"Yup," I nodded. "Would you guys be okay if I did that?"

"Yeah," Jennie waved her hand. "Go enjoy some time with your lover. Can we call him that? What's going on with you and Warrick anyways?"

"I mean, I guess you can," I said. "I have no idea what to call us right now when we're still in the stage of trying to figure things out."

"Well, you two should enjoy some time together. We don't have hardly anything planned anyways," Bev said.

"Yeah we do!" Jennie chimed in.

Joe let out a little groan, "We're not going back to the club again, are we?"

Jennie giggled, "We are. Might as well. There are no services or anything, and besides, that would be a fun way to celebrate."

"We could use some fun after everything," Chris said coming to her defense.

Bev put her hand on Joe's knee, "We'll go, but we may not stay the entire time."

"Oh, that's totally fine," Jennie said. "We'll do some other more traditional stuff and it'll be great to have Lou over on

Christmas. Is Warrick joining us, too? I want to make sure we have enough food."

I shrugged, "I don't know yet, but once I have it figured out, I'll let you know."

I finished my food, hung out for a little longer, then made my way up to bed. Not even bothering to change, I collapsed on my bed and instantly fell asleep. When I woke up the next morning, I had a text from Lou giving me the next few days off since it's a big holiday for me.

I pranced my way downstairs, placing my friends' wrapped gifts under the tree so they were ready for tomorrow. After I had everything arranged the way I wanted, I settled into the couch turning on Christmas movies. I hadn't given myself the time I usually do to enjoy the season and I was missing the traditions. Ice skating, looking at Christmas lights, Christmas markets, the movies, cookie making. The list could go on for miles.

Everyone else woke up one at a time, each drifting to the couch to join me. We hardly talked since we were enjoying the simplicity of the morning. When our movie marathon was finished, we moved to the pool table downstairs having a mini tournament while laughing our heads off reminiscing about our funniest Christmas memories.

The day flew by and I found myself sitting in my dad's office during a lull in the activities. I was absentmindedly scrolling through his email more thinking about how I missed spending this season with him rather than paying attention to anything that may have been new. I was just about to finish my scrolling to get ready to go over to Warrick's when I saw an email from him.

Clicking on it, Warrick was informing my dad that I was able to monitor the inbox now which prompted a response of acknowledgement. The last sentence in my dad's response asked if I would be willing to have a quick video call with him. I rubbed my eyes not sure if I was reading that correctly. *Why does he want to talk to me? Isn't he on the wrong side of this war? Could I talk to him considering all the damage he's caused?*

I slowly started typing out a response telling my dad I'd be available for a call later tonight. After sending it, I grabbed the laptop to pack in an overnight bag. My phone buzzed with a message from Warrick: *You coming over tonight?*

I texted my response back letting him know he'd be seeing me in about an hour if that was okay. I got a thumbs up back in response and went back to getting ready. I decided to go all out, curling my hair and doing my makeup then throwing on a cute, oversized sweater and completing the look with leggings and some high-heeled boots.

I followed the directions Warrick gave me to get to his place, including the parking instructions to keep my car protected. As I let myself in to his apartment, I started to call out, "Knock kno – "

The words escaped my mouth at the sight in front of me. His normally modern apartment was completely decked out in Christmas decorations. He had none of his normal lights turned on letting his home be filled with the soft glow from the Christmas lights scattered around the space. Garland covered every flat surface complete with lights and other decorations like small deer and snowflakes. There was even glittery decorations adding an extra sparkle to the evening. It was like something out of a magazine complete with Christmas music playing softly to fill the space.

I was drawn in by the perfectly decorated Christmas tree not realizing Warrick had entered the room. I reached out to cradle an ornament when his voice made me jump, "Glad to see you made it over here before the snow, love."

"Don't do that!" I whirled around to face him, a hand on my chest.

"Sorry," he chuckled. He handed me a glass of wine then stood next to me. "There is something about these decorations, though. I got them put up last night and have felt at peace ever since. Makes me wish I did this earlier."

"You said it's supposed to snow?" I asked.

"Yeah, it just started."

I peeked around the tree to see large, fluffy flakes make their slow descent to the ground. *Now tonight is perfect.*

"I see you responded to the email from your dad," Warrick said cutting through my thoughts.

"Oh, yeah. Would I be able to take that call from here?" I asked.

He gestured to his office, "Be my guest. He mentioned he's available for a little while, so you should do that now to make sure you get that time in."

I gave him a skeptical look before moving to the office, Warrick trailing me. I set up my dad's laptop, logging in and getting the video call software pulled up, "How did you know?"

"You hit 'Reply All', love. You kept me in the loop," Warrick said settling into the chair near the window so he could watch the weather. "Mind if I sit in here? I'll stay off screen."

"Sure," I said. I read through my dad's response confirming what Warrick said then entered in the info he provided for me to call him. Nerves fluttered through me as it rang and rang.

I thought he wasn't going to pick up, feeling disappointment flashing through me just when his face filled the screen.

"Hey dad," I said.

"Hey, Val-pal. How are you?"

I winced a little at the childhood nickname knowing Warrick would ask me about it later. I took my dad in for a quick second noting he looked far older and more tired than the last time I had seen him. He must've lost a decent amount of weight, too, judging by the way his cheeks were sunken in.

"I'm fine. How are you?"

He looks over his shoulder, but I couldn't tell what he was checking for since he was in a dark room. He turned back to the camera, "Surviving. Look, I really don't have long, but I wanted to take a moment to talk to you since I'm sure you have a million things running through your head. Yes, I created those bombs, but my intention was to keep as many people as safe as I could by transporting them away from the epicenter of this war. No, I'm not truly on the enemy's side. I'm undercover to try to get as many details as I can. Yes, I'm teaming up with Warrick because he's providing a lot of helpful insight into our enemy's motivation and potential next moves. This may not be the most popular opinion given what's happened between you two, but you need to listen to him. He's not wrong in that this war is about to spread to other worlds and he needs your help. This war is no joke, Val. I've never seen more destruction happen so quickly than what's going on here. And this has all been caused by one person. If you can, try to jump in as much as possible. If you can get more people on our side, the better. I have to go, but it was really good seeing you Val-pal. I love you and I hope this reassures some of those thoughts barreling through that head of yours."

"Love you, dad," I managed to squeak out before the call ended. Sitting back in the chair, I swiped a couple of tears away letting out a deep breath. I don't know what I was expecting, but it wasn't a call as quick as that. I guess I can be appreciative of him answering some of my biggest questions, but I didn't have a chance to get a word in.

"You good, love?" Warrick asked.

"Yeah, just letting that all settle in. It may have been a lighting quick conversation, but a lot was said," I turned to face Warrick. "Thank you."

"Anytime."

I watched Warrick a little longer. My dad isn't normally one to harp on how bad things are. He's always been someone who looks at the bright side of things and makes everything look better than what it is, but he wasn't lying about how serious this war is. On the other hand, at least I had considered the possibility of him not being completely on the wrong side of the conflict. And this man in front of me who I wasn't sure I could trust was now becoming the golden ticket to surviving this. Something sent the butterflies in my stomach soaring. Maybe I could trust him some more, give him the benefit of the doubt. Maybe we could give this thing between us a shot.

Chapter 17

As I was sifting through my thoughts, Warrick turned his attention back to me, "Something on your mind, love?"

"Are you wearing Christmas pajamas?" I asked, trying not to smile.

He moved to get up, retrieving a gift bag from his room, "I was hoping you'd join me."

I felt tears spring into my eyes, my heart bursting with how nice this gesture was. However, there was a small part of me reminded of what I had received the last time Warrick handed me a bag filled with tissue paper. I shook off the feeling of dread trying to creep its way in and told myself I wasn't about to pull a head out. I nodded my head, taking a steadying breath. I accepted the bag and a soft kiss from Warrick. When I pulled back, I said, "Let me get changed."

He gave me a genuine smile, "I'll be out in the living room."

I ditched the outfit I carefully picked out earlier to replace my clothes with the silky soft fabric of these red and green pajamas. I had no idea how Warrick found something like these in a place that doesn't celebrate Christmas, but I wasn't complaining. He probably wouldn't tell me anyways.

I headed back out to join him in the living room. He had laid out a hearty breakfast dinner. I sat next to him on the floor noticing the fire burning in a fireplace I hadn't seen before, "Did you make all of this?"

"Yeah, I wanted to give you something special," Warrick said scooting closer to me. "Merry Christmas, love."

"Merry Christmas. Thank you for all of this."

He grinned at me before plopping some whipped cream on my nose. It took me a moment to realize what had just happened, my mouth opening in shock, "Did you just?"

Warrick sported a childlike grin trying to contain his laughter while he shook his head. I kept my eyes on him as I loaded up the spoon with plenty of whipped cream to get him back. He was still trying to hold back laughter when I returned the favor. His eyes widened, surprised by me actually catching him off-guard. Unlike Warrick, though, I immediately started laughing. I wiped the cream from my nose, savoring the sweet flavor as the golden sound of Warrick's laughter finally filled the space, his head thrown back. I hadn't heard that laugh in such a long time, my heart rate picking up in time with the butterflies once again fluttering in my stomach.

He brought his icy blue gaze back to me, light dancing in his eyes. Completely caught up in the moment, I leaned in to kiss him this time savoring the feel of his soft lips on mine rather than pulling away. Warrick pulled me closer to him, his hands sliding down my back. I reached up to cradle his cheek, tracing my thumb along his cheekbone. His tongue lightly traced my bottom lip. I could tell he was being tentative, not sure when this moment would end but making sure to enjoy every second. There was a hunger behind his kiss that only reminded me of my own. This was the Warrick I missed. The one who genuinely smiled and laughed. The one who was attentive and gentle.

Warrick pulled away, a groan of protest escaping my lips. His thumb followed the path his tongue had taken just seconds ago, "I've missed this. I've missed you, love."

"I've missed you, too, Warrick. Can we just stop time and stay here like this?"

He chuckled, "I wish. Trust me, I do."

We went back to eating, casually talking about all things Christmas to bring Warrick up to speed on what the holiday is about. I glanced back at his tree noticing there were gifts. As in more than one.

"Why are there so many gifts under the tree?" I asked, curiosity getting the best of me.

He got up, bringing them all over, "They're for you."

"No, that's too much. I can't take all of these," I protested. I felt bad for only getting him one thing and here he is spoiling me.

"Please, love. I insist. Open them," he smiled. Warrick looked so excited to see my reactions.

I adjusted myself so I was squarely facing him as I started tearing through the paper on the first box. The box was thin, but longer. Enough of the wrapping paper had been removed to reveal the back of a picture frame. Even more confused than I was when I picked it up, I started to flip the frame over to see what picture he possibly could've picked out. I don't think we've ever taken a picture together.

I gasped when I could make out the image. It was Warrick and I at the ball back in the vampire world. My head was back, eyes were closed as I was laughing at something Warrick had said. He was leaning in close, a smile taking up his entire face. There was one thing I couldn't take my eyes off of: Warrick looked at me with an expression full of love. It was written all over his face, something you couldn't mistake. *I can't believe I hadn't noticed that before.*

"Conor snapped that and I can't begin to tell you how thankful I am that he did," Warrick said, drawing me out of my thoughts.

"It's beautiful, thank you," I said. I couldn't say the other thing that was on my mind. The three words just waiting to be said. Why? I have no idea, but something was holding me back.

He handed me the next gift, "This one isn't as sentimental, but I hope you like it."

The box was slightly smaller, but not nearly as flat. When I got it open, I pulled out a thick, chunky sweater made of the softest material I had ever felt. Underneath that were a pair of heeled boots and faded jeans. He knew my taste a little better than I did. I smiled at him, "I love it."

We went back and forth like this until I got down to the last two boxes. So far, he had showered me with a couple new outfits, the picture, and a painting showing the whale creature we saw the night he told me we were fated. He handed me the larger of the two and I could instantly tell it was a book. Warrick explained that this was one of his favorite books from when he was a teenager and that he couldn't wait for me to read it so we could talk some more about what happened. Then, came the last box. It was a small square that I was convincing myself wasn't a ring.

I let out the breath I had been holding when I discovered a necklace in the box. It was simple: a thin silver chain with one small diamond dangling. As soon as it caught the light, millions of little rainbows danced around the room catching me by surprise. I hadn't expected something that small to shine so brightly.

"It's not too much is it?" Warrick asked, worried I may not accept this gift.

"No, I couldn't have asked for anything better. Can I have some help?" I asked holding out the necklace.

He gingerly took the necklace from my hand. I turned around, sweeping my hair to one side all of a sudden incredibly aware of every movement the two of us made. Warrick clasped the necklace, securing it in place then let his fingers linger before dropping his hand and returning to his dinner. I took a couple more bites of my food trying to keep my thoughts from wandering to the kiss we just shared or how he would feel on top of me again.

Instead of getting lost in my fantasies, I decided to get up to head back to where I left my bag. I could at least give him my gift in return even if it was nowhere near the level of what he got me. I joined him back in the living room holding out the small box I wrapped, "I hope you like it."

He gave me an appreciative grin, accepting the gift and wasting no time unwrapping it. Warrick held up the small whale creature, beaming, "What do you mean? This is amazing, love. Thank you."

He got up to place it on his mantle to join the stockings that were hanging. I gave a quick shake of my head marveling at everything Warrick had done to give me a Christmas worth remembering. As soon as he was done cleaning things up, he came back over with a plate of Christmas cookies in hand, "Dessert?"

"You didn't make all of this, did you?" I asked trying to see if there was something he paid someone for because I couldn't figure out how he had all the time to work the long nights at the office *and* get everything ready for tonight.

"You caught me on this one, love. I ordered them from a bakery," Warrick confirmed in between bites.

I grabbed one off the plate, "I knew you couldn't have done all of this without some sort of help."

He put his arm around my shoulders while we settled under a blanket to watch a movie, "Don't think I didn't try, though. The burnt ones are still in the trash."

That got a little laugh out of me. I helped myself to another cookie, letting my head rest on his shoulder while *The Polar Express* filled the screen. "How did you get your hands on this movie?" I asked.

"Your friends work magic. It helped having you out of the house working at the pizza place," he answered.

I was about to give him a hard time for sneaking around, but his phone ringing ended the thought as fast as it came into my head. Warrick let out a low grumble as he stood up answering the phone.

"There better be a damn good reason why you're calling me this late at night, Holly," Warrick barked out making his way to his office.

I paused the movie, skin prickling with nervous energy. I checked the clock to see it was almost 11 at night. There should be no reason why anyone at his company should be calling him at this hour, especially his assistant. I thought about following him, but ultimately decided against it. The last thing I need tonight is to set him off because I'm nosey. Although, I didn't have to be near him to hear his side of the conversation.

"You called me for that? Save it for when I'm back in office. I don't fucking care what they said! It's your job to filter what's urgent and what's not. This is a lesson in what's not urgent. Next time, call me when the building is on fire or someone breaks in," he shouted.

Something slammed on his desk, echoing throughout the apartment. When it was quiet for a while, I moved towards his office to check on him. Warrick was holding his head in his hands. I could see the frustration oozing off him since his night was interrupted, but there was something else lurking beneath the surface that I couldn't put a finger on. I knocked on the doorframe, "Hey, are you okay?"

Warrick's head snapped up, "Yeah, love. Sorry for all the yelling."

"Something go wrong at the office?"

"Nothing that can't be handled in a couple of days," he said offering a small smile.

I took a couple steps closer, "Would it help to talk about it? You seem really frustrated."

He smoothed his hair back, "Just a new development in the war, that's all."

"I mean, I don't blame her for calling you about that. She knows what's going on?" I asked.

"Not really," he answered with a quick shake of his head. Warrick stood up to make his way out of the office, me following right behind him. He made it to one of the windows overlooking the city below, hands in his pockets as he continued explaining, "She knows there's a lot of important research going on, but she doesn't know what it's for. I'd like to keep it that way and tonight she mentioned someone from one of the departments I have monitoring the war had an update regarding the conflict. She started asking me what conflict he was talking about and that's when I shut her down."

I put my hand in the middle of his back, moving it in small circles to provide some sort of comfort, "Is it a bad thing for her to know about it?"

He dropped his head, sighing, "Not a bad thing, no, but she's one who will run her mouth to the first person she sees. I'd like to keep the knowledge of this war under wraps to minimize panic. The last thing I need is a world full of people stressing about a war that isn't here yet."

"But, clearly some of your people already know about it," I pointed out.

"Those who are in my inner circle know. Their hands are legally tied to keep that a secret. Now, I have to reprimand that individual for even hinting at something happening. The amount of questions I'm going to be getting about this ..." he trailed off.

"I appreciate you telling me and Lou about what you know," I said trying to lighten his mood a little.

Warrick slightly turned his head to show me the appreciative grin, "I'm glad you also got a chance to hear it from your dad, love."

"You know, that conversation reaffirmed how dire this war could be. I just don't know how it's going to come to an end," I said, shaking my head as I moved to stand next to Warrick.

"Unfortunately, nothing in your world is going to do the trick."

I glanced up at him, "What do you mean?"

"The enemy is not a human. Your world is going up against a wolf and the only one who knows about it is your dad. However, if he said that, not only would no one believe him, but – "

I jumped in, cutting Warrick off, "But he would be a laughingstock. So, you've been trying to help out my dad by providing him insight?"

Warrick was being so forthcoming with information, I didn't want to miss out on this opportunity. I was making sure I could ask any and every question popping in my head before he shut down again. I guess I can thank Holly for one thing.

He gave a quick nod, "That and trying to find weapons that'll do some damage. You remember the knife you so kindly stabbed me with, love?"

Warrick glanced at me again with a smile tugging at a corner of his mouth. I grimaced at the memory popping up in my mind, "Yeah, sorry about that."

"Don't be," he chuckled. "Anyways, that was one of the things we were researching. Thankfully, you sped up the results for us. Turns out the venom I put on that knife does a decent amount of damage to a wolf, plus makes it take longer to heal, but nothing permanent beyond a scar."

I tucked that away for later when I could check his leg for any sort mark to serve as a reminder of the days when I thought I'd be able to move on from Warrick. It's not a common occurrence for Warrick to have scars. I rested my head against his shoulder, "What other weapons have you researched?"

"You're not going to like me for saying this, but everything I've used against Lou has all been for research. I had to find a powerful wolf to try them on and I, selfishly, didn't want to be the first volunteer. Those silver teeth I'm sure you've seen by now and the silver in the water both have impacts, but again, not exactly what we're looking for," he explained.

Warrick's admission turned my stomach again. He just casually threw it out there that he was experimenting on Lou to see what could cause the most damage to a wolf. *I wonder if Lou ever suspected that.*

"Anyways, enough about that. There's actually a couple of other things I wanted to get off my chest tonight," Warrick said turning so he could face me.

I took in his handsome features, illuminated by the glow of the lights. Shadows were being cast in all the right places, stirring up heat in my core despite the unsettled feeling from telling me what he did to Lou. *Can you keep it in your pants for one night, Val? C'mon.* He reached for my hands, intertwining his fingers with mine as his icy blue eyes met mine again, "Val, love, I'm really sorry for what you had to see today. I didn't intend for you to see that. It may have seemed over the top, but know the pack has been restless in my absence. I needed to remind them who the alpha was because the last thing I need right now is more chaos. I'm only explaining what happened, not trying to make an excuse. This pales in comparison to how sorry I am about what I let happen in Cian's world."

At the mention of that place, I tensed. Warrick sensed the change in my body language and he tried to give my hands a reassuring squeeze. For what? I'm not sure. It could be a silent promise that he won't let anything like that happen again, at least not willingly, or it could be his way of acknowledging the pain that he caused me. Either way, I knew what was coming next and wasn't quite sure how I feel about it.

"I should have never let things get that way," he said, genuine remorse in his eyes.

"I get that, I guess," I held up my hand to silence him. "But I struggle with everything you said to me. I struggle with the pain you caused. Did you really mean what you said back there?"

Warrick instantly shook his head, "No. I really didn't. You have to know it nearly killed me to say those awful things to you, and don't get me started on how it hurt me to physically cause you pain."

"You know that broke me, right?" I asked. "I was ready to give up. I told Cian and Liam to kill me, so you did your part."

The last words dripped with poison, but I wasn't expecting them to affect Warrick the way they did. I swore I saw tears form in his eyes, but they vanished as quickly as they made their presence known.

He traced some of the scars that the pajamas didn't quite cover up, "Fuck. There's no amount of apologies that will make up for what I did. I know this may not change how you feel about this, but I had a plan in place to get you out of there."

I nodded, "I know. I'm thankful for Melody. I'm also thankful for Lou, Chris, Jennie, and Raf because without them, I wouldn't be standing here. Warrick, I appreciate you being willing to tackle this head-on and for listening to how I feel about it. I don't want this to ruin our night, or tomorrow. Speaking of tomorrow, are you going to come over? We're doing a little celebration with the six of us."

He cocked his head to the side, thinking, "I'm assuming part of that count includes Lou?"

"Yeah," I said, knowing he might say no because of Lou.

"I'll be there," he sighed. "I need to work on putting aside our differences for now."

"How very noble of you," I teased. I was thankful we decided to move on from the more serious topics of conversation. It was good to clear the air and get that all out there, but I've worked hard to keep it all in the past in order to focus on moving forward. I sent a quick text to Bev letting her know to expect one more for the festivities tomorrow.

I didn't get the chance to put my phone back down when Warrick was taking it from my hands, placing it on the table, and picking me up by my legs. I had no other choice but to wrap my legs around him, immediately comforted by how familiar this feeling was. Warrick tightened his grip as if he wasn't ever going to let me go, "Is this okay, love?"

"And what would happen if I said no?" I asked, resting my forehead on his.

He grinned slowly, "I don't know if I'd be able to let you go."

Shaking my head, I leaned in to give him a kiss. Our lips melted together picking up where we left off earlier. After all his confessions, my internal battle had quieted no longer trying to steer my conscience one way versus the other. It was easier to give in, to trust him. I bet Warrick wasn't planning on giving me an extra gift this night, but it was the one I needed the most.

He carried me to his room slowly lowering me on his bed, "Do you want to?"

I nodded my head a little more enthusiastically than I thought, "Of course I do. I've missed you in every way."

"You have no idea how much I've missed you, love," he crooned into my neck.

Warrick's hands slowly moved under my shirt, following the lines of my back before moving to trace the bottom of my breast. His lips traced kisses from my neck to my collar bone, barely brushing against my skin causing it to erupt in goosebumps. Between the soft feel of his lips and the gentle caress from his hands, I arched my back to get closer to his touch. He let out a satisfied growl at my reaction before ripping off his shirt. I immediately brought him back to me so I could trace the hard edges of his muscles. I sat up to pull my shirt over my head and moved so I was now on top of Warrick.

"Merry Christmas," he said softly.

I glanced over towards the clock on his nightstand to see we made it to a new day while grinding my hips into his. When I looked back, his eyes were closed from pleasure. I leaned down to give his ear a little nibble then whispered, "Merry Christmas."

I left a trail of kisses from his neck to his hips teasing the edge of his waistline. A moan escaped from his lips as his hands became entangled in my hair, gripping me hard enough to prove he was holding himself back to take things at my pace. I pulled his pants down just enough to tease his tip with my tongue earning a twitch and a louder moan. I made my way back up to his lips to give another long, slow kiss reveling in how right he felt. I was enjoying this slow introduction back into making love with him, but Warrick didn't want to wait any longer. He worked my pants off, discarding my underwear, then took a moment to appreciate my naked body, his fingers drawing loose, teasing circles all over me.

He wasted no more time with letting me sit on top of him. Warrick flipped me under him and threw his pants off faster than I could blink. He traced his fingers down my body until they teased my entrance. A smile lit up his face, "I don't think you've ever been this wet for me, love."

"Are you going to tease me or do something about it?" I asked, cocking an eyebrow.

He thrust his fingers in me heading straight to the spot that drives me crazy. I gripped the sheets and my moan filled the room. Warrick worked his fingers causing the pressure to build in my core, my climax right around the corner. I wasn't ready for that quite yet, still wanting to savor this moment, so I directed his hand from between my legs up to my lips. The two fingers he had inside me were coated, but that didn't stop me from putting them in my mouth. Warrick raised his eyebrows while I watched his pupils dilate, "That's new."

I slowly brought his fingers out of my mouth, a popping noise signaling their freedom, "Care to have a taste?"

"Don't have to ask me twice," he said lowering himself in between my legs. He took his time swirling his tongue around me before alternating between my clit and pushing through my entrance. I could no longer keep myself from the edge. My climax washed over me before I had a chance to try to catch my breath, every inch tingling with pleasure. I screamed out his name, tightening my grip on the sheets. Warrick let out a moan of approval as he kept circling my clit to make the sensation last a few moments longer.

When he noticed I went limp, he crawled up so he could tuck a strand of my hair behind my ear, "Good girl. I could hear you scream like that all day."

"It's your lucky night, then," I said slightly out of breath. "It's my turn to return the favor."

Warrick wasted no time rolling on the condom then sliding into me. It was his turn to moan, his head falling back and eyes closing again. He slowly pumped his hips gradually picking up speed as I adjusted to his size. Our moans were ringing out together the closer we both got to an orgasm. He pulled me up so I was now sitting on top of him, the both of us working our hips in a synchronized rhythm, never missing a beat. His body gave a couple of twitches telling me he was close to finishing. I tilted his chin up, leaning in for a kiss, and as soon as my lips touched his, he shuddered, tightening his grip. Warrick pulled back just enough to whisper my name which was all I needed to hear. I collapsed on him once again out of breath, but I wasn't the only one this time who got to feel the sweet ecstasy of an orgasm.

Warrick eased me back down to his bed, "You're incredible, love."

"So are you," I responded.

We laid there for a little bit longer before we both moved to clean ourselves up. I settled back in his bed, Warrick wrapping his arms around me and pulling me back into him. He planted a soft kiss on my shoulder then said, "Thank you for coming over tonight."

"I should be the one thanking you," I turned to face him. "You went all out to make sure I felt at home here. You covered your entire place in Christmas decorations and celebrated a holiday that doesn't even exist in your world just to give me a night to remember. Then, to top it all off, you opened up to me in a way I didn't expect you to. I can't even begin to describe what that means to me."

Warrick caressed my cheek, placing a kiss on my forehead, "You're worth it, love."

We didn't have to say it, but those three little words floated around the air until they nestled in between us to add extra warmth.

Chapter 18

It had been a while since I actually got good, uninterrupted sleep. I may have been able to keep the nightmares at bay up until this point, but sleep was still challenging. It had been even longer since I had woken up feeling safe and secure. There was nowhere I had to rush off to nor was there something that immediately needed my attention. I was able to confirm my dad was doing alright, although he didn't mention anything about mom and there wasn't enough time for me to ask, but I pushed any of those thoughts to the side. Work was off the table for today and there wasn't a so-called mission I was working on. No, I was able to just enjoy the holiday and myself today.

I rolled over finding Warrick's space empty. Not quite sure if I was imagining things, I felt around confirming I was indeed alone. Slowly sitting up, I hugged the covers close to me and rubbed the sleep out of my eyes. I sat there for a few beats until I persuaded myself to leave my warm cocoon. Warrick's apartment was quiet almost as if it were slowly waking up, too. *Did he leave me here?*

I poked my head out of the room listening for any signs of life. After scanning the hallway, I noticed Warrick's office door was closed and the muffled sounds of his voice were trying to escape. I padded my way over, cautiously pushing the door open to see what he was doing.

"I need you to be more discreet when talking to Holly. She may be able to get me to answer the phone when I'm away from the office, but she can't know about this war. There's a reason only a select few of you actually know what's going on and I'd like to keep it that way," Warrick quietly lectured into his phone. He paused while the person on the other line responded. Thankfully, he hadn't noticed me creeping into the office since his back was to the door.

He continued, "No, I'm taking today and tomorrow off. Something else has come up that I need to make sure I'm fully present for. Thank you for letting me know the update. Pass the message along. We need to speed up production and reinforce security. It's even more imperative now to keep this all a secret."

I watched his shoulders slump as he rested his forehead against the window. Warrick sighed, and in that moment, I could tell something was very wrong. His posture was the same way it was back on the island when he was talking about his past before he got drunk. I closed the distance between the two of us, placing a hand on his back, "Are you okay?"

Warrick jumped a little at my touch, "I didn't realize you were up already, love. I was going to sneak back into bed for a little longer."

I pushed against his shoulder to get him to turn to me. I checked his face for any signs of negative emotions, but he already had his walls up. I gave him a small grin, "That's okay. We'll probably want to head out in a bit anyways. I'm starving and I heard there's going to be breakfast. You didn't answer my question, though. Are you okay? You seemed upset after you got off the phone."

Warrick's eyes softened as he tucked some hair behind my ear, "Yeah, something's come up at work, but it's handled."

"Are you really taking today and tomorrow off? No more phone calls?"

"Yes," he leaned in to kiss my forehead softly. "I want to spend this time with you."

I smiled up at him, "Who knew I'd be getting this lucky on Christmas?"

"I had a hunch," Warrick winked at me. His stomach growled interrupting the moment and reminding us we had somewhere to be. I checked my phone relieved when there wasn't a message or missed call notification. Taking a step toward the door, I looked over my shoulder at Warrick who hadn't moved an inch, "Well, I think your stomach agrees with me that it's time to go."

"We're taking one of my cars," he announced from his spot.

"Why?" I asked already in the hallway moving towards the living room.

It wasn't long before Warrick had closed the distance between us. He was helping me gather everything as he answered, "The snow's too deep for your car. The roads haven't been taken care of yet, so I don't want you to get stuck."

"Got it, boss," I said while I went to the bathroom to change into my clothes for the day and to freshen up a little bit. It was like Warrick was my shadow, following me into the spacious bathroom so he could get ready, too. I rolled my eyes, "Don't you have your own space to get ready in?"

He came up behind me, wrapping his arms around my waist as he leaned down to whisper in my ear, "And miss seeing you naked again? Not a chance, love."

Heat rose to my cheeks and any chance of responding was gone as I felt the words rush right out of my mouth. Warrick's lips barely brushed against my neck sending shivers down my spine, "You better start getting ready or we may have to change our plans for today."

"I think they'd understand if we were a little late," I smirked.

Warrick smiled then pulled me in for a long kiss, his fingers making the trek back down between my legs. His fingers moved in and out of me while his tongue traced my bottom lip. I moaned into his mouth giving him the perfect opportunity to deepen the kiss. Warrick could tell I was getting close and intensified the movements his fingers were making.

"Warrick, please," I moaned.

"Please what, love?"

"Don't make me beg, just make me come," I forced out as my head dropped back.

I felt his lips curl into a smile against my neck, "But I love to hear you beg."

He tried to slow down his pace, but I reached down, grabbing his arm to keep it moving at the pace I wanted it to. Warrick chuckled, "Be that way, love."

He removed my arm and after a few more moments, I was arching into him blinded by pleasure.

We took a second to catch our breaths, Warrick keeping me from returning the favor, "Rain check. We really won't be leaving here if I let you get your hands on me."

Sighing, I reached for my clothes on the counter, "I guess I'll listen just this once."

Warrick nipped my neck earning a giggle from me. Despite not wanting to, we both got ready and made our way to the garage. I settled in the passenger seat of Warrick's SUV admiring the high-tech features within it while trying not to let the thoughts of what we did last night and this morning consume me. I don't know what it is about this world and their cars, but the technology is leagues beyond what we have back home. Warrick joined me after getting everything tucked away in the back and we made our way out of the sheltered space into a winter wonderland. There was at least a foot of snow and the drive wasn't an easy one. Considering it was still snowing a good amount, I'm happy Warrick made the call to drive me. There's no way my car would've made it through all of this.

"Do you guys normally get a lot of snow in the winter?" I asked.

He chuckled, "Oh yeah. We usually get hammered with it, but once the weather starts warming up, it melts pretty fast."

It was so quiet outside this morning. There wasn't another soul in sight as we made the drive back to my house. I took in the peaceful, snowy landscape hardly able to contain my inner child knowing we're getting the perfect white Christmas. When we pulled up, Lou's car was already parked in the driveway. Warrick shifted into park then turned to face me, "There's the very real possibility we might get snowed in here. Think you can handle Lou and I under the same roof again?"

I shrugged, "It wasn't that long ago you two were sharing the same house. There's plenty of room in here, but you have to be the one that answers that question."

"I'll take the chance. Just wanted to give you some warning."

"Thanks," I said opening the car door to be met with a cold blast of air. I hugged my sweater closer to try to keep the warmth in as I made my way around to the back of the car to help

Warrick carry things. When I joined him, he was already unloading things. Surprised, I pointed to the neat pile of newly wrapped gifts, "When did you have time to do that?"

"I already had them in the car before you came over yesterday," he said, not missing a beat with his task.

I started loading up my arms, "Did you know if you'd be coming over?"

He shot me a quick smile over his shoulder, "No, but I wanted to make sure I got everyone something. It's part of the whole playing nice in the sandbox thing I promised you I'd do."

We managed to get everything in one trip. His admission to putting in the effort to be nice to my friends warmed my heart. Warrick really was trying to uphold his end of the deal, and even if this change was a result of him almost losing me, I don't know that I cared. I was just appreciative of him going the extra mile.

As soon as we walked through the door, we were smacked with the mouth-watering smell of Bev's freshly baked cinnamon rolls. We took off our shoes, adding them to the pile by the door to avoid tracking in any of the slush, and started making our way to the tree. "Merry Christmas!" I called out.

To my surprise, everyone returned the response. Chris, Joe, and Lou were on the couch playing video games while Bev was finishing things up in the kitchen and Jennie sat next to Chris watching them play. Jennie threw me a huge smile getting up to help us unload our arms as she said, "Well, look who finally decided to show up."

I waived her off avoiding eye contact, "Cut me some slack. You guys probably didn't wake up too long ago, either. At least you and Chris, that is."

Jennie moved her hands to her hips, a knowing smile replacing the one that was there a moment ago, "I know that look. It's a merry Christmas indeed."

Warrick came up behind me, putting a hand on my waist. The blush didn't start making its way on my cheeks until Chris looked over his shoulder at me before glancing at Jennie and returning his attention back to the game, "Oh, hey, Val. What are you talking about, J?"

Jennie wiggled her eyebrows leaning towards Chris and lowering her voice, "Val got laid."

I smacked a hand to my face. Warrick chuckled beside me. *Why is she so invested in my love life?* Before I had the chance to respond, Bev swooped in with two plates each holding a giant cinnamon roll, "Here, come join me in the kitchen."

I don't think she truly knew the level of appreciation I had for her timing. When Warrick and I settled at the island, I said, "Thank you, Bev. For breakfast and rescuing me back there."

"Of course, and this is a Christmas tradition. Besides, I more wanted to see Warrick's reaction."

Warrick looked from me to Bev, "Should I be worried about what's in these?"

Bev smiled, leaning against the island and throwing her hand towel over her shoulder, "Only if you want to be."

I put a hand on his arm, "She makes the best cinnamon rolls I've ever tasted. The only thing you have to be worried about is falling in love with her cooking. Seriously, take a bite."

"You two are the first to have them since everyone else is distracted," Bev said drawing her gaze to the group huddled in front of the TV. "They're like a bunch of teenagers."

I opened my mouth to add on to her statement when Warrick's moan distracted not only Bev and I, but the rest of the group, too. When he opened his eyes, his pupils were dilated and I could tell he was in love, "These are absolutely amazing."

Bev looked satisfied with that response, "Now I can see why you have a hard time saying no to sleeping with him if that's how he sounds."

I had to mark this day in history because Bev just got big, bad Warrick to blush. I burst out laughing while he scrambled to explain his reaction. Meanwhile, the group at the couch realized what was going on and Joe was the first one to speak up, "Hey, are you already serving up your cinnamon rolls? Without us?"

"I think she's perfectly happy with letting us starve," Jennie joked.

Lou started making his way over to join us, "I don't know what you guys are waiting for, but I'm going to help myself otherwise I don't think I'll get any with Warrick's reaction to them."

My eyes widened realizing Lou actually joked with his mortal enemy instead of immediately going into defensive mode. I glanced between Warrick and him to check if this a genuine joke or the start of something hostile, but nothing ever escalated. Warrick just nodded his head as if Lou had a point, "If it were up to me, they'd be gone in a heartbeat."

"Who are you guys right now?" I asked still too stunned to focus on anything else.

Lou shrugged, "It's a holiday. I can be nice for a day."

"You know I already made that promise to you, love," Warrick added on.

"Shit, it needs to be Christmas every day."

"Does that mean we'd get to have these every day?" Lou asked with a mouthful of food. "I don't think I've ever tasted anything like this."

"Well, there's plenty," Bev turned around to grab a plate full of them. "There was more than enough time last night after Joe and I left the clubs early. We couldn't quite fall asleep, so I kept my hands busy."

Joe gave her a quick kiss on the cheek, "Thanks, babe."

Our playful banter went back and forth until everyone was full from breakfast. We made our way over to the tree to start opening presents after that, each of us trying to fight off the sleep that was threatening to overtake us all before we could do anything. Bev was the first to recover from the cinnamon roll coma and started handing out presents. For having a short timeline to get everything ready, there was more than enough giving going around. You would've thought we had months to plan for this. Even Warrick and Lou had a stack of gifts begging to be opened.

"What are we waiting for?" Jennie asked. "Let's dig in!"

Tearing paper combined with oohs and aahs filled the room. There was a lot of laughter at some of the gag gifts, many hugs going around, and a whole lot more thank yous as each gift was revealed. Despite everything we had faced up to this point, Christmas had a way of shoving that all aside and replacing it with joy. Warrick even leaned over to me at one point, whispering, "Now I know why you love this holiday. People are so happy."

"Generally, yeah. It's nice to be able to push aside the day-to-day things for a little bit and let your inner child come out."

Bev and I cleaned everything up while Joe started passing around glasses of wine. Christmas cookies were being shared and the smell of Christmas dinner wafted throughout the space. Warrick ended up taking Lou's spot for the game they were playing while Lou worked on dinner in the kitchen. I wandered over to see if he needed any help. I was leaning on the island as I said, "Thank you for being so civil today."

"Don't worry about it," he said moving from the stove to the oven to check on things. "Something's off about him again today. The same scent of fear I caught back in the other world is coming off him in waves."

I noticed Lou was talking quietly in the hopes of avoiding curious ears. I quickly glanced over my shoulder towards the couch, happy Warrick was so engaged in the game that he didn't have a clue we were talking about him. Returning my attention back to Lou, I said, "He had a phone call this morning that upset him, but he didn't give me too many details. I'm worried something really bad has happened and he's shouldering the problem."

Lou was leaning in closer to me now so I could hear him a little better, "Something I've told myself that wouldn't hurt for you to remind yourself about is that he's been having to go through a lot of this alone. Up until now, he was the only one trying to figure out how to combat this war. It's helped me explain some of his actions and temporarily brush aside our differences."

I was shocked. When it came to Warrick, Lou never acted this mature. He was always the first one to let Warrick get under his skin. When I recovered, I told Lou, "I got more information out of him last night, by the way. I'll tell you the specifics when we have a quiet moment in the pizza place, but I don't think you're going to be super happy about it. Although, it might clear some stuff up for you, too. Just be ready to go through the emotions."

"Odd," Lou started. He opened his mouth to say more, but a timer interrupted us and he was back to checking on the food he was cooking. While he was busy with the food, Lou's phone lit up as new text message came in. Curious, I leaned over to see Holly's name but no other details. I picked his phone up when he turned around, "Holly, huh?"

"You're allowed to date who you want and so am I," Lou reached for the phone.

I pulled it back so it was just out of his reach, "So you're dating her?"

"I'm not here to be interrogated about this, Val," Lou reached for the phone, this time grabbing it. "We only went on one date and she's been blowing up my phone trying to get a second one."

"Isn't she a lot younger than you?" I asked, genuinely curious.

He started typing out a response then said, "Which is why she isn't getting a second date. Although, she was pretty good in bed."

"Hold on," I put a hand up. "You slept with her, too?"

"Who did Lou sleep with?" Warrick casually asked, pulling up a seat next to where I was standing.

I looked at Warrick from the corners of my eyes, "Your new assistant."

His eyes nearly popped out of his head, "Really? Why on earth would you do that?"

"And this is why I didn't say anything," Lou mumbled. He straightened up, "Look, I've been lonely for a while and needed a release that wasn't just my hand. She seemed pretty nice when she came into the restaurant the other day, so I thought I'd give her a shot. Turns out she's not my type, but I was able to enjoy the feeling of a woman's body for a little bit."

"I could've told you that. Next time, ask me my thoughts and I can probably steer you in the direction of someone who's more your speed," Warrick said before taking a long sip from his wine glass.

"I never thought I'd see the day where you two were actually working together," I observed.

Lou rolled his eyes, "I can handle my own love life, but thank you for the offer, Warrick. You might want to know that she was asking a lot of questions about you and what your company does, though."

That stopped Warrick in his tracks. He calmly set down his glass staring into its contents, "What did you tell her?"

I could immediately tell something was up by the sudden shift in Warrick's demeanor. His warm and cheerful voice from only moments ago was now the typical cold and calculating one I've grown used to hearing. It wasn't hard to pick up on the fact he was starting to lose his faith in his new assistant between how he's acting now and how he was acting last night.

"Nothing," Lou answered, watching Warrick carefully. "I redirected the conversation because the last thing I want to talk about is your company. Especially on a date when I'm trying to get to know the person sitting across from me."

I couldn't ignore how Lou's tone had changed to match Warrick's. It was like there was an unspoken language being shared between the two and I was being left out of the party.

Warrick lifted his gaze to meet Lou's, "Watch your back with her. She's been getting too nosey about things, especially the war. One of my team members almost spilled the beans and now she's even more curious."

"That explains the text," Lou said handing his phone over to Warrick.

I held up my hands as my thoughts spilled out, "Hold on. Lou's now willingly handing over his phone to the person he despises the most while Warrick is looking out for him. Are you sure we're not in another dimension or something? We actually came back to the werewolf world, right? You guys literally go at each other's throats every chance you get, but now you're acting like you've worked together your entire lives or something."

They both looked at me, surprised. Lou was the first one to speak since Warrick was studying the messages on the phone, "Believe it or not, we have acted civil before. I worked for him, remember? Besides, something really weird is going on, but I can't quite figure it out. I'm not that proud to admit it, but Warrick is a little smarter than I am when it comes to the head games department."

I crossed my arms, "Please, fill me in, then."

Lou turned around to pull the mouth-watering roast out of the oven and shut off the burners. He readied the plates to be filled then responded, "Warrick has been working closely with Holly since he's been back in a way I've never seen him work with an assistant before regardless of how new she is. That's the first flag for me. The second one was the interrogation she put me through on our date trying to get any details about Warrick that she could, especially the top secret stuff the company is working on, which means she's fishing for information. She even mentioned that it wasn't Warrick who directly hired her since he was out of town. She basically showed up the same day his old assistant left, and since there wasn't anyone willing to make the decision, they told her to start taking meeting notes. That's how she got her job. No one would bother to talk about that shit on a first date if they're genuinely interested in the person they're on the date with. The last red flag is the questions I've been getting from her via text."

"Change your number," Warrick said.

"Will someone please fill in the blanks for me?" I asked.

Lou started carving the giant roast he cooked up and started serving the plates, "Basically, Holly's shifty and no one knows where she came from. She's clearly trying to get specific details about the company and what exactly Warrick is doing. Warrick's had suspicions the minute he got back here which is why he's been working as hard as he has. He wants to keep an eye on her. What I don't know is what exactly his suspicions are. By the way, I have a new phone coming. She's not going to be getting my number and I have no intentions on hooking up with her again, either."

I turned to Warrick, "Care to share what your suspicions are?"

He handed the phone back to Lou, "Thank you for keeping things quiet and trying to steer her away from her questions. I have a hunch she's been sent to spy on me."

"This sounds like the plot to a movie," I noted.

Warrick turned to face me, "I don't care what it sounds like, it's the truth. Anyways, that's enough about this topic tonight. I don't want to be the one who takes away from the spirit of the holiday."

I studied him for a moment longer watching as the defensiveness was slowly replaced with the happiness from earlier. Lou also changed his demeanor as he let everyone know dinner had been served. Everyone happily sat around the table with their plates piled high with food, talking about the things that have made them thankful and filled with joy. Meanwhile, I was sitting there processing everything Lou and Warrick just said about Holly. I knew Warrick had an idea as to who sent her, but he wasn't willing to share that information. My bet is on this "enemy" whose identity still remains a secret, and I knew Lou was thinking the same thing. This would explain why Warrick went off on her last night. He's feeling tense about letting someone that close to him when he doesn't even really know them.

When everyone was looking at me expectantly, I realized I had missed a question. Setting my fork down, I asked, "What did I miss?"

"We were all talking about something that made us really happy in the last week leading up to Christmas. Chris and I have been able to go on actual dates without having to look over our shoulders. Bev and Joe have been getting back into their hobbies of baking and gaming, respectively. Lou's happy to be back in the groove at the pizza place. Warrick's was getting to spend some quality time with you last night, which we could all tell was what he needed judging by his facial expression when you two walked in this morning. Now, it's your turn," Jennie explained.

"Ah. Well, is it cheating if I have a few things?" I asked.

"Nope!" Jennie answered.

"Alright, the first thing is seeing each of you truly smiling again and seeming to enjoy yourselves. The second thing was getting to talk to my dad last night, even if it was brief and mostly one-sided. The last thing was getting to enjoy some time with Warrick last night. You should've seen his place. He went all out on the decorations," I said. With each word, I felt a smile crawling across my face.

"You got to talk to your dad? How?" Jennie screeched.

"That's amazing, Val," Chris said.

"Yeah it is! How is your dad doing, by the way?" Bev asked.

I took a sip of wine to try to steady myself a little bit, "Warrick has some crazy tech setup that allows for a connection between our worlds. He seems to be doing alright. The war is definitely taking a toll on him, but at least he confirmed what Warrick said."

Warrick reached under the table to put a reassuring hand on my knee while Jennie chimed in, "I'm sure you don't want to spend all night rehashing the conversation, but it does make me happy you were able to talk to him. Seems like he managed to clear a few things up."

I only nodded as I dived right back into my meal. I took a couple of bites, everyone else doing the same, then looked at Lou, "Thank you for cooking everything. It's delicious."

A chorus of agreement followed and we all held our glasses up. I looked around the table, "Here's to all of us surviving hell and still getting to celebrate."

Glasses clanked together then Jennie did what she always does best: lightened the mood and conversation by sharing embarrassing stories. We were all in stitches by the time she reached her last tale and I noticed we had gone through a couple of bottles of wine already. I glanced around the room again wishing this moment would never end, but even I knew that from this point on, it would be an uphill battle.

Chapter 19

I finished cleaning the dishes while everyone else moved on to a round of Monopoly. It had been far too long since this place was filled with the sounds of constant laughter, sadness creeping in at the memory of our friends' weekend. Even then, the people here hadn't been this happy, but I wasn't going to say anything to ruin the mood.

Warrick snapped me out of the daze I was in by rushing up and scooping me in his arms. I let out a surprised squeal as he spun around finally stopping in the living room. We were both dizzy from the combination of the wine and the spins, so we fell on the couch. Warrick started genuinely laughing bringing my own laughter out of its shell.

"Hey, you two," Joe started. "If you're going to get naked, at least take it upstairs."

That only made us laugh even harder. Warrick sat up to respond to Joe, "That's saying a lot coming from someone who was just making out moments ago."

I lifted my head up to see his reaction, perfectly timing it so I could see the blush on his and Bev's cheeks. He nodded acknowledging Warrick's point. Lou leaned back in his chair jumping into the conversation, "Warrick, I don't think I've ever heard you like this. Are you under a spell? In some sort of danger? Just say the word and I'll get Val out of here."

Surprisingly, Warrick leaned into the joke, "Please, rescue me. I don't know what she's done, but she won't let me be my brooding, normal self. She's turned me into some sort of loving creature. It hurts!"

"And I can never let you go," I said, wrapping my arms around him. It was hard to explain this feeling of being in the present while also feeling like I'm watching from the outside. This moment in time felt so undeniably normal that it hurt knowing something bad could come and ruin this at any time. I caressed Warrick's cheek, butterflies wreaking havoc on me as he leaned into my touch while closing his eyes.

"I think it's time to go upstairs," I whispered. "Grab a bottle of wine."

"Yes, love," he said in a robotic tone. Clearly, he wasn't done with the joke from earlier. As he stood up, he looked towards Lou, "She's doing it again, commanding my every move."

The moment Lou opened his mouth, he leaned too far back in the chair and fell to the ground. He had a dazed look on his face before he was consumed with laughter. When we all realized he was okay, we joined in. Nothing like a classic fall to round out the night.

Warrick clasped my hand to lead the way upstairs. I shouted goodnight to everyone then wished them all a merry Christmas one more time. Once on the landing, Warrick swept me into his arms to carry me to my room, "Can every night be like this, love?"

"You have no idea how I wish I could make that happen," I responded. "Maybe one day."

"Maybe one day," he echoed, gently placing me on the floor of my room. He closed the door while I opened the bottle of wine. We each took a sip then turned some Christmas music on to slowly dance around the room to. It didn't take long for us to succumb to what we were wanting, not able to keep our hands off each other. We were more passionate than last night, making sure we filled every need that's been neglected.

We woke up the next morning a tangle of limbs. My mouth was bone dry from all the wine, my head slightly throbbing. I glanced around the room to get my bearings. The sun was fully up reminding me to be thankful we drew the curtains last night. Warrick's arm was draped protectively over me, his nose buried in my hair. Judging by the sound of his breaths, he was still very asleep. I didn't dare move a muscle to disturb this peaceful moment. Rather, I settled in a little more relishing in the continuation of something normal.

"Love," I heard Warrick mumble behind me. "I need to get up."

Confused, I said, "I'm not stopping you."

His arm tightened around me somehow pulling me closer to him, "But you are. I'm too damn comfortable in this bed to want to move."

I tried to wiggle away from him, but he wouldn't let me, "When I try to help you, you stop me."

I felt a little nip on my shoulder. I managed to roll over to face him, bringing my hand up to brush his hair out of his face. His glacial eyes were half open and he sported a soft grin, "I could lay here forever."

"Trust me, I could, too."

We stayed there a little while longer before Warrick finally persuaded himself to get up to use the bathroom. I hugged the blankets around me tighter instantly missing the warmth of him. The faint sound of a phone buzzing got me to prop up on my elbows. I took a look at my screen to see nothing there, so I scooted over to where Warrick's phone was. Frowning, I skimmed the message from Holly asking about a specific lab division. I was so distracted I didn't hear Warrick approaching. He carefully took the phone out of my hand, "She's incredibly persistent and annoying."

"Why does she keep bugging you?" I asked feeling bold.

"She's getting desperate," he started while crawling into bed. I cuddled into him as he continued, "She hasn't been getting clear answers and now she's feeling the pressure. The one who ordered her to work for me is probably getting impatient. Holly also hasn't had any luck going through other avenues either, like Lou."

"Do you think you have any other moles in your company?"

Warrick chuckled, "Probably, but they haven't shown their faces yet. If they do, they won't be around for too much longer."

"Why don't you fire her?" I asked. It might be the obvious question, but it was one that wouldn't stop dancing in my mind.

"I have no reason to right now. She's performing as expected, I haven't had to officially reprimand her for anything. If I fired her, it would be too suspicious at this point. The last thing I need to do is sound any alarms and bring the war here sooner than expected, but trust me, the thought has crossed my mind," he explained casually.

At least he can follow some standards when it comes running a company. We laid there letting the silence settle around us while I debated about asking him another obvious question. Finally working up the courage, I tilted my chin up to him, "She works for the enemy, right?"

"Yeah," Warrick sighed. "She does."

"Still not ready to tell me who this mysterious enemy is?" I blurted clearly still riding the high from the recent burst of courage.

He only shook his head, a shadow crossing his features. His silence indicated the conversation was over, so I looked back in front of me trying to clear my mind of the barrage of questions threatening to burst through the dam. Thankfully, the rumbling of his stomach stopped the train of thought. I got out of bed throwing on some pajamas, "Ready for breakfast?"

"Yeah," he answered quietly while also getting dressed. Warrick was avoiding eye contact, immediately filling me with guilt for prodding on a topic that is still very sensitive for him. I stepped over to where he was standing, reaching out to him, "I'm sorry. I should know better at this point than to try and get you talk about something you're not ready to. It's just eating me ali – "

Warrick brought his hand up to mine, cutting me off, "This one is not on you. All I ask is for a little patience, love. I'll talk when I'm ready, there's just a lot I have to work through before I get to that point."

I nodded my head to show him I understood then led the way downstairs. Jennie and Lou were the only two sitting at the island talking in hushed tones. When I cleared my throat, they snapped up ending their conversation. Jennie painted a force smile on her face instantly raising my suspicions, "Good morning, love birds."

"What are you two up to?" I asked slowly.

"Just catching up on some things," Lou answered a little too quickly. He flinched realizing his response didn't do anything to convince me to move on. "Look, Val. We were talking about Holly."

"Funny enough, so were we. Care to share?" Warrick asked cooly from behind me.

Jennie brought her coffee to her lips leaving Lou to deal with Warrick's question. I looked between Jennie and Lou, placing a hand on Warrick's chest so I could get my question out, "Jennie, do you know Holly, too?"

She gave me a hesitant nod, "She joined us at one of the clubs. I liked her for about the first hour, then she got annoying with all her nonstop questions."

"What did you tell her?" Warrick asked, his anger creeping into the end of the question.

"Chill. I didn't tell her anything. She kept going on and on about your company, so I told her she was ruining my fun and left. There was another day she came into the pizza shop when we were there, Val was gone, and she acted like we were best friends after practically throwing herself at Lou," Jennie paused to take another sip of coffee. "Lou was just catching me up on his love life and letting me know to be careful around Holly."

Warrick studied Jennie for a moment then asked, "What else were you two talking about?"

She narrowed her eyes a little. Lou stiffened and I don't blame him. Warrick was reminding us he was always one step ahead. He apparently knew enough about Jennie to pick up on her tells. The only way I knew she was withholding any information was because I've known her for years. I shot a quick glance at Lou who gave a slight shake of his head. Apparently, there was no way Warrick should have been able to pick up on what they were talking about when we came downstairs, so I turned back to Warrick. He wasn't breaking eye contact with Jennie which meant I wasn't going to be able to pick up on his silent messages.

"Fine," Jennie huffed. "You win. Lou was bringing me up to speed on your conversations last night while he cooked dinner. It might actually be beneficial for you three to loop the rest of us in on what's happening. You don't know what skills we can bring to the table. We have nothing going on while we're here, so let us help."

"I think I know a little more than you'd like me to," Warrick said crossing his arms.

"What does he mean?" Jennie asked me.

I started nervously tapping my fingers on the island, "Well, he dug up a whole bunch of things on me. I wouldn't be surprised if he did the same for all of you guys."

She shot a glare towards Warrick. Before she could say anything, Lou leaned in to join the conversation, his alpha voice coming out, "Look, we could all drop the tempers a little bit. I know it's an invasion of privacy, but we have to move on. We're not going to be changing anything that's in the past. Warrick, you just got a few more hands to help you get ready for whatever you need, so make use of them. Who knows? We could probably help you reach your goals before your deadlines."

Warrick leaned back in his chair considering what Lou said. Jennie also relaxed a little which meant Lou said the right thing.

"Okay," Warrick said.

"Okay what?" I asked waiting for him to start diving into what he needed my friends for.

"Jennie, can you become friends with Holly? I need eyes on her, but don't make it too obvious. I need to know where she's going when she's not at the office, who she's talking to, and any other details you could give me. Again, don't make it too obvious. Have Chris join you," Warrick ordered. He turned to me, "I need you to keep resting and relaxing. You've gone through enough and you're not going to provide any sort of benefits if you're not at full strength. Lou, I'll send you research that's falling behind schedule, if you're okay with that?"

Lou gave a quick nod even though he didn't look happy about it. I guess this was his way of showing Jennie that if he could help Warrick out, then she could, too. Warrick rounded out his grocery list of things as he said, "Joe and Bev can keep doing what they're doing. There's enough on their plates."

"What do you mean?" I asked.

"Later, love," Warrick dismissed me. *How is Warrick in the position to know more about my circle than I do? I have been distracted with other things, but that's no excuse.*

"So, it's settled, then," Lou said. "We each have our roles. We'll carry on with that and report back regularly. Want to use the pizza place? There shouldn't be any prying ears."

Warrick considered that offer for a second thinking about how he was going to respond. He put a hand on my knee as he said, "I'm good with that. We meet every Thursday evening after close except for full moons."

Lou stuck out his hand for him and Warrick to shake on it. Warrick hesitated. I'm sure this was a lot for him even though he'll never admit that. It's been a long time since him and Lou actually worked together on something. They've spent so many years warring against one another and now they have to switch their mindsets. Props to them for trying, but I didn't let myself overlook yet another sign of how serious this war is. Warrick shook Lou's hand officially putting the deal in place.

Bev and Joe finally made their way downstairs looking as happy as ever. Jennie took this as her cue to start getting the leftover cinnamon rolls reheated for us all to dive into. There was no mention of the conversation we just had. I figured Jennie and Chris would bring them up to speed soon enough, so I didn't bother. Joe and Bev were too busy reminiscing about past holidays using this chance to share embarrassing stories of me when I drank a little more than I should've. Warrick and Lou were soaking up every moment of it. *No surprise there.*

The sun set and board games came out. Jennie leaned over to me, whispering, "This has been such a nice break from things."

I responded, keeping my voice low, "I can't remember the last time something felt so normal. Everyone may not be here, but this is what I wanted for that friend's weekend."

She gave me a kind smile, "I know, Val. Me too. What did Warrick mean about Joe and Bev earlier?"

"No idea, but when I find out, I'll let you know," I said shrugging my shoulders. "By the way, where's Chris?"

Jennie smiled, shaking her head, "Taking it easy. He went a little too hard last night."

Warrick nudged my knee with his, "Your turn, love."

The way he looked at me made it clear he heard our quick sidebar conversation. I blushed a little then passed the torch over to Jennie for her to take her turn. It was Warrick's turn to lean in, talking ever more quietly than what Jennie was just doing, "Since you two are so curious, they've started trying for kids."

My eyes widened as I turned more towards him, "How do you know that?"

"Believe it or not, Bev likes me. I've also heard them going to town in their room and joked with Joe a little bit. For some reason, they're both willing to share with me," he said giving my knee a squeeze with his hand. "Wait to tell Jennie until later."

That was big for them. They've been on the fence about having kids for a long time, but I wonder what made them finally make a decision. Especially with everything up in the air right now. They don't even know if their home is still standing or even when they're going to be returning back home. They know we're hopping worlds which would make it hard to get the care Bev would need when she is pregnant.

Our game wrapped up after a couple more rounds now that Chris has rejoined us, and as if on cue, Bev and Joe went upstairs for the night. When the coast was clear, Warrick gave me a nod and I whipped around to Jennie, "There's news."

"Is this about Bev and Joe?" she asked with her eyebrows raised.

"Yup," I slowly nodded. "They're trying for a baby."

Her mouth dropped open before being covered by her hand, "Shut up! I'm so excited for them! But how is this going to work being here and jumping to different places?"

"I was wondering the same thing," I said, settling into the couch.

The rest of them joined me, Warrick handing me a glass of wine as he said, "I think I can offer some insight into this. It sounds like they've been having a lot of conversations with Raf and they're looking into buying a house here."

I put a hand out, "Hold on, so they're serious about living here when they haven't been here for very long?"

Lou jumped in, catching me by surprise, "They love this place. Bev has been going on and on about how wonderful it is here and how normal it feels compared to back in your world."

"Wow, I've really been missing out on a lot," I trailed off studying the glass in my hands. I was starting to feel like an unsupportive friend completely caught up in what's going on with me. I've rarely had a chance to talk about this stuff with them.

Jennie put a hand on my shoulder, "Stop, Val. I know what you're thinking. You're fine. There's been a lot of things you've had to balance. This is all news to me, too. Is it the same for you Chris?"

Chris scratched his head a little bit, "Yeah, kind of. Joe mentioned liking this place a lot and asked me if we would consider living here, but that was it."

"So, why have they been mostly talking to you two?" I asked, glancing between Lou and Warrick.

"Maybe because we're the two in charge? We've lived here our whole lives? We have connections that can help them meet their goals? There's a lot of possibilities," Lou said.

Warrick nodded, "Exactly. We've talked about how to get them in a house even though they don't carry our currency and have hardly been here. Raf already knows them, so they have an in with medical stuff. They know what the dangers are here and since we view them as part of our inner circles, they feel confident they're safe."

"Huh," I pondered. "I never thought of it that way. I mean, I haven't really thought of where I'd end up when this is all said and done."

Warrick shot me a worried look. I put a reassuring hand on his knee, "Don't worry, it'll probably be here. What I mean is that I've been focused on taking things one step at a time. I haven't given a whole lot of thought on what life will be like after this war is over. Who knows how long it'll take?"

I watched as Warrick relaxed a little more, but there were still hints of worry left. I kept my hand where it was, leaning into him a little more when I turned towards Jennie and Chris, "Have you guys given any thought about what you want to do when this war is finally over?"

Jennie and Chris gave each other a quick look then their facial expressions were overtaken with warmth and love. Jennie shifted a little when Chris looked back toward the rest of us, "Well, we were actually planning on keeping it quiet for a little while, but now's the right time I guess."

I had a hunch as to what was coming, but I didn't want to steal their thunder. I could tell with the way they were sneaking around, all over each other, and the non-stop smiles that they got engaged yesterday. Chris looked so proud and I knew Jennie was itching to get started on wedding planning.

"The right time for what?" Lou asked interrupting my thoughts of what bridesmaid dress I'd be forced to wear.

"We're engaged!" Jennie squealed shoving her hand in our direction so we could get a glimpse of the giant rock Chris put on her finger.

"Congratulations!" I shouted jumping to my feet to give them both a hug. "I'm so happy for you two. You're honestly such a great couple and I'm not surprised at all. I knew it was a only a matter of time."

"Thank you, Val," Chris beamed. "What better timing than on Christmas?"

"Congratulations," Lou and Warrick said in unison. I happened to catch a glimpse of Lou's reaction seeing he wasn't the most thrilled and Warrick wasn't selling his feelings either. I gave them a frown when I was confident I was out of the couple's line of sight.

"What are we saying congratulations for?" Bev asked, startling all of us.

In all the excitement, none of had known that Bev and Joe snuck back downstairs. I rushed over to grab a couple of glasses and filled them with wine before handing it over to them, "Chris and Jennie are engaged."

"Amazing, congratulations you two!" Bev exclaimed, raising her glass.

We all joined in sending our well wishes to the newly engaged couple before downing our wine. I moved to the kitchen to grab another bottle for us all to share and put together an array of snacks and desserts for us to enjoy when Warrick wrapped his arms around my waist to hug me from behind. I leaned my head back, "Hi, you."

"Hi, love," he mumbled into my hair.

"What's up?"

"All this love in the air is making me want to be close to you."

I turned so I could look at him, "You sure? Because you didn't seem too thrilled back there."

He lowered his voice so it was barely audible, his brows furrowing, "I'm happy for them, but I don't think Jennie and Chris are going to work out. Plus, I haven't been a fan of him."

"What do you mean?" I asked mirroring Warrick's facial expression.

Warrick leaned in to pretend he was nibbling on my ear and continued, "This stays between us, but I think there's something between Jennie and Lou that Chris doesn't see. Anyways, he's jumping the gun. Lou was telling me earlier that he heard them having a disagreement yesterday morning and Chris popped the question to get them to stop. If you watch him, he's been checking his phone every time Jennie turns away from him and sneaks off to the basement for a while. Something's off and I don't quite trust him."

"When did you and Lou have a chance to talk one-on-one?" I asked apparently hung up on that tidbit.

"Earlier this morning before you woke up. We snuck downstairs to talk about the plan we all agreed to because I needed to make sure he would be okay with what I was going to propose. When we were down there, we heard someone heading our way so we hid. Turns out it was Chris chatting someone up on his phone and I don't think it was Jennie, even though it should've been by the words coming out of his mouth," he finished. Warrick pulled his head back placing a kiss on my forehead as I tried my hardest to keep the shock from my face. There was no way I could show any signs of this when Jennie was so happy. She deserved this happiness. The last thing I wanted to do was burst her bubble.

Warrick pulled back searching my eyes, "Not a word of this, okay? There's nothing we can do right now without getting more details."

"But they've known each other forever, Warrick, since they were kids. I don't believe he's doing this to her. And wasn't he sleeping all morning? What you're saying doesn't make sense" I protested.

"Love, it could be heightened emotions given what they've had to go through. He was alone, she was there, and they naturally developed into something more than friends. Now he's in a place where he can relax and where his phone can connect to his old world. It's a perfect storm. Just look out for her, okay?" he said still watching me closely.

I nodded my head letting out a breath, "Okay, I'll try. Shit, I really need to be around for them more."

Warrick rubbed my arms then pulled me into a hug, "You will be. You, me, and Lou will have some time to talk about all this one on one, and I mean *all* of this."

Another kiss was placed on my forehead then Warrick reached around me to grab the platter of food I put together. I grabbed the bottle of wine I rescued from the fridge along with another one before following him back to our place on the couch. Surprisingly, we fell into an easy rhythm, but I couldn't stop thinking about Chris' potential infidelity. When we made it back up to my room, I looked at Warrick, "You were right. He looked at his damn phone every time Jennie's back was turned. Chris was more distracted than I thought he would be with being newly engaged and all."

Warrick opened his mouth to say something when a knock forced him to close it. I yanked my door open finding Lou on the other side. I cocked my head to the side, "What's up?"

"I'm assuming Warrick told you?" he asked flinching at the harshness in my tone.

I only nodded my head then moved out of the way to let him in. Lou ran his hand through his hair then leaned against the wall near the balcony door. He looked just about how I felt: pissed. I closed the door moving away from it in case anyone happened to be listening then asked them both in an inpatient tone, "So, why didn't either of you two say something until now?"

"Because nothing is for certain yet," Lou said avoiding eye contact.

Warrick leaned back on the bed on his elbows, "Lou and I hatched up another plan to handle this."

"During your little secret talk this morning?"

Lou flinched, "Yeah. Warrick, care to share?"

"Sure," Warrick said pretending to pick at a non-existent fluff on the comforter. "I'm going to hack into his phone and monitor things. It's an easy practice. Ethical? No, but it's not the first time I've done it and won't be the last. I just need to get Chris to part from his phone for more than five seconds."

"You guys are acting so nonchalant about all of this. My best friend is engaged to someone who's actively cheating on her all because he wanted a way to get her to shut up. Who's to say we can trust him to do what we need him to do with the Holly situation?" I asked curious if they would be able to explain their way out of this one.

Lou finally brought his grey eyes up to meet mine, "There's no reason to doubt his loyalty to anything related to the war."

"You sound awfully confident," I snorted.

"He's afraid of us, love," Warrick noted, making me whip my head in his direction. "He's afraid that if he doesn't do his part with helping us out, he won't be able to get back to all his multiple lovers at home. He's also afraid we'll kill him."

I rolled my eyes, "Oh sure, but when it comes to Jennie, he doesn't care because he doesn't think you're going to do anything about that."

"Exactly. He thinks that we care way more about you than her. Unfortunately, Chris isn't the brightest. What he didn't factor in is that we happen to care a lot about her because *you* care a lot about her," Warrick said leaning forward to rest his arms on his knees.

"We'll take care of this, Val," Lou jumped back into the conversation. "Don't say a word about this to Bev and especially not Jennie. Keep an eye on things, let us know if stuff starts escalating, but this is something we don't need you to intervene on. You'll know when the time comes.

"Ugh!" I threw up my arms. "Fine, I guess. Thank you for at least telling me what's going on."

"I know it's not fair, love, but things will get sorted out before they sign on the dotted line," Warrick assured me. He quickly switched to his business side as he said, "Now that the three of us are alone, though, let's walk through what needs to happen tomorrow. The full moon is the night after, so that's going to slow some things down. However, I was thinking if Lou would be so gracious as to give you the night off to go partying with Chris, Jennie, Bev, and Joe. Jennie needs to invite Holly and you clearly need some time with your friends so you don't miss any other major life updates."

"You're starting to impact my business, Warrick," Lou informed him not exactly in the happiest tone. "But, I guess I can let her have a dinner shift off. Val, I'm going to need you to run the place on the day of the full moon and for the next couple of days after that while I recover."

"That doesn't exactly seem like a fair trade off," I started, but quickly changed where I was going with that once I saw the look on his face. I rolled my eyes, "But, I'll do it."

Warrick clapped his hands together, "This will be a good way to kick off the plan. Now, let's finish enjoying a night off from the craziness. Thanks, Lou."

Picking up on his dismissal, Lou gave a quick salute then made his exit. I turned to face Warrick, "I hope you have it all figured out."

"Believe me, I do," he said, his cocky smirk making its way across his handsome face. "Now, get over here, love."

Chapter 20

When I woke up the next morning, Warrick was staring out the balcony window. He came to sit on the bed as soon as he saw I was awake, "Good morning, love. I'm going to have to head out soon to get to the office, but I didn't want to leave you before you woke up. Are you doing alright?"

I rubbed the sleep out of my eyes taking in the sight of Warrick wearing his typical business attire. It was hard not to want to rip those clothes off him when they hugged his body so well. I shook my head to clear those thoughts and hopefully wake up a little more. I wanted to tell him that of course I was alright, but then it occurred to me that he was asking how I was doing after the news about Jennie and Chris. He wanted to make sure I wasn't going to run my mouth the minute he walked out of the door.

"Yeah, I'm alright. Don't worry, I won't say anything. I won't even act like I know anything," I said doing my best to give him a reassuring smile.

"Call or text me if anything changes," Warrick said as he leaned in, tilting my chin up so our lips could meet in a passionate, goodbye kiss. Then, he was gone.

I threw myself back on my bed, arms stretched out as I watched the ceiling. I had to give myself a pep talk before heading down there or I was going to ruin everything. I had to trust that Lou and Warrick would take care of everything.

A light knock sounded on my door snapping me out of my thoughts. I pulled the covers up even though I was decent, "Come in."

Lou poked his head in, "I saw Warrick head out."

I cocked an eyebrow, "So you're trying to sneak in here, why?"

"I wanted to check in on you," he finished letting himself in, closing the door softly behind him before settling on the edge of the bed.

I nervously played with my fingers, "Warrick mentioned something last night I thought was interesting."

"What's that?"

"That there might be something between you and Jennie. Is there?" I blurted.

Lou sighed running his hand through his already messy hair, "I mean, I like her, but I don't know that there's anything going on between us in that way. We have spent a lot of time together, but Chris has always been there. Also, if you remember, she was the one who made a move on me in the last world we were in because she was mad at Chris, so I don't think there's actually anything there."

"But, you're not ruling it out?" I prodded.

"I don't know, Val," Lou said shaking his head. He let out a small laugh, "My feelings are not a place I want to spend a lot of time in right now. They're a mess."

"Sorry," I said casting my gaze back down to my hands. I definitely played a part in that.

"Don't worry about it," he said. "Are you ready for what's about to happen?"

I noticed the change in topic, so I dropped all the other questions running through my mind about him and Jennie. I sighed, "Do I really have any other choice? I mean, I knew I didn't like Holly, but I thought that was because she was trying to throw herself at Warrick and then you. I had no idea she could be tied with the enemy. I know that Warrick's stress about the war has gone up recently which is not a good thing."

"Speaking of Warrick, you mentioned you had more to tell me," Lou said.

"Oh, that's right. Well, I first need you to promise me that you won't go taking your anger out on Warrick," I started.

His eyes slightly narrowed, "I promise."

I straightened my shoulders, "Okay ... Warrick has been focusing a lot of his company's resources on research for the war and he has an inner circle looking into weaknesses of the enemy. Basically, he's looking into ways he can do permanent damage since the enemy is a wolf. You should know how hard it is to do any real damage. Anyways, the weapons he's been using against you haven't been because he wants to eliminate you or hurt you, it's because there's no one more powerful that he can test them on. Unfortunately, that meant you had to become his test subject so he could get the best results."

I could see the rage starting to bubble up, but he swallowed it back down, "You mean to tell me that he's been using me as a way to test his research? That all the pain, the trauma, the attacks, everything has purely been so he can get an upper-hand?"

"I told you that you weren't going to like what I had to say," I reminded him. "And remember, you promised me you wouldn't take it out on him."

"I know," Lou slowly nodded his head. "I don't promise what my wolf will do, though, and before you get all defensive, we'll be fine. There might be a little bit of a scuffle, but nothing life-threatening. Actually, I appreciated you clearing the air a little bit. It helps me know what to expect from him."

"I can appreciate you being a little more mature about this," I told him.

"I have my ways of getting revenge," Lou said as he faced me. I wasn't surprised to see the eyes of his wolf staring back at me indicating how pissed he was. I also couldn't help but feel like I was now a target as part of his revenge plot. *I better give Warrick a head's up later that I told Lou about the weapons.*

Lou clenched his eyes shut while taking a few calming breaths. My stomach growling interrupted his meditation, and when he snapped his eyes open to look at me, I shrugged, "Didn't mean to stop you from what you were doing. My stomach on the other hand has no respect for these kinds of things."

He at least grinned, shaking his head, "Come on, let's go eat."

I waited for him to move before I got out of bed to wrap myself in my robe. No way was I going to be making any sort of movements with his wolf so close to the surface, especially when a full moon wasn't far away. Each movement I made was being carefully scrutinized reminding me how dangerous being around an angry wolf could be. I stopped before my door that Lou was holding open and motioned for him to lead the way. When he didn't budge, I started to cross my arms, but thought better of it. "Lou, you're freaking me out," I said.

"Why?" he asked, tilting his head to the side in a way that wasn't quite human.

"Because I feel like I'm a part of your revenge plot," I answered while still holding my ground.

Lou's facial features finally softened, "You don't need to worry about that. Seriously, Val. You've gone through enough; I don't need to cause you anymore pain."

"Then, will you please be the one that leaves this room first?"

"Fine," he huffed. To my relief, he did just that. Lou casually walked downstairs to the kitchen and started putting together a quick breakfast. I made myself comfortable in my chair at the island just in time for a bowl full of cereal to slide my way. We ate in silence, neither of us taking our eyes off the other. The only thing that distracted us was the sound of someone talking quietly as they tried to go down the stairs. We both turned our attention finding Chris attempting to sneak down to the basement. When he realized he had been caught, he hung up his phone slapping a smile on his face, "Lou, Val! I didn't think anyone else would be up this early. Where's Warrick?"

"He had to head into work," I answered.

"That's a shame, I was hoping we could all hang out a little more this morning," Chris said. It was hard not to analyze every word he said for any signs of truth to what Warrick and Lou told me last night.

"Duty calls, I guess," I mumbled.

Chris checked the time on his phone, "That man really does dedicate himself to his work. I don't know of anyone who goes into the office this early."

"Part of being a CEO," Lou said jumping in. "How'd the two love birds sleep?"

I glanced back at him appreciative of him taking over. With Lou driving the conversation, I wouldn't get myself in trouble with any sort of accusations. Chris got comfortable in the chair next to me before answering, "Jennie's still passed out. Wine will do that to her, though. It was hard for me to go back asleep after I woke up to use the bathroom, so I figured I would come hang out down here until everyone else was up."

"Sounded like you had some company until you saw us down here," Lou casually observed.

"Yeah," Chris nodded. "A guy we met when we went out the other night. I was just planning a double date with him and his girl."

"Nice, I bet Jennie would like that," I added.

Our conversation went back and forth a little while longer until Jennie finally joined us. I made my promised plans with her and it was settled that we'd be going out to the best club in town. I shot a text to Warrick letting him know where we'd be going and when so he could pass the message along to Holly. Things were falling into place so far.

Lou and I eventually made our way to the pizza place, relief flooding me when I saw my car parked in front of the restaurant. *Thank goodness Warrick dropped it off. That'll save me from having to mooch off others for a ride.* We had cut the timing close, so it wasn't long before we were rushing around filling orders. Eventually the rest of my friend crew came in, laughing and looking happier than ever. I actually got the chance to help them out since I wasn't having to run around to buy gifts or talk to Warrick, so it was refreshing to be a part of their conversation for once even if I was still having to bounce around from table to table.

They were getting ready to head out when Jennie called over her shoulder, "Are we still on for tonight?"

"What?" I asked not remembering what she was talking about.

Jennie playfully rolled her eyes at me, "The club, remember? Come join us after closing and make sure to change."

I had completely spaced we were doing that tonight. I gave her a thumbs up, but as soon as she left, I dropped my head shaking it. If I would've remembered that, I would have packed everything I needed to get ready and used Lou's place. *Oh well, I'll just have to resist the temptation to collapse on my bed.*

Lou walked up behind me, resting against the bar, "You forgot, didn't you?"

"Yup," I slowly turned to face him. "I don't even know what to wear or if I have anything that would look good."

He chuckled, shaking his head, "I think you'll be able to figure something out with what you have in your closet. Wear something that you would if you were going to a club in your home world. A lot of black typically works. Add some heals, makeup, and do your hair. You'll be good to go."

I put my hands on my hips, "Are you planning on joining us?"

"We'll see how the night goes," Lou said, poking my buttons. I gave him an eye roll then tended the few customers remaining from the lunch rush. Checking the clock, I noticed neither Holly nor Warrick made their way over to pick up the usual order. I went back to the kitchen seeing the order prepped on the rack just waiting to be picked up.

"Hey, Lou?" I called, making my way back into the dining area. The place was empty again except for a familiar blonde leaning over the bar to give Lou a teasing glance at her breasts. Neither of them broke eye contact to respond to me, so I leaned against the door frame crossing my arms over my chest. I didn't care they were talking so quietly I couldn't hear them, but I did care that Lou was shamelessly flirting with Holly when he said nothing was going on there.

"Val," he started without looking my way. "Can you grab their order?"

"Sure," I answered cooly. I plopped the pizza box on the bar top getting a satisfying jump out of Holly. A fake smile pasted on my face, "Here's your order."

Her eyes took a quick scan of me, head to foot, before muttering her thanks. She turned back to Lou, "So, will I see you tonight?"

"Sure," he answered with a lazy grin.

As soon as she sauntered out of the door, I whirled around to Lou, "What the hell was that?"

"What?" he asked trying to play dumb.

I reached across the bar, lifting his chin, "You know exactly what I'm talking about. I thought you were done with her."

I watched his pupils flare in response to my touch making me draw my hand back. He watched me for a moment before saying, "I said I was done hooking up with her. Look, she was sounding on the fence about going to the club tonight which would impact our plan, so I made the decision to go to make sure she shows up."

"How noble of you," I turned to head back into the kitchen to start knocking out the dishes.

Lou followed me in cornering me by placing a hand on either side of my head, "I haven't been able to figure something out and I need to hear it from you. Why do you care so much about who I'm with if you don't want to be with me in that way?"

Swallowing, I searched for the words to say, "I-I guess it more has to do with who."

"What do you mean?"

"I don't like Holly. I don't like the thought of her getting her slimy hands all over you when there are better people out there for you. I care about your happiness, as a friend. I get helping us out by keeping our plan on track, but don't lose yourself in the process," I explained.

Lou started to move closer to me then thought better of it. He dropped his head then ran his hand through his hair, "That's fair. Don't worry about me, though. Anything between Holly and I is strictly for the benefit of the plan, not to satisfy my own needs."

I could've sworn Lou was about to make a move on me with how he just acted. I glanced towards the clock on the wall noting we weren't too far from the dinner rush and then we'd be able to get out of here. Maybe then I'd be able to breathe a little more at least until the club. It was hard for me to not go back to what my heart felt for Lou. He must be going through hell sorting through all his feelings and trying to keep everything straight.

My thoughts were quickly interrupted by the sound of the door indicating someone had walked in. Lou and I looked at each other surprised a customer came in at this time considering the restaurant is typically empty between lunch and dinner. We poked our heads around the corner to find a lone guy getting comfortable at the bar. The hairs on the back of my neck stood up, my gut telling me to run. He was wearing a baseball cap he kept low to hide his face, a black hoodie, and some jeans. I could tell he wasn't small, height or muscular build. He picked up one of the menus we leave scattered there to start figuring out what he wanted. Lou and I tucked ourselves back in the kitchen. I wiped my hands getting ready to go out there to grab his order since that was our routine, but Lou put a hand on my shoulder to stop me, "I got this one."

The tone in his voice told me he was feeling the same way about this guy as I was, but at least he had a better chance of standing his ground than I did if something were to go wrong. I kept an eye on Lou as he walked over to our lone customer. Lou jotted down his order, served him a beer, then came back into the kitchen.

I looked at him, "Well?"

Lou gestured for me to be quiet and shuffled us into the back corner, keeping his voice down, "He's a wolf. Don't talk too loudly."

Doing my best to follow his instructions, I asked, "How do you know?"

"Scent," Lou said glancing over his shoulder. "He's definitely suspicious and not one I want to mess with. He almost feels like another alpha, but I haven't heard of any others anywhere close to us. There's something familiar about him I can't quite put my finger on either."

"Weird. Do you think Warrick would know of any other alphas?" I asked.

Lou looked in the direction of the dining room, "Maybe, but I don't want to raise any unnecessary alarms when nothing has happened. Let's keep this between us for now, but if something changes, we will let Warrick know."

"Got it boss," I nodded.

I stayed in the kitchen finishing up the cleaning and prepping some food for the next crowd of people, allowing me to steer clear of our shifty customer until the dinner rush started. Every time I went out into the dining area, I felt as if I was being watched, but I wasn't sure if it was Lou or the guy from earlier. Lou and I barely said anything to each other to minimize the chances of this guy picking up on anything he didn't need to know, testing our ability to silently communicate with one another. He finally left about ten minutes before closing, and as soon as the door closed behind him, I let out a breath. Lou came over to me, "Looking forward to the club now?"

"Surprisingly, yes. That was too tense. Why was he here for so long?" I rubbed my arms to bring some comfort back.

Lou only shrugged. He stared out the windows a little longer before saying, "At least he kept ordering stuff and paid. Plus, he gave a good tip, but he didn't say anything except when he ordered. As far as I could tell, he kept his head down."

"I felt like I was being watched the whole night. It was unsettling," I said moving to a chair.

"Watch your back when you go out and you don't have Warrick or I with you," Lou instructed.

I toyed with the corner of a napkin, "Good thing you're going tonight."

"Yeah, it is," he trailed off. "Do you know if Warrick will be joining us?"

I shook my head, "I haven't heard anything, so I'm assuming that's a no."

"That's a shame," Lou said, a smirk slowly inching across his face. "I'm sure he'll be missing out."

I shot him a look, "Lou, what are you up to?"

"Nothing," he answered. "I'm just looking forward to not having to force niceties, that's all."

My phone buzzed with a text from Jennie asking where I was at. I typed out a reply as I said, "Time to go. I'll see you there."

We made our way out of the restaurant after finishing the rest of the closing activities. I pulled into my garage noting Lou following me into the driveway. I crossed my arms watching as he got out, "Are you stalking me again?"

Confused, Lou's head snaps up, "What?"

I waved him off making my way into the house, "Just giving you a hard time, Lou. I've been thinking a lot about when I first got here and you followed me home to bring me my dress for the ball and make sure I was safe. Feels like that was years ago, but it really wasn't that long ago. So, I wanted to throw in a joke with everything that's been going on. Trying to lighten the mood a little before we go party it up tonight."

Lou chuckled, "And I'm still making sure you're safe to this day." He cocked his head to the side reaching for me to tuck some hair behind my ear, "Even though we've gone through hell, I'm glad we crossed paths, Val."

I leaned into his touch, "Me too, Lou."

As soon as I made it up to my room to get ready, I noticed Jennie had saved me some effort from trying to figure out what to wear by laying an outfit out on my bed. Shaking my head, I lifted up the triangular piece of shimmery fabric that was supposed to cover my torso. It was open backed and when I held it up in the mirror, it barely covered my breasts. Lou leaned against the doorframe at that exact moment, eyes widening when he saw what I was holding, "Not something I'd expect you to wear tonight."

"It's courtesy of Jennie," I informed him.

"Ah," he nodded his head. "It suddenly makes sense now."

I didn't give Lou any more chances to say anything before I hunkered down in my bathroom to get ready. Paired with the top were a pair of black leather pants that left nothing to the imagination. I completed the look with a pair of black pumps. I slapped on some glittery eye shadow with some mascara and false lashes, minimal makeup, and a natural colored lipstick. Feeling caught up in the moment, I took a selfie then sent it to Warrick with a quick text to let him know I'd be missing him tonight then met back up with Lou who was waiting in my room. When he saw me, he let out a low whistle, "I've said this before, but I'll say it again. You clean up nice, Val."

"Thanks," I smiled at him.

He led the way back to his car opening the passenger door for me, "Figured you'd probably be drinking tonight, so I'll be your chauffeur for the evening."

"Not a bad idea," I mumbled back looking at the response Warrick sent back. His words made me blush, but more than that, I got the sense he'd be joining us at some point tonight if he could get away from the office.

Pulling up to the club, I could feel the bass emanating from the building. It had been a long time since I've gone out to a club. Most of the places I frequented were bars, but Jennie's managed to pull me out to whatever the best club is a few times before the war happened to have a night where she can dance without a care in the world. There is a certain appeal to that, but it's usually not enough to persuade me to go more than I already do.

Lou looked over at me once he turned the car off, "Managed to talk Warrick into joining?"

I stared ahead watching people head in wearing less clothing than I was, "He might be. Depends if he can get away from the office or not."

"Well, I would hope he would prioritize you over his work," Lou said sitting back. It was almost like he was as hesitant as I was about going in there.

I threw a glance his way, "He's carrying a lot of weight on his shoulders. I get it."

"Is that what you tell yourself to make it okay?" he asked, his question perfectly hitting my doubts on the nose. It's been a little frustrating that Warrick has been working non-stop since we've been back especially since he was so willing to sacrifice some of his time when I first showed up in this world. At least he took some time off to spend Christmas with me even though it's not a holiday they normally celebrate here.

I held Lou's gaze a little longer, "There's still a lot I need to work through in order to be okay with having a relationship with Warrick. The space has been helping me clear my mind a little bit."

Lou shook his head, "You don't need to defend yourself to me. I'm just calling it like I see it, and Val, you look upset that Warrick may or may not show up tonight."

"I may be a little annoyed, but we're only doing this for him. We're here for support as Jennie starts working on getting closer to Holly," I reminded Lou. He had a point, though. I wanted

Warrick here. I wanted to have another night where we could be all over each other, not a care in the world.

We finally headed into the club, pausing a few feet in from the entrance. On the outside, the space looked like an old warehouse, but on the inside, it was like we were taken someplace entirely new. Lights in the shape of glass bubbles filled the ceiling looking like stars, hanging at various lengths to give a rippling effect. The bar was on the upper level overlooking the massive dance floor packed with people having the time of their lives. Booths and tables surrounded the outer edges of the building on the bottom floor to give people a place to sit if they needed a break. There were a lot of blues, blacks, and purples throughout to give it more of a galaxy feel. All the fixtures were modern and fit so perfectly in this space. I could see why so many people came here. You definitely got what you paid for.

Scanning everyone around us, I was thankful for what Jennie picked out for me. Most people were wearing less clothing than I was, but I still fit in. Anything I would've picked out of my closet would have made me stand out like a sore thumb.

Lou placed a guiding hand on my lower back making me jump at the feel of his touch on my skin as he leaned down, "Shall we?"

"Sure," I nodded following his lead. The way Lou was carrying himself confirmed he still wasn't going to let anything happen to me. He was positioned in such a way to keep any unwanted hands off me while we searched for the rest of our group. When we didn't find them on the upper level, we descended the stairs to start our search. My phone buzzed and I read a text from Jennie letting me know they were in a booth on the opposite side from where we were. I shouted this to Lou and he brought me in front of him as we made the tight squeeze through the dance floor.

Jennie's face lit up as we finally emerged from the sea of people, "You guys finally made it. Here, take a shot!"

She thrust a couple of shot glasses filled with a blue liquid into our hands and let out a cheer as we downed the alcohol. I had never tried anything like that before. The burn was more intense than anything I'd ever had, but was replaced with a sweetness that coated my mouth. Lou leaned into me again, speaking at a volume only I could hear, "Don't take any more of those. They'll fuck you up pretty good."

"What is it?" I turned to him.

"Something you can only find on this world and it's made to get werewolves drunk. It's pretty popular here because people can start feeling it quick, but just be careful with it."

Holly stood up right as Lou was finishing his explanation and pressed her body into him while pushing me out of the way. I gave Jennie a look that she reciprocated then sat down next to Joe and Bev. Clearly, Holly had one goal tonight. Bev pushed a glass of wine in my direction, "We got you this to save you from the shots."

"Thank you," I shouted back at her. That would make it easier to follow Lou's advice. I took a sip of it grateful I knew what to expect with this one. Lou wasn't wrong, though, the shot was already starting to affect me. I was feeling light and warm, a giggle escaping my lips just to prove that point. Lou cast a glance over his shoulder in my direction and I shook my head to let him know I was good.

I leaned into the table, raising my voice a little, "Thanks for the outfit, Jennie! There's nothing in my closet that would've worked here, although I was a little worried about flashing someone."

"Oh I know," she winked at me. "About the clothes part. The flashing, well, jury's still out on that but I bet you're going to be safe there. Let's go dance."

"I'll hang back here," Chris said. When Jennie gave him a look, he squeezed her hand, "To keep an eye on the drinks. Someone can tap me in when they need a break."

Joe and Bev both waived Chris off, "No, you go out there with your fiancé. We'll hold it down here."

Jennie mouthed a thank you to them and I gave both their hands a squeeze before following Lou, Holly, Jennie, and Chris into the throng of people. Watching the two pairs dance together worsened the ache of loneliness I was feeling with Warrick not being here. I leaned over to Jennie, "I'm gonna head back to the booth for a little bit."

She smiled and nodded her head before closing her eyes again to get lost in the music. Lou watched as I headed back there, but didn't move to follow me. *Do what you need to and stay with Holly tonight.*

Joe and Bev were surprised to see me when I came back so soon. As I sat down, I answered their silent questions, "Just feeling a little lonely tonight."

"Warrick's not coming?" Joe asked.

I pulled out my phone to see if there were any updates from him then held it up so they can see the empty screen, "Probably not. He's caught up at the office. Perks of trying to date a CEO, I guess."

When Bev started to offer comfort, I waved her off then downed the rest of my wine. Holding up the empty glass, I was about to ask if they wanted anything else to drink when a waiter snuck by to replace the empty with a filled one. I stared at the new glass in my hand, "What? Do they read minds here?"

Bev giggled, "Jennie paid for VIP service courtesy of Warrick, so we don't have to worry about trying to make our way upstairs."

"Fair enough," I shrugged.

We chatted a little more about surface-level topics despite me wanting to ask them more about their decisions about trying for kids and making this world their new permanent residence. Those would be things to talk about another time. They kept looking out towards the dance floor, and when they did it the fifth time, I said, "Get out there, you crazy kids. I can hang back here for a little bit."

They beamed at me and wasted no time joining the rest of our group. I sighed, taking in all the drinks they must have consumed while waiting for Lou and I to get here. Judging by the empty glasses, tonight was going to be a party. I took another sip of my wine making a mental note to slow things down so I didn't get too drunk too fast then started playing on my phone. Someone walked up to the table and I muttered, "We're all good here, thanks. Maybe another round later."

"Didn't think I was carrying a tray of drinks, but maybe that's what'll get you to look up from your phone."

The British accent floated over me snatching the feelings of loneliness right out of me. I snapped my head up to meet Warrick's icy blue eyes, "I didn't think you were going to make it."

He moved to sit down with me, "The thought of missing the chance to have a night filled with dancing started to eat away at me."

"I'm happy you made the right choice," I batted my lashes at him.

Warrick reached up to caress my face, "Did I tell you how gorgeous you look tonight, love?"

"Maybe," I felt myself blush again at the thought of his text from earlier.

Seeing my reaction, he grinned. I moved closer to him, resting my head on his shoulder, "Want anything to drink?"

"I actually took a couple of shots before making my way down here. Figured that would make dealing with Holly easier."

"Lou told me not to have any more of those tonight," I noted.

He ran his fingers through my hair, "He's not wrong about that. Stick with the one and the wine, that's all you need."

It wasn't too long before the rest of the group made it back to the booth to take a much needed drink break. Bev smiled at Warrick, "We're happy you made it."

"Me too," he said before taking a sip of my wine.

Lou just gave a subtle nod of his head and went back to focusing on Holly who hadn't seen that her boss was here now. Jennie and Chris were whispering something to each other, and Bev moved so she was sitting in Joe's lap. With everyone being consumed with their partners, Warrick and I took this moment to escape to the dance floor. This time, I was feeling even more excited to be out here. Crazy what having someone to dance with will do.

Following the rhythm of the music, I started grinding on him, throwing one of my arms around the back of his neck. I closed my eyes leaning my head back while Warrick joined me in moving to the beat. I felt his lips brush against my ear making my skin erupt in goosebumps, "If I would've known this was how the night was going to go, I'd have gotten here sooner, love."

"Mmm," was I all I could respond with. One his hands tightened his grip on my waist while the other moved up to rest right under my breast. He pulled me in even closer eliminating any space between our bodies and I didn't ignore the fact that I felt at home.

"Remind me to thank Jennie for this," he said, his voice growing husky with desire.

Knowing how to play the game, I turned to face him wrapping both arms around his neck keeping my body pressed against his, "I didn't take you as the clubbing type."

He smirked at me while his hands travelled to my ass, "I'm full of surprises. You should know this by now."

"Oh, I do," I confirmed then gave him a kiss. Before he could take control of it, I pulled away.

"That's what we're doing tonight," Warrick said.

I batted my eyes again, feigning innocence, "I have no idea what you're talking about."

"Be careful how much you play, love," he growled into my ear. I knew by that reaction that I had him right where I wanted.

Chapter 21

We danced for a little longer, but decided to take a break as Warrick started to get more handsy. If we weren't careful, we were going to make a scene I'm sure people would prefer we kept private. By the time we'd gotten back to the booth, only Lou and Chris were there.

"Where'd everyone run away to?" I asked.

"Joe and Bev headed out for the night. Jennie and Holly ran away to the bathroom," Chris informed us while handing each of us another one of those blue shots. Warrick threw his back then grabbed mine to repeat the motion. Lou raised his eyebrows at him, but Warrick ignored him. Instead, he leaned over to start kissing my neck whispering what he wanted to do with me once we left here. I felt my nipples harden and I put a hand on Warrick's chest. I leaned in to whisper, "We have company."

He slightly turned as if confirming the other two guys were still here by looking at them. Warrick sat back up letting out a disappointed sigh, catching me off-guard. The Warrick I knew wouldn't typically let that stop him. Heat rose to my cheeks and I shifted uncomfortably when I noticed Chris was watching me very carefully. Warrick must've picked up on that, too, because he pulled me to his lap while staring Chris down. As soon as Jennie and Holly came back, Chris dropped his gaze. I felt Warrick tense beside me. He got up, straightening himself up, "I'll be back. Have to run to the restroom."

The moment he was out of earshot, Holly asked the table, "Why is Warrick here?"

"You really have to ask that?" Jennie snorted.

"What?" Holly asked looking between us all. I smirked, casually taking another sip of my wine. If she really didn't know, she was about to have her little world rocked considering she kept flirting with Warrick and wasn't my biggest fan.

Jennie furrowed her brows trying to figure out if Holly was being serious or not. As soon as it clicked, she said, "Oh, you really don't know."

"Don't know what?"

"Warrick and Val have a thing," Jennie stated. "He's only here because of her."

Holly's mouth dropped open, "What does he see in you?"

Everyone's reactions besides mine were pure shock. Both Lou and Chris' eyebrows shot up while Jennie sucked in a breath, her hand instinctively moving to her chest. Me? Well, I just laughed.

"What?" Holly asked looking around at each of us. "I'm being serious. I'm not trying to be a bitch, I just genuinely want to know."

"Want to know what?" Warrick asked in that calm voice of his I knew not to mess with. Holly hadn't figured out that she should leave Warrick alone when he used that tone. She blinked at him a couple of times repeating her question, "I'm just curious about what you see in her."

I let out a bark of laughter at the fact she couldn't even bring herself to say my name. She really didn't like me. Warrick threw an arm over my shoulder, practically undressing me with his gaze, before turning back to look at Holly. He was taking his time before he responded to Holly's comment, throwing another shot back. Lou shook his head and headed in the direction of the restroom while Holly started impatiently tapping her nails on the table. Warrick drummed his fingers once in response then finally said, "She's a hell of a lot more of a woman than you'll ever be. She can stand her ground, she's a fighter, and I can't forget, she's the most beautiful woman I've ever seen."

Holly's face reddened with anger, but I didn't get the chance to fully enjoy her reaction before Warrick pulled me into a deep, passionate kiss as if to prove his point. When we separated, he called a waiter over for some wine. There was an awkward silence hanging over the table, so when Lou came back, he held out his hand to take Holly back on the dance floor. Judging by Lou's expression, he wasn't looking forward to another round of dancing with her, but he knew it was going to ease some of the tension.

Jennie followed with Chris hanging back to keep an eye on things. Warrick and I waited until more wine was brought back then we headed out to join everyone else. Holly was so absorbed by Lou at this point, she didn't even know we were dancing next to them. Instead of grinding on Warrick, I spent more time dancing with Jennie. Every now and then, Warrick's eyebrows would raise as he watched us, but him and Lou were talking in hushed tones. I saw Warrick's body tense at one point after something Lou had said. Warrick pulled me closer, "I'll be right back. There's something I need to check on, love."

"Everything okay?" I asked searching his face for any signs of what may be going on.

He gave me a reassuring smile, "Yeah, I won't be gone for long. Behave yourself until I get back."

Warrick gave me another deep kiss accompanied with squeezing my ass then disappeared into the crowd. Jennie came over to me, "Where's he going?"

I shrugged, "He has to take care of something."

Holly joined our conversation now, "You're so lucky, Val. Do you know how many women would kill to be in your position?"

I waived her off, "Thanks, I guess? I'm gonna head back to the table, though. I just got really thirsty."

Jennie and Holly resumed their dancing, Lou kind of dancing while keeping an eye on the two of them, his gaze occasionally wandering over to me. I wasn't really thirsty, but I didn't want to keep talking with Holly when she kept making jabs, intentional or not.

I flopped into the booth taking a moment to settle myself. It was too easy to get caught up in things and Holly was driving me crazy. With my eyes still closed, I felt the booth shift a little. I brought my head up noting Chris had moved closer to me. He leaned over so he didn't have to shout over the volume of the music, but I wasn't comfortable with how close he was to me. His face was inches from mine, his lips almost brushing my ear as Warrick had done the whole night, "You look stunning tonight, Val."

"Thanks" I replied before taking a sip of my wine.

"You know? I think about that kiss we shared. A lot," he continued.

I froze in place at his admission. It came out of left field and made all the alarm bells ring. I shot a glance in Jennie's direction, but she was completely absorbed by the music. Chris placed a hand on my thigh, a little too high for my liking. Moving to put more space between us, the hairs on the back of my neck stood up when he followed. I placed a hand on his shoulder hoping he would get the message to stop, "Chris, you're engaged to Jennie. Nothing is going to happen between us tonight or ever. I would suggest you give me some space."

He chuckled, "Don't lie, I know you think of what could've been between us, too. Why don't we try to find out?"

Before I could say or do anything, he buried his face in my neck. He started kissing me, not budging when I shoved him. I shot another glance out to the dance floor, but the rest of our group was gone from my line of sight which meant they wouldn't be back for a while. I scanned the rest of the club hoping for some sign of Warrick, but there wasn't one. *Shit, Chris is reeking of alcohol and not getting the message. Jennie is busy wooing Holly with Lou's assistance, and Joe and Bev are gone for the night. I'm on my own for this one.*

Chris took a deep breath, "You smell so damn good."

I gave him another shove trying to make my escape. His hand painfully gripped my arm, yanking me back to be next to him. I tried to pull my arm from him, "That hurts, Chris."

"Where are you going?" he asked still not releasing me.

"Just to join the rest our group out there," I nodded my head in the direction of the dance floor.

"You just got back," he observed. Cocking his head to the side and studying me, he asked, "Why leave so soon?"

I gave my arm one more tug able to breathe a little easier when he let it go. I put both hands on the seat to help me make a quick escape if it came to that. Holding his gaze, I answered, "I feel refreshed. I only came back for a sip of my drink."

Chris leaned back stretching his arms across the back of the booth. He nodded towards my glass, "Take a load off, Val. I'm not going to do anything."

My guard was fully up at this point. He was all over me one second and the next he's acting normal. I don't know what happened to him, but this is not the version of Chris I recognized. Gone was the kind man I was introduced to, and in his place, a predator. I stared at my glass wondering if he tampered with it. My heart rate spiked and sweat started forming. I didn't know what game Chris was trying to play, but I really didn't like it. Disappointment filled me when I still didn't see anyone else from our group when I looked out towards the dance floor.

"I didn't spike your drink if that's what you're thinking," Chris said coolly. "See?"

He brought my glass to his lips taking a sip. His throat moved to prove he swallowed the liquid in his mouth then smiled, "Would I have really taken a sip if I messed with it?"

"Probably not," I said willing myself to speak. The last thing I wanted to do was to piss him off by not responding. Chris passed the glass back to me, watching my every move as I downed the rest of the wine. It burned a little more than usual, but I didn't know if I was imagining that feeling with what was happening in our booth or if it was real. Chris nodded in approval and went back to bobbing his head in time with the music with his eyes closed. I leaned back, but decided it was time to get away from this loose cannon. The moment I stood up, Chris' eyes snapped open, "Trying to leave again?"

"I'm going to dance and probably get another drink," I said allowing myself to turn my back to him. I only managed to get a few steps away when his hands latched on to my waist. His breath was hot against my neck as he whispered, "Dance with me."

"No," I squeaked out cursing myself for letting my nerves show.

Chris chuckled rubbing one of my arms, "As friends. Jeez, Val, relax."

I clenched my jaw together feeling as if I had no choice as he led me out to the dance floor away from the direction I had seen the rest of the group disappear. Both of his hands were back on my waist not daring to leave while he kept my back to him. The minute I stumbled from the wine hitting me, Chris tightened his grip, "Probably shouldn't chug your drink."

My mouth went dry. I may have drank a good amount so far, but I shouldn't be stumbling right now. I made sure to drink plenty of water in between the alcohol.

Chris finally stopped us when we reached the spot where he wanted to dance. Hands still on my waist, he started grinding my ass against him. I became nauseous when I could feel how hard he was. This was exactly what he wanted in this moment, and because I was feeling loose and light-headed, my will to fight against him was weakened.

"There you go. See? Just dancing as friends," he hummed in approval.

"This isn't how I dance with friends," I mumbled, my words trying to slur together. "Are you sure you didn't do anything to my drink?"

One of his hands snaked up my torso resting directly under one of my breasts. The same motion Warrick had done what felt like minutes earlier, except I felt sick to my stomach now. He pushed me back into him, his lips brushing against my ears, "I only added a shot of the house special and a little something extra."

My body tensed. Lou had told me to stay away from that stuff because of how potent it is. Mixed with more alcohol, I knew I was only going to get more drunk as the night went on, and who knows how whatever "extra" he added is going to play with all the alcohol. I tried to step forward, but Chris crushed me into him. I let out a gasp earning laughter from him. He kept my hips moving in his desired rhythm as he traced the bottom of my breast with his thumb. Chris started to kiss down my neck, pausing only to say, "I've spent so many nights thinking about how you would feel, jealous of Daryl, Lou, and Warrick getting to sleep with you. You've been busy, haven't you?"

I felt like I was going to throw up. As he kept kissing my neck working his way to my sweet spot, my body erupted in goosebumps. Chris may have interpreted it as me enjoying this, yet it was anything but that. My body was starting to go into full-on panic mode. I could feel my throat starting to close, my hands starting to shake. I tried to look back towards our booth, but couldn't really see anything between the other people dancing. From what I could tell, there were still no signs of anyone in our group being there.

Chris finally removed his hand from under my breast, lacing his fingers through mine as he tugged me in the direction of one of the many dark hallways on this side of the club, "Come with me."

I tried to keep myself rooted to the spot, but my legs betrayed me, dealing with the effects of the alcohol. I stumbled after him. Chris didn't take the same care this time as he did when we were leaving our booth behind.

"No," I protested even though the dark hallway was looming ahead of us. Chris threw me against a wall knocking the breath out of me. *I don't remember him being this strong.*

"I don't think you're in a position to say no to me right now," Chris sneered as he pinned me and forced my legs to spread. He crushed his lips against mine and my panic reached a whole new level. I struggled against him, doing my best to throw my weight to knock him off balance or to loosen his grip on me, but that only encouraged him to press harder. The burning sensation of tears prickling against my eyes wasn't enough to distract me from what was playing out. I looked back towards the crowd writhing to the music being played hoping to see some sign of a familiar face. The only one I saw was the man in the baseball cap from the pizza place. He happened to be walking by, but only smiled at what he was seeing before tugging his cap back down and making his way out of the club. I looked up, squeezing my eyes shut as I accepted what was about to happen.

Chris traced the waistline of my pants, slowly unbuttoning them then slipping his hands between my thighs. He groaned when he rubbed his fingers against my underwear, "You can't tell me you're not wanting this as much as I do right now. Not when you're feeling like this."

How wrong he was. I wanted to run and to never look back. I never wanted to see him again. I tried to break free one more time, unsuccessful in my attempt. Chris only snickered as his fingers kept stroking against the fabric. Just as he was about to push aside the last layer of protection I had, he was thrown across the hallway.

"You must have a death wish," Lou growled.

Warrick wasn't far behind him lifting Chris off the ground and slamming him against the wall again, "You better give me a one good fucking reason as to why I shouldn't kill you right now," Warrick spat.

Not giving Chris the chance to respond, Lou said, "Because we need info from him."

Warrick's head whipped around so he was watching Lou carefully. I crumpled to the ground, no longer able to stand on my own. Lou moved so he was standing by Warrick who was still holding Chris by his shirt, "Your fiancé is going to be wondering where you're at in about ten minutes. I suggest you clean yourself up in the restroom then make your way back to our booth. I also suggest you break off the engagement before I tell her what I caught you doing. Then, when you go back to Val's house, you're going to pack your shit and leave."

"I'm not breaking things off with Jennie," Chris muttered.

Lou slid over to replace Warrick now holding Chris up. He gave him another slam into the wall making Chris cough, "And why the hell not?"

Warrick crouched in front me scanning for any signs of damage. I could tell he wanted to reach out and touch me, but he held himself back in case I wasn't ready to have someone place their hands on me again.

"I don't want to deal with that," Chris started. "She'll kill me. Plus, I have nowhere to go."

"You're not fooling me. I know you've been changed. Jennie doesn't deserve this and you know as well as I do that she doesn't have a chance when it comes to killing you now. Go stay with whoever was stupid enough to change you. If I see your face around Val *or* Jennie again, I won't be as nice next time," Lou snarled, his lip curling up to reveal his teeth.

Shock replaced anything I had been feeling minutes ago. No wonder he felt stronger. He was a new wolf and his first full moon is tomorrow. But, who changed him? When did he get changed? Why did he want to be changed? I glanced over to Warrick to see if he knew this information as well, but he didn't give anything away.

Lou put a pause on the questions building like a storm in my mind when he came back over to me, joining Warrick. Both of their attention was on me now, Lou doing the same scan as Warrick. Warrick cradled my face, his eyes searching mine, "Are you okay, love?"

"Just unsettled," I answered with a shaky voice.

His thumbs brushed away the tears hat had spilled over, "Are you okay with telling us what happened?"

I gave a small nod then took a deep breath to try to keep the emotion out of my voice. He wiped away any remnants of tears then helped me to my feet. Lou positioned himself so he was blocking me from view of anyone walking near the hallway as Warrick helped me up. I took some more time straightening myself up, buttoning my pants and making sure my top was in place so nothing was revealed. Once I felt a little better, I looked up at Warrick, "I needed a break from the dancing, so I headed back to the booth to sit down and drink some of my wine. Chris started off by complimenting me, which is normal, but then he mentioned something about when we kissed before."

Both of the men in front me furrowed their brows, but it was Lou who jumped in before Warrick could say anything, "You kissed him before?"

Sighing, I said, "Yeah, like an idiot. It was the first night of the friend's weekend before Daryl confessed his feelings to me. Jennie was trying to set me up with Chris so she could get with Daryl."

Lou shook his head, "You guys have a messy friendship, you know that?"

"Yeah," I nodded, dropping my head, "It's a mess."

"It's okay, you're doing your best, love. You can't control other people's actions. What happened after Chris mentioned that?" Warrick asked.

"Right," I said bringing my gaze back up to Warrick's. "He was too close to me, then put his hand on my thigh. I put some space between us and things started to become tense with him smelling me and starting to kiss my neck, but it was like nothing happened after that. He went back to listening to the music and telling me to chill. I thought he might've spiked my drink, but he played it off by taking a sip from my glass. I decided it would be okay and finished off my wine. We headed out on the dance floor where Chris told me he added a shot of the house special to my wine and the alcohol started to hit me. That's when he started taking advantage of me. You both stopped him before he could actually do anything."

"Right," he nodded. I could see the gears turning in Warrick's head as he processed everything I said.

Lou jumped in, "Did you see anyone else around? Anyone that you might've recognized?"

"Why does that matter?" I asked not following where Lou's questions were going. My knees gave out and both Warrick and Lou jumped in to help me up. They helped me over to an empty booth flagging a waiter down to get us some water. Warrick whipped his phone out typing furiously away on it while Lou made sure I drank some of the water. The two of them scooted in close to me so we didn't have to shout over the noise while still keeping me shielded from any curious looks. Lou started, "I'm trying to figure out who the hell changed him. I don't know if one of Warrick's wolves have gone rogue and is changing people without our knowledge. It would explain why Chris has been acting so differently, though."

Warrick shook his head, "All of my wolves just confirmed they have no idea who Chris is. Most of them have never seen him before, and if any have, they never talked to him, so I think it's safe to say we can rule my pack out. What about yours, Lou? Would anyone go behind your back like that?"

Lou stiffened but relaxed as he pulled out his phone to check with his pack. After a few moments, Lou shook his head, "It's none of my wolves either."

I just sat there still wondering why this is related to what just happened. "The only person I recognized was that weird guy form the pizza place earlier."

Warrick tensed, "The guy with the baseball cap you were telling me about?"

Lou nodded, a muscle twitching in his jaw. That must have been what they were whispering about earlier. Lou regained his composure, "We need to head back to our group."

"O-okay," I stammered. I looked between the two noting they were sharing some unspoken thought about the mysterious newcomer. There was something I clearly didn't know, but I would try to remember to ask them later.

Lou dipped the corner of a napkin in one of our glasses of water then moved to wipe my face. I tried not to flinch, but my attempt was unsuccessful, making Lou hesitate and a small growl to escape from Warrick. Lou flashed an annoyed look at Warrick, but continued moving to clean up my face. He held my chin carefully wiping away the aftermath of my tears.

Lou grabbed our waters, Warrick helping me out of the booth then holding me tightly to help me back to our original booth. Everyone was there, including Chris. Clearly the news hasn't been broken to Jennie judging by how happy everyone looked. Holly gave Lou a doe-eyed look, fluttering her eyelashes at him, "Where did you sneak off to?"

"Just helping out a friend," Lou said, his muscles tensing as he watched Chris. "Can you please grab us some drinks, Holly?"

"Don't we have waiters for that?" she asked. Lou gave her a look and she quickly changed her tone, "They've been a little slow tonight, so I'll be right back."

Warrick was still holding me up whispering words to try to bring me some comfort. The three of us didn't show any signs of moving to sit with Jennie and Chris. Jennie's smile slowly faded as she replaced it with confusion. Looking between us and Chris, she asked, "What's going on?"

"You want to tell her or do you want me to?" Lou asked in a cold tone.

"Tell me what?" Jennie turned to Chris. "What the hell is going on?"

Chris wisely dropped his gaze from Lou's then faced Jennie. He held her hands as he said, "I think I rushed into this, Jennie."

"Rushed into what?" Jennie asked, panic starting to rise in her voice.

"Our engagement," Chris sighed. "I think I need to take a step back to rethink things."

"What the hell, Chris?" Jennie asked hysterically. I watched as tears filled her eyes. "Is it something I did?"

"No," he shook his head. "This one's on me. A lot has changed and I'm having a hard time adjusting. I just need some time alone."

"Asshole," she muttered as she started crying. She ripped the ring from her hand, throwing it at Chris, "Why even bother? Why waste our time? I didn't want my feelings to be jerked around which is why I said yes. You were my safe place, the one thing consistent in my life. You promised me that we would be for forever."

"I know and I fucked up, J. I really did."

Jennie whipped around to me, "Is this because of you? Did you and Chris do something?"

Warrick immediately stopped whispering to me. I felt every muscle go taut and knew he wasn't happy about the accusation, but this wasn't anything new to me. Chris turned Jennie back to him before I could explain what he just did, "No, Val has nothing to do with it. It's all me. I've had a change of heart, that's all."

"Fuck you!" she screamed earning a couple of startled glances from people near us. Jennie wasted no time storming out.

Chris dragged his eyes up to ours, "Happy?"

"Leave," Lou said.

"If you're at her house by the time we get there, I won't hold back," Warrick promised, his tone sinister.

Chris took his time getting out of the booth, clearly not caring about Warrick's threat, then headed towards the exit. Warrick helped me get into the booth with Lou getting in on the opposite side. Holly bounced up to the table with a new bottle of wine, her smile falling when she realized Jennie and Chris had left, "Where'd they go?"

Lou fixed a flirty look on his face, "They got tired and decided to head out. Did you have a good time?"

"Yeah, Jennie's super nice. I was hoping to get to know her a little more," Holly pouted. I could tell by her demeanor she had been drinking heavily and that apparently brought out the child in her.

Lou reached out to rub her arm, "I know. There'll be other opportunities to hang out with her. I called you a car and it's here, you should head home. You look tired."

I hadn't realized Lou had done that, but then again, I wasn't in the best state to be paying attention to every little thing.

"I don't want to," she said sounding like she was about to have a toddler-sized meltdown.

Lou stood up, "I know, but I'll rest easier knowing you made it home safely. Text me, okay?"

I don't know what alpha powers Lou was using, but I watched as she went from getting ready to protest to nodding as if everything was okay. Holly gave him one more pout which earned her a kiss on her forehead then headed towards the exit. When Lou collapsed back into the booth, Warrick asked, "Laying it on thick are we?"

Lou's eyes were closed as he said, "This is why I hate going out."

Before they could bicker amongst themselves, I quietly said, "Thank you both for taking care of things tonight."

"This is not something you need to thank us for, love. We will always have your back," Warrick said.

"Always," Lou agreed.

We waited a little longer, sitting in silence when Warrick stood up giving me a forehead kiss before saying, "I'm going to head out to see if I can catch that asshole before he's gone. I need to make a point."

"We'll head out, too," Lou said moving to get out of the booth to help me up.

Warrick watched as we both stood up, his eyes resting on the spot on my arm where Chris had grabbed me earlier. I followed his gaze watching as a bruise in the shape of Chris' hand bloomed on my arm. When I looked back at Warrick, his eyes no longer looked like his, but his wolf's, "I'm going to kill him."

Neither Lou nor I had a chance to say anything in return. Warrick stormed out. "Shit," Lou muttered under his breath. My head rolled back as he looked over to me, "Val?"

"Hmm?" my eyes were closed at this point.

"Val?" he asked more urgently. I felt his other hand try to bring my head back up. "Fuck. Val, I need you to lift your head up and look at me."

I tried to do what he told me, but my attempt was unsuccessful. Lou let out a few more curses before I heard him talking on the phone to someone. I had no idea what he was saying, but as soon as he was done, he started dragging me towards the exit.

Chapter 22

We raced back to my house. I didn't know what was going on, but it was a struggle to retain consciousness. When we pulled up, Warrick was there just emerging from his car, Raf not far behind him. Chris came out of the house carrying his things when Warrick threw a punch knocking Chris to the ground. Warrick kicked him before dropping a knee to his chest, "I was feeling nice earlier, but that changed when I saw the bruise you left."

"Warrick!" Lou shouted. "We still need to get info from him." He lifted Warrick off Chris to give him the chance to get back on his feet. Raf helped me out of the car sitting me down on the driveway so I could still see what's going on while he got to work helping me. We stayed silent as the scene played out in front of us.

"Who the hell turned you?" Lou asked while struggling to keep Warrick back.

Chris smirked, "I think you already know."

"No, we don't. Enlighten us," Warrick spat.

"I don't see this as being my problem. Clearly there's another player trying to make moves on your territory," Chris said, a cocky air to his voice.

Warrick slipped out of Lou's grasp landing a couple more punches when Jennie walked out of the house. She tightly wrapped herself in her robe and clearly had been crying. When she saw what was happening, she yelled out, "What are you doing to him?"

She rushed over to where Chris and Warrick were, pushing Warrick off.

"Jennie," I mumbled. I tried to get up. Raf put his hands on my shoulders guiding me back to my original sitting position. I didn't hear what Raf was trying to tell me because I was back to getting on my feet focused on getting to my friend.

I started stumbling over to the group on the ground when Lou grabbed me, "Val, no. You need to listen to Raf. Go back over to him."

Pushing out of Lou's arms, I said, "No. Let me help her."

I made it over to Warrick, Chris, and Jennie falling to my knees from the effort. I reached a hand towards Jennie's shoulder, "You can't be here right now."

"What the hell is wrong with you people?" she asked, tears streaming down her face.

"You don't know the full story," I said.

She shook my hand off her shoulder, Warrick having to catch me. Jennie snapped at me, "I don't want to know the full story. All I know is I had my heart ripped out tonight and now he's going to be beaten to death."

"Jennie," Lou started, keeping his position. "You really don't know what's going on."

"What are they talking about, Chris?" she stroked his face.

"Nothing, J. I'm sorry for the pain I caused you," he said, changing his tone from earlier to one that's softer, sweeter.

"Let me come with you," she pleaded.

I felt sick at the thought of losing her once again, especially to someone who couldn't care less about her. I turned to Warrick, "I'm going to throw up."

He quickly held my hair back shifting me away from everyone just in time for the vomit to come up. Raf rushed over and took over from Warrick, but not dragging me away from the commotion. I felt like I had emptied everything from my stomach and wiped my mouth with the back of my hand as I turned back to talk to Jennie, "Please, let me explain."

"Why would I want to hear from you? You've barely been here. How would you know anything?" Jennie shot at me. "We've done nothing but take care of you. When it comes to us, you wouldn't do the same thing."

Her tone was so bitter I flinched. I glanced towards Chris seeing him smirk. He knew this was how it was going to go and was happy things were playing into his hand. I shook my head bringing my attention back to my friend to try to keep things from crumbling any further, "Did you know he's been cheating on you?"

She looked like I slapped her, but it was the last card I could use. I continued on not giving her or Chris the chance to derail my thoughts, "He spiked my drink tonight, Jennie. Then, he dragged me out to the dance floor before hiding us away in a hallway to take advantage of me."

"No, that's not true," Jennie protested.

"We saw everything," Lou chimed in gesturing between himself and Warrick. "He was kissing her, one hand up her shirt while the other was down her pants."

"Is this true?" she asked Chris, fresh tears in her eyes. A tiny glimmer of hope flickered within me. There was a potential she was believing us.

He immediately denied the accusation, "No! She was the one who threw herself at me. She wasn't over what we had started that night. I tried to keep her off me, but she was just so drunk."

Jennie sat back shaking her head. She finally looked at Raf, "Has she been drugged?"

That question confirmed what I was hoping for: she was coming to our side. Her rose colored glasses were coming off and she was starting to see the truth instead of rushing to Chris' defense.

"Yes, which is why she needs to sit still and let me help her," Raf confirmed. That explains why it was so hard to hold myself up.

I finally collapsed when I saw Jennie nod her head. Raf went back to work to help get the drug out my system when I heard a slap. I propped my head back up, Raf supporting my neck so I could see what was happening. Jennie was now walking away, "I can't believe this shit." She whirled around, "Is that the only reason why you're attacking him, Warrick?"

"No," he answered calmly. I recognized this tone as the one he uses when he's about to lose it. "Since we've been back here, have you noticed a change in your ex?"

"Stop toying with me," she pinched the bridge of her nose. "Get to the point."

"He's a wolf, Jennie. Someone changed him. Someone who isn't Lou or myself or any of our pack members," Warrick informed her.

Her eyes widened. Jennie watched Chris who started laughing. Gone was the man trying to convince her of his innocence. Instead of saying anything else, she turned towards the house making her way back in.

"Lou, help me get her out of harm's way," Raf ordered.

Lou started to move towards me when Warrick held out a hand. Everyone stopped moving unsure of what was going other than happen next. Warrick looked down at Chris, "Consider yourself lucky tonight. I fully planned on killing you, yet something is holding me back. If either I or Lou see you around this place, there will be no other chances. If you lay another hand on Val, I will kill you myself. And if you go near Jennie, yo – "

Chris cut him off finishing the sentence, "I'll be dead. Got it. Can I go now?"

Each of us knew Warrick was only letting Chris go because he was going to have someone follow him to get leads on who turned him. Although, I had a hunch that Warrick already knew who did it and wasn't ready to offer up that information. Before I had a chance to ask him, Warrick looked at Raf, "Take her up to her room and don't let anyone see her. We'll be up shortly."

That was the last thing I remembered hearing before I finally passed out.

When I came to, it was light outside and snowflakes were falling from the sky. Warrick was in a chair lost in thought watching the snowflakes make their graceful dance to the ground while Lou was sleeping in another chair. Raf was checking my vitals, smiling when he saw I woke up, "We have to stop meeting like this, Val."

"Job security, Raf," I croaked out. My throat was so beyond dry I would've thought I'd been wandering through a desert for months on end with no water. My head was pounding, my stomach still nauseous, and the edges of my vision were blurry.

At the sound of my voice, Warrick and Lou both sprang to life coming to my side. Worry was etched in their features. I looked between both of them, "Don't you two have work?"

"We've taken the day off. Between you and the full moon, love, there would be no way we could focus on things," Warrick said tucking a stand of hair behind my ear.

"Besides," Lou started. "I don't know what I was thinking when I said I was going to keep the pizza place open during a full moon. I've never done that because no one's going out, so why would I change that today?"

Warrick shook his head then turned his attention back to me, "Can you two describe the guy you mentioned last night?"

"He was wearing a baseball cap and was in jeans and a zip up jacket. I got nothing but bad vibes off him and Lou told me to stay away, but he was at the club last night. When he saw what was going on, he just smiled at me like he was in on what Chris was doing," I explained.

Before I could say anything else, Lou jumped in, "I was getting wolf vibes from him in the pizza place, but it was hard to tell for sure. It felt like my senses were being dulled a little. I have no idea how. You don't think it could be someone from another pack in this word, do you?"

Warrick considered that for a second then said, "It could be. I'll call a meeting with the other alphas in a few days."

I was shocked looking between them, "Lou, why didn't you share your concern with me? Are you thinking he could have been the one to change Chris? And before you answer that, Warrick, how can you just call on all the other alphas?"

Warrick was focused on his phone, so it was Lou who answered, "Warrick's the alpha of alphas. Remember the whole power conversation we had? This is where it comes into play. As for the other guy, I didn't share my suspicions because I didn't want to share something I wasn't entirely sure of. I don't need you upset with me on that one, either."

"Got it," I said. Not caring to be a part of the conversation anymore, I started to get out of bed. I grabbed the pole holding my IV fluids and headed towards Jennie's room despite Raf's protests.

Her door was closed, so I quietly knocked. I waited for a while getting no response. I started to turn when the door slightly opened, "Val?"

Jennie looked like a mess. Her eyes were so red and swollen, makeup smeared everywhere. Her hair was all over the place, and looking behind her, I could see food wrappers scattered all over the floor.

"Can I come in?"

She hesitated before nodding her head. I settled on the edge of her bed, Jennie closing the door behind her as she joined me. She wouldn't look at me, but I didn't care. I put a comforting hand on her arm, "How are you doing?"

"Did he really do those things you said he did?" Jennie asked almost in a daze.

"I wish I was lying, Jennie. I really do, but he did try to take advantage of me."

She slowly turned to look at me, "Was that the only time?"

"Thankfully, yes," I answered. She gave a small nod and I continued, "I wasn't the only one he was trying to get with, though. He was texting and calling other women."

"I had a feeling, but I guess I trusted that he wasn't going to be that way when he proposed," she said.

"I'm so sorry," I said reaching over to pull her into a hug. As soon as my arms wrapped around her, Jennie's body was wracked with sobs. She cried until there was nothing left, and when she was done, I said, "I'm sorry I haven't been around more. You were right with what you said last night. The part where you were wrong was where you said I wouldn't take care of you guys. I'm here for you, Jen. I won't let you go through this alone."

"I shouldn't have said that," she admitted.

"Don't. I'm leaving it in the past," I started. "You just let me know what you need."

She looked up at me from where her head was resting on my shoulder, "I don't think you're going to be getting very far toting an IV with you."

I winked at her, "We have Lou for at least a little bit today."

Lou poked his head through the door, "I heard my name?"

Jennie sniffled sitting up straight while I leaned back in her bed getting comfortable. She wiped her eyes then asked, "Can you get us some food? If that's okay with the doc for Val."

He gave her a soft grin, opening the door up a little more to reveal Raf and Warrick standing behind him, "Sure, but you'll have company if you're up to it."

Jennie patted the bed next to me looking at Warrick, "Make yourself at home."

Raf went back to work checking on my vitals and making sure the IV was in place before heading out of the room to grab more supplies. Before making any move, Warrick asked, "Does this mean we're entering a truce? No more feud between the two of us?"

I watched as a small smile stretched on Jennie's face, my heart warming at seeing the sight of her sadness slowly fading away. She nodded, "I think we can move past that considering I'm probably stuck with you as long as I'm stuck with Val."

He nodded his head as he moved into the room. Warrick lifted my IV tubes out of the way making sure they were in the right spot while we moved further in the middle of the bed to make a space for him. Warrick settled in and Jennie clicked on one of her favorite movies, *The Breakfast Club*, her head resting on my shoulder. "Thank you," she whispered.

I patted her hand. Warrick looked at Jennie, "Thank you, by the way, for being willing to take Holly on."

"She's really not that bad, but you're welcome," she said. "Although, she *really* doesn't like Val."

I let out a laugh, "Only because I'm with Warrick and friends with Lou."

"Well, even if you weren't here, she'd have no chance in hell to get with me," Warrick noted.

We went back to watching the movie, Lou eventually joining us but laying on Jennie's side so he gave Warrick some space. She eventually switched who she was resting on, going from me to Lou. I saw him stiffen, but eventually relax when he was sure she wasn't trying to make a move. Raf came in a few minutes later to grab another round of vitals, talk through my symptoms, and replace the near empty IV bag.

Warrick and Lou stayed there as long as they could, but by the time the sun was starting to set, they moved to get up. Warrick placed a hand on me, "Love, we'll be staying here tonight to keep an eye on things and to make sure you all aren't left alone. Raf is leaving instructions on how to keep caring for yourself if you're still feeling bad, but please stay inside tonight. Rest. Get better."

"Okay," I nodded.

"When we knock on the door in the morning, don't be shocked when we're naked," Lou said casually from the doorway.

"Got it," I said. "Now, get out of here before we have a couple of wolves we don't know what to do with. I don't want to deal with you two fighting."

Warrick chuckled leaning over to give me a kiss. Lou gave us both a wave then they were gone. Raf dropped off some instructions walking me through what he wrote down then made his exit as well. Jennie was still staring out the door when she asked, "Are they really naked when they change back? Even if they turn when they're wearing clothes?"

"Yeah," I nodded. I laughed thinking of that time Lou changed back while he was laying in my entryway and I became so flustered. "They really do. It can catch you off-guard when you're not expecting it."

"I don't think I'd mind seeing Lou naked. Or Warrick, but I won't go there," Jennie mentioned. We looked at each other then burst out laughing. At least that was a sign of progress of her moving on.

Bev poked her head in the doorway, "Lou told me to check on you. What did I miss?"

The mention of Lou's name sent us into another fit of giggles. When we finally calmed down, Jennie waved Bev in, "I was just saying I wouldn't mind seeing Lou naked."

"Probably wouldn't be the worst thing to see," Bev said. She glanced at the IV in me, "What happened last night?"

"Oh, you missed a lot, Bev," I started. "Where should we begin?"

"Maybe with the fact I'm no longer engaged," Jennie causally said. There was no sign of emotion in her voice surprising me. Either she has nothing left in her or she's quickly moving on.

Bev's jaw dropped, "What? I'm so sorry, Jennie."

She waived her off, "It sucks and I'm sad, don't get me wrong, but I think it's for the best. I'll let Val explain what happened. I'm going to get more snacks."

"Oh, don't worry about that," Bev said. "Joe's coming up with some food. He made pasta."

"Please tell me you guys made some bread to go with it?" I asked.

Bev nodded and I clapped my hands together. Their homemade bread is the best. Add some garlic butter and it was heaven. I reached across Jennie giving Bev's arm a squeeze, "You guys are literally the best thing that's ever happened."

Bev waved me off, "Don't mention it. Anyways, tell me what happened after we left."

"Well, I'll give you the short version. I don't know that Jennie and I need to relive the full story," I started, taking a steadying breath. "Chris decided to spike my drink then take advantage of me. Lou and Warrick rushed in to get him off me and then they figured out someone changed Chris into a wolf and he wasn't willing to share that info."

"Crap, you guys had a night. Who would've thought Chris would be like that?" Bev asked.

Jennie shrugged her shoulders, "Apparently he had been cheating on me before what happened to Val last night."

Bev shook her head, "I don't get why anyone would do that to you, Jennie. I'm sorry."

Jennie rested her head on Bev's shoulder, "Thank you for being here for me. Both of you."

Jennie squeezed my hand. We focused our attention back on the movie. Joe came in with plates piled with mountains of pasta, including one for him. He poured a couple glasses of wine for those who wanted it and passed along the bowl filled with bread. We turned some music on instead, letting light conversation fill the space. Jennie seemed to be back to her old self which made me wonder how she truly felt about Chris. Maybe she was just trying to tell herself she loved him when he proposed or maybe she has her sights set on someone else, but who knows.

At this point, night was upon us and a couple of howls rang out. Bev headed towards my room then came back, "Guess we have two guards tonight."

"Not surprised," I said appreciating them keeping their word. I could tell everyone else felt that way, too. We all laughed a little easier, conversation back to flowing freely. When yawns started to take over, I looked at Jennie, "I think I'm going to head across the hall."

"Thank you for spending the day with me, Val. It meant a lot and really helped," Jennie smiled at me.

"Of course," I said returning the smile. "I wouldn't have had it any other way."

I took the slow walk back and got ready for bed. I went through the list Raf gave to me, happy to be removing the IV. I still didn't feel 100%, but I felt a hell of a lot better than I did when I woke up this morning. I stepped on to my balcony earning a couple of stares from Lou and Warrick, but they turned their attention back to monitoring the landscape for anything suspicious. Warrick looked back at me one last time to see me blow a kiss in his direction before starting a walk around the house.

I tucked myself in, falling asleep the minute my head touched the pillow. Morning snuck up on me and I was woken up by a couple of quiet knocks coming from downstairs. No one else was moving to grab the door, so I headed downstairs to open the front door. Lou was laying there breathing hard which meant he must've just changed back. I opened my mouth to say something when more knocks came from the door leading out to the patio.

I moved to open the door when Lou said, "Don't be shocked."

Furrowing my brow, I went back to opening the door. Warrick was laying there also breathing hard, but was covered in blood. "What happened?" I asked louder than I meant to.

"Help, love, please," Warrick croaked.

"Lou?" I asked whipping my head around. He only shook his head. He wasn't ready to get up yet so I was on my own. I leaned down hooking my arms under Warrick's shoulders doing my best to lift him up. He let out a groan as I started to bring him into the house. Jennie was coming downstairs, but stopped when she saw what I was doing, "I'll grab some towels, Val."

"Thank you," I said over my shoulder. Returning my attention to Warrick, I repeated my question, "What happened?"

"Got attacked," was all he could say. That wasn't news to me, but the fact he wasn't healing was really bad. I glanced over my shoulder to see Lou on all fours trying to get up. Jennie rushed past him armed with a pile of towels. She laid them out and I finished bringing Warrick in from the cold shutting the door when I laid him down.

"Lou, do you know what happened?" I asked as I grabbed a few wet washcloths to start working on the cleanup. *This is like when Warrick would attack Lou, but there shouldn't be another wolf who can do that.*

"He got blindsided."

Warrick was covered almost head to foot in blood. There was no way of telling what belonged to him and what belonged to the mystery attacker. "Please tell me the other guy looks worse," I said.

Lou shook his head, "I wish I could say that, but the other guy got away the minute I was able to help Warrick out."

Jennie crouched down to inspect Lou for any injuries. She helped with the few that were on him. I hadn't even noticed the damage on him, but I was thankful it wasn't worse considering what I've seen him go through.

I returned to tending to Warrick. There were cuts all over his face, and as I wiped away the blood, bruises were revealed. He winced every time I wiped near a cut making me take more care. "Warrick, do you know who did this to you?" I asked not expecting any response.

To my surprise, he nodded his head, but wasn't willing to offer up anything else. Jennie was done with Lou and came over to help me giving me a worried look. Her and I were thinking the same thing: Warrick has been untouchable never losing a fight, but here he was defeated and hurt.

We continued wiping the blood away. I had my work cut out for me judging by the number of cuts still open. There were a few deep ones needing stitches, but most could be covered with gauze. I instructed Jennie to go find the first aid kit and she wasted no time with getting up. Warrick tilted his chin up to me, whispering, "I need you to do a couple of things."

"Anything for you," I said wiping his hair out of his face.

"First, can you run a bath for me? Next, can you read me the new emails from my phone? And the last thing, love, can you – "

Before he could finish that question, he was consumed with coughs. Blood trickled out of the corner of his mouth adding to my worry. I whipped around to Lou, "You need to call Raf, now. Then, I need your help with getting him into a bathtub."

"What's going on, Val?" Lou said limping over to me. He stopped the minute he saw Warrick's condition. His eyes widened when he looked back at me. Clearly, he wasn't going to be moving fast.

"Jennie!" I shouted. I had no idea where she went. She jogged up the stairs from the basement and over to us. "Call Raf and tell him to get his ass over here right now. Warrick's coughing up blood."

I instinctively placed my fingers along his neck to check his pulse. It was beating, and it was beating strong, but I could tell it was starting to slow. Jennie was already talking to Raf telling him to get over here when I said, "Tell him Warrick's pulse is starting to slow."

Lou moved to help me lift Warrick up. At this point, I was sure he lost consciousness. We moved him to the closest tub as gently and quickly as we could. When we had him settled in there, I started the water thankful the cold water was only on for an instant. *Jennie must've started some laundry to take care of the bloody cloths.*

Warrick came to as I started cleaning him, barely able to open one of his eyes. The other one was swollen shut. He held my hand, stopping me from cleaning him, "Thank you, love. I'm not going to be leaving you, I promise."

A couple more powerful coughs took over. When he removed his hand from his mouth, it was covered in blood. I felt emotion start to rise up my throat, "Don't you dare talk like that, Warrick. You hear me? Don't you fucking dare. You'll be fine. Raf is on his way over. I'll get you cleaned up and you'll recover. You hear me?"

He nodded his head then rested it against the wall again. Raf burst through the door, "Talk to me, Val."

"What do you want to know that you can't see?" I asked.

Raf knelt down beside me checking Warrick's pulse and taking stock of the damage. He pulled out his stethoscope gesturing for me to move Warrick, "Lift him up, please."

I did as I was told grunting with the effort it took to lift his heavy body. Raf signaled for me to stop then listened to Warrick's breathing. I didn't dare move a muscle or make sound even after Raf finished. He helped me lower Warrick back in the water and helped with getting him cleaned up. I kept glancing at

Raf hoping he would say something, anything. When he didn't, I finally asked, "Well?"

"It's not good, Val. I can't even pretend to lie on this one. We need to get him dried off and over to hospital ASAP. There's a lot of internal damage judging by the amount of liquid in his lungs, but I need you to keep Lou away. If Warrick comes to and isn't all there, he will attack Lou. The last thing we need is another injured alpha, especially mine. That would put me in an incredibly hard position," he instructed me, his brows knit together in concern.

"Okay," I said doing my best to keep the shake out of my voice. I started to feel sick at the thought of anything happening to Warrick. I helped Raf with drying Warrick off then got to work covering his wounds with gauze to keep him from getting blood on everything. When we finished with that, I ran out of the bathroom nearly knocking Bev over in the process.

"Val?" she asked rubbing the sleep from her eyes. "What's going on?"

"Sorry, Bev. I'll explain in a little bit," I said over my shoulder as I ran down the stairs. Jennie and Lou whipped their heads up before I made it over to them, "We're going to the hospital. It's worse than we thought. Lou, you have to stay here. Raf made it clear he's not going to be dealing with two injured alphas today."

Jennie stood up, "How can I help?"

"Just stay here," I held up my hands. "I need you to keep an eye on things here. Please. I'll keep you updated."

Raf was starting to make the descent down the stairs dragging Warrick. "Val, I could use your help here," he grunted.

"Right," I said rushing over to him. I slung Warrick's other arm over my shoulder and we loaded him into Raf's car. None of us expected this to be the state of things this morning. When I went to bed last night, everything seemed fine. Calm. No one even heard any sounds of a fight. And where the hell was Lou? Weren't they both keeping an eye on the house? How had he not heard a fight breaking out?

"Lou was in the city taking care of a problem breaking out near Warrick's office," Raf interrupted my thoughts. It was almost as if he was reading my mind. "He was helping me out when we heard a few yelps coming in the direction of your house. He took off as soon as he heard the noise, but it was too late by the looks of it."

I looked back at Warrick. He still hadn't come to. He grew paler by the minute and his breathing was slowly becoming more shallow. Raf picked up on the decline of Warrick's condition and jammed his gas pedal to the ground, "Why can't this fucking hospital be closer?"

After Raf called in to the hospital to let them know what was headed their way, we spent the rest of the drive in silence. The minute we pulled up in front of the glass doors, a team rushed over to the car and removed Warrick. They moved so fast, I barely had a chance to keep up. "Wait in the top floor waiting room, Val. That's where we'll be," Raf called over his shoulder.

The team carting Warrick disappeared into the elevator leaving me no choice. I stopped to catch my breath dropping my head into my hands. *This is not happening. I can't lose him.*

"Ma'am?" a kind voice asked.

I looked up at the short nurse who was reaching out to me. She offered a kind smile, "I'll show you where you can wait for him."

"Thank you," I nodded. I followed her into another elevator, different from the ones I had seen Warrick pushed into. We headed up to the top floor and she led me through a maze of hallways to a secluded waiting room. Light piano music filtered out of the speakers accompanied by the sound of typing. She directed me to a chair and brought me a cup of warm coffee before heading back behind the desk to join her colleague.

I stared out the window not completely focusing on anything. My coffee went cold by the time I finally brought it up to my lips. I heard the nurse's voice talking quietly to someone then heard my name. I slowly turned finding my friends standing in front of me. Before anyone could say anything, Raf rushed out focusing only on me, "Val, it's not looking good. Can you come back with me really quick?"

"Won't that compromise things?" I asked worried I would cause more damage by not being dressed in scrubs.

"Don't worry about that, we'll take care of you," he said lifting me by my arm. I handed my coffee to one of my friends feeling numb as I followed Raf. Raf's team took me through the process of getting ready for entering an operating room preparing me for what I might see. I didn't hear a word they said, the blood pounding in my ears.

When I pushed through the doors, I couldn't breathe. Warrick lay there, cut open from the procedure. I picked up his hand, tears forming in my eyes. I looked up at Raf, "Please tell me you're not giving up on him."

"No, but I wanted to give you the chance to say what you want in case he doesn't make it," he said somberly.

I swallowed nodding my head. I turned my focus to Warrick brushing his hair back again, "Warrick, I love you, so I need you to pull through this so we can take out whoever did this to you. You promised you wouldn't give up on me so don't do it. Keep your promise. I love you, Warrick. Don't leave me alone after putting me through hell and back. You don't get off that easy."

I brought his hand up to my masked face giving it a kiss then let it rest back on the operating table.

"Doc, she needs to get out of here. His heart rate's dropping," a nurse informed everyone.

Raf immediately went back to work, the nurse watching the monitor handing her duties over to the next available person then ushered me out of the room. The tears came back as I stripped out of the scrubs not wanting to leave Warrick's side. The friendly nurse from earlier came back to bring me to the waiting room. When I came back out, Jennie was the first to come up to me, talking in a soft tone, "What's going on, Val?"

I looked at her before looking at everyone else, my eyes lingering on Lou's, "It's not looking good right now. Raf isn't sure if Warrick will pull through."

Chapter 23

Lou's face paled. Jennie gasped. Bev and Joe dropped their heads and sank into a seat. The tears spilled over and I collapsed in the nearest chair holding my head in my hands, "I can't lose him, Jennie. I don't know that I'd be able to live through another loss like this."

"Shhh, he's not gone. Raf just said there was a chance we wouldn't pull through. It's not guaranteed," Jennie quickly said, rubbing my back.

"It's killing me not knowing what's going on in there," I choked out between tears. "I wish Raf would've let me stay."

"Come here," Jennie pulled me into a hug.

She was rubbing my arms when I said, "I'm sorry you guys are having to take care of me again."

"Stop, Val. I told you I didn't mean that," Jennie gently scolded. "There's no way in hell we'd let you go through this alone."

"She's right, you know," Joe said sitting on the other side of me. He put a hand on my knee, "We're sending up all the positive thoughts and manifesting he'll pull through this."

Bev crouched down in front of me wiping my face, "Don't cry those tears yet, there's no reason to mourn."

Lou was the last to come over, "I've never known anyone tougher. If he told you he'll make it, then he will."

We sat in the waiting room in silence. I kept my attention focused on the world outside of the windows not allowing myself to think. I jumped every time the sound of a door opened disappointed when it wasn't Raf. Lou was pacing along the row of chairs where Jennie, Bev, and Joe sat. There was one time the two nurses abandoned their computers to rush back behind those double doors. I froze not able to tear my eyes away from where they went. No one else seemed to notice their absence, but when they came back, I let out a breath. The friendly nurse smiled at me, "Something else came up."

Despite being vague, I completely understood her words. Their rapid response was not for Warrick. I turned back around to continue looking out the windows. Lou's steps from his pacing echoed louder the longer we had to wait.

The sun was starting to set washing the world in its golden color. It sparkled off the snow the same way the light caught the necklace Warrick gave me the night before Christmas. I instinctively reached for my neck where it rested holding on tightly to the stone. I didn't pay attention to Lou's footsteps stopping or the keyboards silencing, so when Raf tapped my shoulder, I jumped.

"Sorry, Val," Raf started. I didn't let myself get hopeful when Raf sported a small grin as he continued, "We wrapped everything up. He's going to be okay."

I grabbed his arm as I fell to the ground, relief overwhelming my senses. More tears spilled over. Everyone rushed over to us concerned there was bad news, but I looked up at Raf, "He pulled through?"

He nodded helping me up, "He pulled through. I'm going to take you back there now. He's just waking up. The rest of you guys will need to wait until we know for sure he isn't going to lash out, especially you, Lou. You shouldn't even be here."

"It's my fault," Jennie admitted. "I-I couldn't drive us, so Lou volunteered before Joe or Bev could say anything."

Raf pursed his lips then returned his attention to me, "Just so you know, Val, he's pretty weak right now."

I swiped the tears away and followed Raf back to Warrick's room. His head was resting against a pillow, eyes closed. I hesitated in the doorway until I saw the rise and fall of his chest. I slowly made my way over to the side of his bed reaching for his hand again. The moment I touched him, his eyes flew open and his head snapped up. Warrick's eyes almost glowed with signs of his wolf. I was just happy he was able to open his eyes again, the worry of him lashing out the least of my concerns. I let a soft smile take shape noting the swelling was already down. I stood my ground, "Hey, it's just me."

At the sound of my voice, his defenses went down. His fingers tightened around mine and he tugged me into him. As he wrapped an arm around me, he mumbled into my hair, "I told you I'd make it through, love."

"I know," I sniffled. "Thank you for keeping your promise."

"Did you mean what you said back there?" Warrick asked.

I stilled. I had no idea he was able to hear me. Warrick released me so I could look him in the eyes, our faces inches apart because I didn't want to be any further. Honestly, if I could climb in this hospital bed to be with him, I would.

"Did you?" he asked again. "Do you truly love me?"

"Yes," I nodded feeling the tears come again. "I love you, Warrick. I didn't know that for sure until I was about to lose you."

Warrick wiped some tears away with his thumb then cradled my face, "I love you, too, Val. I'm never going to leave you."

He pulled me in for a kiss. It was light, but it didn't need to be anything more than that. If I ever thought the butterflies went wild before, they had nothing on what was happening now. My heart swelled with a feeling I hadn't felt since Gabriel had been in my life. The piece that had been missing was now there.

Raf cleared his throat, "I'm terribly sorry to ruin such a moment, but there's a couple of things I want to say before I let the others come back here if you're okay with that Warrick."

Warrick nodded and Raf pulled a chair up for me so I didn't have to let go of Warrick's hand. Raf stood at the edge of the hospital bed and explained what he found, "You got hit with a lot of silver, your cuts are going to take a while to heal. Your smaller cuts and the majority of the bruises have already healed. However, you ingested something causing the internal bleeding. You had a cracked rib which punctured your lungs allowing your blood to have another place to go. We got that rib back in place, but that's going to take a little longer than expected because of whatever you had swallowed. Do you remember anything from the fight?"

"I remember everything, but I didn't think I swallowed anything," Warrick said coldly.

"Maybe it got in you through one of your cuts, but either way, it did some serious damage. You're also going to have a limp for a little bit. We had to set your femur back in place which also contributed to the major loss of blood. I'll check on you in a couple of hours. We may be able to discharge you. Oh, and you don't happen to know who did this to you?" Raf asked raising an eyebrow.

"No," Warrick answered curtly.

Raf looked like he didn't quite believe him, but left to grab everyone from the waiting room. I watched the door until Warrick squeezed my hand. Bringing my attention back to him, I asked, "You really don't know who did this?"

A shadow crossed Warrick's face, "I do, but it's still not the right time to explain."

"You're killing me, Warrick," I sighed. "I can keep it between us. I can tell you know."

"Val, love, please let me focus on recovering right now. I will tell you, I promise," he said holding my gaze.

"Fine, but I'm holding you to it," I pressed my lips into a thin line.

Raf took that moment to come back in the room with the rest of our group in tow. I don't know how they had time to do it, but they came in with balloons and flowers and even a stuffed animal. Raf flipped on the lights giving all of us a good look at Warrick. I knew he was looking better than this morning, but there were at least two people who hadn't seen him. I watched Joe and Bev take in the sight of Warrick's battered body grimacing as they did so.

"Thank you all for trying to take care of me this morning," Warrick said clearing his throat.

"Glad to see you made it out alive," Lou returned.

Warrick gave him a nod, "Me too. I think it's safe to say we have someone new in town."

"Yeah, but let's not focus on that right now," Lou said curtly.

Jennie came up to the edge of the bed on the opposite side of me. She reached across handing me the teddy bear, "This is more for you than Warrick."

"Thanks," I smiled. I tucked it in close to me and watched as Jennie focused on Warrick, "You gave us a big scare this morning."

"Eh, I'm fine, Jennie," Warrick said trying to play it off. His words fell flat as we remembered how bad he was.

"Alrighty, I think Warrick could use some rest," Raf said stepping in before it got too awkward to usher the four of them out.

I turned back to Warrick putting the bear on his bed. He was watching me carefully, "I'm really glad you called Raf when you did."

I shifted in my seat, "Me too. I thought you were going to be mad, but as soon as I saw you cough up blood, I knew there wasn't going to be anything I could've done about it."

"I also appreciated everyone being here to support you," he said.

I reached for him again, "They were here for you, too."

"I don't know. It felt like they were just going through the motions," Warrick said looking out the window.

"I can guarantee that's not true," I said turning his head to look at me. "You have no idea how scared we all were, especially those of us who saw you in that condition. I had never seen someone so bloody. It's hard to know what to say to someone you thought was gone. And I'm sure Raf warned them before coming in here that they could set you off."

"I'll let you win this one, love. I'm just happy to have you by my side," he said. Warrick adjusted himself so he could sit up as the nurse brought in a tray of food. He poked some of the food items clearly not wanting to eat what was in front of him.

I poked his arm, "I bet you could convince Raf to discharge you and we could get you some good food. I could even ask what they're making at the house."

He grinned, "I do like the sound of getting out of here."

I stood up leaning in to kiss him. I gave him another kiss, smiling as I pulled back, "I love kissing you when you're smiling."

His face was filled with his golden smile and I went in for one more kiss. Warrick entangled his hand in my hair and he deepened the kiss. I ran my tongue over his bottom lip earning a groan. His other hand reached over cupping my ass. We were so caught up in each other, neither of us had noticed Raf entered the room. He cleared his throat and we pulled apart like a couple of teenagers getting caught red-handed, "Well, I have a few things I need to check, but I think we're going to discharge you. Although, it may be a while before you're cleared to engage in any extra curriculars."

I turned away making myself look busy with getting settled back into my chair, my cheeks red. Raf chuckled and shook his head checking all of Warrick's vitals. When I looked up, Warrick was watching me, his pupils dilated indicating the desire he felt for me.

Raf finished checking on things and sat in the only other chair. He wrote a few notes then looked at both of us, "You're good to go, Warrick, but you still have to be careful. Your lungs are in a fragile state even though they're sounding better. There's a risk you could undo everything we fixed and then we're back to square one which definitely means no sex."

"How long?" Warrick asked still watching me.

"At least a few days? I'll be checking on you every couple of days. Also, I normally wouldn't discharge people at this stage, but I need you to listen to me very carefully. Both of you," Raf said his tone becoming serious.

We stopped staring at each other to focus entirely on Raf. He set his shoulders, "The wolf who did this is clearly still out there. He got close to Val's house and knows there's something in there that means a lot to you, Warrick. You need to watch your back, and if you can jump worlds, now might be the time. I've never seen you with this level of damage, Warrick, and it scares me to know there's someone who can do that to you. I know Lou feels the same way and as the other wolves learn about this, they'll share the same feeling."

Warrick held up a hand, "The other wolves aren't going to find out about this. I'm not going to let them see me hurt, you're going to make sure no one who works here knows about this, and we're going to carry on like nothing happened. Got it?"

"Yes," Raf said dropping his eyes. "Let's get you out of here. Start getting ready, I'll be right back."

Warrick moved slowly to the edge of his bed. I moved to his side to help him up, but as soon as he put weight on his right leg, he sat back down on the bed grimacing, "Guess I'm truly waiting for Raf to get over here."

As if on cue, Raf came back in with a wheelchair and some new clothes folded neatly on the seat, "Get dressed. I'll take you down in the freight elevator and we'll get you in my car. Don't worry, no one's going to see you. The staff I had in your surgery are not wolves and only know you as the CEO of your company. Due to patient confidentiality, they are legally bound to keep their mouths shut. You'll want to use this chair for a little bit until you can put weight on both of your legs. Any other questions I didn't cover?"

"No," Warrick said watching Raf carefully.

"Good, I'll be waiting right outside the door for when you're ready," Raf turned to leave.

I helped Warrick get dressed then moved him to the wheelchair and pushed him into the hallway. Raf took over picking up speed and we made our escape in silence. We got Warrick into my house and Bev greeted him with a plate topped with a perfectly cooked steak, "Welcome back."

Warrick dove right into the food muttering his appreciation in between bites. I joined him and everyone left us alone. I could tell it was bugging Warrick that they stared when he came in the house still in a chair. He wasn't one to let people see him hurt. Warrick turned his head to me, lowering his voice, "Can you help me up to your room? I think I just want to rest tonight, love."

"Of course," I said. I helped him out of his chair and we slowly ascended the stairs one at a time. When we got to the top, Warrick let out a growl making me pause, "Are you okay?"

"Yeah," he gritted out. "Just frustrated I can't do this on my own."

I squeezed his arm, "You'll be back to normal before you know it."

He dropped his head then continued with moving forward. We got him settled in my bed and I ran down to grab his wheelchair. I kissed his cheek then asked, "Anything else I can get you?"

"Besides you on top of me, love? No, I'm good. I'll just watch a movie for a little bit. Go back downstairs and spend some time with your friends. The alone time will be good for me," he ordered.

I nodded putting his phone next to him, "Okay, but let me know if you need anything."

I didn't completely close the door, but it was closed enough to offer him a lot of privacy. I headed back downstairs joining everyone who came back out of their hiding places and their conversation stopped. I looked around, "Really guys? We're just going to keep making things awkward?"

Lou sighed, "Sorry, Val. It's been a day. It's hard to imagine who could do that kind of damage to someone at Warrick's level."

"I'm in the same boat as you," I sighed. "Even Raf said he was scared, but Warrick doesn't want this to get out, so don't go sharing this with your pack."

"Got it," Lou said.

I sat back in my chair and Jennie looked over at me, "How are you holding up?"

"I'm just happy he didn't die in there," I said.

She nodded, "I'm sure that was incredibly hard for you."

"Yeah, I was getting flashbacks to what I went through when Gabriel died."

Joe jumped in at this point, "Who's Gabriel?"

"Val's fiancée who died in the war," Jennie explained.

Bev gave him a smack on the arm, "You knew that. Daryl told you."

"Ah, yeah, that's right. I'm sorry, Val," he said.

"Don't worry about it," I waved him off. "I don't think I have anything left in me to get emotional tonight."

"Well, on the bright side," Jennie said perking up. "I got to see both Lou and Warrick naked and I didn't mind it."

That got a laugh out me as I recalled our conversation from yesterday, "Got to cross that one off your list, Jennie."

Lou turned his head, but we all caught his red cheeks. Jennie was watching him very carefully as she said, "Definitely did not disappoint. You have nothing to be embarrassed about, Lou."

"I don't know, Jennie," he nervously chuckled. "I wasn't planning on you seeing me like that this morning."

"Don't worry about it," Jennie said. They stared at each other a little longer and looked away thinking no one caught that moment. I wasn't blind, though, I was picking up on something that was more than the angry, drunken kiss Jennie gave Lou back in the fae world.

Awkwardness aside, we joked a little bit longer before I got a text from Warrick asking me to help him with something. I let out a yawn and told everyone goodnight. When I got into the room, Warrick watched every move I made, "How can I help you?"

"There's quite a few ways you can help me, but the first one would be helping me into the bathroom," he said. Heat rose to my cheeks as electricity cracked through the air. It was going to be hard to keep us off each other for a few days.

I got him setup in the bathroom and made my exit waiting for him to call me back in when he was done. We got in bed and settled in for the night, exhaustion settling in. Warrick leaned over and wasted no time with picking back up with where we left off in the hospital. I moved so I was straddling him, but not putting any weight on his legs. I pulled back to catch my breath, "Warrick, we need to stop. I don't want to hurt you."

"Come back here, love," he said with a gravelly voice. "I'll let you know if you're hurting me."

"Doctor's orders, though."

He frowned at me, "Fine, but the moment I'm cleared, we're locking ourselves away."

"Deal," I said kissing his neck. I trailed kisses down his chest pausing when I reached the waistband of his pants. I pulled them down a little marveling at his size before teasing his tip with my tongue. Warrick's head fell back, a moan filling the room. I glanced up at him, "Raf never said anything about this, though."

"Be my guest, love," he said, his hand gently grabbing a handful of my hair. I let him tell me what rhythm he wanted as he filled my mouth. As Warrick's grip tightened, I knew he was ready to climax, but he wasn't allowing himself to enjoy that release yet. He lifted my head up bringing my mouth to his. I smiled leaning into our kiss bringing one his hands up to my breasts. "Love," he moaned into my mouth. "You're killing me."

I pulled away, "And here I thought you were enjoying this."

"Death by pleasure. There are worse ways to go," he chuckled. I shook my head at him and made my way back down between his legs. This time, he let me choose the pace until he finally let himself go. He moaned, my name escaping his lips, then brought my mouth back to his for one last kiss. Warrick caressed my cheek, "You're incredible, love."

"I figured you could use the release," I said settling in by his side.

"It helps, but I do miss the feeling of you," Warrick pretended to pout.

"Focus on getting better first, then I might just let you lock me away," I said.

He gave his approval and we got ourselves comfortable. The movie ended and he asked for another one. I headed downstairs noting everyone else had migrated to their rooms for the night except for Lou. He was just sitting on the couch staring towards the doors where Warrick was at this morning.

"Hey," I said putting a hand on his shoulder.

He jumped, but relaxed when he saw it was me, "Hey, Val."

"What's up?" I asked moving to grab a couple of movies from the shelf.

"Just thinking, that's all."

"About?"

Lou sighed running a hand through his hair, "Do you think the enemy Warrick keeps talking about was the one who attacked him?"

I dropped down into a seat, "I hadn't really given it a ton of thought, but probably. It would make sense."

"I can't believe we almost lost him today," Lou mumbled.

I shook my head, "I can't either. Raf said we need to jump if we can. He also mentioned we need to watch our backs because Warrick's attacker knows there's something in this house he's willing to protect."

"Shit," Lou rubbed his face.

"We'll be fine, Lou. We have to be," I said trying to sound confident. Then, a question popped into my head I couldn't keep to myself, "Do you think this guy is the one who changed Chris?"

"He could be," Lou said watching me. "I don't know. We need Warrick to talk."

"I tried," I sighed. "He's not willing to say anything yet."

"That sounds about right."

We sat there for a little longer in silence before I started heading upstairs. I paused at the edge of the couch, "Lou?"

"Yeah?" he looked up at me.

"Don't be afraid to give Jennie a chance. You two could be good together," I said feeling a small part of me crack at that admission. Even though Lou and I wouldn't be together, I still really cared about him and treasured that short time we were in a relationship.

"Where did that come from, Val?" he asked confused.

"Just an observation," I said then waved, "Goodnight, Lou."

When I got back in my room, Warrick asked, "What took you so long?"

"Just talking to Lou," I said starting another movie then crawling back in bed.

"About what, love?" he asked cautiously.

I met his gaze, "About today. And about Jennie, to tell him they'd probably be good together."

"Hmm," he thought about it. "I could see that."

We cuddled together eventually drifting off with the movie still playing.

At least a week had passed with no other incidents. No Chris showing his face. No signs of the weird guy we had seen the night we all went to the club. No needy texts from Holly. Warrick made progress each day and was able to walk with only a slight limp after a couple of days. He was back to going into the office to keep up appearances more than anything else, but came back to my house every night for Joe and Bev's cooking and my love. The day he was finally cleared to do things was the day we spent in bed together making up for lost time, and you could tell he missed being together.

On the last night of the week, we all converged at Lou's to enjoy a meal out of the house. This was the first time I had been back to the pizza place since Lou wouldn't let me come back to work with the threat of whoever attacked Warrick still out there. Much to my dismay, Warrick had agreed to this arrangement. When we were hanging out at the tables we pushed together in the middle of the restaurant, I looked at Lou, "Anyone asking for me?"

"Oh, everyone," Lou laughed. "All of my customers prefer you to wait on them than me. Warrick can back me up on that."

Warrick chuckled at that bringing his beer to his lips for a long drink. I glanced down at the table taking in the scene of my friends laughing, too. We were so relaxed finally able to enjoy a break from the chaos. Every now and then a customer would come in to pick up a to-go order and Lou would take care of them. A couple of people filtered in for a late dinner, but once they had food on their table, Lou was back to hanging out with us.

The door opened right before closing with one final customer hoping to get something before the door got locked. Lou glanced in that direction, "Hey, buddy, we're clo – "

He stopped before he could get the rest of the word out and immediately stiffened. Lou slowly rose out of his chair. I studied the man slowly making his way over instantly recognizing him as the one wearing the baseball cap, but this time, he wasn't wearing it. There was something familiar about his features and the way he carried himself, yet I couldn't place it. It was almost as if I had seen him before. When I caught a glimpse of the wolf tattoo on his arm, I knew where I had seen him before: the pictures on Warrick's desk back in Cian's world. Yet, I felt like that wasn't the only place I remembered him from.

Before Warrick could turn around, the mystery man clapped a hand on his shoulder, asking in a familiar British accent, "Is there room at this table for family?"

Acknowledgements

Third time's a charm, right? Again, thank you sooo so much to my incredibly supportive husband. Kyle, without your input and encouragement, this book wouldn't have happened and this series would cease to exist. I am so appreciative of you being willing to be my guinea pig with the first drafts of my books. You give great insight into what things may need to be changed or what is solid. I've also enjoyed seeing you laugh and get emotional as you read, too. You've been so wonderful for always telling me to keep going when I want to stop. You quiet that voice of doubt that whispers in my ear so I don't let my fears keep me from pursuing this dream. There are never enough "thank you's" for how you've helped me get this far.

Thank you to my mom for catching edits and providing some solid input - I told you this one wasn't as spicy! But, thank you for having to put up with my spicy scenes, too. I know it was shocking at first, but now it's a good laugh. All jokes aside, I do really appreciate the time you have spent to make sure my writing is polished. I've become a stronger writer because of your inputs. Thank you for walking in this journey with me!

A huge thank you to the Miblart team for the beautiful cover art they always do - you all know how to capture my vision! I get so excited whenever I get a draft in my inbox and I don't think those little happy dances will ever stop.

For all my family and friends, thank you for the patience you give! There have been a lot of times where I've had to hide myself away in my house to get writing stuff done which has translated to a lot of "I'm busy" or "Can't make plans today." One of these days, I hope that'll start to turn around. Also, thank you for all the support! It puts a huge smile on my face to see the people I hold near and dear to me get excited to get their hands on my books.

Finally, THANK YOU times a million to my readers. It took a while for me to get something in your hands, but here we are three books later with plenty more to come. Without you all picking up my books, this wouldn't be happening. Your support helps me keep going. Your reviews give me an idea of what you truly feel. When I hear that one of you are looking for the next book, I have a hard time holding a smile back because I know you're enjoying Val's adventures as much as I do. So, thank you for being willing to give me a chance.

Thank you again for taking the time out of your busy schedule to shove the world aside and escape into *Whispers of Moments* I really hope you enjoyed it, and if you did, please leave a review!

Did you know?

Indie authors are small business owners (yay for supporting small businesses!). Reviews are our bread and butter, and mean the world to us. Fun fact – it takes 50 reviews *minimum* for exposure on Amazon. The best way to support an author (after reading their book, of course) is by leaving a review, even if it's just a few words!

Thank you sooo so much for your support!

Want even more content? Check out my website and socials to be in the know for all the latest and greatest updates:
www.toriegwriting.com
www.facebook.com/toriegwriting
www.instagram.com/toriegwriting
www.goodreads.com/torie_gaylord

About the Author

Torie is a passionate adventurer who finds inspiration in the beauty of the outdoor world, especially in her backyard of Colorado. When not hiking through the mountains or torturing herself with running, she enjoys the company of her loving husband and their two cats, who serve as her trusty sidekicks as she types away . A lover of engaging storytelling, she often loses herself in a good book, movie/tv show, or video game. Eager to create her own worlds, Torie is excited to share her adventures through writing, inviting readers to embark on journeys of their own.

Read more at toriegwriting.com.